PRAISE FOR JULIE PARSONS
AND
THE COURTSHIP GIFT

"As well-written and carefully plotted as Parsons' first effort."

—*Kirkus Reviews*

"A superior thriller; a terrific read; a most welcome addition to the canon of contemporary Irish fiction."

—*The Irish Times*

"Parsons' book is a skillful, high-quality suspense thriller in the Ruth Rendell mode."

—*The Times* (U.K.)

"*THE COURTSHIP GIFT* superbly reinforces what has become obvious about Parsons' talent: that she is one of those rare authors who can successfully combine psychological style, literary style, and heart-stopping suspense. Haunting, evocative, compelling!"

—Jeffery Deaver, author of *The Blue Nowhere*

"*THE COURTSHIP GIFT* is intelligent, engaging, and rarely predictable. . . . Parsons rations out the adrenaline-pumping, palm-dampening scenes to good effect."

—*Peterborough Evening Telegraph* (U.K.)

"You won't be able to put it down and you won't be able to sleep."

—*Irish Tatler*

"A mesmeric portrait of obsession and evil."

—*The Sunday Telegraph* (U.K.)

"Julie Parsons is one of those writers readers constantly long to discover and so rarely find—a writer whose alluring style beckons us word by word, whose mastery of suspense tempts us to continue reading long after we should have turned the lights out. *THE COURTSHIP GIFT* is a haunting, well-told tale of vulnerability and desire, of innocence and self-deception. It should not be missed."

—Jan Burke, author of *Flight*

MARY, MARY

"Packs a wallop. . . . very well written. . . ."

—*The Boston Globe*

"If this debut is an example of her talent, Julie Parsons appears to have a long, successful career as a novelist ahead."

—*Midwest Book Review*

ALSO BY JULIE PARSONS
Mary, Mary

JULIE PARSONS

THE COURTSHIP GIFT

POCKET **STAR** BOOKS

New York   London   Toronto   Sydney   Singapore

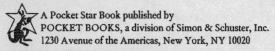

A Pocket Star Book published by
POCKET BOOKS, a division of Simon & Schuster, Inc.
1230 Avenue of the Americas, New York, NY 10020

Previously published in hardcover in 2000
by Simon & Schuster, Inc.

Originally published in Great Britain in 1999 by Macmillan,
an imprint of Macmillan Publishers Ltd.

ISBN: 0-7434-2665-7

First Pocket Books printing October 2001

10 9 8 7 6 5 4 3 2 1

POCKET BOOKS and colophon are registered trademarks of
Simon & Schuster, Inc.

For information regarding special discounts for bulk purchases, please
contact Simon & Schuster Special Sales at 1-800-456-6798 or
business@simonandschuster.com

Front cover illustration by Anna Dorfman

Printed in the U.S.A.

Grateful acknowledgment is made for permission to reprint the following: "Since you, sir, went away" by Chang Chiu-Ling from *The Penguin Book of Chinese Verse* translated by Robert Kotewall and Norman L. Smith (Penguin Books, 1962), translation copyright ©N. L. Smith and R. H. Kotewall, 1962. Reproduced by permission of Penguin Books Ltd.

ACKNOWLEDGMENTS

My special thanks to:

John Caden, for the remarkable feat of holding my hand, keeping my nose to the grindstone, and making me so happy.

Dr. James O'Connor, Curator, Natural History Museum, Dublin; Dr. Declan Murray, Dept. of Zoology, University College, Dublin; Éanna Ní Lamhna; John O'Mara; the late Bill Mellon; Bernard Condon B.L.; Det. Chief Supt. John McGroarty; Brian Hanney of the Coroner's Court for sharing their immense knowledge and expertise with me.

Joe Bollard and Whiskey for helping me try to understand the world their way.

Sarah Caden, Brendan O'Connor and Paul Caden for their love, support and encouragement.

Rory Johnson, official photographer and geographer.

Alison Dye for the crisis counseling and the fun.

Renate Ahrens-Kramer, Sheila Barrett, Phil McCarthy, Cecilia McGovern and Joan O'Neill for their comments, suggestions and continuing friendship.

Brian and Alice Conroy for their front room.

Laura Kay for giving me peace and quiet in her upstairs room.

Treasa Coady of Town House, Suzanne Baboneau of Macmillan, Alice Mayhew of Simon & Schuster, and Nina Salter of Calmann-Lévy. Thank you for all the insights and wise words. It's always such a pleasure . . .

FOR HARRIET

for the future

Michael had watched them both for weeks. The man and his wife. Watched them in the tall redbrick house in the busy street that backed onto the river. Stood in the park on the far bank, saw the shadowy figures as they moved about their business. The man, tall and spare, his hair gray, his face thin and lined. The woman, younger, with long legs and a small waist and round applelike breasts that he had seen just once, as she stepped from the shower and reached for a towel.

He had watched them at home and at work. Seen him leave his car in the reserved space in the multistory car park and walk quickly to the lift, a stack of beige files crammed under his arm, his briefcase banging against his leg. Seen her rushing from the house with a pile of books and a big wicker basket. Strapping them onto the carrier of an old bicycle, humming a tune as she put on her gloves and snuggled a soft woollen hat down on her fair hair. Watched her in the museum where she spent her days, the yellows, reds, blues of the dresses she wore reflected back from the glass and polished mahogany of the rows and rows of display cases.

Watched him at lunches and dinners. In high-ceilinged

rooms, pools of soft light refracting on silver cutlery and sparkling crystal. And the men with whom he ate, self-satisfied, knowing, fingers clicking for service, bread rolls gutted on white tablecloths, red wine stains in interlinking circles. Listened to his laugh, loud, confident, watched for the small signs of insecurity, the face in repose, hollows under the eyes, lines deepening around the mouth.

Knew him. Waited for him. Waited for her. Until the house was quiet, then slipped in through the back door. Careless, unlocked. Stood in the rooms filled with heavy furniture. Gilt mirrors, mahogany sideboards. A grand piano in the bay window of the sitting room. Paintings, faded, dusty. Figures in eighteenth-century dress. Walked upstairs quietly, slowly. Opened each of the doors in turn. Found the large bed, neatly made. Books on a table. A basket filled with discarded clothing. Bent to run his hands through silk and linen and lace. And lay down, his head on the pillow where hers had been, his arms folded over his chest, fingers trailing on the cotton coverlet, his legs crossed at the ankle.

And thought of the times that had been, and the times to come.

2

It couldn't have been an accident. She just didn't believe it. Accidents don't happen like that. But the Guards had told her, off the record, of course, after the postmortem, that there would have to be an inquest but the preliminary findings seemed clear. David had died of anaphylactic shock. From a bee sting.

"You did know, didn't you, that he was allergic? And he knew, too, didn't he?"

And she had said yes, of course. And remembered how he had laughed about it, said that it was great, that it meant he never had to do any gardening. Said that he couldn't eat honey either, hated the taste, the cloying stickiness, hated the thought of the bee sucking the nectar from the flower into its honey stomach, then regurgitating a drop, holding it between its jaws, opening and closing its mouth until the water in it evaporated, and it became concentrated sugar.

"Ugh, disgusting."

Refused to accept the importance of bees in pollination, all the useful attributes they possessed.

"The cruelty of the hive. Don't you agree? The way the bees are selected. Controlled by the queen, and the way the new queen stings, kills all her rivals. It's like some kind of fascist state. Don't you agree?"

One of the first conversations they ever had. Years ago, fifteen at least, maybe more. When she was a teenager, and he was one of her aunt Isobel's favorite visitors. One bright summer day when the garden hummed. Alive with movement. Wings beating, mouthparts opening and closing. The whole cycle of birth, death, destruction, renewal taking place. Invisible to their human eyes. Unheard by their human ears.

And she had thought to impress him. Told him that she was going to be an entomologist when she left school.

"A scientist, eh?" He had sat back in the wooden deck chair, taking a swallow from the tall glass at his elbow, the tone in his voice mocking. "Rather you than me."

And she had stood up, annoyed, and turned on her heel, glad all the same that she was wearing her bathing suit, the stretchy material tight, riding up just enough to show a firm half-moon of pale skin.

All those years ago. Different people now. Transformed by their experiences. Old and weary David looked as he lay on his side, his arms and legs curled up, as if to protect himself. His gray hair stood up stiffly from his forehead. He had pulled off his shirt, and it lay beside him in a crumpled heap. The muscles of his chest and back were flaccid and withered, his skin very white apart from the angry red patches all over his upper body. His eyes were wide open, their bright blueness dulled, as if a fine gauze curtain had been drawn across them.

But still the chemistry of his body unchanged by age.

Still the deadly reaction to the venom that the bee had pumped into him. She touched his cheek with her hand. His skin was cold and hard. It reminded her suddenly of an india rubber ball, small and bouncy, that she had had when she was a child. She remembered hitting it with a tennis racket, high up into the sky, almost as high as the roof of Isobel's house. Standing, gazing upwards, trying to see where it would land. Spinning around, her eyes blinded by the glare from the sun. Sickened suddenly by the movement. As she was sickened now by the feel of David's face, the look in his eyes and the rank smell that filled the small room.

3

Of course it was intended that she should find the body. That was the way with a courtship gift. Michael had read about it in one of those children's encyclopedias that his granny kept for him, for when he came over to visit in the summer, during the holidays, from London and school. It was called *The Wonder Book of Why and What*, with a picture of a boy with very short hair and a white shirt and a model airplane on the cover. Granny had a stack of them in the bookcase behind the black-and-white telly. His mother's name was written inside, in big looping letters, but the books didn't look as if anyone had ever read them. The pages were stiff and clean, although they smelled like everything else in his gran's house. Of damp, and fried food, and the disinfectant she used in the outside toilet.

The bit about the courtship gift was in one of the illustrated sections. Insects, all shapes and sizes. What they ate, how they built their nests, how they mated. He was interested in that. He knew about mating—insects, animals, people. It was how his mother earned her living, most nights, although she didn't have any more babies. He was supposed to be asleep, in the cold little room at the back. And she was in the front room, where it was always warm, and the light came from the pink lamp on the table. She usually waited until she thought he was asleep before she went out. And usually he was asleep, but there were always the noises that dragged him back. The front door banging. Heavy steps on the narrow stairs. Men's voices, laughing. Then a wedge of light from the landing that fell across his face, as she tiptoed into his room, rummaging in the bottom of the wardrobe for the box where she kept her money. Holding it up, so its scratched tin glinted, as she turned the little key, and put away the folded notes, carefully, put it back beneath a pile of old blankets.

Once he got out of bed and crept to her door and listened. Once he pushed his toe against the chipped cream paint and the door opened. A man was standing in front of the fire, no clothes on, and his thing sticking out. Red and hard. He put his hand up to his mouth to stop the giggles, the man looked so funny. And then he saw his mother. She had no clothes on either.

It was mating. That was what it was. Like the dogs in the alley, and the cats in the corrugated iron shed in the back yard, the insects in the book.

And that was where the courtship gift came from. He'd read about it, how the male had to give the female a present, so she would choose him instead of any of the others. He might give her a piece of a flower petal or a seed wrapped up in a parcel of silk, or it might be the body of another insect, a fly, perhaps, stolen from a spider's web. So instead of trying to run away, her attention would be caught by the corpse. And she would eat it, and keep still. So he could do with her exactly what he wanted.

4

The night that David died was a Wednesday night. She was sure of that. She had gotten home from the museum at about six, rushing to cook dinner before choir practice at seven thirty, irritated by the next-door neighbor waving a large padded envelope at her as she fumbled in her bag for her keys.

"The postman left it with me. I didn't want to accept it. I told him he should have put a notice through the box and then you could have picked it up from the post office, but he kept on and on about it."

"Yes." Anna looked at the woman's face. It was animated with malicious curiosity. "Did he now? That was a bit sloppy, wasn't it? Expecting you to do his job for him. A word, perhaps, to his supervisor?"

"No, no, I didn't mean that." Mrs. O'Donnell squirmed, wringing her hands together. "No, it's all right really." Her features crumpled, loneliness lying just beneath her fine lined skin. "Perhaps you'd have time for a cup of tea, a drink?"

But Anna was already inside the door, rushing upstairs to shower, dropping the parcel and the rest of the letters addressed to David onto the desk in his study.

He arrived home just as she was leaving.

"Dinner's in the oven," she shouted, as she slammed the back door. "See you later. Love you."

It was the night of the comet too. It followed her as she hurried down Anglesea Road, a long smear of yellow lying low in the northern sky. With her as she crossed the Dodder at Ballsbridge, and turned left under the plane trees to the church hall in Clyde Road. Waited for her as she eased herself into her place next to Zoë, as she opened her mouth and sang. Final rehearsals for their Easter performance, *St. Matthew Passion*, tears slipping from the corners of her eyes as fifty voices joined together in the agony of the music.

She didn't go with the rest of them for a drink afterwards. She was drawn again to the light in the sky.

"Do you see it?" She took hold of her friend's plump shoulders and turned her around in the right direction. "Isn't it beautiful?"

Zoë shrugged. "Ice particles, that's all. Pieces of frozen water. Not that much to get excited about."

But Anna had gone already, towards the dark space of Herbert Park. Slipping through a gap in the railings, walking quickly across the football field as far away from the polluting city lights as she could get.

It was cold that night, too cold for mid-April—clear with no cloud cover, perfect for stargazing, frost stiffening the new growth on the roses and glazing with the thinnest layer of ice, like spun sugar, the water in the oval pond. Her footsteps were loud on the grass, her breath condensing in pale clouds in front of her, while farther away the city's traffic sang its metallic song.

She could see the back of her own house from where

she was. The third set of chimneys counting from the dark space where the laneway connected Anglesea Road to the river. She stopped for a moment, and watched. Lights in the downstairs room, and a sudden burst of yellow in the window at the top of the house. David's study. A long drop to the garden below. His silhouette moving around, standing for a moment looking out. Can he see me? she wondered, suddenly feeling exposed, vulnerable, knowing how he would disapprove. Asking for trouble, he'd say, wandering around on your own at night. Silly girl.

She turned away, and headed for the darkest part of the park, far from the spreading bloom of the streetlights. She lifted her eyes to the sky. The Milky Way, a delicate sparkling spiral, stretched from one horizon to the other, and the moon, a mottled helium balloon, floated to the south, while there in the north lay the Hale Bopp. Four thousand years since it had last been seen here in this place, at a time when the longest day and the shortest day were known and marked by men and women who dragged huge stones hundreds of miles to stand them in patterns whose meaning was still elusive. Who lived in fear and wonder of what was to come and for whom life was a series of mysteries, of riddles and puzzles, of answers still to be found.

Riddles, puzzles, unanswered questions? She backed away from David's body and huddled in a corner of the room, her hands over her face, as the Guards who had arrived soon after the ambulance tried to calm her, reason with her, ask her where she had been when her husband was dying. She could see they didn't believe her when she told them she'd been standing in the middle of Herbert Park watching the comet.

"Closed, isn't it, to the public at night?" one of them said, before the other older one frowned at him, and put an arm around her shoulder. She laughed. Hysteria crashed through the wide smile on her face, turned now to the color of milk.

"So. Arrest me," she said, and put her head in her hands, as her shoulders began to shake, and sobs burst from her while they stared helplessly at each other, and waited for the doctor to stand up, pronounce the man on the floor to be dead, then stepped back out of the way so the ambulance men could carry their heavy burden down the stairs.

5

It usually took a couple of days for the death notice to get into the papers. There was the whole routine of the postmortem to be gone through in these cases of sudden death. And then the undertakers got involved, and they were the ones who prompted the family, reminded them that there needed to be some kind of public notification.

However, just to be on the safe side, he bought both the daily newspapers every day, and went through them carefully. Just in case there might be a small news item, the kind you'd find down the left-hand side of page 4 in the *Irish Times*, or somewhere at the bottom of page 7 in the *Independent*.

And his vigilance was rewarded. Both papers had a small piece, noting that "well-known Dublin solicitor David Neale" had died accidentally at home, listing his academic and professional accomplishments, mentioning some of the cases in which he'd been involved, stating his sporting interests—part-owner of a successful racehorse, played for the under-21s international rugby team. All that sort of bullshit. Survived by his wife, Anna. And then the next day the formal announcement:

NEALE (Ballsbridge, Dublin 4) 9th April, 1997.
David Sebastian, suddenly.
Sorely missed by his beloved wife, Anna,
his brother James, aunts, uncles,
sister-in-law, and a wide circle of friends.
Funeral arrangements later.

To be cut out and kept, along with the others. For those days when his life didn't seem to amount to much, when he didn't feel that he had fulfilled his potential. That he had got as far up the ladder as his teachers all said he could. All those nice women who had minded him and mothered him, whose thick thighs he pressed against as they listened to his reading and corrected his addition and subtraction. Felt sorry for him. Talked about him at break time, and on playground duty.

"Lovely kid, Michael Mullen, isn't he? Ever so clever, nice-looking, sweet."

"Such a shame."

"Women like her shouldn't be allowed to have children."

"Wouldn't do, though, to have him taken away from her. He's better off with his mum no matter what she's like."

They wouldn't like it, all those Miss Clarks, and Miss Joneses, and Mrs. Prescotts, if they could see what he was getting up to.

But at the end of the day, he didn't care. Because he was quite happy, thank you very much, quite happy and perfectly content.

6

She hadn't been able to stay in the house. Not for the first few days, anyway. She couldn't stand the thought of that room up there, and the marks on the rug where he had died. She had moved herself from their bedroom directly below to the small sitting room that led into the garden, and made up a bed on the sofa. A couple of blankets and a pillow. A hot-water bottle to try to keep the chills at bay.

She had lain there that night after they had taken his body away, sleep beyond her. Whenever she closed her eyes all she could see was David's face. His eyes and mouth wide open, staring at her, trying to speak, his hands dragging at her clothes, pulling at her body. As soon as she felt the hour was decent she phoned Zoë and told her to come and take her home with her.

Not that it was much better there. They were kind and polite, Zoë, her husband Kevin, and Tom, their five-year-old son. But what could they say or do? How could they explain to her why her husband had died? She could see them moving around her as if she were a piece of sharp, jagged glass, on which they might snag their skin if they got too close. Eventually she could no longer endure the comments they whispered about her when they thought she had gone to bed, and the long sighs that seemed to hang in every room, waiting for her. So she went home, or rather to David's house, which had once felt more like a home to her than anywhere else.

It was warm inside now. Bright sunlight poured through the front windows and fell in colored blocks, tinted by the stained glass in the panel in the door, on the cream hall carpet. She stood on the front step, the door open behind her, and waited. She listened. David's grandfather clock ticked slowly, steadily. As if it was the heart of the house, she thought, as she took a step inside and pushed the door shut behind her. She listened again. Waiting for the sound of music coming from upstairs, or from the piano in the sitting room. She stepped forward once more and called out, "David. Are you there?"

But there was silence.

Silence upstairs too. Nothing to hear but the creak of the floorboards beneath her feet as she placed them carefully on the step in front of her, one hand sliding up the polished wood of the banister. And stopped outside his study, and pushed open the door.

It was exactly as she had left it a week ago. She walked forward and righted his chair, which was still lying on its side. She picked up the papers that were strewn across the floor, the *Irish Times* folded in half and half again. He must have been doing the crossword, she thought. Each square was filled in, a neat grid, completed. She could see him, balancing the paper on his knee, one foot resting against the edge of the desk, his chair teetering dangerously backwards. She piled them neatly beside the old portable typewriter he still used even though its keys were bent, its letters uneven.

She got down on her hands and knees, the wooden boards hard, uneven, catching in the fine wool of her long skirt as she leaned forward, picking up the objects that lay scattered in every direction. A heavy glass ashtray, the butt of a cigar and a smear of ash, trodden in. A mug, lying on its side. Dried coffee a sticky skin on the floor, and a glass, broken. She picked up the shards. The remains of their contents still coated them. She smelled her fingers. Brandy, she thought. She looked again at the objects on the floor. A pair of scissors, paper clips, a couple of Biros. And as she reached out to pick up a small framed photograph of herself, which had ended up in the far corner, she saw a bee. Missed, somehow, by the Guards when they collected the rest. She crawled forward slowly, carefully, and picked it up, using one of the paper clips as a tweezers. She sat back on her heels and looked at it. It was a queen: bigger than the others, the drones and the workers; laid in a special egg chamber; fed on bee milk, royal jelly; vitamins, proteins, sugars, DNA, RNA, fatty acids, to make her grow and grow, to lay eggs for the hive, thousands every week during the summer, and to be discarded when she got too old to reproduce.

She got up off the floor, sat down on David's chair and laid the insect on his desk. The queen had come in a rough wooden box inside the padded envelope. Anna knew the kind. A neighbor of her aunt's who made honey every summer had shown her once: the partitioned section for the queen, the sugar candy she would feed on, and the larger compartment for the workers who travelled with her. Fifty or so, he had said, to mind her and care for her. They had died to protect this queen. She had died of hunger and cold, unable to survive without them. Anna looked at her closely. The queen's sting was intact. It was hypodermic, not barbed like the other bees. She could sting and sting and sting and still not die. She did not rip out her abdomen as they did for the sake of the safety of the rest. The queen only ever stung for one reason: to kill off the other queens, her rivals, as they lay in their egg chambers, not quite as ready as she was to fly.

She remembered that she had left the package on his desk with his other letters. She had looked at it as she walked upstairs that evening. Turned it over, backwards and forwards, a couple of times, feeling it, like a child with a Christmas parcel. There had been nothing to show its contents. David's name and address were printed on the outside. No sender identified, no return address. Documents, legal papers, a book maybe, she had thought, if she had thought at all. Bringing more work home. Too much these days. Now she leaned back into the chair, resting her forearms along its polished wood as he always did. She crossed her legs, the toes of her right foot resting against the floor, jiggling up and down as his did. She thought of the package, lying on the desk. She could see his hands, with their long thin fingers. Holding a cigar, lifting the mug of coffee to his lips, taking a sip from the glass. Finally picking it up. Using the point of the scissors to rip open the seal. Pulling out the box. He wouldn't have known immediately what it was. He would never have seen anything like it before. He would have turned it over, noticing the mesh, the little compartments. And then he would have slid back the lid. And done what? Dropped it? Thrown it against the wall, driving the bees to distraction? The air in the room tainted with the smell of his fear. Sweat beginning to break out on his forehead. A scent they would recognize, and to which they would react. Instantly. Flying at him to frighten him away. To keep him at a distance from their queen. And what would he have done then? Screamed and screamed as the first barb went in. Ripped off his shirt to try to pull the stings from his body. His arms flailing uselessly as he twisted and turned in his agony. They knew how to attack. She had seen them once in her aunt's garden turn on a wasp that had tried to steal their honey. It was all over in a couple of minutes.

As it would have been for David, the allergic reaction to the bees' venom making his blood pressure collapse: nothing for his heart to beat against, no force to keep the blood flowing through his arteries, no precious oxygen travelling to every cell in his body. His brain beginning to shut down, his brain cells dying. His breath stopped by the swelling in his throat. Slipping down into a deep, dark hole, gasping for the precious bliss of air that now could not save him.

But still she didn't understand. Why didn't he leave the room as soon as he saw the bees? Why didn't he do something to get rid of them, open the long window that looked out onto the garden? Try to throw out the box with its malevolent contents?

She stood up and looked out and down to the garden below. She unlocked the brass catch and pushed hard. It didn't budge. She pushed again and again. Still no movement. She paused with her hands pressed against the glass and saw the ground far below. Her palms were wet, her heart pounding, her knees weak. She stepped back one, two, three, four steps, and gripped the corner of the desk. Anything to stop the sensation of helpless slipping and sliding that flooded through her. She had never felt at ease in this room. It was too high above the garden, the trees, the river. She waited, until her breathing slowed and her pulse began to calm, then pulled herself forward, hand over hand, gripping the back of David's heavy mahogany chair, the bookshelf against the wall, the edge of the sill, and reached up to grasp the brass handles on the window, pushing it again, so it loosened and opened, just enough to let in some air. Then she moved away quickly, so she could not look down to the garden below or across the river to the smooth green of the park.

"YOU SHOULDN'T stay here on your own, you know. It's not good for you." Anna sat in the kitchen with James, David's younger brother. If she closed her eyes she could imagine that it was David who was here with her. The same accent, the same deep rumble in the throat as they spoke. But that was where the resemblance began and ended.

"You'd never know you were brothers," she said, and watched the flush creep up his fleshy white face, starting somewhere below his collar and ending at the hairline of his high, domed forehead. He shrugged his shoulders and opened his briefcase, laying file upon file on the kitchen table.

"I'll have more tea," he said, "before I begin to explain to you the gravity of your situation."

It would have to be James who revealed to her the extent of David's deception. He was the executor of his will. She remembered a conversation she'd had with David not long after they married. Or at least a conversation he had tried to have with her. She had been reading at the time, stretched out in front of the fire, one arm bent at the elbow, her head leaning on her hand. David was sitting on the sofa behind her, talking about wills and money and the house. His words drifted above her head, like dark wisps of cloud.

"Are you listening to me?" He prodded her in the back with the toe of his shoe. "Are you?"

She didn't reply. She looked at her hand in the firelight. Its blood vessels glowed a deep, vivid pink. She turned it this way and that while, behind her, David's voice rumbled on. She listened to its rhythm, its cadence, its change of pitch. But not to the individual words. The way she had once listened to the voices that came from her aunt's drawing room, her father's hoarse and hesitant, her mother's barely audible, and Isobel's loud and angry, making her creep backwards, up the long staircase to the landing where she had left her favorite doll. She didn't want to know then what they were saying, as she didn't want to know now what David was saying. All she wanted was to lie in front of the fire, and feel its warmth spreading through her body. That was all she wanted. Then and now.

She sat in the kitchen, with James across from her. Outside it was bright and sunny, the sky rainwashed light blue. James spread the sheaves of paper out on the table. It was seven days since the funeral, and they had walked side by side behind David's coffin. She had done what was required of her. She had worn her most sober black skirt and jacket, taken her place in the front pew next to James and his wife, listened while some of David's oldest friends and colleagues stumbled over the readings and the lessons. She had sat in the back of the big black car, the cracked leather seat pricking her thighs, while Isobel lit yet another cigarette. She huddled against the door, her body concertinaed, a tight ball of grief, her face suddenly without its familiar angular structure, a mass of lines and sagging wrinkles. They drove in silence out of the city to the new cemetery beside an unfinished housing complex. Anna threw the first handful of dry dust on top of the polished wood of the coffin. It landed without a sound, and lifted once again into the still spring air. She had wanted to stay, to watch the gravediggers cover David over, but James took her by the arm and pulled her away, back into the car and home to his house.

She had stood, clutching a glass of wine, while all around her stuttered the rhythm of a dozen conversations, an occasional loud laugh rushing in to fill an awkward space. She had wondered, who were all these people who told her how sorry they were for her loss, brushing her cheek with theirs, pressing her limp hands as they said goodbye, their promises of help and comfort as empty as the aching space she felt within her.

"Look. Here." James kept pointing at bank statements and balance sheets. Letters with broad bands of red across them, from debt-collection agencies and the Dublin county sheriff. "Didn't you know? Didn't you even suspect?"

She shrugged her shoulders helplessly, gazing past his neat fair head at the pot of house leeks that sat outside the window on the wide sill. *Sempervivum* was the botanical name for the fleshy star-shaped rosettes. Always living. David had told her once that the Romans planted them on rooftops to protect against lightning. He should have taken their advice, she thought, as James held up yet another threatening letter.

"You're bloody lucky," he said. "I can't understand how he managed to get so much credit for so long."

"But he had money. He always had money. Plenty of it. He was always spending, buying things. Paintings, furniture, wine. You know what he was like. And anyway, there were the rents from the building in Dame Street. His office only took up the first floor, the rest must have been bringing in plenty."

James smiled at her. He reminded her suddenly of the way David had looked when they first met. When the skin around his eyes had been tight, only the slightest hint of the lines that would crease and crosshatch, and make it look like crumpled tissue paper.

"You didn't know that either? Come on, you must have. I can't believe that, in this day and age, you didn't know what was going on."

But what was to be gained by knowing? Knowing just made it worse. That was how it always seemed to Anna. Better not to know that your father was ill, that your mother was desperate, that your aunt, your father's sister, was angry. Better not to know what was said about you on those dark winter nights, when their voices rose and fell behind the drawing-room door, and you curled up on the window seat on the landing and watched the stars spring into the shapes that decorated the wallpaper in the room in which you now slept, that had once been your father's when he was your age.

"What?" She lifted her hands in confusion, holding them palms outward towards him, the sunlight picking up the grooves and wrinkles, the lines and creases of her pale skin. "I knew nothing. I've told you, we never talked about it." Because they never talked about anything much anymore. Silence in the house, more complete than the silence now.

"He sold the Dame Street building last year. And," he shuffled through the pile again, "he sold his boat, and that piece of land that your aunt gave him when you got married."

"But why, I don't understand, what did he do with it all?"

James shifted in his chair. He seemed awkward suddenly, ill at ease. He fiddled with the cuffs on his shirt, and plucked at the skin on his neck. "What do you think he did with it? He spent it of course. On himself, for himself. Satisfying himself, making himself feel good. Do I have to spell it out to you, Anna? Can't you imagine what he did with it all? And how it took more and more to keep feeling the way he wanted to feel?" He paused, and looked away, then looked back at her. "You are listening to me, Anna, aren't you? You are hearing what I'm saying? Because you're going to have to make some hard decisions." James had taken out his pocket calculator and was totting up a long column of figures.

She got up and walked to the door. She opened it and

stepped outside onto the flagged terrace. Apple blossoms flecked the bright rainsodden lawn with pink and white, and lay in a brown scum across the stones at her feet. The crop would not be good this year. Spring had been cold and windy, bad weather for pollination. The bees didn't like it: they didn't fly when the sun didn't shine.

"I still can't understand how he could have died like that. Can you?"

"Look, Anna, please, I'm trying to help you here. You have to concentrate on the matters at hand. There's only one way out of this mess. You're going to have to sell all David's paintings, the good furniture, and I'm sorry to be the bearer of such bad news, but you're going to have to sell the house as well."

David's house. Where he had always lived, or so it seemed. Long before they met, that summer when he came to stay with Isobel and she was home from school, and he flirted with her, and teased her, and promised to take her out on Sundays. Drove up the long school driveway, and presented himself to her housemistress. I am Anna's cousin, he said, holding out his hand, looking so tall and straight and strong and handsome. Knowing that all the other girls were watching from the dormitory windows. Envious, jealous. How had poor, pathetic Anna Bartholomew managed to find someone like that to take her out? The boys, hanging around on the playing fields, were envious too, of his black BMW, and the ease with which he lounged against its shiny body, swinging the door open for her, ignoring the deliberate ugliness of her uniform, making sure that her legs in their thick navy tights and her feet in her heavy lace-ups were safely inside before slamming it shut with a flourish.

They didn't have sex the first day he brought her here. There was a woman in the sitting room when David pushed open the front door and led Anna in by the hand. He introduced them. Her name was Marion, he said. He kissed her on the mouth, pulling her close, and whispered something in her ear. She smiled, her pretty mouth opening to show white teeth.

"She's wonderful, Anna, a fantastic cook. Can you smell what we're having for lunch?" Meat, roasting meat, dark brown in its tray, topped with ridges of yellow fat, crisp and succulent. And potatoes, nestling in the gravy that gleamed as it swirled around the meat. Saliva darted into her mouth, so she had to swallow hard.

"Not for me," she said, as David handed her a plate. "I'm a vegetarian."

"Oh? Since when?"

She shrugged. "A month or so."

"A principled decision? Or a whim?"

Again the shrug. "You pick."

It had been a game, that lunch, and she had won it. She didn't realize immediately the extent of her victory. David had kept her waiting and teased her, spoiled her so she had no interest in boys of her own age. All the way through her years of university. Even when she went to England to do her Ph.D. he had written to her, come to see her in her dingy student flats, bought her presents, given her money. He had tormented her with his flattery, and his faithlessness, until the day he told her he loved her and wanted to marry her. To make her feel secure, comfortable, protected. Her hand swaddled in his, her head flopping on his shoulder, his body heavy and solid, keeping her anchored, pinned down, like the weights used to press and preserve wildflowers.

Until that night when she opened the front door and stepped into the hall. Heard the sound of music. Recognized it. Bach's double violin concerto. Stopped to listen. Something wrong. The record was one of his favorites. Old and scratched, warped and damaged.

Why don't I buy you a CD, much better quality?

No, I like it like that, it's more the real thing. Like a performance, imperfect.

But now the needle was stuck. The same half-phrase repeating, over and over. She listened and called out.

David, David. The record.

She took off her coat, hanging it from the carved newel-post at the end of the banisters. Called again.

David, can't you hear it?

She put her foot on the first step, walked quickly up the first flight of stairs, past their bedroom, the door open, dark. Switched on the landing light, then faster, faster up the next flight. The music louder all the time. The click, the phrase beginning, then stopping midway, and going back to the beginning. Again she called out.

David, David, the music.

And walked up and up, the stairs twisting away in front of her. The violins getting louder as she got closer. What could he be doing? What crazy game is he playing? And the same demented half-phrase, over and over, as she pushed open the door, and saw simultaneously, it seemed, the old record player on the low table, the playing arm hopping as the buckled plastic swirled around on the turntable, and David on the floor. His eyes open, staring at her as she screamed at him.

The music, the music, turn the music off.

7

Billy Newman had never met David Neale. But he knew his wife: the touch of her hand, the fragrance that came from her as she leaned towards him, the feel of her elbow in his grasp as they walked together, her step matching his own. She had mentioned her husband a couple of times. Once when they were walking along Dame Street together, their heads close so they could hear each other above the clash of the traffic, and she had stopped him, and taken his hand from his dog's harness and removed his glove and placed his fingers on something cold and smooth, letting him run them over the deep indentations in the metal. And asked him what he could make out, and he had paused, as he put together the shapes in his head. The D, and the A, and the V and the I and another D. Yes, she had said, David, and moved his fingers down to the next line, and waited as he spelled out the word. Solicitor, she said, and then, shall we go in? But he had told her he didn't want to, that he was in a bit of a hurry, although they both knew this wasn't true. Billy was never in a hurry when he was with Anna. And she had said, of course, no problem, and would he like to have a cup of tea in Bewley's, before she had to go back to the museum?

He supposed that Anna would have told him that her husband was dead, but he hadn't met her for a week or so. And as it happened, he found out anyway, when he was having afternoon tea with old Winnie who lived next door. They had a routine, a standing invitation on Tuesdays and Thursdays, after she had come back from her regular visit to the small cemetery in Donnybrook. She would always be cold then, the wrinkled skin on her hands icy when he brushed against them, even though she wore padded gardening gloves when she pulled up the weeds and swept the fallen leaves from the smooth gray tombstones. She would bang on his wall when she was ready and he would put on Grace's harness, just so she'd behave herself and not chase old Winnie's cat, and take his seat in the chair that she had placed carefully for him where he could easily find it. He would sit square, both feet on the threadbare carpet and the palms of his hands grasping his knees, the smell of the toast that she was buttering in her little kitchen making his mouth water. And listen. To the sound of the liquid pouring from its pot into the china cups she always used.

"Milk?" she would ask, in her polite little voice, and he would look in her direction and say, "Yes, please."

"Sugar?"

This time he would nod, listening for the tiny tinkle of the tongs as she put two lumps into his tea, stirring it briskly, the spoon making a sound like miniature chimes.

It was always quiet in old Winnie's. She didn't listen to the radio or watch TV. She preferred the newspaper, the *Irish Times*, every day, choosing the articles, the items of news that she would read aloud to him as he drank his tea and ate his toast, spread with her own homemade damson jam. It was warm and clean and calm with old Winnie. Sometimes he would doze off after he had finished eating. And she would do her ironing. The comforting hiss and thump of the heavy metal on cloth trickled in and out of his consciousness as his head dropped forward, and the only color he could remember, red, from the time before he got meningitis, would flood through his dreams, until suddenly he would jerk awake, opening his eyes, back in the darkness again.

She had said to him that day as she put his hands around the cup, "Here's something that will interest you. Listen," and she read to him the death notice. "Isn't that the husband of the nice pretty girl with the fair hair, the one who comes to see you sometimes? The one that works in the museum, the insect expert?"

Trying to remember if Anna had told him the names of any of David's family. But he was sure, then, as he listened to old Winnie's clear little voice. It must be him.

And he was glad. Sometimes when he got very close to her he could smell the man she lived with. Smoky, sour, rancid. Overlaying her sweetness. He didn't like it. It made him feel anxious and angry. Ill at ease with the reality that he had to share her with someone else. Who could see her.

"Tell me," he said to old Winnie, "you said she was pretty? What does that mean, what does she look like?"

"Well . . ." Old Winnie moved away from the ironing board and took his hand and drew him down onto the sofa beside her. "She's tall and very slim. And she has long legs and such graceful arms."

"I know that, I can feel that myself." He was impatient now. He knew the shape of Anna's body. He had felt it alongside his so many times. He knew the shape of her small breasts, the curve of her waist and the roundness of her hips. "It's her face, I want to know about her face."

And old Winnie had tried her best. To describe the smooth fairness of her skin, the bright sheen of her hair. "It's a bit like yours, Billy, it gets more blonde in the sun, but yours is very straight, whereas hers is wavy, not exactly curly. And it stands up around her forehead, even when she wears it pulled back in a bun or a plait."

"Her mouth, tell me about her mouth and her eyes."

"Well . . ." Again the pause, and she took his index finger and placed it on her face so he could feel the difference between the skin of her cheeks, roughened and ridged, and the smoothness of her lips. "Feel that? Feel the difference? Except her mouth is firm and full like mine once was when I was a girl, and I was as pretty as she is now." His finger rested on the deep indentation of her upper lip, sticky now with her makeup.

"And this here, is hers like yours?"

"Mine is deeper, more marked. Hers is more shallow, her lips don't have quite as much curve as mine do. Feel it, Billy, can you feel it?" And he felt just for an instant her mouth open as his finger slipped down over the gap between her lips and he felt her breath, warm and damp on his skin.

Afterwards, when he had thanked old Winnie for the

tea and the toast, he realized that she hadn't mentioned the dimple in Anna's chin. Maybe it wasn't so noticeable to sighted people who had so much variety and choice in what they could see. He put his finger on his own chin, and felt the little dip. He remembered, one day in the park, she had said to him, "You've got the same thing as me, here." And she touched the cleft in his chin, running her finger backwards and forwards over the little indentation.

"You have one too?"

"Here, feel it on my face." She took his fingers and held them to her skin. He had felt slightly sick, nervous tension making his stomach jittery. He let his fingertips travel over her chin the way they travelled across the raised dots of Braille, reading the little imperfections, a slight round roughness, like the marks he had on his chest, from what his mother had said was chicken pox. Her lips were just within reach, and he wanted to feel their fullness, but instead he said, "My mother always told me I got mine from her. It means, you know, that you want to be loved."

"Does it?" She dropped her hand and he felt her move away, her dress stirring as she crossed her legs. "My mother never said that to me."

Anna's voice was bright, and light, and musical. He had heard it for the first time last December, just before Christmas, the time when the carol singers come to Grafton Street, cluttering up the place, making it difficult for people like him to walk easily up and down. All the extra voices and the boxes of money shaking and rattling, confusing, getting in the way of the regulars, who had their pitches and their patrons, as he liked to call them, who stopped every day, to listen for a few minutes, call out hello or goodbye or how'ya doing, then drop their money on his leather satchel before walking away, their footsteps getting lost in the layers of all the others. And he had felt annoyed and bad-tempered, unable to find his opening note in the cacophony.

Until he heard, somewhere to his right, a voice. And he put down his tin whistle and turned, reaching for Grace's harness, pulling her to her feet, urging her forward, closer to the sound that slipped into his body as if through every pore in his skin, making the hairs stand up on his arms, and his eyes, sightless since he was a baby, fill with tears that flowed like a flood tide down his cheeks.

> *I heard a maiden sitting and sing,*
> *She lulled her child, a little lordling,*
> *Lullay, lullay,*
> *My dear son, my sweeting,*
> *Lullay, lullay,*
> *My dear son, my own dear dearing.*

The din of the street faded into a muffled, muted background. He felt himself bathed in the beauty of the sound. And he began to pray, Hail Mary, full of grace, the way his mother had taught him.

"Pray, Billy, to Our Lady. And she will bring back your sight. Have faith, Billy, Our Lady will intercede with the Holy Father on your behalf. Pray, Billy, pray with me."

The pavement was coated with a thin film of ice, but he

sank down on his knees anyway, holding on to his dog for support, while all around him he heard the voice, like the angels his mother told him flew wherever Our Lady was to be found. Felt her touch on his hands as she lifted him to his feet, asking him what was wrong, leading him away from the noise that howled at him now, pulling him in every direction. Putting an arm around his thin shoulders, her breath on his cheek, the feel of her soft breasts through her coat, pressing into his side as she drew him away from the din, bought him tea and listened, offering friendship and understanding as he told her how his mother had promised that his eyes would get better. Promised, and lied. And left him with no one and nothing. Darkness and silence. And fear.

8

There was a phone call first. A man's voice she didn't recognize.

"I'm looking for Mrs. Neale, Mrs. Anna Neale."

She didn't answer immediately. She tried opening her mouth. Her jaws felt stiff, locked shut. No saliva moistened her tongue and her throat was tight as if swollen. Like David's, she thought, her eyes moving slowly around the room.

"Hallo, hallo, is there anyone there?"

She was lying on the sofa, her legs half covered by an old sheepskin coat. She moved slowly, swinging them down to the floor, feeling the carpet underneath her feet, avoiding the mugs and glasses that were strewn in a semicircle around her.

The voice continued in her ear. "I'm sorry to disturb you but I was wondering if I could come and see you. It's to do with your husband. I know it's probably not a great time right now, but perhaps we could just talk . . ."

The voice trailed off and there was silence again. She tried to remember why she was here on the sofa, in front of a fire that had been cold and dead for hours. She stood up slowly and carefully, the phone in one hand, and walked towards the window. Sunlight seeped through the heavy cream material of the curtains. She put out her hand to pull them apart and again she heard the voice.

"Is that you, Mrs. Neale? Please, I just want to ask you a couple of questions."

He had said he would call in an hour if it was convenient. He said his name was Alan Murray, that he had met David a few times through his job. He didn't tell her then, on the phone, that he was a sergeant in the Garda, that he was working with the Drug Squad, and that he and David were familiar to each other from the cramped and squalid District Court and occasionally the echoing grandeur of the High Court. He waited until he had drunk the tea she had prepared for him, commenting on how nice it was to get the real thing, a properly made pot, warmed, with three teaspoons of tea leaves, stirred and left to draw before it was poured.

"It's delicious. I thought I was the only person who still cared about making a decent cup of tea." He stared at her over the rim of his cup. She was looking at the floor, the index finger of her left hand twisting a lock of hair into a tight knot, then letting it go, smoothing it out and twisting it even more tightly again. He watched as he spoke, fascinated by the parade of expressions that crossed her face. Her mouth and chin trembled, just for a moment, then tears began to slither silently over her cheekbones and onto her hands. He reached into his pocket and took out a handkerchief. He held it out to her. "It's okay," he said, "it's clean. Fresh from the drawer this morning."

She smiled again, this time a deep dimple appearing

just above the left side of her mouth, and lifted it to her eyes.

"The real thing, in hankies too. No tissues for you?" She looked at him properly for the first time, noticed the dark red hair, light blue eyes, the kindness of his expression.

She poured more tea while he explained why he had come to see her.

"I got this phone message, you see, from your husband, saying he wanted to talk to me about something personal. But I didn't actually receive it until two days after he died. I'd been off work for a few days. My wife is pregnant, and she's been quite ill. Terrible morning sickness. She had to go into hospital, just for a bit of a rest, really, so I'd taken some leave to look after our little girl. So I wasn't in the office when he phoned."

"David phoned you? Were you friends?"

"Well," he pushed his dark red hair back from his freckled forehead and smiled, "we weren't exactly friends, but we'd known each other, first by sight and then to have the odd conversation, oh, I'd say for the last three years or so, since I was transferred to the Drug Squad."

"The Drug Squad, you're involved in all that?"

"Yeah, all that." He mimicked her tone of voice. "You know the way it is, David's clients were in and out of court like cuckoos in a clock. Up on remand, tried, sentenced, released, up on remand. You know what junkies and small-time dealers are like. Unstoppable."

"But, hold on a minute." She leaned across the table towards him. Her face, he noticed, had regained its color.

Her cheeks reminded him of his daughter's, her skin as smooth and perfect as Emily's. "David wasn't that kind of solicitor. He didn't do that sort of thing. He wouldn't have been in court." Conveyancing, personal injuries, corporate work, contracts, wills, nothing that involved drama, she seemed to remember him saying. No family stuff, no criminal work. Too messy. Keep it simple, he had said, and for Christ's sake, it's the last thing I want to talk about when I come home. What I want to talk about is you, and how do I love you. So much I can't count the ways. That's what he said. And what did she say? What did she think? Could she remember?

"No?" Murray raised his eyebrows, then continued. "We are talking here about *the* David Neale, aren't we? The one whose mobile phone number is written on practically every cell wall in the Bridewell." Scratched with safety pins, stubs of pencils, scrawled in lipstick, even, he remembered the station sergeant telling him, smeared in blood after a savage brawl. His name passed in whispers. Get on to Neale, he's the fuckin' business. He'll get one of his fellas to come down here and get you out of this fuckin' dump.

"In the Bridewell?" She repeated the phrase as if struggling to master a strange language. "Such a pretty name for such an awful place. I didn't know David was ever there. He didn't tell me." She thought of the pictures on the television news. Prison vans, armed police, men in handcuffs, their coats slung over their heads trying to conceal their identities. And always anger, rushing from the waiting crowds.

He smiled at her and held out his cup for more tea. She lifted the large blue teapot in her two hands, as if it was far too heavy for her to manage. He reached over and took it from her. He poured for both of them.

"Oh, he was there all right. Regularly, often."

There was silence in the kitchen now. The fridge motor switched itself on and hummed loudly, setting up a vibration that rattled and banged unevenly.

Anna looked over at Murray.

"So, you met him in court. So?"

"So, you know the way it is, everyone gets to know everyone else because it's the same cast of characters week in, week out. And then every now and then, when there was a really big case, when we thought we'd landed ourselves a prize, there would be David Neale." He paused and drank some of his tea. "I knew I'd seen David somewhere and then I realized, of course. I'd seen him play in an under-21 match against France years ago, rugby, you know?"

"Oh." She smiled.

"Yeah, when I was at school. He was brilliant, scored three tries. And I play a bit myself, club games, that sort of thing, or I used to until we had the baby. So one day when we were all hanging around, I asked him about it, the rugby that is, and he was amazing, had this incredible memory for games. So after that we'd always say hello. But I really got to know him a couple of years ago, just after Emily was born."

"Emily?"

"My little girl. You see, she was nearly six weeks' premature when she was born. I got the call to go to the hospital when I was in court. It was right in the middle of a case, one that David was involved in. There was a bit of a panic about it, she was so tiny, and Sarah, my wife, had a hard time. I was in a bit of a state and I'd been down in the Rotunda with her, and I came back up to court, and somehow or other I started telling David all about it, and he was so kind and understanding. So after that, if he was around at lunchtime we'd have a sandwich together and sometimes we'd have a pint when whatever case was all over."

"But surely, surely you were on opposite sides, weren't you? I do have this right, don't I? He would be defending the person who was on trial, and you would be prosecuting them, isn't that what you mean?"

"Yeah, but he was the solicitor, instructing, as they say, the barrister. He didn't actually handle the case in court, and anyway it's not like that, really, it's nothing personal. Afterwards, well, everyone wants to relax a bit and let their hair down. There'd always be a gang of people in the pub afterwards."

The air thick with smoke and loud with congratulations and recriminations. Barristers in their sleek black suits, their clients dressed in their best, their cleanest, their neatest. Jeans and sweatshirts, washed and pressed for a change. A suit dragged out of the back of a closet and given a lick with a hot iron. Lank hair slicked back, pallid faces shaved, buying rounds, wads of money strewn across the counter. And David Neale, always in the thick of it. Taller than everyone else, lounging against the bar, swapping jokes with everyone, from the street junkie who would be dead in six months to the barrister who came to court in a vintage Bentley, chauffeur-driven. And beside him, Alan Murray, the sergeant from the Drug Squad, charmed and beguiled like the rest.

"Did he talk about me?"

"Of course he did." What harm to tell a lie now? What was it his mother used to say? If it's told for a good reason, then God won't mind. And his father would snort with derision. Your God, he'd say, your Catholic God, he's so understanding of all your weaknesses, isn't he?

The fridge clicked off again. Loudly. He watched her finger, twisting and turning in her fine fair hair. He shouldn't have come. Whatever it was that David Neale wanted had nothing to do with this pale, pretty girl who looked like she had stepped from the pages of a children's storybook, in her long gray skirt and fine wool sweater, a scarf the color of ripe rowan berries looped around her shoulders.

"So strange," she looked down at the floor, then back up at him, "I keep on waiting for David to come home and tell me that it was all a mistake, an illusion. It's a really powerful feeling, but somehow I don't think it's going to happen. Not now. And I feel so tired, all the time."

He left her then, handing her his card, watching the way she dropped it on a stack of newspapers, by the front door.

"Don't lose it," he said, and reached down to pick it up again. "You might need it sometime." He looked at the paper on the top of the stack. "Is it you who does the crossword?" He smiled. "Pretty difficult this one. I only got half of it done, but you must have had help to finish it." He pointed at the squares. Most were filled in in blue Biro, large, sprawling letters that strayed out of the boxes, but interspersed between them were tiny, neat letters, written with a fine black pen.

She took it from his hand. She shook her head. "No, it wasn't me, it was David who did it. Always, every night. Before we went to sleep." Sitting up beside her in bed while she dozed against his side, inhaling his warm smell, cigar smoke and alcohol. And she would wrap her legs around his and draw him down beside her into the comfort of sleep.

Like the sleep that dragged her back to her place on the sofa, pulling on an old nightie, twisting and turning like a cat making its bed, until she was safe again, and again she could let go of the present.

UNTIL SHE woke. And she was standing. It was cold and very dark, and her feet felt wet and sore. She looked down, rocking slowly from side to side, trying to feel what was beneath her. She shifted awkwardly, reaching for the comfort of the sofa and chairs, the warmth of the fire. But there was nothing but angular shapes that would not identify themselves. She stepped forward one pace, and realized as her pupils slowly dilated that she was not in the house. Somehow she had found herself in the garage. Below her was a rough concrete floor, above her, bare crossbeams and a corrugated iron roof. She stepped forward again and tripped, her foot hitting something hard and unyielding. Pain shot up her leg, and she cried out. She put out her hands to protect herself. And felt underneath her fingers a scrap of paper. Shiny, smooth. Irregular edges, as if torn. She stepped farther into the middle of the floor and reached up. Somewhere she knew there was a light switch. She turned around in half-circles, swinging out her arm until she felt the cord brush against her. She grasped hold of it and tugged hard. Light everywhere. Sunbursts in front of her eyes so they hurt, as the pupils spiralled inwards. She blinked and blinked. And noticed first of all the orb web. Suspended from the roof beams. A near-perfect circle. The sticky silken threads glistening. And waiting in the center, *Araneus diadematus,* its white cross shining. She reached up on tiptoe to look more closely, noticing the flies and daddy longlegs trapped.

As she lifted her hand to push back her hair from her face, she saw what she was holding. A photograph: David, smiling, a cigar in his hand, a glass on the table in front of him. He was half turned to his left, looking at someone. But the other part of the picture was missing. She ran the tip of her index finger down the rough edge. She looked again at the photograph. It had been taken with a flash, held too close. David's eyes were bright red. An unnatural color, like the kind of lollipop that children are given as a treat. She squatted down on the cold, dirty floor, looking for the other half of the picture. But there was nothing. Only a scattering of dried leaves blown in from the garden, and a handful of rusty screws and nails that pricked her feet as she moved. In one corner was propped a fork, spade, and hoe, and next to them the lawn mower. She pushed it away from the wall, and began to move the other garden tools. And behind her the door to the garden banged, swinging open on its hinges, a sudden gust of wind swirling through the dust.

She turned quickly, still holding the photograph, and stepped outside. A fitful breeze pulled at her hair and flicked up the cotton of her nightdress and soft drops of rain spattered on her bare arms. Beside her a screen of shrubs, leafless still, jerked their branches. She walked towards them, picking her way carefully across the grass, her feet cold and sore. Shrubs and shadows swayed together, branches entwined like lovers' arms. Then as she watched, one seemed to detach itself and move in her direction. Three slow steps. And stopped. And backed away. And in a swift and graceful movement leaped for the wall and was gone.

She began to cry then, her mouth open in fear and horror, both her hands covering her eyes, pulling a pall of invisibility down over her. And realized that she no longer had the picture, that she had let it fall from her grasp. She dropped to her hands and knees, feeling in the dark, the wet grass, scrabbling around searching for her piece of paper. Until, finally defeated by the cold and the rain, which now was sluicing down, she struggled back into the kitchen.

She told James, when he came to see her the next day with more papers to be signed. But he just looked at her ashen face and the way she sat huddled up on the sofa staring at the bars of an electric heater and said, "Grief does strange things to people, you know."

She didn't reply. She knew all about grief. And she had for years.

9

Michael always travelled by ferry whenever he had to go to England on business. It wasn't that he had anything against planes or flying, quite the contrary: he loved the power that pushed him back into his seat, the vibration that worked its way from the soles of his feet up through his body. He especially liked the denial of the laws of gravity, Newton's apple flung up into the air with such force that it could stay there forever. Or, at least, until the fuel ran out. But the problem for him was that security in airports was oppressive. Far too thorough. He could never be sure who was logging his movements. Times and dates stamped on everything: the ticket for the car park, the cup of coffee bought in the restaurant, the trip to the toilet. Cameras all over the place, some whose positions he could see, others whose presence he could assume. He knew too many people who had been picked up by the cops after a flight, who hadn't realized what Customs knew about them or what they were carrying, who hadn't anticipated the grainy black-and-white pictures the surveillance cameras had recorded, kept for safe-keeping. Until they might be wanted.

It was the terrorists who had screwed it all up. So much

paranoia about hijackings. Now there were always too many police around, with too much time on their hands. Getting the big picture, making the connection between the guy waiting in the multistory car park in Birmingham or the high-rise flat in London, with the man passing through the boarding gate on the ten-fifteen flight to Heathrow or Gatwick or Stansted. Taking note of just another link in the growing chain of evidence, that one day, if he wasn't careful, would wrap itself around his neck and drag him down with the rest.

So it was the boat now or the high-speed catamaran when he wanted to travel to and from England. No baggage checks. A cursory glance at his ticket, the cold in the bleak little station at Holyhead or the windy pier in Dun Laoghaire driving away all thoughts and desires from the Customs officers and the harbor police, except to be tucked up in bed with the missus.

He liked it all, the lights of the port, orange, yellow, white, shimmering back up at him from the dark, oily water in the harbor. He'd watch through the windows until they left behind the twin lighthouses, and wait until he could feel the change in the engine as it met the surging, lifting, rolling swell of the Irish Sea. Then he'd walk to the bar, his feet gripping the carpet tiles beneath them, holding him upright even though the passageway tilted to one side or the other. He'd find himself a table on his own and take out a book. And he'd listen. To the raucous, drunken conversations that surged around him, getting louder and louder as land was left farther behind.

A couple of times he actually came up with some useful

information. There was one trip in particular, a few years ago, that had paid for itself more often than he could possibly compute.

It was funny how it happened. He'd been sitting, as always, carefully minding his own business, but that hadn't lasted for long. The bar was full of Travellers. People his granny referred to as tinkers. They must have all been drinking before they got on board, because they were well pissed already. One of the women stood up and began to sing. She had long rust-colored hair piled on top of her head, and huge pendulous breasts underneath a shapeless black sweater. One hand held a bottle, Newcastle Brown, he thought, by the label. A cigarette burned down between the stubby fingers on her other hand. And her chins vibrated as the words of the song poured out of her large red mouth.

He knew it well. It was one of his granny's favorites. She'd sing it as she kneaded the dough for tomorrow's brown bread and rolled out the pastry for the tarts that were her specialty:

> *If I was a blackbird, I'd whistle and sing*
> *And I'd follow the ship that my true love sails in,*
> *And on the top rigging I'd there build my nest*
> *And I'd pillow my head on his lily white breast.*

Listening to the music pouring out of the radio on the bookcase in the corner, big and brown, with tattered stubbly material stretched across the speaker. As he lay on the sofa, his thumb jammed behind his teeth, his gaze wandering around the cobwebbed ceiling. His granny kept him up at night, company for her through the school holidays until his mother sent the letter with the money for his fare home, back to London and winter.

The Traveller woman could sing. In spite of himself he lifted his eyes from his book to watch her. A mistake. She swayed towards him, and stood with one hand on her hips, her bright blue eyes fixed on his face, while all around cheered and urged her on. And when the song was over she sat down beside him and put one hand on his thigh, while she asked him, her spoken words slurring in a way that her singing words didn't, "Come on, mister, will ye buy me a pint?"

He tried to back off, politely, averting his eyes from the unstitched scars that puckered and twisted the skin on her chin, but suddenly she was gone, yanked to her feet by her hair, then lying sprawled and screaming on the filthy floor, a booted foot crashing down on her ribs. And before he really thought about it he was on his feet too, pushing the man away. Stupid move. There were six of them and one of him. He could handle himself all right, but not when the odds were so against him, and the opposition had already started smashing glasses.

Backing him against the wall, something sharp sticking into his neck and the smell of the whiskey foulness of the man who had him pinned with his knee against his groin. As he tried to speak, to smile, to reassure, but now he could feel the drop of blood rolling warmly down his suddenly cold, sweaty skin.

And then as quickly as it had begun it was over. Two men from a group who had been standing around the bar had pulled off his attacker, and shoved back the rest of the pack, waving what he realized were police identity cards. He felt like laughing. At the irony of the situation, as they threatened and warned off the Travellers and drew him into their circle, handing him a clean handkerchief to wipe the blood from his neck, giving him advice about doctors, hospitals in Dublin he could visit, offering him brandy for the shock of it all. What could he do except thank them, and accept their help gracefully?

There were twelve of them in all. Off-duty Guards and sergeants. Detectives, they told him. They had been to Manchester for a football match. Some were nearly as pissed as the Travellers, who now had settled down in the far corner. He should have known by the look of them. As identifiable as the other lot. It was the way they had of looking at everyone else. Defining them as "civilians," as outsiders. A group apart. One of his rescuers, tall and lanky, with a thick Cork accent, pulled out a stool and waved him onto it, pressing another drink into his hand. Michael listened to the talk. Mostly about the match they'd seen, the standard of play. Comparison of one star with another. Criticism of the referee. All so predictable.

Suddenly he felt sleepy, as the adrenaline began to seep from his body, lulled by the alcohol, and the gentle vibration from the boat's engines, the only clue really that they weren't in some pub in the city center. He leaned back against the wall and closed his eyes, a sense of warmth and well-being flooding through him. He slept, his head dropping forward onto his chest for a moment, then jerking awake again, opening his eyes, blinking in the bright neon lights.

"Are you all right, boy?" It was the Guard who'd bought him the drink, leaning over him, swaying, his eyes glazed, his face wet with sweat. He sank down on the seat beside him. "Sure you're all right? Wouldn't like anything to happen to you now, would we, after saving your skin from all those." He jerked his head towards the Travellers, who had retreated farther away from the bar. "Here . . ." He stuck out his hand. "My name's Andy Horgan, pleased to meet you."

Michael took hold of his warm, damp grip. "I'm Mick," he said, "Mick Burke. Can I get you another?" He stood up, and pushed his way to the bar. Careful, be very careful, "boy," he thought, as he ordered brandies, doubles.

Horgan swayed slowly from side to side, keeping time with the rhythm of the boat. Ash from his cigarette drooped, then broke off and fell in a long neat tube on Michael's thigh. "Sorry, sorry. Mick, is it?" He peered blearily at him through the smoke and made as if to brush it off. "Where you headed?" Horgan had a look of careful concentration on his thin, unshaven face, but the slightest slur in his voice and the erratic, uncoordinated movements of his hands and arms gave him away.

Michael answered him equally carefully. He was going to Dublin to visit his relations.

"Where you from?" Horgan leaned on the table for support, one hand curled around the glass.

Michael told him. He was from Kilburn, worked in a shop, a newsagent's corner shop, you know the kind. Rambled on about nothing much, the price of drink, the weather. Watching Horgan's eyes, closing, opening, watching him shaking his head from side to side as if to keep himself conscious.

"Come on, drink up, I'll get us another." Horgan pushed himself up from the seat and lurched the few steps to the bar. Michael sat back and listened to the other conversations, to the left and to the right, looked at the two men, sitting at the next table, spotted them for what they were. Younger than the rest, their clothes more casual. Runners, jeans, leather jackets. Drug Squad, he was certain.

But drunk as well. Too much booze for their own good. They were talking about someone they'd seen at the match, how they weren't sure who got the biggest surprise.

"Jesus, business must be good, did you see the jacket on him? And the tart he was with? Christ Almighty, and us busting a gut for the miserable pittance we take home after tax every month. You'd wonder, wouldn't you? Really, you'd have to ask yourself if it's fuckin' worth it."

"Yeah, and he was inside until last week, and now he's out enjoying himself, that piece of shit Joey Roberts. Christ, I'll tell you I'm gonna get that bastard if it's the last thing I fuckin' do. I hate that cunt."

Michael covered his smile with his hand as he listened. He'd have to tell Joey. They'd have a real laugh about it. Everyone in the business knew the coppers were useless gobshites. Still, he reached out to take the glass that Horgan was waving in front of him, it wouldn't do to underestimate them all the time. One of these days they'd get their act together, and then there'd be trouble.

"Christ, I'm fuckin' knackered." Horgan slumped down beside him, and lit another cigarette.

"Hard weekend, eh?" Michael raised his glass. "Thanks, mate."

"Hard? You said it, fucking unbelievable. And unbelievable fucking too." Horgan grinned. "Jesus, unbelievable." He repeated the words slowly, and his tongue slipped wetly along his bottom lip.

Michael fixed an interested expression on his face. "Tell us."

Horgan half rose and tried to loosen the denim of his jeans where it caught tightly around his crotch. "She practically took the balls off me. Jesus, she wouldn't stop. Fuckin' gorgeous."

"Yeah?" Keep it going, keep it casual, sound interested.

Horgan grinned again, animated now, his voice steadier. "Incredible, tits out to here, legs up to here, and what a cunt."

"Sounds like true love to me." Michael drank, and wiped his mouth with the back of his hand. The liquid warmed him from his throat to the pit of his stomach, but he felt more sober now than ever.

"Would be except that she's married. Husband was away this weekend."

"Oh, you struck it lucky then, did you? Or was she out touting for business, looking to earn a few bob while the cat's away?"

"No, you've got it all wrong. She's not like that. An' anyway I'm a fuckin' Guard. I'd know better than to go near any of those cunts." Horgan dragged hard on his cigarette and blew a couple of smoke rings, his mouth forming a tight, muscled circle. "You see, the way it happened, I met her first a few weeks ago, she was over in Dublin from Manchester on a hen night. Her best friend was getting married. Somehow or another we ended up in her hotel room. So I decided to pay her a visit. The return match so to speak. Great excuse, go over for the football with the lads. Say goodbye to them at the station. Spend the night with her. And the next morning, and the afternoon, and the fuckin' evening. Jesus, am I wrecked! But it was worth it."

Michael shrugged, draining his glass. "I dunno. One slag's pretty much the same as another. They all look good in the middle of the night."

Horgan's face darkened. He fumbled in his jacket and pulled out an envelope. "Here, look at these, if you don't believe me." He flung it on the table and stood again, dragging a wad of notes from his pocket. "You just look at those while I'm getting us another and then you tell me, is she amazing or is she what?"

Polaroids, their colors bright and garish. The girl kneeling on the bed. Then, sitting back, her large breasts hanging down, one hand caressing a nipple, the other reaching between her legs. Horgan lying on his back, the girl seated on him. His eyes closed, his mouth wide open. More and more of the same, skin so white, mouth so red, her body wide open, looking like a piece of fruit on the cusp between ripeness and rottenness. Michael could smell the stale air in the room, and hear the shouts and groans of pleasure. He flicked through the photos again, keeping an eye on Horgan's back as he pushed his way to the bar. He knew which one he'd take. A keepsake. Just in case. To remind him to be on his guard. At all times. Unlike the stupid copper who was lurching back to the table again, glasses grasped tightly in hands grown careless and clumsy with alcohol.

"What do you think?" Horgan asked, picking up the envelope, and slowly and deliberately putting it back in his jacket. "What a woman. Had the whole thing set up. A stand thing, you know what I mean, for the camera, automatic timer, the fuckin' works. Click, click, click. Wasn't I right about her?"

"Dead right, that's what you were. Dead fuckin' right." He raised his glass to Horgan and smiled. "I can't tell you how glad I am that we met tonight." As Horgan drank, he slipped and slid slowly and gracefully from the bench to the floor, his head resting gently on Michael's polished boot.

"Sleep well, dear friend." Michael reached down and carefully moved his leg away. "And when you wake, may you have the gift of forgetfulness."

He finished his drink and eased himself carefully from the crowd, pushing in through the swinging door to the toilet. He smiled at his reflection in the mirror and turned on the tap, sluicing cold, clean water over his face and neck. Michael would not forget. He never forgot. Keep it all, his granny used to say, don't throw anything away. You never know when it might come in handy. She was right about that, as she was right about so many things. Keep it all, it'll be useful one day. As sure as there's a God in heaven and his Holy Mother sitting at his right hand.

10

Friendship. Now, there was a concept unknown in the insect world: whole colonies, tens of thousands of tiny creatures, mutually dependent, working as one organism, for the benefit of all, without love or fellowship, motivated by a single notion, the survival and perpetuation of the species.

Anna sat by herself in the silent house, a bottle of wine and a glass on the table in front of her, thinking about friendship. She hadn't, she realized now as she waited for the phone to ring, been a good friend. Perhaps the ways of friendship had to be learned, didn't come naturally, instinctively, like the ability to breathe, to eat, to sleep, to wake. Perhaps we need models, examples, templates to copy, she wondered. She tried to think back, to remember. Her parents must have had friends when they lived in London, before her father became ill, when they had a house of their own and jobs they went to every day, a doorbell that rang, visitors that called. And Isobel, too, had friends, David among them: neighbors who drank tea with her in the kitchen and talked about the price of milk and the cost of winter feed, discussed the progress of the salmon from the bay up the river. She had heard them all, listened from the corridor to the ups and downs of their voices.

She had tried herself to have friends, girls to skip with and play dolls in the windy playground at the national school in the village near Isobel's. But they had turned their backs on her, laughed at her accent and her difference. And then there were her friends at boarding school when she was older, girls who would invite her to their houses for half-terms, or weeks during the summer holidays.

"Go, do go," Isobel would always say. "Be with people your own age. You don't want to come back here and sit around with an old woman like me."

But Anna heard not the words of encouragement, only the relief in her aunt's voice. Anything to keep her at arm's length. So she would go, to big, beautiful houses in Dublin, or in the lush pastureland of Kildare and Tipperary, where she would try to fit in, not to mind that she was being patronized, pitied, offered charity. And then there would always be the moment. She poured herself more wine as she thought about it. Always, the same thing, in every house. She would watch to see who it would be, which one of the male members of the family would try it first. The hand casually brushing her thigh at dinner, the suggestion that they visit the lake, the mountain, the forest. The offer to help with whatever household task she had taken it upon herself to do, ending in a clumsy embrace, a wet mouth stuck to hers, a hand reaching for her breast. Once there was even a father who fell drunkenly on top of her bed, and refused to leave until she had done what he asked. "Don't make such a fuss about it," he whispered, taking her hand. And she wondered the next morning why she had made such a fuss. It wasn't that bad. But he wanted more and more. So she left, hitching a lift into town in the early morning, catching the train back to Isobel's.

And what about the friends of her adult life, that she had shared with David? Already since his death they had ceased to call, to show any interest. They had, she supposed, been David's friends. He had made the effort, arranged the parties, organized the nights at the theater, booked the restaurants. She had gone along with it all, dressed as he had asked her to, done her hair, put on her makeup, been sweet and pleasant, smiled when he talked about her as if she were a small, pretty child. A pet to be admired. Gliding on the updrafts that David's energy created. Rising without effort, and floating, serenely, happily, in his slipstream, then landing softly, gently, unscathed. Until now.

The Guards had come to see her a couple of times, asked her questions and more questions about David and his allergy. Was it common knowledge? Who knew about it? How much did she know about his business affairs, how he had managed to accumulate such debts? They didn't believe her, she could see it in their frank and open expressions, when she said she knew nothing. She remembered what James had said. He was right. It was better to be ignorant, but she didn't feel good about herself. They thought she was stupid and gullible. She watched the looks that passed between them, the pen poised, paused over the notebook. Waiting for her to say something, anything that might give them reason to write it down. But she had nothing to say. I didn't know, she kept on repeating, and heard the rejoinder, How could you not know? The unspoken rebuke. In this day and age. What kind of a marriage did you have?

She wondered now, as she realized that everyone had moved on, while she sat in the empty silent house, and felt herself become invisible, her identity blurred and faded. A nonperson, she thought, alive only to her colleagues in the museum, the people in the local shops she visited every day, and Zoë, ever constant, ever true. But Zoë, her friend from the university, had her own problems. A child born with hemophilia, a constant struggle with his illness, and a permanent feeling of guilt for having brought him into the world.

"See," she could hear David's voice, "people like her shouldn't have children. It's enough of a risk when you know everything there is to know about your family, as we do. But an orphan like Zoë, no one knows anything about her parents. Even she doesn't. What was she thinking of?"

She had struggled to keep their friendship alive, but David had made her choose. She was ashamed now, when Zoë was so good to her. "I'm sorry," she said, out loud. But there was no reply, only the creak of a floorboard above her head, and a soft sigh as if someone had just sat down on one of the deep armchairs in the sitting room next door.

It was cold here in the kitchen. Too much stainless steel, too many white tiles. It was more like an operating theater, a place of dissection, than a warm haven where food was cooked and eaten, she thought, as her gaze wandered over the shiny pots and pans that hung on the walls, the kitchen knives in order of size beside the stove. David's choice. David's house. It had never become hers. Never in the five years they had been married. It was marked by David and his family: the heavy mahogany dining-room table, the dark patterned wallpaper in the sitting room, the family portraits that lined the stairwell, the precious Spode porcelain, which he kept locked away. She had taken out one of the vases, flower-covered, ornate curved handles on either side, and filled it with a large sprig of damson blossom. It sat now on the table in front of her. David's voice scolded, "You'll break it, I know you will, it's worth at least seven hundred pounds." But she didn't care. She leaned forward and breathed in the flower's musky perfume. It hung in the still air, reminding her of the tree that grew in the churchyard by the sea. The white petals dropped down into the marble bowl that sat on top of her mother and father's grave. Rainwater dripped into it too, covering the white stone with a pale green patina. She used to believe when she was a child that the water in the bottom of the bowl could work miracles. Like the well in the woods on the long steep hill to the lake. *Tobar na súl.* The well of the eyes. So cold and clear that the small stones that lay in the little hollow shone as if coated with lacquer. Scraps of cloth, tokens they were called, tattered holy pictures and photographs of the afflicted hung from the branches of the hazel that grew all around. Talismans of hope. She collected her own special water from the marble bowl in a bottle with a dropper and carried it with her to ward off evil. To make the teacher like her, to keep the big girls from teasing her. If only she had her little bottle now.

She put her hand in the pocket of her long cardigan and took out a small package. She laid it carefully on the table in front of her and looked at it, moving it slowly around on the smooth wooden surface with the tip of her finger. It had been waiting for her when she went into the museum this afternoon, sitting with a bundle of unopened letters in the middle of her desk. She had stayed at home until late. She wanted to miss the crowds of schoolchildren who came in noisy, hectic groups, whose voices bounced around the main gallery, rising in echoing waves to the glass roof high above. She would be lucky, she thought. She'd probably manage to slip in with just a nod to the security guard. She could hurry up to her stuffy little office, collect her mail, maybe make herself a cup of tea, and be soothed by the familiarity of her surroundings. The springy wooden floors of the corridors, the mahogany filing cabinets and display cases that filled every spare inch of space, the portraits of all the former curators who stared benignly at her as she walked past.

And she was right. The building was virtually deserted. Only the two security guards were still there. Smiles and nods as she walked past, their eyes and the low mutter of their voices following in her wake. She cringed to think what they were saying, the pity that was coming her way. She didn't want any of it. She began to climb the long staircase to her room.

And the package. Her name printed carefully on the front. She picked it up, and felt through the wadding. It was hard, boxlike. She shook it, holding it against her ear, and it rattled slightly. She turned it over, backwards and forwards, sudden panic rising up through her body. She put it down on the desk and walked to the sink in the corner. She turned on the tap and half filled the smeared glass that was on the windowsill. She drank. She put down the glass and picked up the package again. She slid one finger under the flap, feeling what was inside. Plastic, smooth, hard. She pulled it out, turning it over again in her hand. A cassette tape, her name typed on the inlay card. The tape she now put into the radio in front of her on the kitchen table. She poured herself more wine. She pressed *play*. She listened.

11

Michael Mullen supposed that the first death had been an accident. Or that was how it had seemed at the time. Too much drink, too much excitement. New Year's Eve. Fifteen years ago, although it didn't seem that long when he thought about it now.

He had been out drinking in town with a few friends. Were they friends? Depends on what your definition is, really. Now he'd probably say they were acquaintances, or more to the point that he was in their company from force of habit.

There was Christy Dillon and his girlfriend Tessa. And Eamonn Power and Joey Roberts, of course. And Martin, that mad guy from Derry, the one who ended up in Portlaoise prison. The newspapers called him a "bomb-making supremo." Yeah, right, great with a lump of Semtex and a detonator.

Christy, now, he was a bit more than a friend or an acquaintance. Because Christy had in his inside pocket a plastic bag and in the plastic bag was a beautiful, smooth block of the best Afghan black. It smelled like heaven on a sunny day, and it was worth at least five grand. To be split between them when the right moment came. To be the start of his new business venture.

sobering up as the wind blew down the Grand Canal, little drifts of snow fluttering across the dull gray patches of ice. The others had dropped away, so there was just the two of them, lurching along the path by the water. "No fucking money for a taxi, that bitch took it all." Christy kept on and on about it, moaning that Donna was nothing but a fucking slag, and how he'd be in dead shit with Tessa the next day. And the streets were getting more and more silent, the red-brick houses smaller and meaner and narrower as they followed the arrow-straight line of the canal away from the city center.

It was at Portobello that it happened. So quickly that at first he didn't know what to do. They were crossing the rickety footbridge. Christy was ahead of him, still mouthing on, drunker than he himself realized. His foot slipped on an icy patch and suddenly he was in the lock, the water pouring over the gates above his head. And dark shapes and shadows that could have been anything down there with him.

He shouted, "Help me, for fuck's sake, help me. Please, Michael, please."

A few more times, splashing and trying to swim around and around in a circle that got tighter and tighter, his hands scrabbling on the limestone walls covered with luscious slime that shone green in the streetlights, nourished by generations of rat droppings.

And Michael waited and waited, watching the bobbing shape of Christy's head, hearing his cries turn into sobs. Wondering, puzzling, thinking about the alternatives. Waiting for the crippling cold of the water to slow down the movements of his arms and legs, for his saturated clothes to pull his head under. For first his stomach, then his lungs to fill with the putrid liquid that would drag him beneath the shiny, glittering surface, blind his eyes to the lights from the street, deafen his ears to the sound of the traffic, the laughter of a couple who were staggering hand in hand on the other side of the road.

Now that was an interesting one, wasn't it? The choice that presented itself to him. He could have rushed to the nearest house, banged on the door, screamed that his friend was drowning, that he needed to phone for an ambulance. Or he could have knelt down on the cold grass at the lockside, taken off his jacket and held it out to Christy, something to grab hold of. Then he could have pulled and pulled with all his strength, hoping that Christy's frozen fingers would be able to cling to the saturated material, that the jacket wouldn't rip apart at the seams, so that as soon as Christy got close enough he could lean over, reach down, grab him by the arm, the shoulder, the neck, the head, the hair, and pull him to safety. He could do that. Or he could sit on the heavy wooden beam of the lock gate and wait until there was silence, then walk to the nearest phone box and call the ambulance.

He watched as they dragged Christy out of the water and laid him on the cold ground and gave him mouth-to-mouth resuscitation, and he cried when the doctor came over and put his arm around his shoulder and tried to comfort him, saying, "You did everything you could. He'd been drinking, hadn't he? The alcohol and the cold, there was nothing more you could have done."

He cried again the next morning when he called to see Tessa and sat beside her on the settee in her front room and looked at her long pale face, her light blue eyes puffy and red, and her small slender body curled into its pale pink quilted dressing gown. When she crossed her legs he could see how white they were, the blue veins showing through the fine skin.

She was distraught when she went with him out into the garden, three days later. They'd all gone back to Christy's house after the funeral. It was so cold, a sleety rain snapping at the washing on the line, that they went into the shed. He held her tightly to warm her up and told her he was so sorry that he hadn't stopped Christy from having it off with that girl in the alley, that if she hadn't taken all their money they'd have got a taxi home and none of this would have happened. She looked at him, her face suddenly red with anger, and she said, "What was that? He did what?" And then she was really crying, harsh, angry sobs pouring out of her throat, and he began to kiss her gently on her cheek and her mouth and on her white neck. And laid her down on the old sofa, the one where Christy hid his dope. He thought she'd push him away, that she'd say no, or something. But she didn't. Her pussy was as open and wet as her mouth had been. And suddenly it was all clear to him, as the sun broke through the solid gray of that winter morning and spread its light in rainbow shafts over her pale hair. And he remembered the courtship gift, from the children's encyclopedia on his granny's bookshelf. The body of the dead insect, presented to a potential mate, wrapped in a fragment of silk. And as his breath forced itself out of his body in sudden gasps, a voice called, "Tessa, are you there? Mam says it's time to go." She flung him off her, pulling up her tights and smoothing down her skirt, and opened the door.

A fair-haired boy was standing outside, his blue eyes wandering from side to side, his hand outstretched. And she said, "Okay, Billy. I'm here. I'm coming now."

He watched them picking their way through the mud, the tangled winter grass clutching at their legs as he did up his jacket, feeling in his pocket the comforting smoothness of the Afghan black in the plastic bag. All his now, no need to divide it. A great way to start the year. And sweet Tessa. She'd always been too good for Christy. There'd been talk of them getting engaged next Easter. What a mistake that would have been. He'd done her a favor really, and she'd done him one too. Shown him how to shroud the dead in the silken cloth of betrayal. And the effect that could have. On her, and on him. He'd never forget what he owed her. Never.

12

Anna had pressed *play*. She had listened. She had found a pen and some sheets of lined paper and begun to make notes. She had stopped the tape, rewound it, listened again, made more notes, stopped the tape, rewound it, made more notes still. Then stopped it, rewound it, and listened, no need any longer for the pen. The words and the voices that spoke them floated around the room. Above her, in front of her, behind her. And when she finally crawled onto the sofa and closed her eyes, the words and the voices that spoke them were there too. In her, of her, with her. And nothing could take them away.

But who had sent it to her and why? That was what she wanted to know.

She sat on the floor in front of the fireplace. The room was cold, the fire long dead. James had phoned her in the morning, woken her from a restless, dream-filled sleep and told her he needed to talk, that he would come and see her at lunchtime.

"You will be there, won't you? It's very important." Now she rocked back and forth, the rhythm of the movement soothing, comforting, while James, a younger, duller version of his older brother, gave her the details. How much David owed and to whom. That he was about to be sued by a client who claimed he had misused his account. That there had been a possibility that it might have become a criminal matter.

"If David hadn't died when he did, well . . ." James's voice trailed off.

"Stop. Do you hear me? Stop. Right now." Her voice came out in a shriek as she wrapped her arms over her head, rocking backwards and forwards, her fingers stuffed in her ears.

"Come on, Anna, you've got to know all this."

She raised her head from her bent knees. "No, I don't, James, I don't have to know anything at all. Just leave me alone."

"Anna, you'd better get used to all this, and quickly. Basically, you'd better decide where you're going to live after the house has been sold, and I tell you, you'd better be hoping that you get a good price for it, because David owed a lot of people a lot of money, and now he's dead there's only one person who can pay them back."

She stood up slowly, her legs stiff, her joints aching. "I'll make some coffee." She walked slowly into the kitchen, reaching automatically for the kettle, turning on the tap, putting spoons of coffee into the glass jug. The pen and the sheets of paper lay where she had left them the night before. She straightened them into a neat pile, the written words running easily through her head. Behind her she heard the click of James's well-shod feet on the tiled floor. The sickly sweetness of his aftershave prickled her nostrils. It was on her cheek too, she knew, transferred to her skin when he bent to kiss her. She poured the boiling water into the jug, and thought, just for an instant, of the scream that would come from his mouth if instead of inclining her cheek towards his kiss, she had flung the kettle at him, scalding his pink skin, driving the smug, supercilious grin from his face with its savage heat.

"Do you know something?" His voice was so like David's that it sent a small shiver of anticipation prickling up and down her spine. "It would be much better for you if you had someone here to help you with all of this. Isobel could come and stay for a couple of weeks. She'd be a real support. She'd make everything so much easier."

Would she? Easier? Isobel, her father's sister, younger by years but with the same gray hair, dark eyebrows and large brown eyes. Who never forgave him for assuming that he could come home when he became so ill, that the house and farm he had left when he was a teenager were still his. Who had never "taken to" his wife, Anna's mother. And who had never forgiven them both for dying, drowning, one fine sunny day, when the breeze was light, and a small swell gently lifted and lowered the fishing boats at anchor, leaving behind their seven-year-old daughter, her responsibility now.

"Will you be my mummy, Issy?" Anna had crawled onto her lap one evening not long afterwards. "Will you look after me like Mummy and Daddy did?"

But Isobel didn't answer. She just picked up her glass and drank deeply, pushing Anna away to reach for the bottle again. Isobel with her face ruined by whiskey and anger, her capacity to love buried beneath a hard callus of disappointment and resentment.

"Did David ever talk to you about me?" Anna lifted her head and looked straight into James's pale blue eyes.

"Talk about you? Yeah, of course he talked about you, all the time."

"What sort of things did he say?"

"Oh you know. Chat about what you'd both been up to, this play, that film, such and such a party. You know the sort of thing."

"No, I don't. That's why I'm asking. I've realized that I don't have any idea what David was like when I wasn't there. And I want to know."

James giggled, a soft, silly, nervous sound, and poured himself more coffee. "You don't have anything stronger, do you? Something to perk this up a bit."

"Help yourself." She gestured towards the whiskey on the countertop. His chair clattered noisily as he stood, reached over for the bottle, unscrewed the cap and poured himself a generous measure.

"So," she said, "tell me. What did David say about me? Did he tell you what I was like in bed? Did he tell you how often we made love? Did he talk about how much he wanted me? Did he?" Her voice trailed away to a whisper. "Tell me, I want to know, tell me the truth, for Christ's sake."

DAVID HAD told the woman on the tape.

"I don't know why I married her," he said, more than once. "She was beautiful when I met her first. So young, so perfect."

"Aren't they all," the woman had replied, "aren't they all."

"And she was clever too, not just beautiful. She had a

wonderful curiosity. She wanted to know everything, she wanted to find it all out and keep it for herself. And she was clever in other ways, my perfect girl."

"I bet she was," the woman's voice slurred.

"Yes, she was a clever thing. A funny mixture, completely independent and completely dependent. She used to drive me mad when she was a student. I never knew where to find her. Sometimes she'd vanish for weeks at a time, and I'd be going crazy not knowing where she was. And I'd phone her aunt, and ask her. And then she'd turn up, arrive on my doorstep, full of stories of adventures. And I'd be driven to distraction with jealousy. I couldn't bear to think that someone else had put their hands on that perfect skin."

"Is my skin perfect?" the woman spoke again.

And David replied, "Oh yes, yours is absolutely perfect."

That was the first place where she had to switch off the tape. Get up, go out into the garden, stand in the cold and turn her eyes to the sky. Counting off the stars, Betelgeuse, the huge, the glorious, low on the horizon, the Pole Star, bright and constant, the stars of the Plough stretched far to the north, elongated by the twist of the earth that would bring the hemisphere southwards towards the equator. And when she had calmed herself, dried her tears, she went back to listen to more. And heard him say, "Of course I thought I loved her, but what's love really? A phase, that's all in any relationship. It never lasts, not for long. Power's the thing that's really important. Which of you has the power to hurt. It used to be her, but not any longer."

Then there was no more speech, just sounds that said

more to her than any words. She remembered he had said to her a long time ago how much he admired her ability to be silent. "I can't do it," he said. "I always feel I have to say something, to keep the conversation going, but you can just sit there doing nothing. Not reading, or watching television, or even obviously thinking. You seem to be able just to be. It's extraordinary to watch. It tells me so much about you." Like the long silences on the tape, framed by the sounds that came from David and from the unnamed woman. Telling her more than any conversation they could have had. Driving her up the stairs to his study at the top of the house. Bringing with her his heavy bunch of keys. Fanning them out, separating each from its neighbor. Trying them in turn, opening the filing cabinets, the locked drawers in the desk. Looking for the letters that he always kept, which she had never wanted to read. Filed according to date. Everything, he said, from the letters his mother had written him when he was at boarding school to the postcards Anna had sent him from her summertime field trips. He had laughed once, holding open the filing-cabinet door and flicking with his fingernail across the stiff cardboard dividers, and said, "If you want to know my secrets you'll find them here." She had leaned around him and pushed it shut and sat on his knee and kissed his forehead. "I trust you," she had replied. "You can keep your old secrets, they don't worry me."

But there were no letters anywhere to be found. Only an accretion of checkbooks, bank statements, gas, electricity and phone bills, and appointment diaries, covered in dust, all the entries in David's large, sprawling hand.

Dust, too, in his office on the first floor of the building on Dame Street, the light from below casting a tangerine wash across the ceiling and over the walls. She had been here many times at night. When she was still a teenager and they would meet in one of the bars on George's Street or somewhere closer to the river where no one would know him, or the woman, Marion, wasn't it, with whom he lived. And after a few drinks, he would take her by the hand and bring her here. To the long narrow room that looked out onto the alleyway at the back, littered with beer kegs, and rubbish bins, the smell of coconut and unnamed spices from the Indian takeout next door seeping in through the gaps around the window to the room where there was a sink and a kettle, and a low fold-up bed. She lay on it now, feeling the roughness of the blankets underneath her, and closed her eyes, listening. To the traffic, and the shouts of a drunk, disjointed syllables, meaningless except to him.

She had opened everything. Drawers, cupboards, filing cabinets. All were empty. There were none of his clients' files, his accounts, the records of his business. There was nothing. She had caught the flash of a silverfish, *Lepisma saccharina,* as its flattened body slithered down a tiny crack. Paper-eaters, the scourge of archivists, she thought. But silverfish weren't responsible for the disappearance of the mounds of paper that she had seen so often piled high in these rooms.

"YOU TOOK them, didn't you?"

"What?"

"All the files from his office."

"How do you know?"

"How do you think I know? I was his wife. I have his keys."

James poured more whiskey into his cup. "I had to."

"Why?"

"For Christ's sake, Anna, use your imagination, if not your intelligence. Don't you see that David has been a bad boy? He's been doing things he shouldn't."

"Like what? I don't understand. And I don't understand why I didn't know this was going on."

"Yeah, well, David always said you lived in a world of your own. I always thought he meant it metaphorically, not literally. But you're actually better off this way. At least if anyone asks you about it, you don't have to pretend the dumbwife routine. You're much more convincing than that."

"How dare you speak to me like that?" She was standing now, her face flushed, her fists clenched. "Who do you think you are? Get out of my house."

James stood up. A slick of sweat gleamed from his forehead. He opened his mouth as if to speak, then stopped. He shrugged his shoulders, then buttoned his jacket, taking his car keys from his pocket. He smiled at her, a neat grimace, his lips tightening over his teeth. Then he turned and left.

She waited until she heard the front door slam. Then she took the tape from the pocket of her cardigan, slotted it into the cassette player and reached out for the button. And listened again. David's laugh filled the room, bouncing off all the hard surfaces. "I'm so glad I met you," he said, over and over again. "You are so wonderful, so extraordinary. When I think about you I am lost, when I look at you, I am found again."

Tell me, who are you? Anna listened and listened and the bright light of day seeped away. She sat in the dark, and remembered how she had thought that David would protect her. He would keep her safe and look after her. You will, won't you? You'll never leave me, will you? And he had soothed her and kissed her cheeks and rocked her to sleep. But she had been wrong. Not only had he left her, but he had made sure that her memories of him would be destroyed. That every good and wonderful moment between them would cease to be.

James had told her once, years ago, that marrying David was a mistake. "He's cruel, you know, he likes hurting people."

"You're drunk," she had said, unpeeling his fingers from her wrist. "Don't be ridiculous, you're jealous."

"Yes, I am," James had replied. "Of course I'm jealous. But I'm telling you the truth. You'll be sorry, if you marry him, he won't look after you."

She thought she had proved him wrong. But she hadn't. Somehow David's death had released the demons. She thought she had kept them at bay with magic spells and sorcery. Blowing kisses to a single magpie, not stepping on the cracks in the path, never looking at the new moon through glass. She sat in the dark and she wondered. Who had sent her the tape, and why? That was what she wanted to know.

13

Andy Horgan, that was his name, the cop from the ferry. It had taken Michael Mullen the best part of half an hour to remember it and then to remember where he knew him from. Half an hour, watching him over the shoulders of the men who were crowded around the bar. Seeing the top of his head, catching sight of his long, thin face, then losing him again as someone pushed forward to shout an order at the overworked barman. Finding him, losing him, as one or another of the lads engaged Michael in conversation, whispered a request in his ear, reminded him of a past favor, confirmed a friendship that went all the way back. To the days of his granny's corner shop when they were all kids, buying penny bars and lucky bags and later on single cigarettes. Before they were bringing in any kind of money. Before they could afford the packet of ten or twenty.

It was a Sunday night, six months or so after the incident in the bar on the boat. He would have forgotten all about it, except for the hassle it had caused him with Joey Roberts. He'd wondered at the time what Joey was doing in Manchester. But he'd been so taken with everything else that happened that night that he hadn't really stopped to think about it. Until later. And then it began to disturb him. The Joeys of the world didn't do much travelling. They had their routines, their areas of influence, if you could call it that, their clients, their regulars, their suppliers. Their lives were circumspect, controlled by their need for the drug, and the money to buy it. That was what kept the whole merry-go-round working so smoothly. The Joeys of the world knew their place. It reminded him of the hymn he used to sing when he was a little boy at school in London.

> *The rich man in his castle,*
> *The poor man at his gate,*
> *God made them high or lowly,*
> *And ordered their estate.*

So his ears should have pricked up when he heard the cops talking about him that night. And it all became crystal clear a couple of weeks later. Joey had organized his own supply. All by himself. He'd gone straight to the source and cut out the middleman.

Or so he thought. But Michael had other ideas. Poor old Joey was a perfect example of how you can definitely have too much of a good thing. The overdose that killed him was so pure, so powerful that for a moment before he lost consciousness his expression was that of a mystic who has seen the face of the Lord. He was a sweet bloke, really, Michael thought afterwards. But too trusting. When he had called to see him, Joey seemed unconcerned for his own safety, as if he didn't realize that Michael might have a problem with his newfound independence. And when Michael handed him the plastic bag and said, "Here's a present for you, Joey, just to show there's no hard feelings," he took it, even thanked him.

That was a problem solved. But right now, here on this Sunday night in his old local at the far end of the South Circular Road, there was another problem in the making. And it was coming from the family who were sitting around a table over in the corner near the dartboard. He knew them well. The Delaneys. Father and mother and five children. Four sons and their darling daughter Bernie, the apple of their collective eye. Who was snuggled up, holding hands with the cop from the boat, Andy bloody Horgan.

He tried to remember what he'd told him. Something about coming over to visit relations, worked in a shop in Kilburn. A story so clichéd and hackneyed that only the very stupid or the very drunk would have fallen for it. Michael knew that it wouldn't square with what the Delaneys could tell the cop. He watched them all carefully. Horgan had seen him. There was a puzzled look on his face. Michael could imagine what was going on in his head. How much did he remember about that night on the ferry? He'd be anxious, ill at ease. He'd want to try and find out what Michael was doing in this pub where everyone knew everyone else and no strangers ever drank, unless they had a very good reason.

And Michael certainly knew everyone here. Seed, breed and generation as his granny used to say, as she sat on her high stool behind the counter, with her ledger in front of her, every Sunday evening, adding up what each family owed. Charting the changes in their lives through what they bought. Tins of milk powder, bottles of gripe water when they had their new babies. Packets of crisps and Snack biscuits when the kids started going to school. Big bottles of minerals, balloons, colored candles and icing-sugar for their birthday cakes. And the endless demand for tins of beans, packets of soup, fish fingers, instant this and instant that.

"Do none of them know how to cook?" she would sneer. "Do they not know they could make themselves a dinner for half the price that I'm charging them? No better than animals, that's what most of them are," as she totted up the long column of figures in her head.

But the Delaneys were different. Even Granny, hard to please where Dublin people were concerned, acknowledged that. The kids had all gone to secondary school and stuck it out to the Leaving Certificate. Bernie had a good job in the civil service, and the boys were all working too. One was an electrician, one a plumber and the other brothers had set up their own security company. Maybe that was where Horgan came in, Michael thought. Doing a bit of moonlighting. Wasn't that the way with Guards? Always game for a bit of extra work.

Suddenly the noise level dropped, as two of the older men at the far end of the bar began to sing. Tonight was a Sinatra night. The regulars were mad for his music. Michael watched the singers, the way they closed their eyes and swayed in time to the tune. He swayed too, his fingers drumming out the rhythm on the pitted bar counter. The song ended and he joined in the applause, then turned away from the crowd and raised his hand, gesturing to the barman to buy a round for the singers. And saw that Horgan was standing at the other end, a tray of drinks in front of him. Their eyes slid past each other. Michael watched as Horgan carried the tray to the table and sat down again, slipping his arm around the shoulders of the girl and whispering something to her. Then he stood up and walked towards the battered door in the corner with the hand-painted "gents" sign on it. Michael picked up his pint and drank half of it in one long swallow. He wiped his mouth on the back of his hand and picked his way through the crowd, nodding to some, greeting others, a word in an ear here, a pat on the back there. He stopped at the Delaneys' table. He shook hands with the da and ma and asked politely after the others. "You're looking well, Bernie, great. When's the baby due?" She frowned and stared into her orange juice. She was always a snooty bitch.

"A couple of months, Michael." Her mother spoke for her.

"Great stuff, glad to see you all."

He pushed open the door to the toilets. He thought of the photograph that he had put away carefully, somewhere safe. You could see that Horgan was a skinny bloke, not much flesh on his ribs. Wiry, though, tougher than he looked. Michael was sure that they could come to some mutually satisfactory arrangement. Everyone had secrets after all. And what was to be gained by telling them, by sharing them? He was sure he could persuade Horgan to see things his way. There'd be a reward, of course. For both of them. Bernie Delaney would never need to know what her new husband had been up to, and Michael was sure that there'd be a load of useful information that Andy Horgan could pick up for him around Garda headquarters. Everything he'd need to keep one step ahead of the posse. Yes, there'd be a reward all right. And it would be where his granny always said you should get it. In this world and not the next.

14

It was ten miles or so from the city to the cottage where the beekeeper lived.

"You didn't tell me," Anna said, "how you found this guy."

"That's because I didn't." Murray glanced over at her. "He found us. Simon Woods is his name. He phoned Donnybrook station, said he'd read about your husband's death. Actually he said he was away at the time, but when he got back the whole beekeeping fraternity was buzzing about it. Sorry, sorry," Murray paused, "bad pun, ouch and all that."

She didn't respond.

"Anyway, he'd heard about David's death, so he just wanted to give whatever help he could."

"And did he say why he sent the bees?"

"He said that it was all perfectly straightforward. He has a regular ad in one of the beekeeping magazines, a coupon you fill in, you know the kind of thing, and your husband sent it off, with his credit-card number and his address, all that was required. So Woods posted the order out to him, just the way he would to anyone else. And, in fact, he went away on the same day. He had no reason to

But it never seemed that night to be the right moment. And it was all because of that girl from out Dun Laoghaire way. Donna was her name. She was, Michael remembered, with a sudden flush of sensation, a real cracker. Tall and strong-looking, long legs with muscled calves and a cleavage just waiting to be stroked. He had sat and looked at her in the pub that night. Just watching how she moved, slipping from foot to foot on the high stool, so that her short satin skirt rode up over her thighs, easing her hand into her tight little blouse, fiddling with her bra straps, as if she was feeling the weight of her breasts. Christy was after her too. Thinking about nothing else. He kept on leaving Tessa without a drink, forgetting all about her, ignoring her, pretending not to hear when she asked him for a cigarette, when she tried to demonstrate her claim. Christy wasn't having any of it. Not that night.

There was a bar extension until two, and a disco. But Tessa didn't stay for it. She walked out, her back straight, her head held high, although Michael was sure he'd seen tears. For Christy's benefit, of course, although Christy didn't notice. He was dancing with Donna, if you could call what he was trying to do dancing.

All the time that lump of dope was burning a hole in his pocket. And Michael wanted his share, and wanted it badly. After all, he'd paid for half of it, doing his granny's dirty work. Collecting overdue repayments on the money she lent to those she called the "less fortunate," in the area. And he wasn't going to let that drunken slob make off with his investment. He remembered that eventually he followed Christy into the gents', shoved his hand inside his jacket, and pulled out the dope while Christy was still fumbling with his zip and his prick. And backed away quickly, looking at the size of his forearms and hands.

But Christy was past caring. All he wanted was the girl. Grabbing hold of her tits in the sweating, yelling mob that crashed around on the dance floor. While she gazed over his shoulder towards the corner where Michael lounged, her eyes wide open and sober, then walking away without a backward glance as the disco lights were switched off, the neon flooded the room, and the barmen started sweeping up, lifting her coat and her bag from the chair, taking a cigarette from Christy's packet, lighting it, then almost as an afterthought pocketing the rest.

She took whatever else he had, too, three tenners, a couple of fivers and a handful of loose change, when he'd finished fucking her up against the wall at the end of the side alley. Michael couldn't quite see how Christy would manage it. He was so drunk he could barely balance, his jeans down around his ankles, leaning forward with one arm pushed against the bricks, the other pulling at her hips. Michael stood underneath the streetlamp and watched them. And she watched him right back, the cigarette still burning between her fingers, then reaching down to rummage in Christy's pockets, before he'd even caught his breath and pulled up his underpants. She didn't smile as she walked past Michael. She just folded the money into a tight roll and put it in her bag. And left without even saying goodbye.

Michael laughed. He admired her style. But Christy didn't see the funny side. "Why didn't you stop her, the lousy bitch?" He cursed and swore all the way home, was a dirty evening, cold, with a blustery east wind and a drenching rain. Murray had opened his umbrella, holding it low down over his face as he walked, but the wind kept grabbing it, whipping it inside out. Finally it pulled it from his hands and sent it spinning, in a series of demented somersaults, into the middle of the traffic. Then a passing car had slowed and stopped, the door opening. David Neale had beckoned to him. Murray could still feel the warmth in the car and smell the leather of the seats. What was it his father always said? "That's the smell of money and don't you forget it."

Neale had offered to drive him home, protested that it was no problem, that he wasn't in a hurry, but Murray insisted that the station was far enough. What had they talked about? He tried to remember. Neale had asked after Emily, he was sure of that. He always did, and Murray had pulled out the most recent photographs. Christmas, Emily opening her stocking in front of the fire. They hadn't talked of anything of any real importance, he was certain about that. It wouldn't have been appropriate. At the end of the day David Neale was on the wrong side. And that was the sum of it.

It was funny, though, how much Murray liked him. For no particular reason, really, except that he had that graceful charm. He looked down again at Anna's pale face and closed eyes. It had been a surprise to see that he was married to someone like her. She didn't fit the picture he'd imagined. She looked too young for David Neale. Not his type at all.

Two miles outside Rockallen, they crested the hill.

Below them was a long valley bisected by a deep, fast-flowing stream. Murray remembered paddling in those same foaming brown waters years ago on a hot June day, his toes carefully negotiating the tumbled slippery stones, until he overbalanced and fell backwards with a yell, and heard above the splash of his body, in the rushing cold water, the laughter of the blonde girl with the rosy cheeks who lay sunbathing on the rug on the bank.

"See that?" He slowed and pointed to the spot where the stream widened out into a circular pool. "That's where I asked my wife to marry me. For the first time, that is. She laughed me out of it. I think I had to ask her four more times before she said yes."

Anna didn't respond. Idiot, he thought. Why don't you think before you speak? He glanced sideways at her. "Sorry, that wasn't very considerate, was it?"

She shrugged. "It's not your fault. It gets to the stage where everything that anyone says is wrong. And at that point silence takes over. And that's not a good thing either, if you see what I mean."

"Okay." Murray paused, then pointed. "Look, isn't that it? See the sign, hanging from the tree?"

SHE WALKED on ahead of him, up the flagged path towards the two-story cottage. Algae bloomed greenly on the gray stones. A wind chime sounded gently, breathy notes moving through the pipes. She looked to see where it was hanging and found it among the branches of a rowan. Behind her Murray peered through the small downstairs windows. Inside was a large room, sparsely furnished. A fire was burning in the grate and the cat inside, on the windowsill, stood, arched its striped back and mewed loudly. Anna walked on, around the house, to the meadow beyond. This year's grass peeped, a pallid green, through the tangled brown of last year's growth. No sign yet of the wildflowers, the corn cockles, poppies, oxeye daisies, loosestrife, and purple spires of foxglove, which in midsummer would brighten it and bring it to life. The beehives were placed at regular intervals, angled to make the most of the fragile shafts of early summer sun. Like tiny ancient monuments, Anna thought, positioned exactly so the light could animate them, bring them to life with its golden warmth.

She stood still and listened. A gentle hum vibrated in the quiet. She walked forward slowly, then stopped again, watching the small dark shapes as they darted in and out of the slatted openings. Every movement was filled with purpose, worker bees going about their business. She took another few steps forward, her feet sinking into the soft ground. She felt a gentle touch on her hand. She looked down at the bee that had landed on her skin. She lifted her hand slowly upwards. The bee's antennae twitched and its wings fluttered as it maintained its balance. It looked so sleek and brown. Like toffee with a stripe of butterscotch, she thought, as it rose from her hand and hung in the air in front of her before flying away.

"Well done." The voice was loud behind her. Her heart jumped inside her chest. She turned around. "A perfect way to handle a honeybee. . . . You're his widow, are you?" Simon Woods said. He reached out his right hand

and took hold of hers. His fingers were warm and callused. "I'm so sorry for what happened. I had no idea that your husband was allergic like that. Absolutely no idea."

"How could you? It's not your fault, please don't think that I came here to try and lay some blame on you, because I didn't."

"So why did you come? And who's he?" He jerked his head towards Murray, who was leaning against the wall of the house, his eyes closed, his face turned towards the sun.

"He's a friend of my husband's. He thought it would be good for me to meet you. Because I'm trying to understand why. Why my husband did something so irrational, so dangerous, so completely crazy. Tell me," she paused, "did you have any other contact with him, he didn't phone you at all, did he?"

"No, nothing."

"But surely you must have some conversation or something with the people who buy your bees."

"Why?"

"Well, how do you know that they know how to treat them, look after them, manage them?"

"You don't, but neither do you have any reason to think that they won't. They pays their money and they gets their bees. Sometimes they phone me afterwards to say that they're delighted with what I've sent them, but quite often I never hear from them again."

"So you really have no idea why my husband contacted you?"

"I've told you already. To order bees. I got the coupon, filled in—legibly filled in, which makes a huge difference.

I wish more people would use typewriters like your husband did, although these days there are so few of the old mechanical ones left. And quite often I can't decipher the handwriting, and that's a real hassle."

Woods fumbled in the pocket of his creased denim jacket and pulled out a worn tobacco pouch and a small hooked pipe. "Look, I'm really sorry, I wish I could help you in some way, shed some light on this whole business. But all I can say is, when you think about it, the coupon was filled in with the address and credit-card number of a man called David Neale. That's all that is sure and certain."

"What do you mean?" Anna looked up at him. His fingers, stained bee brown with nicotine, filled the carved bowl and tamped down the tobacco. He lifted the pipe to his mouth and lit a match, his hands curved around the tiny flame to protect it from the breeze. He inhaled deeply, then breathed out, yellow smoke tainting the air with its vanilla scent.

"I've nothing more to say, really. I'm sorry. I wish I could help you. I love my bees, you know, they're special to me. They've brought peace and order to my life. They're doers, producers, makers of goodness. I hate to think that they could destroy. I'm really very sorry that this happened to your husband. If I could turn the clock back I would. But . . ." He shrugged again and put out his hand. His fingers rested lightly on her shoulder. "I'm sorry, I've upset you, haven't I?"

"It's not you." She stepped back so his hand slid from her. "I just don't understand how this happened. None of it makes sense. None of it seems real to me." She could feel the tears pricking at her eyes and her mouth begin to quiver. She shouldn't have come out here. It was pointless. Acceptance was the only way forward. She was beginning to see that now.

MURRAY OPENED his eyes, blinking quickly, massaging the skin around his eyebrows and the rim of his eye socket as his pupils dilated. He watched the two of them from the sheltered warmth of the gable wall. The tall thin woman, her fair hair shining in the sunlight, and the equally thin figure of the man, who inclined his narrow gray head towards her in conversation. Simon Woods was looking well these days. A hell of a lot better than he did in the black-and-white photographs in his file in Garda headquarters. Living out here in the mountains must be good for him. It would have been a calculated risk coming forward after Neale died. The last thing Woods would want was any hassle from the Guards. But he probably reckoned, Murray thought, that he'd excite less interest if he volunteered whatever information he had. After all, he said he had nothing to hide and the Donnybrook Guards were quite happy with his statement.

Murray straightened up as Anna and Woods turned away from the beehives and walked towards him.

"You'll have coffee, won't you?" Woods pushed open the back door and stood aside to let them both in. "Please, have a seat. I won't be a minute."

The coffee was strong and dark. Its smell mingled with

the others in the dusty house: the powdery ash from the turf fire, a faint underlying scent of cat and the sickly sweet smell of incense, sandalwood, Anna thought, or patchouli oil. An essential accessory of every student bed-sit she was ever in. Large abstract paintings hung on the bare stone walls, flower shapes and flower colors, but dis-torted and exaggerated.

"Are they yours?" she asked him, as he handed her a mug. "They're very beautiful."

He nodded and drank, stroking the little tabby who had settled, stretched out along his thin thigh.

"Did you go to art school?" she continued.

"I had lessons for a while, I had a very good teacher."

Murray leaned forward and helped himself to sugar. "They remind me of the work of a man called Peter O'Malley. Did you know him?"

Simon Woods smiled, a tight, painful grimace. He stood up, the cat tumbling from his lap and landing per-fectly on all four feet. "I knew him. For a while I knew him very well. But that was then. I don't live in the past or the future. I live in the present."

There was an awkward, strained silence. The cat mewed, rubbing itself against Anna's legs, then rolled over on the floor, exposing the soft white fur on its belly. She bent down to stroke it, murmuring endearments. The two men moved away, towards then through the front door. She could hear their voices, but not what they were saying. She began to hum to herself. Over and over again, the same little tune. The way she used to when she was a child, sitting on the landing at Isobel's, hearing the voices, rising and falling, falling and rising. Hearing the sounds but not the words.

The cat rolled over on its side, and jumped to its feet, disappearing up the stairs. Anna stood up and walked outside. Murray was by himself.

"Where's Simon?" she asked, looking around.

"He had to go out, he said to say goodbye to you. He asked me to give you this."

Murray pressed a glass jar of honey into her hand. "He wasn't sure you'd want it. He said if you didn't just leave it here on the windowsill."

She opened the jar in the car on the way home. She dipped her index finger into its silken sweetness and dropped some on her tongue. The taste was strong, tangy. The Egyptians had used honey to embalm their dead, she remembered, to preserve their mortal remains, to keep corruption at bay. She tasted it again and remembered the touch of the honeybee on her hand. Nothing could keep David's memory intact for her now. Not the way it used to be. It was ruined, it was gone, and nothing would ever bring it back again.

15

"It must be difficult," Sergeant Murray had said to her, as he dropped her off outside the house, after they had gone to see Simon Woods. He gestured towards the For Sale sign lashed to the front railings.

She said nothing. She busied herself feeling around in her bag for her keys, her eyes lowered. He thought he saw tears on her cheeks, but when she spoke her voice was steady. "Difficult isn't the word for it," she said, holding out her hand. He felt her fingers, cold, bony, dry, in his. Then she was gone, the door slamming hard behind her. He waited until she had disappeared inside the house, then he put the car in gear and moved away slowly down the road towards the city center. What a strange and contradictory person she was, he thought. At one minute helpless, childlike, almost sexless in her presentation of herself. She reminded him of Emily, with her lack of self-consciousness, her apparent openness and innocence. And then the transformation, as if she had grown a glossy iridescent skin. He had watched her with Woods and seen it happen. He wondered what they had been talking about that had triggered her metamorphosis. He hoped he had been right to bring her out to see him. Woods had always been unpredictable, a bit of a wild card. And hard to pin down. It had been a long time since they'd been able to pin anything on him. Woods had learned his lessons the hard way, and he'd learned them well.

"Don't forget you've got my mobile number, just in case you need anything. Keep in touch, won't you?"

"And you with me, Sergeant, won't you?"

They had both smiled, her gray eyes crinkling up at the corners. And now there was a message from her. He listened to it as he sat beside Emily's cot, watching the yellow teddy bears on her sleeping suit rise and fall in time with the sighing breaths from her half-open mouth.

"Just to let you know, I'm going to stay with my aunt in West Cork for a few days. If you need me for any reason, this is her number," repeated twice, slowly, carefully. Good, he thought, as he put his phone back in his pocket and bent over to rest his lips against Emily's warm, rounded cheek. Better that she should be with someone who cares about her than on her own. Emily stirred against his face. He wanted to reach down, lift her from her blankets and let her sleeping body mold itself against him. He knew exactly how her head would feel drooping onto his shoulder, her arms flopping around his, her strong arched feet curling into the small of his back. She was getting so big and already he mourned the loss of the infant who once would lie cupped against his chest, her tiny arms and legs folded froglike beneath her. But soon there'd be another baby in the house. Sarah was due to give birth in five months. He wanted another child, he was sure of that. But Emily was special. His firstborn. His precious one. He couldn't imagine that he could ever feel anything that would match the way he felt for her.

He stood up and moved away from the cot, backing out of the door, and stepping into their bedroom down the passage. Sarah was asleep too. She had dropped her nurse's uniform in a pile on the floor. He picked up her white smock and baggy trousers, her discarded tights and underwear, and took them with him into the bathroom. He pushed them into the linen basket, which was already stuffed full. He'd put a wash on tomorrow before he left for work. Sarah had enough to do already. He stood in the doorway, his toothbrush in his hand, watching her sleep, and thinking of Anna Neale, all alone in that big, quiet house. He'd been speaking to the lads from Donnybrook today. Casually. He'd been tactful about it, felt his way around to asking if they thought there might be more to Neale's death than just the accident. They didn't have much to say, except that they knew about his debts, and that there was a bit of suspicion about the kind of people who were his clients.

"Why?" Brady, the sergeant, wanted to know. "What's your interest?"

He backed off quickly, assured them that he had none. "Just that, well, you know the way it is, Neale wasn't a bad bloke, and his wife seems like a nice girl."

"Yeah." Brady laughed. "Too bloody nice, if you ask me. Some guys have all the luck." Anyway, they were keeping an open mind, they'd let him know if they came up with anything. Would that do him?

That would do him just fine. He rinsed his teeth,

switched off the light and slid as quietly as he could into bed. He curled into Sarah's warm body, feeling the heavy curve of her breasts beneath his hand. He slept.

THE ANTS' wings hung from their small black bodies. Stiff, transparent, veined. Three times the size of the tiny insects that dragged them along as they poured from their subterranean nest chambers, drawn by the warmth of the day, to take part in their annual nuptial flight. Up into the air in a swarm to mate, then back to earth where the males would soon die and the few females who had survived the appetite of hungry birds would vanish back underground, shedding their wings, voluntary prisoners waiting for their eggs to ripen.

Anna sat in Isobel's garden and watched them. It was two days later. She leaned back against the kitchen door and waited for the moment when, as one, they would lift off the ground. She put her hand down, palm pressed flat on the brick path. Gradually one ant after the other turned towards her, crawling up and over her skin. She sat completely still, watching as they dragged their neat waisted bodies across the back of her hand. She could, she knew, have shaken herself vigorously, dislodging them, then trampled them as they fell back to earth. So easy to massacre the entire colony, pour boiling water down the crater-shaped hole that poked up between the bricks, destroy their laboriously constructed nest. But she would never do that. She lifted her laden hand and held it in front of her face, then blew gently at the insects until they rose, circled and flew. Transformed, wings vibrating in the sun, the swarm following suit so that soon all there was to see on the path was the occasional earwig, its flattened body insinuating itself along the grooves in the old brick.

She stretched out her legs and kicked off her runners. She leaned back against the peeling paint on the door and closed her eyes. She undid the top button of her jeans and pulled off her sweater, pulling up the T-shirt underneath, so the sun's rays fell on the pale skin of her stomach. She listened. Around her the garden sang, chirruped and whistled. Legs rattled against external skeletons. Mouthparts sucked noisily and wings hummed as they beat. Up and down, up and down. She smiled sleepily. Isobel's garden, always her sanctuary, her place of safety. Her first and best hunting ground: by day with her net, by night with her light trap, her killing bottle filled with the leaves of crushed laurel, giving off their almond-scented cyanide vapor, using her father's large magnifying glass with its ebony handle and his collection of books to identify what she had caught. That was how she had begun. In this garden that sloped down to the sea, where the sun's warmth was trapped in the fuchsia-filled hollows, and radiated back from the shining surface of the large oval pond, alive with dragonflies.

Memories of David, too, in this garden. A teenager reprieved from boarding school, to spend the long summer holidays here in this place that was the closest she had ever come to having a home. Waking late one morning. Leaning out of her bedroom window. Hearing the sound of voices. Laughter, deep and satisfying. An unusual sound in this place, dominated by the presence of women.

Craning farther out, as far as she dared, over the sill, the lush green grass a long way down. A sudden lurch in her stomach, moisture on her palms. Then two figures appeared from the thick shrubbery in the walled garden. One, she could see, was her aunt, wearing as always a broad-brimmed straw hat. The other, a man, tall and slightly stooped, she had never seen before. She watched them walk together beside the pond, stopping now and then to bend over and look into its green depths, examining the water lilies that grew in such profusion that year. And saw them sit on the wooden bench beside the drawing-room windows. Isobel struck a match and leaned across, cupping her hands around his as he angled his cigar into the flame. Anna smelled the scent of smoke as she reached forward to hear what they were saying, but only fragments of the conversation drifted up to her ears. Something about horses, betting, money changing hands. A joke, obviously by the shout of laughter that burst from him. She pushed herself farther out of the window, clutching the frame for support, and a piece of ribbon that had been tied around her hair slid free and floated like a pale pink feather, down, down, down to land in front of them on the table. And he twisted around, putting one hand over his eyes to shade them from the glare of the sun and shouted up to her, "Come out, come out, wherever you are." And laughed again. And she saw his mouth open, his teeth white and his tongue fleshy, the color of raw meat.

She was safe here in the sunlight, safe here during the day, far away from the house in Anglesea Road. She would be free of it soon, she hoped, and free of the nightmares that plagued her. The last one had been so real that it seemed as if, days later, it still hovered out of sight just behind her right shoulder. She could feel the fear it had brought following her around, waiting to flood her awareness if she let slip her guard even for a moment. She could remember it so clearly that it seemed now as if it had really happened. It was as if she had woken sometime in the early hours of the morning. She was lying on her side, both arms curled around her body. It was very dark and very quiet. Even the traffic that passed the house night and day seemed to have gone. She sighed deeply. She was cold. She reached behind her with one hand to pull the heavy quilt up and over her shoulders. And as she did she lifted her head and saw the dark figure standing just inside the door. She gasped out loud. Her heart leaped inside her breast and began to beat so quickly that she thought it would burst through her body. She turned towards the figure. And saw that it was a man.

"What do you want?" she screamed, dragging herself back away from him, pulling the quilt up and around her to shield her from his gaze. "Tell me, please, what do you want?"

He said nothing, and then as she began to cry out, covering her eyes with her fists, pulling at her hair with wild distracted movements, he turned and walked through the door. And was gone.

She waited and listened. She could hear nothing. Only the rapid drumming of her pulse in her ears. She pushed the quilt away and slowly got out of bed. Her legs were weak. Sweat ran down between her breasts, like drops of iced water. She took two steps to the door and switched on the light, crying out with relief as the room revealed itself to her. She moved out onto the landing, rushing from light switch to light switch, the house transforming itself before her gaze. Dark marks on the walls where David's paintings had once hung. Empty spaces in all the rooms where his furniture had once stood. Dusty shapes on the carpets, indentations made by the wooden feet of chairs, sofas, sideboards, tables. Practically all gone now. Almost nothing was left that David had once coveted.

She checked the lock on the front door. The chain was still in place. She went from window to window, trying each of the locks in turn. Nothing had been disturbed. She rushed into the kitchen. The back door, too, was bolted top and bottom. And now she was awake, staring at her reflection, which shivered in the dark glass of the windows. Who was this woman who stared back at her? Hollow-cheeked, gaunt, a white nightdress hanging from her skeletal shoulders, her hair matted, its shine dulled by grease and neglect.

"YOU'LL BE sorry to let it go, I'm sure." The estate agent had been sympathetic, solicitous of her welfare as he warned her that the house would sell quickly. "We've had a lot of interest in it already. A lot of people have come to the open viewing days, and I've had quite a few phone calls from clients who want to have a second and even a third look. I'll let you know when I'm bringing them, just in case you don't want to be there."

But there had been no warning call the day before yesterday. Just the silhouette of a man through the stained-glass panels in the front door and the repeated ringing of the doorbell.

She hadn't heard it immediately. She had been out in the garden, dragging the washing from the line in between downpours, before getting ready to catch the train to Isobel's. He was there, standing in the front porch, as she walked quickly into the hall from the kitchen. She had stopped, her heart banging again beneath her ribs, and stepped back a couple of paces. Maybe he wouldn't have seen her. She didn't want to talk to anyone, whoever he was, or whatever he wanted. And then he pressed his face against the stained glass, his hands up around his eyes trying to see in, and called out, "Hallo, is there anyone there?"

Furious, suddenly, at the intrusion, she jerked open the door. "What do you want?" she asked abruptly.

"I'm sorry." He stepped back, looking surprised. "I did ring the bell, a few times." He held the brochure out towards her. "I've come to see the house."

"Oh, I see. They didn't tell me."

"Didn't they?" He put his hand inside his coat and pulled out a large gold pocket watch. "Two fifteen I agreed with the woman I spoke to on the phone. We agreed we'd meet here." He stepped back out of the porch and looked up and down the street. "Perhaps she's been delayed. The traffic is pretty dreadful."

Anna said nothing. She looked at the long chain from which the watch in his fingers was suspended. It was very beautiful, the links slightly twisted so they would lie flat against a shirt or a waistcoat. Her father had had one like that once. Practically the only thing he had left her. She had given it to David as a wedding present. He had always complained that it ran fast. It was gone now, sold, she supposed, for some reason or other.

"Look, I'm sorry to be a nuisance. But would you mind if I came in and waited? It's starting to rain again." And he smiled, sweetly, so small lines appeared under his eyes and around his mouth. She stood away from the open door and let him in, struggling to close it behind them, her arms full of damp clothes.

"Here, let me." He pushed the door to, leaning his back against it as it closed with a sharp click, his arms folded across his body. She saw his face clearly for the first time, long and thin with high cheekbones, and glossy brown hair parted at the side, which flopped over his forehead, and eyes of the same lustrous color. He leaned back against the door, his legs crossed at the knees.

"Sorry about this," he said again. "It's an awful business selling a house, isn't it?"

She shrugged her shoulders, her hands plucking at the damp clothes in her arms. She gestured towards the sitting room on the right. "Would you like to wait in there? Most of the furniture has gone, but I think there's something or other to sit on. I'm sure whoever it is you're waiting for won't be long. I'm just in the middle of packing, so . . ."

"Of course, thank you, whatever." He walked through the door she had pointed to. She watched him as he wandered around the room, peering out of the window into the small front garden, inspecting the Victorian tiles around the fireplace, looking up at the moldings and the ceiling rose, finally settling down on an upright chair by the long bookshelves. She watched him lean forward separating individual books from their neighbors with his fingers. There was something about the angle of his head that reminded her of the seals on the rocks in the bay near Isobel's house, the ones her father used to take her out to see. Sleek and smooth and very self-possessed. He turned his head back towards her. "Can I help you? Is there something you want?"

"Sorry, no." She backed away, feeling stupid and awkward, and hurried upstairs into the bathroom, piling the washing into the airing-cupboard, searching around on the bathroom shelves for her toothbrush, and all the other bits and pieces she would need for her trip.

She was in her bedroom, just about to zip up her bag, when she heard his step on the landing.

"Um, look." She turned around. "Again, I'm really sorry about this, but I'm running out of time. Would you mind if I just looked around the house by myself. Or maybe you might come with me, a sort of a chaperone, if that's the word."

She smiled. "I don't think it is. I'm sure estate agents have their own very particular term to describe it. But of course. Where would you like to start?"

He introduced himself when they reached the top of the house and were standing in David's study. He told her his name was Matthew, that he was born and brought up in London but he'd been living in Dublin for quite a while.

"Me too," she replied.

"Yes," he said, "you still have some of the accent."

"Yes." She smiled. "So do you."

"But I love it here, I feel very at home in Dublin."

"And so you want to buy a house here?"

"Well, in fact I have a few already. I deal in property, that's my business, but I'm always on the lookout for somewhere that's a bit special."

"And would this be it?"

"Do you know something? It might well be." He crossed to the window and gazed out. "See over there." He pointed to the tall building that rose high above the trees in Herbert Park. "That's where I live now. There's a wonderful view from my flat right up at the top. I can see for miles in every direction." He tugged the brass catch and put his weight to the sash. "Do you mind if I open it? There's quite a view from here too. Your garden and the river look wonderful."

She shrugged, and stepped back into the doorway. He looked at her quizzically.

"It's okay. It's just I don't like heights. It's a bit far down for my taste."

HE HAD been sympathetic, the man who had come to look at the house. Told her how he could not stand tunnels, couldn't bear being underground. That it was one of the reasons why he didn't live in London any longer. He couldn't abide the Tube. He made her laugh with his self-deprecating description of the lengths to which he would go to avoid travelling that way. And she told him how heights were just the first of her problems. The staircase at school with the deep central well made her sick and weak, her legs collapsing underneath her, her heart trying to burst through her chest. Then there were the big buildings, waiting to crash down on top of her. St. Patrick's Cathedral with its high vaulted ceiling. The Central Bank like a modern monolith. Liberty Hall, an elongated shoebox, to be blown over by a westerly gale. Bridges she could not cross, wide-open spaces into which she could not venture. It was all because of gravity. It would fail her, she knew. Release her, let go of her body, so she would spin, like an abandoned balloon, far out into space. Hurtle out of control towards the stars in the darkness.

She felt silly now, remembering the conversation. He had been polite but what, she wondered, must he have thought of her? Still, what did it matter? She would never have reason to see him again, even if he did buy her house. He would just be a signature on the deeds, as she would too.

She crested the hill above Isobel's house and looked down and away from the comfort of the earth to the sea, stretching milky blue, the color of moonstone towards the horizon. And felt again the paralyzing panic, her legs refusing to move, her palms sticky, her heart roaring in her ears. She dropped to her knees, digging her fingers into the ground, catching hold of tussocks of grass, anything to keep her rooted, safe. And called out, "Sammy, Sammy, where are you?"

Until, at last, the little dog appeared, his stubby tail wagging, his tongue flopping from his mouth, licking her cheek as she held on to him tightly, until her heart slowed and she could gradually, carefully, drag herself back up into the sheltering trees and safety.

David had liked this walk. They had often come this way, up through the fields at the back of the house, then down into the wood towards the lake. It was always the first place to be revisited whenever she came back here. And Sammy, Isobel's Jack Russell, the latest in a long line that stretched back into her childhood, loved it too, so she had called the dog and set off. She felt in her pocket for the bottle with the dropper, to be filled with water from the holy well and brought back to Dublin for Billy. She had promised him.

She was safe now in the woods, walking downhill to where the spring bubbled from the ground. Along the narrow lane, grass growing lush and green on its ridged center, moss clinging to the stones in the shade. On either side thick hedgerows of fuchsia, blackberry, gorse and honeysuckle crowded in. A flock of pigeons started up out of an ash tree, their wings dark against the bright evening sky. She tilted her head back and watched as they circled, calling to each other, then settling on another tree farther down the valley. A rabbit rushed from the ditch, slowed, saw her, and dashed off ahead down the lane.

"Hey, Sammy, here, Sammy," she called. "Rabbits, rabbits." And whistled, the high-pitched tone that usually brought him to her knee. But there was no answering yap, no scurry of black and white as he shot past, the scent of his quarry burning in his nostrils. She waited and called again. Then she walked on, her feet falling over each other as the track got steeper and steeper, the stones slippery here on the other side of the hill in the shadow. Down below, among the hazel and beech, she could see movement as the holy medals and scraps of tattered cloth twisted and turned in the branches overhanging the well. Prayers and petitions carried heavenward by the breeze. She stopped for a moment and listened to the sound of the birds and the trickle of the tiny stream, which appeared and disappeared, sneaking in among thick grass and small boulders eventually to fill and refill the pool. And heard another sound, faint at first, a low whimpering. And then, in response to the sound of her feet on the loose stones, a long drawn-out howl.

She stopped on the edge of the grove. It was dark beneath the trees, and quiet for a moment. She stepped forward slowly, her feet scuffing through the leaf mold. Then the noise began again and as she pushed aside the low branches she saw where it was coming from. The soft brown eyes gazing up at her, one paw reaching out, then dropping back, exhausted by the effort, and the ragged gash down the belly, blood saturating the earth beneath the small body and the bulge of the entrails as they strained outwards through the wound.

Again the cry of pain, but this time a human sound as she knelt beside the dog, reaching out with one hand to stroke his head, the other hand held poised, ready, to do what? What could she do? Blood spreading in a slow, dark puddle from his side, seeping into the well like crimson ink, thinning, diluting, in swirls and coils, and already his bright brown eyes beginning to dull, a shadow spreading across their surface in the same way as the darkness of the eclipse spreads across the face of the moon. Until the luster had gone and his stare was fixed and unchanging.

16

Seawater lapped up and around Billy's calves. He stood very still, not sure whether he liked the sensation. Beside him Grace nuzzled his bare knee and waited. He rested his hand on her back, gripping the slippery pebbles under his feet with his toes. Then he gave her a little push, his fingers sneaking through her thick hair.

"Go on, girl, off you go." He listened and heard in front of him her paws moving through the water and behind him the gentle swish and suck as the waves ran up the steep little shingle beach and fell back down again.

IT WAS Monday afternoon. A special day, a collection day. He had dressed more carefully than usual, combing his hair so it fell neatly to one side, feeling the knot of his tie, making sure that it was crisp and tight. Then he had walked from his flat in Cherrytree Court along Mount Street, crossing carefully at the lights and continuing along the side of Merrion Square. He could smell the newly mown grass from the middle of the park, and every now and then, if Grace's path strayed towards the railings, he could hear the rustle of the branches of the lilac bushes that hung out onto the path. He knew they were lilac because when he had walked this way with Anna, a couple of weeks ago, she had stopped him and said, "Smell this," putting her hand on the back of his head and pushing him towards something soft, which brushed delicately against his face. Sweetly scented, the way her skin was. "That's lilac," she said, took his hand and held it around the cone-shaped flower. "Careful, now, the petals are fragile." If he tilted his head slightly to the left he could just about smell it still above the stink of the traffic and the city's dirt.

At the end of Merrion Square he had to turn to the right and cross an awkward junction. Grace had done it many times and he had complete confidence in her, but today as he waited, listening to the rhythm of the traffic as it surged past, he felt someone stop beside him, and a man's voice said, "Can I help you cross?" No point in turning up his nose at a genuine offer, so he looked in the direction of the voice, smiled and said, "Thank you," holding the prof-fered elbow lightly with his fingertips. At the other side of the road he quickly let go, reluctant to prolong the physical contact any longer than necessary, letting Grace take over. She knew they were going to the railway station, to catch the two-ten train to Bray. The real train, with the heavy doors that slammed loudly and the deep leather seats. It was easier to handle than the DART because it stopped only once, at Dun Laoghaire, doors slamming and the guard's whistle blowing before they were off again.

Billy liked his trips. He usually went three times a week. Monday, Wednesday and Friday. He had the route from the station to the amusements on the front carefully worked out. On the left-hand side as he walked he could hear the sea. Sometimes when the weather was bad it roared and crashed against the wall, but today, in the calm sunshine, it was soft and gentle. Swishing and sucking, backwards and forwards. And there were always the smells to guide him. The sticky, sugary candy floss, which made his mouth water, the sickly fumes from the diesel engines that drove the roller-coaster and the other rides. And, above all, the smell of children. They reminded him of Grace when she got wet and lay in front of the electric heater, her thick coat steaming. It was a smell that caught in the back of his throat and made him feel like gagging.

He was surprised at how many children there were in the amusements in the afternoon. He would have thought that they would still be at school. But maybe they were like him, bunking off, running away, as he used to when he was going to the blind school and hated it. Hated the teachers, and how they spoke to him and the other boys, making him feel that they were all worth nothing.

The people in the amusements didn't feel like that about him. He could hear them calling out his name as Grace picked her way through the crowds: Jim, the guy who looked after the little kids' merry-go-round outside on the grassy area, Bobby who stood at the door with a two-way radio that crackled and hissed, and the girls in the café, joking with him over the sizzle of the deep-fat fryer and the burble of the music from the radio. And then he'd turn to his left, heading for the roar and thump of the bumper cars, and Steve would come out of the office at the back and shake his hand, and ask him how he was doing, and bring him in, closing the door behind him, so it was suddenly quiet.

He liked Steve. He treated him well. He'd take out the bottle of whiskey and they'd sit down and talk. Steve would pour the first one, and Billy would drink it quickly. Then Steve would pour another one, and they'd take their time over it. Then Steve would get up and go to the filing cabinet. Billy could hear the banging of the keys on the lock and the scrape of metal on metal as the drawers slid open. Then Steve would stand beside him and put the padded envelope into his hand and give him instructions about where he was to go. Grafton Street, to the downstairs jacks in the first burger joint on the left. Or to the benches by the fountain in Stephen's Green. Or to wait in the bus shelter on Mount Street, the one nearest his flat. Tell him which of the regulars it was who would make the pickup. Or maybe just take it home with him and wait for a knock on the door. And Billy would hold the envelope delicately, as if it contained something infinitely precious and fragile, and press it gently between his fingers, feeling the way the little plastic bags inside would give slightly under the pressure. Then he would put them into his satchel and say goodbye, and off he'd go. Back out into the bang and clatter, the screech and scramble, the crowd pushing against him. And back out into the fresh air of the sea front.

Usually he'd turn left immediately and head straight for the station. So he'd be in the city center in plenty of time to make his delivery. But today he didn't. It was warm out there, with a soft breeze that brushed against his face and blew his shoulder-length hair across his mouth. And he could hear the sea, that lovely repeating phrase over and over again. Swish, suck, swish, suck. It made Anna seem close to him. She was always talking about the sea. Telling him how much she loved it.

"It's so beautiful, Billy, I'll have to take you sometime, down to West Cork where my aunt lives. And we'll go out in a sailing boat to one of the islands. And you can lie on the sand in the sun while I light a fire and make us some tea. Would you like that?"

He'd got a card from her this morning. She knew how much getting a letter meant to him, even though he wouldn't be able to read it himself.

"You'll have to teach me Braille sometime, Billy, won't you? Here, give me one of your books, put my fingers on the words, read them to me."

And he had held her hand with his hand guiding her across the raised marks, while she struggled to understand. "It's no good," she said, "it's too complicated."

"It's not that," he told her. "It's because you don't need to feel, the way I need to feel, and the skin on the tips of your fingers isn't sensitive enough. You have to look after it, you have to keep it soft, because if it gets callused or rough you can't read with it. That's why it's more difficult as you get older."

"A bit like people needing reading glasses, is that it?" she asked, running her fingers across the tips of his. He was silent for a few moments, disappointed in her. "No, of course it isn't," she said, "how stupid of me. I'm sorry, Billy."

But of course he had forgiven her. Old Winnie had read the card to him, twice, three times so he could remember what was in it. He could hear her voice now as he walked across the grass towards where he knew there were concrete steps that led down to a little shingle beach. And as he felt his feet slipping and sliding on the loose stones he heard Anna's voice instead, up close, breathing in his ear. He could smell her, as sweet as the lilac, and feel her hand on his. The smoothness of the skin over the small bones. She was telling him that she was going to go to the well to get the special water for his eyes. He wanted to reach out and hold her close and thank her. "I've been swimming," she said. "It's lovely. Very cold at first, but once you get used to it, it's great. Can you swim, Billy? Will I teach you?"

He sat down and took off his shoes. He rolled his trousers up over his knees and walked out into the water. He'd had lessons once, when he was a kid at school, in an indoor pool. He hadn't liked it: it was too hot and it stank of something that made his eyes water and his nose run. It was noisy, too, echoes everywhere, impossible to tell where a voice was coming from and how close or far away. It made him feel edgy, nervous. Unsure of himself. And then there was the way the teacher touched him. Held him on his hips, his fingers reaching down into his groin. He hadn't liked it. And he didn't believe him when he said that it was all part of the lesson. He wasn't that stupid, despite what the teacher thought.

He had fallen one day when he was trying to get away from him. He had banged his head on the hard edge of the pool as he dropped into the water. He remembered the feeling of someone's foot against his ankle, and the sense of losing control. Then a pain in his head that made him scream, and nothing more until he was lying on his side and vomit was coming out of his mouth and down his nose. He could taste it and smell it even now after all these years. But he was sure that he could also remember how to do what the teacher called the doggy paddle. Not that he'd do it now with all his clothes on, and his satchel with his deliveries still on his back. He just wanted to see what the water felt like. So he'd be more prepared when Anna came back.

But suddenly something was wrong. There was someone else in the water with him. He could hear the sound of splashing to his right, and jeers and shouts. Then a cold wetness all over his face.

"Who is it? Who's there?" He swung around, his arms out wide, feeling his feet beginning to lose their grip. Someone began to push at him, then grip him by his sleeve, pulling him back, so he lurched from side to side. And lost his balance. And fell, face down. Water bubbling into his ears. And as he opened his mouth to scream, the salt sea rushed in and up his nose, siphoning into his lungs and his stomach. Then just as suddenly he was pulled up and out, feeling the sun on his face, and he opened his mouth and gasped for breath, and heard the sounds of the world around him. The ice-cream van's hurdy-gurdy, the screech of a seagull overhead, before he was pushed down and down into the water again, pouring into his ears, his eyes, his throat, as the smooth shiny pebbles slipped and slid away from his feet, and the weight of his clothes began to drag him down and down.

17

The next death was a bit different. It was three years later. Another tragic accident. The verdict confirmed by the coroner's court.

Michael had just bought the first of his houses. He had used the money that his granny had left him. A surprising amount for someone who had lived all her life as if she had nothing. The house he bought was at the far end of the South Circular Road, three miles or so from the city end, where his granny had her shop. It was red-brick, like most of them in that area, two stories with large bay windows and a room up under the eaves.

He remembered that there was a particular smell up there. It got stronger and stronger as he walked up the narrow stairs towards the attic. It was hot under the roof. The sun poured in through a large rectangular skylight, soaking into the bare wooden floorboards and the chipped, stained plaster on the sloping ceiling. A pile of children's clothes had been swept into a corner. He stirred the bundle of rags with the toe of his polished shoe. Faded pink and blue Babygros, a red dress, synthetic velvet with yellowing lace around the neck and wrists. Ribbed tights, stretched by nappy-swollen bottoms, hand-knitted cardigans and a nylon anorak, the zip hanging by a couple of threads, and a fraying rip down the back, the padding, like an old lady's hair, bursting through. The clothes moved as if they were one garment, stuck together by the smears of brown that had spread from them onto the ground and hardened into lumps like clods of earth. The neighbors told him that the mother of the house had died up there in that hot little room under the rafters, that her husband had stayed on with his four children, sitting by the fire in the back room off the kitchen, staring from the red coals in the fireplace to the television and back to the coals again. While around him the house creaked and crumbled, kept in one piece by the layer of chip fat and cigarette smoke that crept up the walls and across the ceiling towards the ornate plaster rose from which hung a twisted brown flex and the single bulb dulled by fly-dirt and dust.

Not that any of that mattered to Michael. He had gutted the house, filling skip after skip with debris and rubble, wiping out all trace of that family, covering the walls with bright white paint and the floors with easy-to-clean nylon carpets. He had turned each of the three bedrooms, the front room and back room on the ground floor into self-contained units with their own front doors and Yale locks and a tiny kitchen inside what looked like a cupboard with a circular sink and a two-ring Belling cooker. The kitchen in the back, which gave out onto the small sunny yard, became a second bathroom and on the landing outside the attic there was just enough room to install a small electric shower and a toilet.

"It's a flatlet," he said to all his prospective tenants, watching the hope on their faces turn to pinched despair as they squeezed through the door into the narrow space under the pitched roof, filled with a bed and an upright armchair, and the same kitchen arrangement fitted into the highest point of the end wall.

And that was how he met Liam Ward. And his girl-friend Máire. They came to look at the attic room. It was September, he remembered. Still warm. The sun slanted through the skylight, making it look cozy, and gave no inkling of how bitterly cold it was in the winter with the frost curling into elegant leaf shapes on the inside of the glass and condensation running down the walls. He liked Liam at first. He was a big guy. Came from somewhere out past Spiddal, by the Atlantic in Connemara. He was handsome, self-confident. He was, he told Michael, a car-penter, but he could turn his hand to anything. Roofing, decorating, electrical work, bit of plumbing. "If you know anyone with any work going," he said. After they'd agreed on a price for the room, Michael told him to call round the next day to the house he was doing up three streets away in St. Anthony's Road.

It seemed as if the whole arrangement would work out brilliantly. Liam could do everything he claimed. Even better, he could take charge, take responsibility. Michael found that he was leaving him more and more to his own devices. After all, he had bigger enterprises to worry about. The expansion of the business that was going to fund everything else. The one that would provide all the cash. Capitalizing on human frailty was how he thought of it. There were boom times ahead, if he could just get himself in the right position to take advantage.

Then he discovered that Liam wasn't quite as straight as he seemed. There was the matter of the invoices for materials, wood, plaster, cement. The deals that he was getting from the suppliers didn't quite match the amounts he was claiming. Michael watched him and waited. He hoped that this dishonesty was a one-off. A lapse, an aberration. But it wasn't. He watched Liam digging himself a very large hole. And he waited.

And went one night for a drink with him and all the lads after the St. Anthony's Road house was finished. Pints flowing. A celebration.

Then Liam made his move. Told Michael he knew all about what he was up to. He'd seen what was going on. He wasn't a thick eejit from the bog. He knew a healthy profit when he saw it. And he wanted in.

"Why should I?" Michael asked him.

Liam smiled, finishing off another pint, and said, "Because it'll be bad news for you if you don't."

It was lucky that Máire was away that night. She'd gone home to see her mother for a few days. Michael didn't think he'd have done it if she'd been there in the bed beside Liam. More to the point, he probably wouldn't have gotten away with it. She wasn't a drinker the way Liam was. She didn't have that obsessive desire for alcohol, which was stamped all over him as he stood at the bar pouring pints down his long, sunburned throat.

Michael watched him and his friends as the night wore on. One of them took a fiddle from its case and began to play and Liam began to dance. By himself. His big body was loose and graceful, his long legs lifting straight up in front of him, the metal clips on his boots clattering on the pub's tiled floor, punctuating the roars from the crowd who had gathered around to watch. A strange sight to see in Dublin on a drunken Saturday night. And Liam was drunk all right. To the casual observer he looked fine. But he was out of it. There was a look in his eyes that said he was on automatic pilot. Walking OK, talking OK, even dancing OK, but away with the fairies all the same.

Michael slipped out just before closing time. He knew Liam was past caring. He sat in his car across the road and waited. Saw him leave with a few of the others. Walk up the South Circular to the chipper. Michael followed him on foot. Waited till he came out. Smelled the vinegar steaming from the paper bag. Watched his thick fingers smearing grease across his mouth, wiping his hands down his jeans. Turning for home, the empty bag dropping from his hand to the filthy pavement.

He gave him twenty minutes to get into bed and fall asleep. Twenty minutes while he stood in the shadows and looked up at the face of the moon. Then he let himself into the house. Carefully, quietly, up the carpeted stairs. Paused outside the door. Heard the snores. Used his own key to get in. Saw in the moonlight that Liam was lying fully clothed on the bed. Felt in his jacket pocket for the packet of cigarettes and the box of matches. Lit one, dragging hard on it, so the tip glowed neon orange, then dropped it on the bed, beside Liam's right hand. Waited just long enough to see the ring of burning brightness on the quilt cover. Then left as quietly as he had come. Back down the stairs and out into the street. Didn't look back. Not once. Slept soundly in his own bed until he was wakened by a phone call, sometime in the early hours.

His granny had been a big one for fire insurance. She had drummed it into him. Read out snippets from the *Evening Herald*. Smoke damage, structural damage, water damage, pounds per square foot for refurbishment, cost per square foot for rebuilding. The biggest sin in her book was underinsurance. "No sense," she'd say, as she lit another Sweet Afton and held out her glass for more Paddy. "No bloody sense. You remember that, Michael. Make sure about it."

Of course he went to Liam's funeral. It was the least he could do, to pay his respects. And Máire was so pleased to see him when he appeared on the steps of the church after the funeral Mass. She blushed a blotchy pink, which came up from below the neck of her white blouse and spread like a rash across her small face. And of course he kept in touch with her, and when he bought his next house he offered her first choice of the new bedsits. He helped her move in, bringing with him a couple of bottles of nice Australian chardonnay, soothing her tears as they sat side by side on her bed, and she told him how lonely she was now. And how could Liam have been so stupid to smoke in bed like that when he was drinking? "You're so good," she said, "so kind. After what he did to your house. How can you ever forgive us?"

And then he explained to her, showed her the betrayal, the silken wrapping around the corpse. Told her how

Liam had laughed about her that night before the fire. Said that he was never going to marry her. Why would he want to tie himself down to a girl like Máire? Who wanted to drag him back to live in a bungalow in the next field to her family, with nothing to look at but the gray of the Atlantic, and nowhere to go but the pub where her father and her brothers drank. Night after night, year after year. She was a good worker, was Máire, but all that saving she was doing, for the wedding, she thought, well, he had other plans, big plans.

Michael had let her off the rent for a while. During the time he was coming to see her regularly. She had a beautiful body underneath the shapeless sweater and jeans she always wore. She made him feel so good, for a while. He could do anything he wanted with her soft breasts and belly, and the silky skin of her wetness, that sucked on him like the touch of a sea anemone around his finger.

Power and possession, the best feelings in the world. Máire drew him into her and thanked him for his kindness. Until he tired of her stories about her home place, and her complaints about Dublin, and told her eventually that he was upgrading the flats and wanted her out.

His granny had been right about the fire insurance. She was a wise woman. "You take after me," she always said. "You're nothing like your mother. I don't know where she got you from. If she'd had half your sense she wouldn't have ended up the way she did. But you'll go far, Michael. Won't you? You'll go all the way. Nothing and no one will ever stop you, will it, Michael, my little love?"

He'd seen what was left of Liam when he'd gone to the

house in the early hours of the morning. It didn't look human, the thing that had to be separated from the remains of the bed. Charred, blackened, only the shape of the bones of the skull showing that this once had been a man. What could he say? The first death had been by water, the second by fire. Who knows what the third would be? But it would come in time, he was sure of that.

18

Anna had seen that dullness in the eyes before. In David's eyes as he lay on the floor staring out into the room. And long before that too. Here in this house. In the kitchen. A large pot on the range. Full almost to the brim with water. Steam beginning to drift from its surface. A metallic clattering coming from inside. From the creature, black and shiny, its hard external skeleton ridged, its claws banging against the side of its torture chamber. Shiny eyes, like beads of ebony, protruded from the top of its head. Then, as the temperature of the water reached its maximum and steam misted the kitchen windows, the light in the eyes faded as the orange pigment spread from its fan-shaped tail to the tips of its long feelers.

"Doesn't it hurt, Issy?"

"Not at all. Lobsters don't feel the way humans do."

"Are you sure?"

"Of course I'm sure. Absolutely certain."

SHE HAD carried Sammy back to the house, wrapped in her sweater, held close, the blood from his wound soaking through the layers of wool and into her shirt as his head lolled back over the crook of her arm. Isobel had been mowing the long rectangle of lawn that ran down to the water's edge. Anna could hear the screech of the machine as it tore into the thick grass long before she saw the slight, gray-haired figure trudging backwards and forwards. She walked towards her, trying to attract her attention, calling out her name as loudly as she could, but Isobel did not hear her, did not notice her until she raised her eyes and saw Anna's bloodied figure and the small bundle cradled in her arms.

She stepped towards her and lifted the dog's black-and-white head, heavy now and leaden. "No," she said, pulling the limp body from Anna's arms, then screaming with horror and disgust at its mutilation. "What have you done?" Her lined face was creased with anger. "You stupid idiot. Can you be trusted with nothing? Is nothing safe with you?"

She pushed away Anna's offer of help, running inside, her cries of anguish bouncing off the flagged stone floor of the hall and kitchen, while Anna followed slowly behind, the blood on her hands already dried, caked beneath her fingernails.

She knew the stains wouldn't wash out of her shirt. Even if she had run it under the tap in the yard until the cold water was as clear as the pool in the woods, the outline would still be there. The darker rusty rim would tell her how the dog had died. She stood in the shower and scrubbed and scrubbed, using the nailbrush on her skin to drive away the feel of the blood and the smell of the little dog in death, the wound she had tried to bind with her belt, and the urine that had dripped from him. She dropped her clothes in a heap in the bathroom, and when she had washed every bit of her body and changed, she stuffed them into a plastic bag and took them out to the far corner of the garden, and tipped them into the pit that Isobel had dug underneath the biggest beech tree.

She had phoned the vet. They stood around in a half-circle while he knelt beside the small black-and-white body laid out on an old feed sack. He looked carefully at the wound, touching its ragged edges with a piece of stick he had picked off the ground. Then he stood up, pushing his cap onto the back of his head so that a deep red line showed where the binding had bitten into his forehead. "I don't know. Looks like it was done by another dog. Must have been a big one. Maybe a greyhound. There've been a few savagings recently. Sheep mostly. But a greyhound would look upon a dog like this as not much more than a rabbit. You should tell the Guards about it."

"What's the point?" Isobel lit a cigarette, her hands trembling. "It's the kind of thing that makes enemies of your neighbors."

"Well," the vet shrugged, "if you don't it'll happen to someone else's dog."

"It wouldn't have happened to mine if she'd been watching what she was doing."

"He'd gone off by himself." Anna's voice was pleading. "He always does that, you know the way he loves to. I thought he was still behind me, in the field. I didn't see him on the lane at all, until I got to the pool and there he was."

They laid the dog on top of her bloodied clothes.

Carefully, lovingly. Anna used the long-handled shovel to shake the dark friable earth down on top of him until only the barest outline showed. Then hurriedly, as the rain began to fall, she piled the rest of the sod on top until there was just a small hump mirroring the shape beneath. She gripped the smooth wooden handle and leaned forward, her eyes closed. Beside her Isobel bowed her head. No show of emotion, no sign in her stiff shoulders and straight back of the way the dog had lain, pressed against her thigh, night after night, ears pricking at the sound of the glass dropping from her hand onto the carpet. Rain rattled loudly on the leaves above them. Anna listened, thinking suddenly of Billy, trying to interpret the world the way he did, ordering sounds, movements of air, changes in temperature. She swayed slightly from foot to foot, listening to see if her perceptions changed as she moved her head.

Beside her the vet reached out his hand and took hold of her upper arm. "Are you all right?" he asked. "You're not feeling faint, are you?"

She opened her eyes and smiled at him. "No, I'm fine."

"Do you remember?" he said. "Your father's dog, the last one?"

"The Wicklow collie?"

"That's the lad. What was it he was called?"

"Merlin." Who sat at the jetty and waited. Even after the bodies of her mother and father had been brought home. Leaving the kitchen first thing every morning and waiting until nightfall. Crawling under an upturned dinghy when it was wet. He only lasted a few months.

"What happened to him? I don't remember."

"I think we said at the time that it was septicemia. From a rat bite on his hind leg that festered and didn't respond to treatment. But there was a bit more to it than that."

"Yeah?"

"Well, I always reckoned, although your aunt doesn't agree with me, that he died of a broken heart. Isn't that right, Isobel?"

"Ask Anna," she said, not looking at them. "She's the scientist. Ask her if such a condition exists."

ISOBEL SAID it again that evening as they sat in the kitchen, a bottle of wine, the second, open between them. She leaned towards Anna, her glass so full that wine slopped over the rim and dribbled down the stem. "Go on, you should know. You're the clever one who went to university. And if you didn't learn it there, then David's death should have taught you something about it, shouldn't it?" She drank deeply so that wine spilled from the edges of her mouth onto her stained sweater. Anna didn't reply.

"Go on, tell me." Isobel stood up, swaying, and leaned towards her, banging her fist on the wall. "Tell me, you stupid bitch, tell me all about broken hearts."

Anna lifted her glass and stared into it. She wanted to push her fingers into her ears the way she had when she was a child. Instead, she got up and went to the oven, opening it carefully and pulling out a roasting tray.

"Why don't you have something to eat, Isobel? Dinner's ready."

"Oh, you want to feed me, do you, the way your mother used to feed your father? Do you remember, when he was dying and he couldn't use his hands at all? When finally it had caught up with him, the motor-neurone disease, whatever you call it, had taken him over. He didn't believe it would happen, not at first. He told me, 'It's not going to be like that for me, I won't let it, I'm different.' But he wasn't, after all, was he? He was just like everyone else, flesh and blood and nerves and bone. And it got to him finally, so your mother had to cut up his food into tiny pieces, do you remember, tiny little pieces so he wouldn't choke. She was like a mother bird feeding her fledgling. The next step would have been for her to chew the food herself, then spit it into his open mouth. I was waiting to see that. That would have been something."

Anna lifted a golden-brown chicken from the oven. Crisp potatoes were piled around it. Behind her she could hear Isobel's voice, rising and falling, falling and rising. She willed herself not to hear what she was saying.

"That was my first broken heart, when your father left here. I thought he'd take me with him. I thought he'd come back and rescue me from this place, and all the responsibility. But he didn't. He went to London and got married to that woman. And I had to stay at home and nurse, first our mother and then our father. Wipe their arses, wash their faces, feed them, close their eyes and bind their jaws shut tight when they died. And all along I thought he'd come back for me. That was my first broken heart."

"Please, Isobel, please." Anna turned towards her, the knife in her hand. "It was all such a long time ago, please have something to eat."

"The first one was bad enough but it was nothing in comparison to the second. I loved him so much. It was exquisite. It was perfect. It was complete."

She poured more wine into her glass and drank again. Anna watched how the tendons in her throat stood out as she swallowed in deep, choking gulps. She thought of the photographs that had once lined the drawing-room mantelpiece. Isobel at sixteen, in a pleated white skirt and blouse, a tennis racket in her hand. Isobel at eighteen, in a long white dress with a halter neck, her hair swept up off her shoulders, her neck long and slender, her delicate body graceful. Isobel in her twenties, a glass in one hand, a cigarette in a holder in the other. She was laughing at something, her open mouth showing even, white teeth. Now her teeth were stained and chipped, her face gaunt, her body stick-thin.

"But he didn't love me. He wanted me. For a while he wanted me more than anyone else, but it didn't last. I knew he was moving on. So, do you know what I did?" She drank again. "Do you know, Anna, what I did? Go on, guess."

Anna tested the blade with her finger. David had shown her how to do it safely. It was blunt. She opened the cutlery drawer, pulled out a whetstone and laid the knife at an angle across its abrasive surface. She tested it again. Not sharp enough.

"Are you listening to me, Anna? Are you?"

Backwards and forwards, the noise of metal on stone, harsh, insistent. She checked it again. Now it was ready. She held the chicken down and began to carve. She concentrated on her task. White meat slipped from the carcass and lay in neat slices on the plate. David had taught her how to do this, too. "It's so easy," he had said. "Why is it that women always think you have to have balls before you can do it? Come on, my little one, I'll show you."

"I'll show you, you little bitch, how much I loved him." Anna felt Isobel's hand twist into her hair, and pull her head back. "I gave you to him, didn't I, when you were seventeen and he came here to see me? I watched how he looked at you, so I gave you to him. And then he rewarded me. He kept on coming back. Year after year after year. Even after you were married. He promised me he would. And he did. Sometimes when the two of you were here, you'd go off for a walk, or out in the boat by yourself. I'd watch you kiss him goodbye and then we'd watch you disappear from sight. And we'd be together. But it wasn't enough. I thought it would be. And now, before I got everything I wanted from him, he's gone. And all that's left is you, and I never wanted you."

It was dark outside now, and so quiet. It was two miles to the nearest house, half a mile to the main road. If she had been able to reach the switch and turn off the lights the darkness would have eaten up the whole house instantly. Sucked it in, swallowed it up. She had been terrified of the blackness when they first came here, a child of the city, used to the lights of the street. She remembered her father trying to calm her down, explain that if she waited just for a few minutes her eyes would adjust and she would begin to see again. The way she knew now that Billy could sense, feel his way carefully from familiar place to familiar place. Now she loved the dark. It wrapped itself around her so that she could move without fear. What she couldn't see couldn't harm her, she had decided. Unlike the open spaces that daylight revealed in those first few months in this strange world. The clear pale sky, stretching unhindered from horizon to horizon. No roofs, chimney pots, television aerials, overhead railway bridges that had edged her world before.

"Where does it begin and where does it end?" she had asked her father.

And he had shrugged his shoulders and said, "Beginnings and endings, only your imagination can tell you that."

The knife was heavy in her hand. The stench of Isobel's fury filled her nostrils. She could feel Isobel's arms around her shoulders, her breasts and stomach flattened against her back. She knew her aunt's naked body so well. She had put her to bed countless times, stripped her clothes from her, wrapped her in a blanket, laid her head carefully on a pillow. And now she saw David too. Touching her, kissing her, his large, strong hands on her sagging, wrinkled skin.

With a sudden jerk Anna twisted her head free from Isobel's grasp. Disgust gave her strength and she pushed her violently away, then turned to look at her. Her aunt swayed from side to side. Her face was flushed, her eyes bloodshot. She picked up the bottle. She poured the last of it into her glass, swinging it wildly around, then flung it as hard as she could at Anna's head. Anna ducked and the bottle crashed through the window. She heard the sharp sound as it smashed on the path outside. Isobel began to cry.

"He's gone and I loved him. They're all gone, even the dog. And all that's left is you and me. And I hate you so much."

IT WAS very early when Anna left the house next morning. She had taken refuge in the room that until now she had always called her own. She had pushed the chest of drawers against the door, then lain awake and listened to the sound of Isobel as she roamed around the house, her voice hoarse with anger and pain. She felt the handle of the knife, smooth and comforting, beside her, as she turned her face into her pillow, and wept. But even her tears could not stop the pictures from flooding her inner eye. Eventually, as the palest traces of light began to creep around the curtains, she got up and dressed. Last night's crescent moon hung in the pallid sky, the morning star like a punctuation mark beside it. She walked down to the jetty. She picked up a flat stone from the water's edge and skimmed it across the floodtide. It bounced three times, then sank with a small, hollow gulp. She turned and walked away, her feet scuffing through the long wet grass, leaving tracks that would disappear as the ground beneath them warmed.

19

It was the kid Michael noticed first, strapped into his seat in the car next to him at the lights. There must have been some holdup because they seemed to have been there for ages. Three rows of traffic in a line, and five or six cars behind, God knows how many in front.

Michael was bored. He fiddled with all the gadgets on the dashboard, pushing in the cigarette lighter, waiting for it to pop out with a click even though he didn't smoke, pushing all the buttons on the radio, hopping from pre-set to pre-set, rock music, phone-in shows, classical music, more chat, backwards and forwards, again and again, drumming his fingers on the steering wheel, tempted to hit the horn really hard, create a commotion. He resisted that one when he saw the blue lights flashing up ahead. "Behave yourself, Michael me lad," he said out loud and laughed, peeling a mint from its wrapping and biting down on its hard surface. And looking around, at the kid in the seat closest to him, and the other one, smaller, strapped in beside him, crying so loudly that Michael could hear his shrieks even through the closed windows. He could see that the older boy was hitting the little one with some kind of a spade or a bat or something. Wham, wham, wham, again and again. A classic case of sibling rivalry, he supposed, glad for the umpteenth time that he was an only child. Not much love doing the rounds in his house, but at least he got whatever there was and didn't have to share it with anyone else.

All was not well in the car in the next lane. The woman sitting behind the wheel had turned around and was shouting at the kids. And then she got out, right there and then at the traffic lights, and came around to the side next to him and opened the back door, yelling at the bigger boy and taking the plastic spade or whatever it was out of his fist, throwing it right across the whole line of traffic. And as she got back into the car again he recognized her. Immediately, as if no time had passed since he had last seen her, lying in her narrow single bed, her face flushed and sweating, and tears rolling down her cheeks.

It was definitely Tessa, there was no mistaking her. She looked a lot better now than she had in the old days, when she had been Christy's girlfriend and Michael's first experiment. She was still very fair, but her hair was short. She was still slim, but much better dressed than before. And by the look of the car she was driving, some kind of fancy Jeep, she'd a lot more money than he'd expected her to have.

As a rule Michael didn't believe in coincidence, but he couldn't force logic onto this encounter. He was out on the road to Bray. Hundreds of cars passed along it every day. Why not Tessa? he supposed. It was funny, though, it had never occurred to him that she might be living here in Dublin. He remembered that he had heard that she'd gone to the States, or was it Australia? Wherever it was, she was home now.

Just as she got back in behind the wheel the lights changed and the row of cars moved forward. He let her pull ahead and sat back and waited. For what? To satisfy his curiosity. And was there any desire left in there? He passed a couple of cars and drew up level with her again. She looked pretty from what he could see, but nothing more. He had wanted her then, but it didn't last. Once he knew that she would respond to him there was no more fun to be had. He had tried out the courtship gift on her and it had worked. And that was the end of that.

He slowed down and fell in behind her. She passed the turn for Cabinteely, the red-roofed Spanish-style church at the turn for Dean's Grange. She left Stillorgan behind on the left, then pulled into the right-hand lane, heading down Mount Merrion Avenue, large detached houses on either side of the tree-lined road that led towards Blackrock and the sea. She was travelling more slowly now, keeping in to the side. He slowed too, maintaining the same distance between them, flicking on his indicator as she did, almost stopping behind her as she turned in through a set of iron gates standing open between large granite pillars. A banner flew over the high wall. Kilduff Woods, it said, with an illustration of Tudor-style houses, pitched roofs and chimney pots and black timbers against red brick.

He pulled into the curb and waited. She had turned again almost immediately to the right, into one of the cul-de-sacs that branched off the main avenue. He got out of the car and leaned against it for a moment, reaching into his pocket for his leather gloves, smoothing the soft skin down over each finger. Then he crossed over the road, and walked slowly past the new houses with their bare front gardens. Tessa's car was parked outside the house, which stood by itself at the top of a small incline. The back doors were open. A red tricycle lay on its side on the front path. As he watched, the little boy in dungarees squirmed feetfirst out of the car. He tottered towards the bike, chattering away to himself. He squatted down beside it, fiddling with the handlebars, his fingers pushing the bright shiny bell so it chirruped loudly. Then he took hold of the metal crossbar and with all his strength hauled it upright, setting it on its three wheels. He eased himself onto the saddle and pushed off with both feet. The tricycle spun down the little hill on to the road. The child laughed, and took both hands off the handlebars, just as the front wheel crashed into a piece of concrete, fallen from the back of a lorry. It twisted to one side and stopped dead. There was a moment's silence as the little boy landed heavily on the ground, then a loud, frenzied scream. Again and again the cry, as he pushed himself up, looking around, his mouth wide open, blood trickling down his forehead. And began to run, still screaming, away from the safety of the house, down the cul-de-sac towards the main road, stumbling and falling, his cries becoming more desperate.

Michael watched the child. He thought of the cars flying by, how none of the drivers would anticipate a little boy in blue dungarees with a cut on his head, rushing into their path. How they would be unable to stop. How they would try to find the brake pedal, try not to think about the other cars so close behind. The articulated lorry, heavily laden on its way to the port, that would smash into them if they slowed without warning. And the child's face turned in their direction, his mouth wide open, his scream cut off suddenly as their car might plow into his frail little body. And the small thump as the front wheels and then the back wheels went over him.

He turned back towards the house. It looked empty, the leaded windows upstairs and down opaque in the sunshine. He turned again towards the main road. He could still hear the child screaming. And then there was silence. He walked quickly back down the cul-de-sac, and saw an elderly woman bending over to pick up the child from the footpath, where he had fallen again, his legs awkwardly twisted underneath him. He heard her soothing words as she wiped his face with a tissue, and kissed him gently on the cheek.

He slowed his step as he approached her.

"Is everything all right?" he asked. "Is he hurt?"

The woman looked up at him as she heaved the child onto her hip.

"I'm sure he's fine. He's a bit of a devil, this young lad. Aren't you?" She kissed his wet cheek again, his sobs sending shudders through his small body. "Always into mischief. Should have a ball and chain around his ankle. Keep him in one place. He's just like his daddy was when he was a wee one. Just like your daddy, aren't you, my little pet?"

She wrapped both arms around him and turned towards the cul-de-sac. He heard behind him the sound of running feet and Tessa's voice crying out in dismay as he crossed back over to his car and got inside, quickly, bending down, putting the keys into the ignition. He looked up carefully, so she wouldn't see him, and watched her, as slender as when she was eighteen, taking the child from the woman, kissing him, hugging him.

He drove past them, the two women and the boy, away from the main road, farther into the patchwork of half-finished houses and open green spaces. There was still a lot of building going on. Rows of scaffolding in front of frames of wood and concrete blocks. A JCB was digging foundations, a huge heap of earth spilling over the road. He stopped the car again to watch. It made him think about the third death. It wasn't that long ago. Another accident, or so it had seemed. The man's name was Adam. He had deserved it. Much more than the others.

Michael got out of the car and walked across the road. Clods of earth lay strewn about. He thought of the feel of the clay, the way it had clung. It had smothered everything with its sticky, cloying weight. Filling Adam's nostrils, his ears, his mouth, his eyes. Clinging to his hair, so that even after he had been washed and dried, when he lay in his coffin, clay dust coated his scalp and lay in the fine lines around his mouth.

Michael looked at the JCB driver, snug in the cab. He was wearing headphones. Probably listening to the radio. It would be hard to attract his attention, to tell him that there was something wrong. That he should stop digging and stop dumping earth in a huge growing heap. Michael remembered that wet day at the end of that summer. He had tried to help Adam, in the same way he had tried to help Christy. It was just too late, that was all. Just too late.

20

Billy had never been sure exactly who it was who saved him that day. He had felt Grace's hard bony head pushing against his leg. Then he felt nothing more until he tasted seawater mixed with his own vomit, and the smooth stones of the beach pressing into his cheek, as someone thumped on his back and lifted his arms up and down pumping the breath into his lungs again.

Someone else, he thought it might be Bobby, from the amusements, pulled him to his feet, wrapping a blanket around him, and Steve was there too, calling out to Grace, taking him by the arm and half carrying, half dragging him across the road and into the arcade. Then they stripped him and rubbed his thin body with towels and gave him hot tea, black with too much sugar, which he didn't like and tried to spit out. But when he heard the tone in Steve's voice he did as he was told. "What kind of a fuckin' arsehole are you, you stupid little blind cunt? Messing around down there by the sea as if you're on a kiddies' picnic instead of doing what we fuckin' pay you for. Swimming, eh? Is that what you want? Well, you can take your dog and you can piss off back to the city, do you hear me?"

And it was only after he had begged and pleaded to be given a second chance that the tone of Steve's voice changed and the atmosphere in the room lightened. He heard the sound of the cap on the whiskey bottle turning, and waited for Steve to put the glass into his hand.

"You're lucky that the boss is away for a few days. And that all the stuff was still in your bag, and none of it was damaged."

"I'll go now. If I hurry I'll be in town in half an hour," Billy stammered, sensing a reprieve.

"Well," he heard Steve get up from his chair behind the desk and come around to stand in front of him, "maybe not just yet."

THERE WERE men who would pay an extra premium for a blind boy. Billy had discovered that over the years. There was, he knew, no threat from him, no risk of betrayal, or blackmail. There was one in particular. He'd been a regular for quite a while. His hands were rough. Like a lick from a cat's tongue. He was convinced, or so he said, that Billy's blindness could be cured.

"It's like the laying on of hands," he said, "except it's not hands."

Billy could never work out what he got from it, but it was harmless enough. At least it didn't hurt. It was just messy. All over his face. And he didn't like the way the smell lingered. For the next couple of days, no matter how much he washed or with what kind of soap.

He'd given up a lot of it since he met Anna. It didn't seem right somehow. He'd never thought about it one way or the other before. It was just something that he did. It brought in extra money, and quite often he liked how it made him feel. Wanted. Needed. Useful. Part of a group. Like when he was in the blind school, and the starched sheets gave no comfort. But the arms of the other boys did.

He didn't think that she would approve, and he wanted approval from her more than from anyone else. So when men came up to him in the street, and put out a hand to touch him, he would pull away, make it plain that he didn't want to know. In case she might be watching, that she might see something that would tell her what he was.

He thought of her now as he walked with Grace from the station in Westland Row, under the bridge and into Trinity College. She had shown him this way, through the university buildings that clustered by the high wall and out onto the wide path that cut across the playing fields.

"It's a much better route to Grafton Street," she had said. "Much safer, and all this lovely fresh air. Don't you feel it on your skin?"

She had guided him over the cobbles in Front Square and out through the arch, wooden blocks beneath his feet and the low vaulted ceiling suddenly throwing the sounds of footsteps, of traffic, of voices up into the air so they bounced around him.

After the girls in the coffee bar had dried his clothes, Steve had sent him on his way. He still had time to make his connections, so he would be paid on Friday as usual. The money was really important. If he was to look after Anna now. Now that her husband was dead and she was on her own. Like him.

Grace took him to his usual pitch next to Bewley's. Most of the regulars were there, the boys who sold papers from the barrow, the old lady in the wheelchair who sold the *Big Issue*, the flower sellers. He laid his bag down at his feet, and felt inside it for his tin whistle. Then he straightened up and began to play. Dance music, jigs and reels, faster and faster, while around him gathered a crowd. He could hear the footsteps, how they stopped in front of him. He listened intently, noting the ones that tapped. Heel and toe. Toe and heel. The air moved around him, as people came and went. And money dropped down into the plastic box he placed carefully on the ground. And three times during the afternoon a hand would feel inside his bag, take something out and leave something else behind. So that when the time came for him to go home, his bag would be lighter, even with all the coins he had collected.

But there was something different now in the warm, noisy street. A pool of quiet slightly to his left. And a sound like the beat of a bird's wing, a displacement of air, as a hand reached out to touch his, and a voice said, "Billy, how are you? It's me. I'm back."

The dog's claws scraped on the paving as Grace stood up, responding to the caress on the rough hair on her head and around her neck.

And Billy opened his mouth and began to sing. Her favorite song. His head thrown back, his eyelids closing over his wandering eyes.

My young love said to me, "My brothers won't mind
And my father won't slight you for your lack of kind."

Then she stepped away from him and this she did say,
"It will not be long, love, till our wedding day."

He held out his hand and drew her in close beside him.
"Sing," he whispered to her. "The next verse."
 He heard her take a breath and then the words,

> *She stepped away from me and she moved through the*
> *fair,*
> *And fondly I watched her go here and go there,*
> *Then she went her way homeward with one star awake*
> *As the swan in the evening moves over the lake.*

And then together, his voice swirling around hers, matching it, dipping below her notes, then rising to meet her
again,

> *I dreamt it last night that my young love came in,*
> *So softly she entered, her feet made no din;*
> *She came close beside me and this she did say*
> *"It will not be long, love, till our wedding day."*

The applause pattered over them like a fine shower of rain,
and Billy laughed out loud, forgetting everything except
the pleasure of being with her again. She looked around
her, smiling at his pleasure and the delight of the audience.
And saw among the crowd a face that she had seen before.
Dark hair, glossy in the sunshine, and eyes as brown as the
back of a honeybee. Just for a moment, and then gone.

21

Anna had thought that she was prepared for it, for the way the house would look when it was empty, but it was the sound that got to her first. The hollowness. Her footsteps on the bare boards as she moved from room to room, looking at the dirty dark marks on the walls and floors, identifying everything that was missing. Paintings, rugs, mirrors, chairs and tables. A lifetime of collecting.

"You should be pleased," James had said, when he phoned her at Isobel's to tell her that the house and the last of its contents had been sold. "You got a very good price."

All that was left in the sitting room was the piano, the beautiful walnut baby grand. "You're not selling that, are you?" she had said to James. "David gave it to me as a wedding present. He said it belonged to his godmother."

"Well," James had steepled his fingers in an unconscious imitation of his older brother, irritating her with his pomposity, "well, that wasn't strictly the way it happened. He obviously didn't mention that she wasn't just his godmother, she was also our aunt. She left the contents of her house to both of us, to be divided equally. I seem to remember that David got rather more than his fair share, but . . ."

But now she didn't want it. If it had belonged to David it meant nothing more to her. She sat down on the faded tapestry stool and opened the lid. They had played duets together, she and David, that first summer at Isobel's, on her old upright, out of tune, the ivory keys yellowed and cracked. His large square hands pushed her angular fingers out of the way, his thumbs caressing her knuckles as they crossed over and above her. The Russian dance from the *Nutcracker*, the Minuet from *Eine Kleine Nachtmusik*, and fragments of Bach. And then he had taken over, playing Scott Joplin. Expertly, a continuous stream of tunes complete with commentary. History, sociology, gossip about the music and the musicians, until Isobel shouted crossly that dinner was waiting.

She lifted the lid and drew her fingers up the keyboard, then down again. She wanted to take a hammer and smash the ivory to pieces. She clenched her fists and banged them down hard, until the windows shook with the sound, and her head began to ache. She stood up then and turned away, walking quickly upstairs. It was as bad if not worse up there. They had left behind her bed, but taken the lovely pier glass that had always been in their bedroom. And the dressing table and chest of drawers, and the ornate chaise longue that David had given her, she remembered, last Saint Valentine's Day. Someone had taken their clothes from the mahogany wardrobe and heaped them on the floor. Everything. Even her underwear, strewn on top of David's suits and jackets. His silver-backed hairbrushes were gone, and the collection of snuffboxes that he kept in a little cabinet mounted on the wall of the room he jokingly referred to as his dressing room.

Upstairs again, where he had died, there was nothing at all. No desk, no filing cabinets, no rug. Just a pile of papers, strewn dustily about. And a couple of cigar butts, crushed.

She ran then, back down the stairs, into the kitchen and out into the garden. A square of brown in the middle of the lawn showed what else was missing. Her sundial, brass, with a furred patina of green. Another present. For her thirtieth birthday. Midsummer, two years ago. Waking her early on a bright blue morning. Pulling her from her sleep, binding her eyes with a silk scarf, then taking her by her hands and leading her, step by careful step, her feet feeling cautiously the cold tiles of the kitchen floor, the warm smoothness of the terrace, the clipped bristles of the grass. And his lips on her cheek, on her mouth, and his hands undoing the buttons on her nightdress, as he whispered the words that were etched into the metal,

> *Since you, sir, went away,*
> *My gauze curtains sigh in the autumn's wind.*
> *My thoughts of you are like the creeping grass*
> *That grows and spreads without end.*

"To remind you of me," he said. The long shadow you cast over me when you were alive, she thought, and the even longer one you have cast now that you are dead. She wished she could cry. But there was nothing left now. Except anger.

It was getting dark. It had already been late afternoon when she got off the train at Heuston station. She had caught the bus to O'Connell Bridge, then crossed the river, and walked quickly to Grafton Street. She wanted to see Billy, to tell him she was sorry that she hadn't been able to get him any of the well water. She heard his music before she could see him, the crowd encircling him was so dense. She pushed her way through to the front and stood and watched for a while, looking around her at the faces, still and appreciative. Marvelling at his skill, the way his fingers arched over the simple metal tube, his breath blowing such beauty from it. He didn't look well, she thought. His pale hair fell damply over his forehead and the reddish stubble on his jaw and chin glinted in the sunshine. She noticed that his shirt collar was badly frayed and there were greasy stains on his carefully knotted tie. Ash from a cigarette had burned a neat brown-rimmed hole in the crotch of his trousers, and he was wearing an old tweed jacket that didn't fit. She stepped closer. There was a small crack in the corner of his mouth, yellow and oozing against the dark pink of his lips, and as he finished a set of tunes and opened his mouth to smile his thanks for the applause, she saw that his teeth were smeared with a greenish film.

David had always warned her about getting too involved with Billy. "You're mad, crazy, nuts. You know nothing about the guy except that he's blind and he's musical. It's not up to you to help him, you know. The state will always take care of people like him if his family won't. Back off, Anna, before you regret it."

She would never have sung in the street with Billy while David was alive. He was prepared to tolerate carols with the choir, raising money for charity, a couple of times coming up to Christmas. In fact, she'd even caught him boasting to one of his legal cronies about her voice. But busking, waiting for people to throw down money, that she would never have done. Just thinking about his response made her anger burn even more brightly. And she stepped forward and touched Billy's arm, feeling the fragile bones beneath her fingers.

The man in the crowd, was it the same man who had come to look at the house? She was almost certain that it was. But she had come recently to doubt the truth of her senses. She had seen David so many times over the past few weeks. Seated squarely at the wheel of the car in front of her as she cycled to work, buying a newspaper from the paper seller at the corner of Dame Street and George's Street, weighing a pocketful of change in his large bony hand, and once she had been sure it was he in the distance far away on the sodden brown beach at Sandymount. She had been looking at the flocks of dunlins that had arrived for the summer, but by the time she had raised her binoculars to her eyes and focused, he was gone. And now she didn't want to see him again.

It was cold in the garden once the sun began to sink. She walked back inside and went into the small sitting room next to the kitchen. She had left her own private belongings here, piled on an old garden table. Letters, notebooks, photographs, her own books, a small jewelry box that had belonged to her mother. On the floor beside it were a couple of tattered cardboard boxes filled with her parents' papers. She had dragged them from flat to flat over the years and finally to this house, never quite able to sort through them, but never sure enough to throw them out. She had told James that they were to be left where she had put them, that they were not to be touched.

"Do you hear me? Are you listening? They are mine, they have nothing to do with this."

She knelt down beside them now and peeled back the flaps, checking to make sure that everything was as she had left it. She put her hand inside and flicked through the piles of paper. But there was something else. She was sure that she had buried the tape deep at the bottom of the box, before she went away. She had held it in her hand and looked at it wondering what to do with it. She couldn't bear the thought of bringing it with her. Carrying the evidence of David's deceit everywhere she went. Polluting the beauty of the place she had thought they had both loved. What a joke. A bitter taste filled her mouth as she thought of her aunt and what she had told her. Was there to be no end to the pain that he could inflict? She leaned over the box and began to lift out the sheaves of paper and old cardboard folders. When she reached the bottom there was nothing more but a couple of bent paper clips. Where was the tape? She sat back on her heels and wondered. Perhaps she hadn't put it here. Had she taken it into the office with her? Or maybe . . . She got up and walked down the hall into the empty room at the front of the house. The bookshelves were still untouched.

"I've a friend who'll take all those," James had said. "He'll give you a fair price."

She remembered that she had walked around the house with the tape in her hand, wondering where to put it. Perhaps, after all, it was somewhere here. She reached out and grabbed handfuls of the books, tearing their spines as she sent them crashing to the floor. What was the point of all this collected wisdom and knowledge? she thought. Hadn't David proved to her once and for all that what mattered most was cruelty and the power to hurt?

She raised her eyes from the growing pile of books and looked out into the garden. And saw the figure of a man standing, close to the window, his face in shadow. She jumped, her legs moving of their own free will, her heart thudding, her stomach churning as he began to walk, step by measured step, closer and closer. She moved towards the door and switched off the light. The darkness would save her now, the way it always did.

22

Her spine pressed against the wall, holding her breath, her feet tensed, waiting for the moment when she would be able to run. Hearing first of all the back door open, footsteps on the kitchen tiles, then getting louder on the hall floorboards. Silence for a moment, then she saw his back as he walked into the room, and stood in front of her and began to turn around.

As she reached for the light switch, her cold fingers finding the small brass knob, and pulling it down, the room flooded suddenly with color. Shining on his glossy brown hair, his thin face, accentuating his cheekbones, his long nose, and the smile on his mouth as he saw her.

"It's you," he said, coming towards her. "You frightened the life out of me. I couldn't think who it was. I thought it might be vandals, kids looking for a hideout for a cider party. All I could see from the garden was someone in here, wrecking the place was how it looked." He stepped closer. "Are you all right? You're shaking, you're cold, is that it?"

She shook her head, relief making her weak. "No, I'm fine, really, I just wasn't expecting anyone here tonight. I didn't know, I didn't realize that anyone else had keys."

"Well, strictly speaking, I shouldn't because the contracts haven't been signed yet, but you know, of course, that I bought the house last week at the auction?"

She shook her head again.

"Yes, you convinced me that day I came to see it. Anyway they gave me a set of keys because I said I wanted to come back and have a look at it again. They also said that you were away and they didn't think you'd be back for a while. I am sorry."

It was the last of David's wine they drank that night. A kind of hysterical gaiety washed over her. They sat in the kitchen with the door open, so, she said, they could smell the night-scented stock she had planted.

"You'll miss it here, won't you? I feel bad about buying it now. Taking your home away from you."

She refilled her glass and drank. "It's not my home, not any longer."

"Because you could stay on living here, if you liked, for a while. I don't have any immediate plans for the house, and it might be better to have it occupied rather than leaving it empty. Empty houses attract trouble."

"So rent it out, or something. I don't want to live here any longer. I only came back to get the rest of my things. I don't want to have anything more to do with this place."

"Really?" He paused for a moment. "Your husband died here, didn't he? So, I'm sorry if I'm being insensitive, but the house must be full of memories for you, am I right?"

"Right and wrong too. Lived here, died here, none of it matters to me any longer." She could feel the alcohol moving through her body. She drank again, rolling the wine around in her mouth before swallowing. It tasted so delicious. She looked at the man seated across from her. "What did you say your name was? I'm sorry, I've forgotten."

"Matthew Makepiece, at your service, ma'am." He raised his glass in mock salute.

"Matthew Makepiece, what a wonderful name. How clever of your mother, or your father, to pick a Christian name that would so perfectly match your surname."

He put down his glass. "They didn't." His tone was flat.

"Oh?"

"I was called Makepiece after the orphanage, the Makepiece Institute that I was brought up in, and I was given the name Matthew because I was found in St. Matthew's Row, just near Bethnal Green in the East End of London."

"Oh, no." She flushed. "I'm so sorry, how stupid of me. Please, forgive me for being so . . . ," she searched for the right word, and reached out to touch his hand, "so presumptuous."

He moved his hand away from hers, and shrugged. "It's okay, you weren't to know." There was an awkward silence. "It was an awfully long time ago. Really. It's a curiosity for me now. I don't think about it."

She wanted him to leave. His dark eyes brimmed with sadness and she couldn't bear it. She wanted to drink and drink and forget it all. David and his cruel deceit, Isobel's despairing hatred of her. All she wanted now was forgetfulness. She poured more wine into her glass, and he took the bottle from her hand and filled his own.

"So where are you going to go? Do you have a flat or another house, or somewhere else to live?"

Zoë would take her in for a while, she knew. Although Zoë had her own problems. And there was always James, except she couldn't bear to have anything to do with him. Maybe someone at the museum would have a spare bed. She didn't care. She'd stay in a guest house or a hotel, somewhere with no memories, no voices, no feelings, nothing to remind her. Until she could sort her life out properly.

"Because I have an empty flat in a house I own just near here by the canal. It's pretty basic. Just a couple of big rooms, with a small kitchen and bathroom. But you're welcome to it, if you want."

She wished she was like the caddis fly, making its own little shelter out of tiny shells, stones, pieces of wood, grains of sand, stuck to the silk that it spun into a long tube to hide its body from predators as it dragged itself across the riverbed.

"Think about it, you can let me know if you'd like it," as he opened another of David's bottles and refilled her glass.

IT WAS late when she got to work the next morning. She couldn't remember what time Matthew had left. She had woken on the sofa, a blanket tucked around her shoulders, a cushion under her head. Her clothes were folded neatly on the floor beside her and she was wearing her favorite nightdress, one David had bought as a present before they were married. Fine cotton with pin tucks down the front and ruffles at the wrists.

She sat up slowly, pleating the soft material between her fingertips. It had been upstairs on the floor with all the rest of her clothes. She remembered she had prowled around the house before she went to bed, a candle in her hand. She must have picked it up then, and decided to wear it. Candle wax had hardened in round drops all down the front. She ran her fingers over them, as if to read what had happened, but they told her as little as the Braille marks on Billy's books.

She made coffee in her office. The museum moved and creaked around her. Footsteps in the corridor outside, the wooden floor springing up and down, snatches of conversation, then a soft tap on her door. Oh, God, she thought, it'll be O'Dwyer. He'll want me to have lunch with him. I can't face it today. But it was Sergeant Murray who stood before her desk, the security guard at his side.

"It's Billy Newman," he said. "You'd better come with me."

GRACE raised her wet nose, her nostrils opening wide as Anna reached down to smooth her thick coat. The dog was lying in her basket behind the door to Billy's little flat. She whined anxiously. It was dark inside, the sun blocked out by the office buildings that crowded all around. Billy would always turn the light on for Anna when she came to visit, his hand travelling without hesitation to the greasy switch.

"What's it like when you do that?" she had asked once. "Does it make any difference to you at all when you put the light on?"

He smiled his customary polite, automatic grimace and shook his head. "Should it?"

The room was usually so bare. His bed was pushed against the wall below the window. There was a small table beside it with his radio and alarm clock. Two wooden armchairs were placed precisely on either side of the fireplace, and in front of it was a large velvet-covered cushion she had given him. Sometimes when he was feeling sad, so he had told her, he would curl up on it, his head on his arms, cover himself with a blanket and lie for hours, his thumb in his mouth, and Grace pressed against his side.

She took a step farther into the room and reached for the switch. A triangular wedge of pale light fell from the bare bulb over the group of men standing together beside the bed. Heads turned towards her for a moment, then back to the still, silent figure she could see lying there.

Murray took her arm and drew her back out onto the walkway from the street. It was bright with summer plants in flower. Gathered in small clusters outside their doors, staring silently at her, were the others who lived in the two-story flat complex. Most were old-age pensioners. Anna knew them by sight, and some by name. They had all tried, at different times, to befriend and mind Billy. But he kept them at bay, deliberately elusive. She could hear his voice now. "I'm not like them," he would say. "I'm young, healthy. I can go where I want, when I want. Don't lump me in with them."

It was cool here out of the direct sunlight, and she was glad she was wearing a cardigan over her short-sleeved summer dress. She fiddled with its mother-of-pearl buttons and said, "Tell me, what's going on? What on earth happened? Is Billy all right?"

Sergeant Murray began to explain. How the lady next door had heard the dog bark. How she had banged on the door and got no reply. And eventually called Sister Miriam, the housing superintendent, who had used her key to get in. Billy was on the floor by the bed. He had been badly beaten.

Anna turned and looked in through the open door again. The ambulance men were maneuvering Billy's prone figure from the bed to a stretcher. "How badly hurt is he?"

"Well, we'll know more after we get him properly examined in hospital."

"But," she looked away again, "he is going to be all right, isn't he? It's not going to be serious, long-term, is it?"

"I can't really tell you one way or the other, but he is conscious, which is good."

"But who would do such a thing? And why? There's nothing here worth stealing. There's only his radio and a few tapes, nothing else at all. And Grace, of course, but no one would steal a dog."

"Actually, that's why you're here. Billy's really upset. He doesn't want her to go into kennels. He specifically asked if you'd mind her." Murray looked at her, a speculative expression on his pale face. She knew what he was thinking, that he wouldn't have expected someone like her to be friends with someone like Billy. She waited for him to say it. But he was silent, frowning.

"Of course," she said, "it's no problem."

"That is, if you can. I'd forgotten, where are you living now? I saw in the paper that your house was sold."

"It's fine, it's okay." She smiled and he saw the relief on her face.

"You've had a holiday," he said, "you're looking so much better. You obviously got the good weather. Did you go to your aunt's place?"

Her smile faded, her face hardened. "Watch out."

She pulled his arm and motioned him out of the way. She had given Billy the little bell that hung outside his front door. It rang now, over and over again, as the men carried him out. She saw his face. One eye was swollen shut, already purple with bruising. The other swivelled from side to side, rolling frantically in its socket. His lips were huge, split open, and blood was caked around his nose. She pushed past the men who were crowded around him and leaned down to kiss his cheek. His open eye spun towards the warm contact, and he tried to speak. But the moment passed as they pushed her back and out of the way.

"You'd think, wouldn't you," Murray said to her, as she found Grace's lead and brought her out of the flat, "that the dog would have done something to protect him. After all, they must be very close."

"It's trained out of them when they're pups, any kind of aggression. Guide dogs are useless guard dogs. The two just don't go together."

He walked with her back towards the museum, through Merrion Square, the sun warm on their faces after the chill of Billy's flat. Anna felt sick. The bright green of the grass and the reds and yellows of the summer flowers looked unnatural, as if they had been specially painted for the occasion. They stopped beside the playground. Children flung themselves down the slide and hung from the monkey bars, shouting and screaming. Two little boys were fighting in the corner. Anna watched their mock karate kicks and elaborate gestures. She could see Billy's battered face in front of her, and imagine the sound of fist on bone and his screams, so pitiful, unanswered.

"I'm curious," she said. "Why are you involved with this? Do you know Billy?"

"Will you be at work this afternoon? There are a few questions I'd like to ask you, if that's okay."

She didn't answer. She was watching a little girl, blonde curls waving in the gentle breeze. She had wandered away from her mother, who was sitting on a bench reading a magazine. The child was walking on tiptoe, chattering to herself, pointing at Grace and waving. And walking right into the path of the swings, as they swung back, up and down. Anna felt dizzy. She remembered the sound of the bang on her head, the bright spots in front of her eyes, then darkness. She lifted her hand. She could still feel the raised ridge behind her right ear where she had been stitched. The little girl slowed and stopped, then sat down suddenly on the ground. Her mother looked up.

"Hey, come here, sweetheart. Mind where you're going." She jumped to her feet and ran over to pick her up.

She kissed both her plump cheeks, and the child laughed. Loneliness swirled over and around Anna. She felt cold and nauseous, the color draining from the world.

"Are you all right? Did you hear me? I'd like to see you later today." Murray put his hand on her arm.

"I'm fine, perfectly okay, but very late for work. I'll be in my office till six. Come in whenever suits you."

And she was gone, half running, with the dog trotting beside her.

IT WAS late when she heard his voice again in the corridor. She cleared a pile of books from a stool and made him tea, dunking a tea bag in a stained mug and adding milk from a carton.

"So this is where you spend your time," he said, peering down at the drawer of specimens open on her desk.

"That's right. This is my sanctuary."

"And you don't get lonely up here?"

"No more so than anywhere else. I have plenty of companions to interest me. There's a million or so pinned insects in these drawers." She waved her arm towards the row of mahogany cabinets that lined the walls. "You know, there are specimens here that Darwin collected. The identifications are made in his own handwriting."

"And could you re-create him, do you think, if there was a mosquito in there who had bitten him?"

"Don't believe everything that Steven Spielberg comes up with. It's a nice idea, but scientifically unrealizable."

She picked up a magnifying glass and leaned over the case again, examining the brilliantly colored butterflies.

One thin hand grasped the glass's handle, the other reached for her hair, her index finger twisting and turning a stray lock into a tight coil, then letting it go and smoothing it out. He watched her face, the way her top teeth caught hold of her bottom lip in concentration. It was so quiet here now that he could hear her breath sighing in and out of her mouth. He cleared his throat. "I wanted to ask you," he said, "if you'd have a look at some of these photos and tell me if you can identify any of them."

She didn't look up. "Is this to do with Billy?" She picked up some tweezers and began to adjust one of the butterflies on its pin.

"That's right. You spent time with him, maybe you saw someone by chance who might have had something to do with the attack."

She put down the glass and tweezers, and looked up at him. "But why are you involved? I thought you were in the Drug Squad, wasn't that what you said?"

He took a mouthful of tea and made a face. "You disappoint me. Your scrupulous tea-making doesn't extend as far as here obviously."

She smiled wanly. "It would be a breach of civil-service practice to enjoy your tea break. It's only allowed if it's to be suffered rather than celebrated. Isn't it like that in the Guards?"

He laughed. "Got it in one."

He opened his briefcase and took out a large manila file. He put it on the desk in front of her. "If you wouldn't mind looking at these, just in case you recognize any of them."

She sat back on her chair, and began to fiddle again with her hair, then pulled the file towards her, and opened it, taking out a bundle of photographs. "You still haven't told me why you're interested."

He poured the dregs from his mug into the sink and rinsed it out, shaking the drops of water from it and putting it upside down to drain.

"Nothing specific, really, but the place where Billy lives is a junkie's paradise. A lot of dealers go there because it's quiet. All those old people, too scared to hassle them. It's close to the city center, but it's out of the way, tucked in behind the office blocks. Have you never noticed the little groups of people who congregate on the green area under the cherry trees?"

She looked up from the pile of pictures. "No, I haven't, actually. Now you come to mention it, I must be very stupid."

"Not stupid, you're not that. You've just never had any reason to see them. You're lucky."

She decided after she had finished looking at the photographs that they were all what were called in the museum "types." Specific specimens, the definitive example of the species. Their labels were marked with a red dot. These should be marked in the same way, she thought, as she turned them over. An archive of abuse and destruction. But she could put names to none of the faces in front of her. She could identify without difficulty hundreds, possibly thousands of species of insect, but this handful of men was beyond the range of her knowledge.

She walked him out through the public rooms, their

feet bouncing on the sprung wooden floors, calling into the security guard's little cubbyhole to collect Grace, who had been pampered and petted all afternoon.

Murray stopped to look up at the basking shark suspended from the glass ceiling. "I love this place. My mother used to bring us here all the time. She liked to draw the birds."

Anna watched the pleasure on his face. "You'll be bringing your own daughter soon, won't you?"

"I'm not sure," he said. "Her mother is one of those eco-warrior types. She doesn't approve of stuffed animals." He shook her hand at the door. "Take care of yourself, and don't worry about Billy. I phoned the hospital and they said he's going to be fine. He's very bruised and sore, but there won't be any long-term damage. I'm sure you can go and see him soon."

"Thanks, that makes me feel better." She turned away from him, and stopped suddenly. He followed her gaze. She was looking through the glass doors, towards the railings that bounded the neat green lawn. Her face was suddenly bright. There was a man leaning against the mottled bark of the old plane tree, whose long twisted branches spread dark shadows in the sunlight. He was holding a newspaper, folded over. He had a pen in one hand, and he was frowning. Then he looked up and smiled too. And began to move, with a graceful long-limbed walk, over the grass towards her.

23

The room was large and very bright. An elaborate cornice, vine and acanthus leaves entwined, wound its way around the edge of the ceiling. Two long windows looked out onto the canal below. Light rippled across the white walls, shifting and changing as the water moved in the gentle summer breeze. Double doors divided the room in two. Anna walked across the polished pine floorboards and pulled them open. She peered inside. It was darker here, with one window through which she could see overgrown sycamores and dense buddleia. And behind, the chimney pots and rooftops of the straight Georgian street that led back to the museum. "I love it," she said. "I can't thank you enough for letting me move in."

She had been so surprised to see Matthew waiting for her. And embarrassed.

"How did you know where to find me? Did I tell you last night where I worked?" She remembered the neat pile of clothes on the floor beside the sofa.

"Let me think." He paused, resting the first finger of his left hand on his bottom lip. "Did you tell me where you worked? Yes, you did. You told me all about the museum, and what you did there, and how much you loved it, and how you were never happier than when you were up in your little room with your favorite insects. What was it you said they were? Parasitic somethings?"

She grimaced, pulling a face of mock despair, and hid behind her hands. "Oh dear, I told you all that, did I? All about me and the parasitic wasps, the ichneumon flies, about how I was practically a world expert, and when I finished my Ph.D. . . ."

"When you finished your Ph.D. they'd be coming from every corner of the globe to worship at your dainty feet."

She laughed. "Sounds like I owe you an apology. Too much wine after a fright isn't good for me."

He had taken her by the elbow, his fingers kneading her forearm through the sleeve of her cardigan. They had zigzagged together in and out of the early-evening traffic, skirting Merrion Square, and walked quickly past the stained white limestone of the Peppercanister Church. He had stopped where the road widened out from the high Georgian houses onto the canal. He took her hand and pulled her to the water's edge. A group of mallard ducks were swimming in interrupted circles in and out of the reeds. Matthew squatted down and took a plastic bag from his pocket. He emptied some scraps of bread onto his palm and crumbled them fine, throwing them beyond the birds, so they turned as if in formation and followed the fine white specks floating away on the widening ripples. He looked back at her, and reached over to run his hands through the thick hair on Grace's neck. "Your dog will have fun with all of this."

"She's not mine, actually, she belongs to a friend. I'm just looking after her for a couple of weeks. Is that okay? You don't mind?"

"Not at all. Come on, I'll show you around."

It was dark behind the hall door. Planks of wood were stacked in heaps along one wall. There was the smell of new paint and wood shavings and from somewhere below the sound of whistling.

"I'm doing the house up, bit by bit. The men have started in the basement. It'll be quite a while before they get to the first floor, so you can stay as long as you like."

He'd arrange, he said, for whatever she wanted from the Anglesea Road house to be moved. It would be no problem.

"No, really, it's too much. You're being too kind. I can do it."

But he insisted, "It's easier for me, it's my business. Buying and selling, moving property around, it's what I do."

"Then please, let me take you out for a meal, if you're free. It's what I can do."

They would go, she decided, to David's favorite restaurant. She walked with Grace back to David's house, and phoned to book a table. She went up to the bedroom. She sorted through her clothes, trying to decide what to wear. She ran her hands over the linens, silks, wools of the suits and dresses that David had bought for her. They felt alien to her now, as if they had belonged to another person. At the bottom of the pile was a large plastic bag, dusty, with small tears where coat hangers had snagged on it. She reached inside and felt the embroidered satin of her wedding dress. She tugged at the skirt, dragging it into the light. It had fanned out behind her like the tail of an Australian lyrebird, heavy on the church's red and yellow tiled floor. David's fourteen-year-old twin cousins had reluctantly lifted it from the car and carried it across the wet gravel, sighing their displeasure and disapproval. She had felt the cold slither of the fabric on her breasts as she walked towards him, waiting for the moment when he would turn and see her and smile. But she remembered now that he hadn't. She could see the back of his head as she walked up the aisle. He was leaning over to Isobel, his face turned down to hers, hers lifted towards his.

Anna's fingers gripped the heavy material, and she ripped at it, but there was no give. She got up and walked into the bathroom, the dress dragging behind her. David's razor lay where he had left it, on the shelf above the wash-basin. She unscrewed it carefully. Dark hairs stuck stiffly to the blade. She lifted it out, holding it gingerly between thumb and forefinger. She held up the dress with her other hand, and slowly cut through the satin, from bodice to hem, hacking at the gathered stitches of the waist, then slipping easily down the long skirt with a high-pitched whine. Again and again, up and down, until the dress lay in long thin slivers on the tiled floor. She flung down the blade, kicking the remains of the material into a crumpled heap in the corner.

She walked back into the bedroom, reaching into the bag again. She felt the springy ridges of crêpe. She grasped hold of a handful and pulled it out. It was one of her mother's dresses. A favorite, she remembered. Made in the thirties for her own mother, kept carefully for years. She should never have left it crumpled and forgotten like this. She took it over to the window to get a better look. It was gray, the color of clouds on a sunless morning, with a skirt cut on the bias, and three-quarter-length sleeves with pearl buttons on the cuffs and the same pearl buttons running down the bodice. It was beautiful. As she held it to the light, she noticed her wedding ring, shining up at her. Carefully she slipped it off and weighed it in her palm. Then she opened the window and hurled it as far as she could into the garden. She held up her left hand and turned it around. Her finger was marked with a broad white band where the ring had blocked the sun from her skin. Soon it would go, she thought, and there would be no trace of her marriage anywhere on her body.

The dress fit perfectly. And there were shoes to go with it. Suede, with an inch-high heel, the leather inside molded by her mother's feet, now slipping perfectly around her instep and toes. Matthew noticed them as they walked towards the restaurant. It had begun to rain, a short intense summer shower that made the temperature drop suddenly, so she shivered and the skin on her breasts rose.

"Mind," he said, catching her hand, "your lovely shoes. They'll be ruined if you stand in a puddle."

They ordered fish. Prawns to start with. She watched the waiters as they looked from her face to Matthew's. She watched how they paused as they hurried from kitchen to dining room, the snatched comments that passed between them, the questioning looks on their faces. She leaned back in her chair, drinking her wine, and watching Matthew in the candlelight. His long thin fingers, as he pulled off the heads of the prawns, swallowing in one mouthful their rich pink and white flesh, then breaking open the bony plates of their skulls to suck out the greenish brain tissue.

"My father always did that," she said. "It was the only time I ever heard my mother annoyed with him. She couldn't bear crustaceans. She said they reminded her too much of insects, and she couldn't imagine eating crickets and grasshoppers. Creatures with long legs and waving feelers."

"And do you feel like that too? Would you like something else?"

"No." She smiled, expertly breaking one open, and holding it up to admire. "But I don't like the insides of their heads, I'm afraid."

She was getting drunk, she knew, and she didn't care. She sat back in her chair, crossing and uncrossing her legs, feeling the soft material of her dress slip over her thighs. When she leaned back and up to fix the clasp that held her hair she knew that her breasts were pushing through the bodice of her dress, which clung and moved as she moved. She leaned forward into the light of the candle and undid the first few buttons. She stroked her neck with her fingers and let them drift down towards her breast. She watched him, and saw how his eyes followed her movements. And she was pleased. She hadn't behaved like this for years. Not since the days when she and David had played their dangerous games, and she had wanted him more than anything else she could possibly imagine.

The same feelings were flooding through her now. She felt bright and shining, like the moon, polished, glowing in the reflection of his attention. She listened to his voice, telling stories, of his childhood in the orphanage, his adolescence in a series of foster homes. He made her feel like laughing and crying. He knew absolutely nothing of his parents, he said. Not a single solitary piece of information. She wanted to reach out and hold him, try to heal the hurt of the little boy he once had been. She could imagine him, small and thin with the same glossy brown hair and eyes. How desperate would you have to be, she thought, to abandon a baby like that.

"But I'm glad in a way," he said. "I have no family baggage, nothing to live down, or to live up to. I can make myself in my own image and in no one else's. And I've done well. I've made my own way. I've been lucky." He smiled and reached over to take her hand.

"So why are you here? What brought you to Dublin?"

"Whimsy, fanciful notions, really. One of my foster families was Irish originally. The kids were all mad about Irish music and dancing. They went to classes, spent most of the weekends travelling to competitions all over England. A couple of times they came here, and they brought me too. And I liked it, so I decided when I was old enough to make decisions for myself that I'd come here to live. And I did. As I said, I can make myself into whatever I want. And there's no one around to contradict me."

He poured more wine into her glass.

"Do you know," he said, "I've been trying to think ever since I met you who you remind me of. And now I have it."

"Who? Go on, tell me."

"There's a painting by Leonardo da Vinci. It's called the *Litta Madonna*. I saw it last year in the Hermitage Museum in St. Petersburg."

"Ah no." She leaned forward and smacked him gently on the hand. "Not a Madonna. Please. It's not much of a compliment. All that weeping and moaning and gnashing of teeth. And wearing blue all the time. It's not my color."

"No, no, you've got me wrong. It's not the mother, it's the child that you're like. Picture this now." He drank deeply, then held up both his hands. "She's framed between two windows, which show the usual view of far-off hills. She's looking down at him, at the baby on her lap. And her gaze has bathed him in an extraordinary golden light. She's wearing a dress that's, what do you call it, sort of drawn together at the neck."

"Gathered?"

"Yes, that's it, gathered. And it has two openings over her breasts, that are stitched together loosely."

"Sort of, instead of buttons or zips, you mean?"

"I suppose so. Yes. Anyway, the baby is feeding from his mother's breast, and he is holding onto it, the breast, that is, with one hand, in a very adult, possessive sort of way. But he isn't looking at her at all. He's looking directly out of the painting, confronting directly the observer. His eyes say that he knows everything, can see and understand everything. And his hair is the palest red gold, curly, soft tendrils all over his head. Just the way yours must have been when you were a baby."

"Go on." She smiled. "This is getting interesting."

He leaned across the table, his eyes bright in the candle-light. "Anyway, the baby is feeding, looking at everyone, holding onto Mary's milk-filled breast with his right hand, and in his left hand, which is close to his mother's belly, there is a bird. A goldfinch. And he's holding it gently, but firmly. He's not letting go. No way."

"Oh, yes." She banged her glass down on the table. "I know the painting. Of course. There's a print of it in Isobel, my aunt's house. The baby is extraordinary."

He smiled. "Isn't he? And you can see he's used to being loved. You can see it in the way he doesn't feel he needs to look at his mother. And that's the way you are. It's written all over you. You're used to having someone to take care of you, watch your back. Aren't you?"

The smile died on her face. "Not so, Matthew. Not so at all. Would that I had been so lucky."

There was an awkward silence for a moment. Matthew leaned forward again and ran his hand around her face. "Of course the other thing about you that's like the painting is that you are so beautiful, and like the painting you should only be on display for a certain number of days a year. Just in case some harm should befall you."

He held her hand as he walked her home. Running his fingers in between hers, gently, letting go, then grasping them again.

"Sing for me," he said, "the way you sang in the street with that blind boy."

"It *was* you." She turned towards him. "I thought it was, but I wasn't sure. I looked for you afterwards, but you had gone."

"Go on, sing that song, just for me."

She laughed, and she sang, watching his expression in the glow from the streetlights. When they arrived at the house she walked before him to the door and opened it. But he was standing outside the gate, already turning away.

"Aren't you—won't you come in?"

He shook his head. "Not tonight. But there'll be a truck here tomorrow morning at nine to move your things. Goodbye, Anna."

"No, wait." She moved towards the gate, but he had already gone, disappearing into the darkness.

24

The bees were anxious. Their queen was aging. For two full seasons she had laid eggs to the maximum of her ability, fifteen hundred, sometimes two thousand a week, fertilized by the drones on her mating flight when she was young. Safe now in the center of the hive, fed and protected by the fifty to sixty thousand workers, who warmed her with the mass of their bodies, cooled her with the fanning of their wings. As they licked her and groomed her, the power of her pheromones, her queen substance, kept them together, kept them as one.

They licked her and groomed her, passing her chemical power throughout the hive, signalling that she was in control, that all was right within their bee world. But as she got older, as her powers began to diminish and the sense of her presence lessened, a decision was taken. A new queen must be created. The old queen must leave, take with her half the colony, find a new home somewhere else.

Eggs to be fed with royal jelly, succored with bee milk. Cells to be enlarged to make room for the growing queens. Twenty days from the hatching of the egg to the emergence of the fully grown bee. And the first one to break through the cap on her cell turns on the others, using her sting, to kill them before they can become her rivals.

. . .

SIMON WOODS stood in his garden, with a large mug of coffee in his hand. Around him in this sheltered valley on the seaward side of Rockallen grew his favorite fruits and vegetables. Loganberries and raspberries, artichokes and asparagus, black currants and strawberries, broad beans, peas and courgettes. He was a selective gardener, some would say an eccentric. Not for him the humdrum carrots, onions, potatoes and cabbage. There was no fun in them. And, besides, they were freely available from the small shop next to the pub at the top of the hill.

He wandered out along the narrow path that wound around the side of the house. A cigarette drooped from his lips. This was his favorite time of day, late morning, when he had cleared the remains of last night's alcohol from his system, boosted his energy levels with at least three cups of very strong coffee and smoked his fifth cigarette.

When he reached the end of the path, where the meadow spread out beneath the trees in his small apple orchard, he sat down as always on the smooth stump of an old oak. Felled by a savage and unexpected storm one early spring, three years ago, it lived on in the bowls and platters he had made from its wood and used every day in his kitchen.

He sipped his steaming coffee, and listened. Peace, perfect peace. Just the way he liked it. No human sounds at all. Just the rush and ripple of the stream edging the garden, as it slipped and slid over the rocks tumbled through it, the mournful lament of a couple of crows high up in the chestnuts, and the low hum of the bees.

He had five hives here in the apple orchard, and another ten farther up the hill hidden among the gorse and the heather. He had gotten his first bees fifteen years ago when he had made enough money to buy this piece of land and the derelict cottage that came with it in what was then the depths of Wicklow. Now he was resigned to the bungalows that poked their ugly tiled heads through the bracken, accepting their bright security lights, which pushed the stars away from the reach of his telescope. But he could not bear the sound of traffic, a constant background noise now as it had been when he lived in the inner suburbs. Which was one of the reasons he always slept late. To avoid the commuters who zipped along the road, barely slowing down to negotiate the hump-backed bridge that crossed his stream at an angle.

He knew he would have to move again quite soon. He was becoming reconciled to it. Lock, stock, barrel and hives. Farther up the valley where the winds were even colder and the ground stony and inhospitable. But it wasn't just the intrusion of his neighbors that was making him think about leaving. He didn't feel right here any longer. Not since the visit by the cop from the Drug Squad and the widow. This place was tainted now, polluted by the death of the man to whom he had sent the bees. What was it the Buddhists believe? That bees carry karma to heaven, was that it? Well, the karma was bad now. He should never have allowed himself to be drawn into this business, to be used in this way. He felt as if a large hand had picked him and his life up and shaken them, so that none of the pieces quite matched any longer. And it made him feel sick and sore. And frightened.

He knew, of course, who the man was who had come with the widow, even though he hadn't introduced himself. He was the new breed of cop. Urban, educated, sussed. And he could see that the cop had recognized him too, in fact probably knew who he was before he even drove the widow out here. That would have been a calculated move. See if he'd be affected by meeting her. Well, the cop was right. He was affected. He didn't feel good. But all he had done was fill the order and send it off. And no matter how sorry he felt for her, he had to keep on reminding himself that he wasn't responsible for her husband's death.

But hold on a minute, the little voice inside his head said. You know who was, and you also know that it would be a smart move to go to the Guards and tell them. Before anyone else gets hurt.

Ah, to hell. He threw the dregs of his coffee on the grass at his feet and stood up. And listened. He turned around, dropping the mug with a curse. One of his hives was swarming, the bees pouring from it in a dark noisy cloud. He should have known this would happen. Midsummer was prime swarming time. Sometimes they could be prevented. Conscientious beekeepers had all kinds of tricks to stop the bees from leaving. Clipping the queen's wings, destroying the queen cells as they were developing, replacing the queen every two years so the spread of her pheromones through the hive was always at its maximum. Sometimes he bothered. Often he didn't. But it would still be a pity to lose his bees when honey production was at its greatest.

He hurried into the house and dressed himself quickly in his overalls and headgear. He walked back to the orchard, carrying with him a folding stepladder, and a large straw skep. He placed them against the trunk of one of the trees and looked up. The bees had settled into a dense elongated cluster. Somewhere inside, her vulnerability shielded, was the queen. Occasionally a bee would separate itself from the rest and dart upwards, from the purple heather on which it always fed, travelling up to heaven, he thought.

It was hot inside his protective suit. He felt clumsy and awkward, claustrophobic. He swayed from side to side, disoriented, his hearing and vision restricted, confused by the thick cotton material that pressed up and around his face. He thought he heard a car somewhere, possibly the sound of voices, but when he swung around towards the house the garden was as empty and quiet as always. Sweat began to drip down his forehead and he tried in vain to wipe it away. Then, with the basket in one hand, he began to climb the ladder, steadying himself with the other hand against the tree. One step, two steps, three steps, balancing, reaching for the branch from which the bees were hanging. And then, suddenly, he was on the ground, the stepladder pushed away from beneath his feet, his head and neck twisted back at an impossible angle. Such a short drop to do such damage. But, of course, it wasn't the length of the drop that mattered, was it? It was the manner of his falling and the force with which he hit the ground. A big man, too big, to be balanced on such an unreliable perch. He should have known better.

25

They only came out at night, the women who worked the canal bank. There was never any sign of them during the day. Nocturnal creatures, Anna thought, perfectly camouflaged, as she sat looking out of the long windows, Grace asleep at her feet, and watched what the darkness revealed.

It began any time after eight in the evening. As soon as the tall silver streetlamps were switched on. That was the signal. The women appeared, in twos and threes. They walked up and down, plainly visible in the pools of orange light, then disappeared again as they moved out of its reach. Over to the canal bank where the cars slowed, stopped, then speeded up again.

Anna watched the points of light. Cigarettes burning brightly as mouths sucked hard, indicators flashing, then the sudden brightness as the car door opened and revealed a woman's face, a man's profile. Then the slam of the door and darkness again.

Anna sat in her own darkness and watched. Once she fell asleep in her chair and woke, a scream dragging her upright, her heart leaping in her chest. A man and a woman standing below her. Shadowy shapes, their features obscured. But a voice, fearless, arrogant. "You fucking cunt, you think you can get away with working on your own. Who do you think you are, bitch? You're nothing without me."

And the response, the woman, pleading, wheedling, no words, just the sounds, which reminded her of the way Grace whined when Anna came home after work. She waited and saw the couple emerge into the light. He had his arm around her, and he was pushing her down onto the pavement. His hands were on her head, his fingers in her bleached hair. Her face was pressed against his crotch. Her head began to move as he leaned back against the railings, his eyes closed, his mouth open, gasping for air. And Anna stood above and watched.

"You should be careful, living there," Billy said to her, when she went to see him after he came out of the hospital. "It's not your kind of place. It's different from where you lived before. All kinds of bad things happen there."

"Don't be silly." She poured him his tea and put his hand around the mug. "I like it. The canal is beautiful. The swans swim there with their cygnets, and there's a fantastic range of insect life."

But he was not to be mollified. He sat huddled up, his face still bruised and sore, and reached out, taking hold of her arm. "Promise me you'll be careful, especially at night. Don't let anyone in unless you're sure who they are. You don't have your husband to look after you any longer."

"But I've got you, haven't I? And Grace, until you want her back."

But it was Matthew she wanted to see. The van had arrived as he had promised. Two men had loaded her belongings into it, and unloaded everything at the other end. And she had waited for him to come and see her. But the days had passed with no word. So she busied herself making a new home in the two high-ceilinged rooms.

She was the only tenant. At night after the workmen had gone the house was silent. She explored the floors above her, a candle guttering in her hand. There was no electricity or water up there. Just huge empty rooms, the plaster falling onto the floor, the moldings sagging, and floors that threatened to give way beneath her weight. But she wasn't frightened. Whatever ghosts were in this house had nothing to do with her. They had been created by others, and would, she knew, leave her alone. She had left David behind in the house on Anglesea Road. Nothing she had brought with her carried the slightest hint of his presence, and soon there would be little there to remind anyone of him. She had cycled past the house a couple of days ago and seen a skip outside, piled high with wood and rubble. She had stopped for a moment, curiosity getting the better of her, then felt anger curdling her interest, making it sour.

The museum and her work were her refuge. She hunched over the displays on her desk, her magnifying glass and tweezers in her hands. It was painstaking, time-consuming, slow, the restoration and recataloging of the entomological collection. Her duty and responsibility. To keep, to preserve, to maintain for future generations. She wanted to show it all to Matthew. She was sure that he would understand how important it was. He had questioned her about it, that night in the restaurant. And she was surprised at the extent of his knowledge. She had asked him if he had studied biology at school.

He had shaken his head. "Not exactly. There was quite a good library in the children's home. Lots of old encyclopedias. I taught myself to read when I was very young. And I read everything there was in the place. The adventures of Biggles, biology, natural history. And I found insects along the way. *The Wonder Book of Why and What.* Do you know it?"

She smiled. "Perhaps its cousin. Isobel, my aunt, had *The Wonder Book of Do You Know*, and the whole set, ten volumes, I think, of Arthur Mee's *Children's Encyclopaedia*. Apparently my grandfather used to make her and my father memorize huge chunks of it. And he used to test them on Sundays after church. She said that was why she was such an atheist. All God's time was taken up with learning the physics of the world, and not the metaphysics."

She had thought about this conversation so many times since that night. Perhaps, after all, she had bored him. David had become bored by her, she could see that so clearly now. The distant look in his eyes, as if he was gazing over the top of her head, at something or someone else. There was a time when he used to visit her here, bring her chocolates, fruit, a thermos filled with ice-cold vodka and orange juice. She remembered that they had made love in her little office. He had sat on her chair, his legs braced on the floor, and she had sat across him, holding his mouth to her breast, silent, while all around them doors opened and closed, voices called to each other, the museum breathed in and out.

She lifted her head from her work. She rubbed her eyes.

She was tired. She got up and stretched her arms above her head, moving her neck from shoulder to shoulder to ease it out. She heard a soft tap, and saw Matthew standing there, smiling at her.

"Are you all right?" His voice sounded worried. "You look very pale."

She smiled up at him. "Matthew." She wanted to say his name out loud. "I'm fine, I'm just surprised to see you here. You're really the last person I would have expected. How did you get in?"

Matthew winked and tapped the side of his nose. "Very persuasive I am, and your security guards are nice guys, if you treat them right."

"I'm not sure I approve, but I suppose in this case . . ."

"In this case they were right to let me in. I said I had a present for you, and they obviously reckoned you needed cheering up."

He put the bottle of wine on her desk, then produced a corkscrew and a couple of glasses from the leather shoulder bag he was carrying.

"Very impressive." She mimed a curtsy. "You think of everything."

"And this, too, is very impressive." He leaned over the drawer she had been working on, bending down to decipher the faded inscriptions on the name tags. "How old are these?"

"They were collected in 1862. By a Church of Ireland clergyman from County Meath. They're caddis flies, his life's work. When he died he left his collection to the museum."

"And what are you doing?"

"Just resetting them. And renaming them, bringing them up to date, giving them the modern versions of their names. Checking to make sure that all the information is correct. So the next lot of entomologists who work on them can be secure that the knowledge they are building on is reliable."

"Show me some more." He stood up again and took her hand.

"What would you like to see?"

"How many are there?"

"Millions, literally."

"So show me your favorites, the parasitic ones, what are they called?"

"Wasps or ichneumon flies. *Apanteles glomeratus,* who lay their eggs in the larvae of cabbage white butterflies."

"What happens?"

"The parasitic wasps feed off the growing larvae. They provide them with a food source, until they hatch. Some of them also inject the larvae with a hormone to prevent them from developing further. It's all very clever. And there are even species like *Mesochorus discitergus,* who will parasitize the parasites. So it goes on and on. Here, look." She pushed him forward over the drawer.

"They don't look very interesting, do they, small and dull."

"Don't underestimate dullness as a means of survival. In the insect world it's highly prized."

"But what about these?" He pulled open another drawer. "Now, that's what I like."

She leaned past him to look more closely at the huge

butterflies whose blue wings gleamed. "Yeah, you would. *Morpho pelaides*. South American. They are lovely. And do you know, their color doesn't come from pigmentation. It comes from the refraction of light from the scales on their wings. So you see them as shiny and metallic, and the brightest blue in the world, but it's the photoreceptor cells in your eyes, the cones that give them that color. Isn't that interesting? But apart from that they're so obvious. No entomologist with any kind of imagination goes for a species like that. They're too perfect. It's like men who are only capable of being attracted to women like supermodels and page-three girls, who can't appreciate the subtleties of beauty."

"Like yours," he said, as he reached out to push back a lock of her hair.

She pulled away, a fraction, so the tips of his fingers scraped past her skin. "My husband loved them. He gave me a brooch once, made of enamel, just that color."

As a payment. To remind her of a holiday in Mexico that first summer they were married. She hadn't wanted to go. She had wanted to go to Isobel's, to walk through fields wet with summer drizzle, to smell the honeysuckle in the hedgerows. Taste the salt on her lips as a gale-force wind flung sea spray up into the garden so the leaves on the oaks and sycamores curled at the edges, singed like burnt toast. But he had insisted. They travelled by train, she remembered, from Laredo in Texas to Nuevo Laredo across the border.

"Come on," he said, "where's your sense of adventure?" But she sat up, awake at night, while he slept, his head heavy and hard banging against her collarbone. Across from her was a young man, equally awake, whose eyes moved from her face to her breasts as his hand fumbled beneath the bundle on his lap. When they got to Mexico City, she struggled for breath in the thin, polluted air, and cried with helpless despair at the poverty she saw.

"What's wrong?" he had asked, impatience turning to anger. "What is it with you?"

But all she could do was stand still and watch the Indian woman with her daughter, her dark eyes impenetrable, squatting on the footpath, a raffia mat spread in front of her, two pairs of shoelaces and three pieces of chewing gum waiting for a buyer. She had fumbled in her bag for her purse, but he pulled her away, holding her tightly with one hand while the other held on to his latest purchase. A pre-Columbian statuette, a carved stone figure, whose empty eyes and downturned mouth made the skin on the back of her neck tighten and the fair hairs rise on her forearms.

They got drunk that night, she remembered. Both of them. He bought mescal from a street kiosk and they drank it in their hotel room after dinner, the ceiling fan whirring like the blades of an ancient helicopter. She lay on her back, with her arms spread out, and looked up at it. Whoosh, whoosh, whoosh. Her head turned with each revolution. She felt as if she was lifting up towards it, sucked in by the vortex it created. As if it was a whirlpool out at sea and she was in a tiny sailing boat, no match for the power of the water. She teetered on the edge, about to fall over, until David caught her and pulled her close, stripping off her clothes and kneeling over her as he kissed her thin body, the chain-mail crisscross of blue veins showing through her pale skin.

"Kiss me," he shouted, holding her head between his large hands, forcing his tongue into her mouth, until she wrapped her arms around his neck, her legs around his back and turned him over so she was leaning over him, her small breasts just out of reach of his mouth.

"Here," he said, "do this." And he reached over to the pile of clothes that lay on the floor and took hold of his plaited leather belt, quickly slipping it around his neck and pulling it tight. "You hold the end," he instructed, his breath coming in short gasps. "Pull it, as hard as you can." And he pushed himself inside her, until she felt as if she would burst open, like the mango she had seen that morning, smashed on the cobbles in the market, its musky yellow flesh covered by swarming flies.

"Tighter, tighter," he screamed, and she jerked at the belt, until he could no longer speak and watched his eyes as they lost focus, became cloudy, began to roll back into his head, as the gasps from his mouth increased their intensity and she felt him surge inside her. And as his head lolled back and to the side she let go, falling off him, the tears welling silently and trickling down her face, into her ears, her mouth, and darkening the white sheet.

He made no attempt to hide the marks around his neck. She noticed, she remembered, in the days that followed, before they began to fade, how he would finger them from time to time. Wincing, then smiling, as his flesh responded to his touch. They had left Mexico City and got the bus to

Oaxaca, farther to the south. A town filled with Aztec pyramids, places of sacrifice and pain. There had been a bundle of photographs somewhere, she remembered. Pictures of David, looking brown and healthy. He was smiling all the time. Happy and at ease. And she was nowhere to be seen.

The first of many such payments. Pieces of jewelry mostly, sometimes money. She didn't care. She'd go on doing it for as long as it suited her, gave her pleasure.

Like the pleasure she felt now as she and Matthew left the museum and walked through the twilight.

"Come on, here, let's have another drink." He took her arm and steered her towards a door, which swung open onto the street. Inside were faces she knew. People who recognized her as David's widow. She walked past them and sat beside Matthew at the bar. They were watching her, she could see, talking about her, gesturing to Matthew. She leaned closer to him as he ordered more wine, putting her hand on his thigh, resting her head just for a moment on his shoulder. He reached into his bag and brought out a large brown envelope. And put it on the bar in front of her.

"Anna, I thought you should have this. The workmen at the house, your old house in Ballsbridge, found it underneath the floorboards in that room upstairs. It must have been your husband's, I suppose."

She waited until he had filled her glass. Then she felt inside. Letters, a couple of notebooks, and photographs. She pulled out a handful, at random. She recognized Isobel's writing. She laid the pictures on the countertop.

David with a baby, David with a small boy, David with a bigger boy. David and the same boy in a boat, swimming, playing football. At a restaurant somewhere. She turned them over. They were named and dated. David and John, ten years ago, eight years ago, seven, six, five, four, three, two, one year ago. David and John two months ago. The resemblance between them was unmistakable.

She raised her glass and emptied it. She held it out for more.

"Is everything okay?" Matthew took her hand. She drank again, and again he filled her glass. She drank again, and stood up, carefully putting the letters and photographs back into the envelope, hugging it to her as she turned to leave.

She heard his footsteps behind her as she ran down the road. Then he was beside her, wrapping his arms around her. Bundling her into a taxi, cradling her head on his shoulder. She began to sob. Tears spilled down her cheeks, and she turned into him, hiding her face against his chest, feeling his hand touching her breasts, his finger circling her nipple, as she lifted her mouth to his neck, running her tongue into the hollow at the base of his throat, and feeling against her chin the cold metal of a chain that ran down beneath his shirt.

Home was where he said he was taking her. To the apartment block that loomed high above the park where she had gone to watch the comet the night that David had died. Where she had often walked with Billy. The building seemed to sway above her as she got out of the taxi. Cubes of light piled one on top of the other. He took her by the hand and pulled her into the foyer, lined with marble. They waited in silence for the lift. The doors opened silently. She hesitated, fearful, but he drew her in, waiting until the doors closed behind them. Then he kissed her. She stood with her arms outstretched, her hands pressed against the smooth walls, keeping them from closing in against her. She looked up. Their faces swam down at them from the shiny metal ceiling. He reached out his hand and fitted a small key into the panel of buttons. The lift began to rise, faster and faster. He pressed her against the wall, forcing his tongue into her mouth, tearing at the buttons on her blouse, dragging it off her shoulders so her breasts were naked. Over his head Anna watched the numbers of the floors as they passed. She could feel the distance from the ground below. It was getting farther and farther away. She could feel the big black hole opening up beneath her feet. She wanted to scream out with panic, but Matthew stopped her mouth with one hand, while with the other he lifted her skirt. She looked up again at the reflection above and saw their bodies, wrapped around each other. Where did his end and hers begin? She felt him slide inside her as the lift stopped and the doors opened. He staggered out, lifting her off the ground, her clothes falling on the floor, as he carried her into a huge room, windows suspended from floor to ceiling, shimmering in their transparency, like the wings of dragonflies. She screamed out with fear, the darkness dragging her forward, but he laid her gently down, pinning her arms behind her head, fixing her to the ground with his body.

"Don't let me go," she cried, "please don't let me go."

She reached up to him, struggling to kiss his mouth, while above her face danced a small silver key, hanging at the end of the long silver chain. Again and again she screamed, while above her he laughed out loud with pleasure.

IT WAS getting light when she woke. They were lying together on a low bed. Matthew was turned towards her. His head was resting on his arm, his legs drawn up to his flat stomach. His brown hair fell over his eyes, and his mouth was half open. A small thread of beaded saliva trickled down his chin. She reached over and wiped it away with the corner of the sheet. He stirred and sighed. His eyelids flickered for a moment, then closed again. The silver chain and key dribbled over his collarbone and onto the pillow. She raised herself on her elbows and looked around. The room was bare and unadorned. Beside the bed was a wooden chest, and on it a silver box. Rectangular, plain, smooth and cold to her touch. She picked it up. Her face moved, distorted in front of her. She turned it this way and that, watching the way her features grew and shrank in the box's convex surface. She tried the lid. It was locked. She turned back to Matthew and gently picked up the chain that lay against his chest. She looked at the key. She held the box up to it, and pushed it into the small fleur-de-lis-shaped keyhole. She turned it slowly. There was a soft click and the lid of the box began to open. Beside her Matthew sighed, and stirred. Anna turned the key again and locked the box, and placed it carefully back beside the bed.

Her legs felt unsteady beneath her as she walked from the bedroom towards the room she had seen last night. She stopped on the threshold. In front of her lay the southern suburbs and the Dublin mountains. And a long drop to the ground below. She drew back, clutching the door for support, sweat prickling her skin, her knees weakening beneath her. And felt a hand on her stomach, naked skin pushing against hers, and lips and teeth at her neck. She looked down at Matthew's hands as they took hold of her. And remembered the photographs she had seen last night, as she screamed out loud and fell forward on her knees.

And saw as his body curled over hers, the way a leaf curls around a silken chrysalis, the silver key dancing in front of her eyes at the end of the silver chain.

26

Billy needed a shave. Thick stubble covered his chin and jaw. He ran his hand over it, pushing it this way and that, and scratching. He liked to do that. To scratch. It took away the horrible sensation that he often experienced. That he could feel the hairs growing out through the follicles on his face and neck. It always sent shivers down his spine.

He had searched his flat for his electric razor, the one he had bought with some of the first money he made from busking, but for some reason he couldn't put his hand on it. In fact, he realized, someone, probably Sister Miriam or maybe old Winnie from next door, had been into all his things while he was in the hospital. Nothing was where he remembered having left it. It drove him crazy, made him wild with anger and frustration, so he stamped his feet hard on the floor and banged his fists against the wall, until he heard Grace get up from her blanket and come and stand beside him, pushing her head into his knees. Did they not realize what they were doing, those stupid old women, when they came in to "tidy up" for him? He had a system, a plan. It was all laid out in his head. He could see, if that was the right word, how his room looked, and where everything was, and then those stupid old bags fucked it up for him.

He would have to wait until Anna came this afternoon. He would ask her to find everything that was missing. To put the world to rights, as she always did. Then he would ask her to shave him, as a treat, although he could do it himself. He wanted his face to be smooth and soft, like hers, so she wouldn't pull away when he kissed her. He was going to kiss her today, he had made up his mind to do it. He would take her hand and pull her close, and then he would reach up to her face with his other hand, and take hold of her chin and turn her around so he would know exactly where her mouth was. And then he would do it. He would kiss her gently with his lips closed first of all, and then when he could feel how she was responding he would open his mouth, and she would open hers, and they would kiss properly, like lovers. He knew how it would feel. Her hair would brush against his cheek, and he would taste the sweetness of her saliva. Maybe she would sit on his knee. He knew how her long legs would feel pressed down on his, and how her body would cleave to him. He would touch the wool of her sweater, and then underneath he would touch the silky material of her underwear, and then eventually the warmth of her skin. And she would enjoy being touched, he knew she would. She was like him, she used her skin as if it were another sense.

He remembered one day when she had come to see him in Grafton Street. It had begun to rain, suddenly, heavily. She had wanted to help him pack up his bag, but he wouldn't let her. He didn't want her to see what was inside it. She had waited until he was ready, and then she said, "Come on, Billy, let's give ourselves a treat."

She had put her elbow into his hand, the way he liked it, and walked slightly ahead of him, inside.

"Where are we?" he asked, as he stopped, over-whelmed. Perfumes, makeup, extraordinary scents prickled the inside of his nostrils so he wanted to hold his head up in the air the way Grace did, and breathe in and out loudly.

"Come on." She pulled him with her, threading through the noise of women, nearly all women, he could tell, talking, laughing.

"Where are we?" he asked again.

"In Brown Thomas," she replied. "Haven't you ever been here before?"

He'd almost laughed at her. How would someone like him ever go into a shop like that? Where would he ever get the money to buy any of the things that were sold there?

"Careful, mind the steps," she said. He could feel a wide spiral beneath his feet, soft carpet so his shoes made no sound.

"Is it all right to bring Grace in here?" he asked, conscious suddenly of the dog's heavy body and the oil from her coat that clung to his fingers.

"Of course it is, no one minds a guide dog." Anna turned back to him as she spoke. "Now," she said, as they moved away from the staircase, "give me your hand." All those different textures. That was what she called them. Textures. Fur, wool, silk, linen, cotton. He ran his hands along the rails of clothes. "Which do you like best?" she asked him.

"I don't know, I can't choose, they all feel so wonderful." But he wasn't telling her the truth. It was the silk he liked best. The way it slithered off his fingers, like water. He remembered he had lifted a long dress to his face, and held it to his cheek. That was the way Anna would feel today when she came to see him.

It had been so lovely that day on the street. He had laid his bag down behind him, up against the shop window. It was full of little plastic packets. Sometime during the day someone would come and take them away, and leave him an envelope filled with money. He'd take that home with him, and the next day he'd go back out to Steve in the amusements. That was how it worked. It was so simple. There were always so many people around that no one ever noticed what was going on. Anna would have, but whoever it was who made the collection would wait until she had gone. It wasn't a problem. He'd told him, the boss, that they were all to stay away when his friend was there. And the boss had said, "Sure, Billy, of course, no problem."

But the street was changing. There were new people coming all the time. Taking over the regulars' pitches. He knew when he got better and went back that he'd have to push his way in again. The Traveller kids were a real nuisance. Most of them couldn't play or sing to save their lives. They upset his ear with their screeching. He didn't mind that they were Travellers. He wasn't prejudiced or anything. There had been a Traveller in his class in the blind school. His name was Martin. He used to play football all the time in the yard, the hollow sound of the big ball as it banged off his foot and onto the hard surface mixed in Billy's memory with the smell that came from his hair and clothes. Wood smoke and sour milk. And now there were refugees from places like Bosnia. Women who whined for money, homesickness and despair in their alien voices. He pitied them, but they got in the way too much. Anna was fascinated by them. He remembered her voice that day.

"You want to see this, Billy. First of all there are two women. One is very pretty, very young. The other is a bit older, fatter. They're wearing what I suppose is some kind of traditional dress. Long skirts and blouses with shawls over their hair. Pretty, bright colors, lots of reds and pinks. They're walking down the street towards us, and a few paces behind them is a man. Thin, and very handsome. Well dressed, shiny suit. He's lighting a cigarette and the nail on his little finger on his left hand is long, really long, and it's painted blue. Maybe he's their brother, minding them, but he looks like their pimp."

What does a pimp look like? Billy wondered, as he played on and on that day. He'd had a pimp for a while. Someone to look after him, take care of his travel arrangements, collect the money and give him his cut. But then his pimp had realized there was more money to be made in other business ventures. And Billy was just as glad. Especially when he had given him the opportunity to move with him. To make his trips to Dun Laoghaire and back and his deliveries around town.

Would he ever be better? He should lie down and rest, the way the nurses in the hospital had told him to. Until Anna arrived. And with Anna would come healing.

IT WAS the bell he heard first, the little chime that hung outside his door. He thought that it must be the breeze that was moving it, making it ring so sweetly, but he could hear none of the other sounds that usually accompanied wind. Like the faint humming that funnelled down his chimney, something similar to the sound he could make by blowing across the top of a bottle. Or the rustling of the leaves on the tall cherry trees outside his window.

And then he heard voices. Low, hushed, quiet. He pushed the quilt from his legs and swung them over the side of the bed, feeling for his shoes, shoving his feet into them, and reaching down to tie his laces. He listened again, heard a soft laugh, and recognized Anna. He stood up and walked slowly across the room towards the door. Grace shuffled to her feet. He paused, leaning against the wall for support, his legs still weak after his time in the hospital.

"No," she was saying, "you can't come in. He still isn't well. He's not up to meeting strangers. Even at the best of times it's difficult for him."

And then a man's voice. And a sickening feeling in Billy's stomach.

"Well, can I wait, then? Out here. Or down at the bottom of the steps. Where it's sunny. I've got the newspaper. That'll keep me occupied until you've finished."

"No, no, really, I don't know how long I'll be. I said I'd

do some cooking for him. A few things he could put in his freezer. He doesn't look after himself properly at all. And he needs taking care of now, specially. It's all so difficult for him."

Billy's heart thumped against his shirt, and his jaw set.

"Look, I'll tell you what I'll do. There's a good deli up the road. I'll go and buy a whole load of food—pies, a cooked chicken, some salads—and then you won't have to hang around all afternoon. It's a beautiful day, Anna, and I'm going away again tomorrow. I want to spend it with you, just you. Please."

There was silence. Billy waited for her response, but he could hear nothing for a moment or two but the tinkling of the bell. Then, the man's voice, again.

"Okay, whatever you want. I'll see you back here at," pause, "at exactly four thirty. That's two hours. I'll be here."

And her voice, hurried, quiet, knowing Billy realized, that he would be listening.

"Not here. I'll meet you in the square. By the Oscar Wilde statue, at twenty to five. Not here. All right?"

Then silence again. Until her knock, her hand lifting the metal flap of the letter box and dropping it back down, twice. Then a pause. Then once more.

He waited again. Counted to ten. And heard the flap lift and her voice.

"Billy, are you there? It's me."

HE LAY on his bed and listened to the sounds coming from the direction of the kitchen. She was humming as she chopped onions. It was a hymn, one of her favorites. He listened and sang along silently, the words she had taught him.

> *He who would valiant be,*
> *'gainst all disaster,*
> *Let him in constancy*
> *follow the master.*

He shouted out the chorus.

> *There's no discouragement,*
> *Shall make him once relent.*
> *His first avowed intent*
> *To be a pilgrim.*

He heard her laugh, and he smelled the onions as she walked from the kitchen towards the bed. "That's more like it, Billy. That's the first time I've heard you sing since you came home."

The springs creaked as she sat down beside him.

"You smell," he said, taking her hand.

"They're very strong, aren't they, these onions? They're making me cry."

"You don't sound as if you're crying. You sound very happy. Happier than you've been for ages." He held her hand and smoothed the skin down over her knuckles. Then he took it and put it against his cheek.

"You will shave me, won't you, after you've finished in the kitchen?"

. . .

SHE LOOKED for the electric razor, but it was nowhere to be seen. She found blades in the bathroom cupboard. They must have been used because they had been taken out of their paper packets. There was a razor too, old, the metal stained with water. The cupboard door squeaked as she closed it, and saw her reflection smiling back at her. It was the only mirror in the flat, already there when Billy moved in. She looked at herself and tried to imagine how she would feel if she could not see her own face.

She sat in front of him, and draped a towel around his shoulders. Then she lathered the soap in one hand and rubbed it over his cheeks and chin and down his neck. He was very thin. He had lost a lot of weight in the last couple of weeks. She didn't like to look at him too closely. It made her feel like a voyeur or even a thief. Stealing his image away without him knowing she was doing it. But this was different. She had to look at him now as she made the soap thick and creamy, and dipped the razor in a bowl of hot water.

"When I've finished, do you know what I'll do, Billy? I'll wrap your face in a hot towel, the way they do in Japan. It's lovely."

She talked to him as the blade etched dark tracks across the creamy snowfield of his face. About the insect collection.

"I've been working on the Cynthia Longfield specimens. Did I tell you about her?"

He shook his head, making the razor jump.

"Shh, don't move. I might hurt you. Didn't I tell you

about the dragonflies and damselflies she collected? Absolutely beautiful. A world-class entomologist. Do you know she used to go to Cambodia and Vietnam, way back in the thirties, on her own? An extraordinary woman." She leaned forward and placed one hand on his left shoulder. "Lift your head back, now. So I can get at your neck."

There was a small puckered scar just below his Adam's apple. It was bright pink. Where the point of a knife had been pushed against him. Just enough to break the surface. His hands were spread out on his knees. Patches of tight new skin were sprinkled across them, like symmetrical freckles. Cigarette burns, they said in the hospital. The same as the ones on his buttocks and his groin. There were scars inside him too. He was lucky, they said. He didn't have any internal injuries, just superficial tears and lacerations. They'd heal in time. They gave him pills to make him sleep, but he didn't take them for long. They made his dreams even more frightening than his memories when he was awake. The feel of the men's hands on his body, the smell of their sweat. He told the police nothing. But what could he tell them that would make sense to a sighted person? How do you give a physical description if you can't say what color someone's hair is, whether they're dark-skinned or fair-skinned, if you can't describe the shape of their nose or mouth?

"You're lucky," one of the men said to him, just before they left. "You won't have to make a choice about what to tell the cops, will you? You won't have to lie and hope they believe you, will you, Billy boy? But you tell your boss that what we did to you is nothing in comparison to what we'll do to him if we catch him trying to take over our areas again. Do you hear me, Billy? We know he won't like what we did, but it's a warning. You tell him."

He shifted on his chair as he remembered the pain. Her grip slackened for a moment.

"Ah!"

He jerked away. A fine trickle of red turned the soapy lather to pale pink. It gathered momentum and dripped onto his shirt.

"God, I'm sorry." She leaned forward quickly, reaching to press the corner of the towel into the small cut.

"No." He pushed her away. "Don't touch me. Leave me alone."

He made as if to stand, feeling with his own fingertips the wetness of the blood.

"Wait, hold on a moment. Let me help you." She put out her hand again, her fingers meeting his. Until suddenly he nudged her hard with his elbow, so she fell backwards out of his path, and he stood, knocking over the bowl, water cascading across the floor.

"Get out of here," he screamed at her. "Go off and meet whoever you want. Don't burden me with your pity. Just leave me alone."

"Billy." She tried to follow him, but he had slammed shut the bathroom door and locked it behind him. "Billy," she called again, "please, let me in. You need to put something on that cut. Sticking plaster, disinfectant. Something."

But there was no reply, just the sound of running water. She went into the kitchen and picked up the mop. She cleaned the mess on the floor and the table, picking up the razor from where she had dropped it, taking it into the kitchen, washing it clean and putting it out of reach on the top of the cupboard. The stew she had been making was ready, so she turned off the cooker, and covered the saucepan tightly with its lid. There were peeled potatoes and carrots in a bowl ready to be boiled. She checked the contents of the small fridge. There was enough milk, butter and eggs to last him for the next few days. And she had put two small loaves, one brown and one white, into a plastic container in the bread bin. She wiped down all the surfaces and ran her hands under the tap. There was a smudge of brown on the index finger of her right hand. Billy's blood, she thought, as the water washed it clean. She knocked softly on the bathroom door again. But this time no voice answered her. Only the sound of the tin whistle. Played quietly. For comfort.

"I HAVE something for you," Matthew's voice breathed against her ear.

She rolled over on her stomach and pushed herself up. Candlelight wavered and shone in the dark brown of his eyes. She leaned over and kissed him, feeling his teeth with the tip of her tongue. He nuzzled her breast, gently at first, then pulled her over on top of him, his fingers digging into her soft skin. She cried out.

"Look," he said, "under the pillow."

She reached behind him, and felt the cold metal of a bunch of keys.

"Take them out, show me," he said.

She held them up in front of him.

"They're all for you. For this apartment, for everything. I'm going away for a couple of weeks, but I want to know that you will come here while I'm gone, to think of me, to be with me." He pushed himself into her. "Promise me you'll look after everything until I come back. Promise me you'll be here for me."

Did she answer? She didn't remember, and in the morning when she woke the bunch of keys was lying beside the silver box. And he was gone.

27

"So, who is he?"

Anna sighed and stood up. She walked over to the sink and turned on the tap, holding the kettle underneath the water, which spat out at her, intermittently.

"Something's wrong with this," she said. "The pressure's gone all funny."

James pushed back his chair and came over to stand beside her, peering down at the gurgling trickle, which appeared and disappeared, drumming against the stainless steel. "You'll have to get your new landlord to have a look at it, won't you?"

She had found him waiting for her when she came home from the museum. He was sitting on the top step outside the hall door, reading the newspaper.

"You look tired," he said. "Are you sleeping all right?"

She didn't answer. She fiddled in her bag for her keys, feeling the heavy bunch that Matthew had given her. She lifted them for a moment, stroked their indentations with her fingers, then tucked them away in a corner.

"You haven't been in touch for weeks. We were worried about you."

She said nothing. She shifted her weight from one foot

to the other, feeling, as her thighs moved, the ache where Matthew's body had been the night before.

"I've been round a few times looking for you, but you never seem to be here. I've had a number of conversations with the workmen. I must say they're doing a terrific job. Didn't they tell you?"

She shook her head.

"And I drove past last night, it was pretty late. I knocked on the door for a while, but you know, Anna, this isn't the kind of place you'd really want to be seen hanging around."

"No, you wouldn't, would you? Not if you were a man."

"Or a woman for that matter, it cuts both ways, you know. Anyway, look, I'm here now and so are you, so why don't you invite me in for a drink?"

It felt odd seeing James here in these two big rooms above the canal. He walked back and forth looking at the white marble fireplace in the room at the front, lifting his head to inspect the moldings and ceiling rose, and peering through the double doors into her bedroom behind.

"A bit of a comedown from the Anglesea Road house, is that what you're thinking?"

He shrugged and took the glass of wine she offered him, instead of tea. "These are beautiful houses, neglected but still lovely." He stood at the window, examining the long shutters, which were folded back into their embrasures. "They're all intact, which is great. It'll be very nice here in the winter."

She said nothing.

"If you're still here then."

"Why wouldn't I be?"

"Well, a friend of mine happened to see you the other night, in a bar in Leeson Street. He said you were with someone."

"So? I also have friends, you know."

"The way he described it, you were being slightly more than friendly."

"So?" She picked up the bottle and poured herself more wine. James held his glass out towards her.

"Here." She put the bottle on the floor between them. "Help yourself."

He raised his eyebrows as he got up and walked over towards her. "The way my friend was talking about you and your 'friend,' well, to be honest, I would have thought that it was a bit soon for you to be looking for a replacement for my brother."

She stared at him for a moment, saying nothing. Then she stood up and went into the bedroom. When she came back she had the brown envelope in her hands. She took out the photographs and handed them to him. She watched him in silence as he looked through them, his face flushing.

"Where did you get these? Who gave them to you?"

"Oh, so you knew then. And who else knew? How many other of David's 'friends' knew he had a son?"

"No one wanted to hurt you, Anna, please believe me. That was why no one told you."

"Like no one told me about the women he was involved with, the money he owed, the life he lived that I knew nothing about."

"Oh, come on. We've been through this before. You could have known a lot more if you'd wanted. It was pretty bloody obvious what was going on, but you chose to ignore it all, living your peaceful little life, with your stupid fucking insects and your choir. Talk about head in the sand, Anna, I've no sympathy for you." He stood up and leaned with his back to the fireplace. "Now, I asked you before, where did you get them? Because I looked for them and I couldn't find them."

"The way you looked for his diaries too, and couldn't find them?"

"Okay, I admit, I did take them out of his office, but I did it to protect you."

"To protect his memory, you mean, don't you?"

"So what's wrong with that? He was my brother and I loved him. In spite of his faults. He was a wonderful man, and what was the point in spoiling it all for you?"

"Spoiling it? You accuse me of having my head in the sand, yet you talk about it as if it were a child's tea party or something. We're talking here about our relationship, and everything that I thought was true and solid and real."

He said nothing. She moved over to the window. The last of the sun played over the water. Behind the rooftops the sky was the color of a blood orange. She turned back into the room.

"So tell me," she said, "who is the child's mother? You know her, I suppose. Do I?"

"She's nothing, a casual affair. He didn't believe her at first. She made him have a blood test. That's all I know, and no, you didn't know her. We didn't talk about it much.

He kept in touch with the kid, paid some kind of maintenance. There was provision made for him in his will."

Anna walked to the door and opened it. The landing
outside was dark. The building was very quiet now.

"Get out," she said. "I don't want to see you again."

THEY HAD talked about children from time to time.

"There's no rush," David had always said. "I don't
want to share you with anyone else. Not for a while."

Once she had thought she was pregnant. She had
waited as the days passed and she did not begin to bleed.
And then she told him. His face darkened.

"No," he said, "it's not the right time. I told you I
wanted to wait."

"But," she had replied, she remembered, "if it happens
now, it happens. Isn't that good? Just to let nature
decide?"

"What's nature got to do with it?" he had snapped back
at her. "We're human beings, not lower forms of life like
your bloody insects. And what defines us is our ability to
choose, to make conscious decisions based on reason, not
instinct. It isn't the right time for us to have a baby. Do
you understand what I'm saying?"

She had woken the next morning with pain dragging at
the bottom of her spine, blood staining the sheets beneath
her.

"Just do it," Zoë had said to her. "Don't tell him, until
it's too late. That's what I did with Kevin. He wanted us to
wait. He said we didn't have enough money, but I couldn't.
I wanted to have a child so much. I just went ahead."

Growing and growing so her already round body and full breasts became like one of those children's toys that roll around on its base and can never fall over.

"You will be there for me, Anna, won't you? Kevin won't be able to bear it." Zoë had made her promise. She had hung on to Anna's hands as if they were her only salvation. Anna watched, silent with amazement, as Tom's tiny screwed-up face pushed out of his mother's body. So this was what it was all about. This was how humans reproduced. It seemed so familiar, so obvious, yet simultaneously so odd. She thought of all the insect species she had studied, understood, admired. The laying of their eggs, their metamorphosis from larva to pupa to fully formed imago. Each stage predetermined. So unlike the noisy, painful, wonderful scene in front of her as Zoë grunted and struggled, her face puce with effort, until this soft, defenseless boy child, his pulse beating rapidly, visible through the transparent skin stretched across his fontanelle, emerged.

"Hold him, Anna. Isn't he beautiful?" Zoë passed him over the bed to her. Anna stroked his wrinkled skin. If he had been a butterfly or a moth he would have been hidden away now, curled under a leaf until he dried off, his small crumpled wings unfurling, blood pumping into their veins, waiting for them to harden, so he would be ready to fly. A matter of minutes, possibly an hour, was all it would take. But this unformed creature, a collection of possibilities rather than certainties, was so utterly confounding that Anna could say nothing.

And then Zoë discovered, when the baby began to

crawl and fall, his arms and legs blotched and mottled with bruises, that her beautiful, perfect son was a hemophiliac. That the reason he cried so much was because his joints were agonizingly painful from internal bleeding. That they would have no more children because the risk was too great.

"But I don't regret it, not a bit of it." Anna had heard Zoë's defiance too often to be impressed. She had watched the toll that Tom's illness had taken on Zoë and her husband's relationship. How he seemed to have stepped back and away from her, so it was Tom who was now the center of her life.

She could hear it, the plaintive, resentful tone in Zoë's voice as they sat having lunch in the museum café.

"Tom was very upset."

"Why?"

"Because he saw you through the supermarket window and he banged on it and called out to you, but you were with someone, a tall man with dark hair, he said, and you didn't hear him. And then he ran out and tried to follow you across the road, but the lights changed, and fortunately he had the sense to stop. But, oh, he was crying when I found him. You know what he's like, Anna. The tears. Great blobs of water. Pouring down his cheeks, and his nose running all over everything. He was so upset. You know how much he loves you. And he kept on saying over and over again, 'Why didn't she see me, why didn't she hear me? I wanted to tell her about the earwig.' "

"The earwig?"

"Yes, we were shopping and there was a huge pile of

globe artichokes in the vegetable department, and Tom was standing right by them, and you know how small he is, well, I suppose he saw, up close, an earwig coming out between the scales. And don't you remember a few weeks ago, it must have been, that party we had in the garden, what was it you told him about earwigs?"

"THEY'RE SUCH good mothers, Tom. Earwigs, the exception in the insect world. Mrs. Earwig loves her babies, and looks after them really well. When they're still inside their eggs she licks them to keep away the fungus spores that might damage them. And then she stays with the eggs until they hatch, and looks after the nymphs, that's what little ones are called, isn't that pretty?, until they're old enough to take care of themselves. In case anything might come along and eat them. Look at them, aren't they sweet? See, if you put your finger down, they'll just walk up and over you. And they won't hurt you at all."

She had taken him by the hand, searching out the fronds of his mother's tall dahlias, even inspecting the washing hanging limply on the line, looking for the familiar curving tail and shiny brown body.

"They don't really wiggle into your ears, do they?" he had asked. "Because Jimmy at school says they do and he says you should stamp on them when you see them. Like this."

And he ground his sandals down into the grass, swivelling his hips for emphasis.

"No, of course not." She had laughed, pulling him close and kissing his forehead. "Why on earth would a creature who lives outside in the sun and the rain want to go and get stuck inside something as dark and smelly as your ear?"

"But why," he had asked later, when he had had the time to think it over, "why would anything want to eat Mrs. Earwig's babies?"

"Because that's the way of the world, Tom. Bigger insects eat smaller insects and smaller insects eat smaller ones again. That's just the way it is. And sometimes birds will eat eggs and nymphs or else they'll catch them and bring them home to their chicks in the nest, so they will grow big and strong and be able to fly away and make babies of their own. That's just the way it is."

"And will I do that, Anna?" he had asked, screwing up his forehead in concentration. "When I get big will I fly away from my nest and make baby boys just like me?"

"And girls too," she had replied, pulling his fledgling thin body onto her knee. "Don't forget about the girls."

"Ugh, girls," he said, getting up and walking away, kicking an imaginary football and striking out with a stick at the flower-laden branches of a fuchsia, so the ground below turned a livid red and purple. Later he came to her and laid his head across her knee and turned around so both his green eyes were staring up into her face.

"Anna," he said, pushing her book onto the ground, "now that David has gone to heaven can I come and live with you and sleep in your bed and drive your car and go on holidays with you too?"

She didn't laugh. She smoothed the thick brown hair from his pale forehead and slowly shook her head and said, "Not all the time, but for special days, like my birthday and New Year's and maybe Halloween if your mother lets you. Would you like that?"

"But that wasn't what I meant," he said, and he sat astride her knees, holding her face between his two grubby hands. "I want to look after you and be with you so you won't be lonely, so you won't cry anymore. So you'll be happy like me and my mummy and daddy. Because now David is in the ground," and he paused and half whispered, pressing his mouth to her ear, "I know because Mummy told me that's where he is—you need someone to keep you company, don't you? A boy like me."

"SO, ANNA," Zoë put down her knife and fork, "who is he?"

"A friend."

"What kind of a friend?"

"Just someone I've met. He's nice, interesting. Different."

"Be careful, Anna. You've been through a bad time. Just be careful."

BUT SHE didn't want to be careful. She walked, after she left the museum that evening, through the crowded rush-hour streets, to his apartment block. She put his bunch of keys in the pocket of her skirt, and felt them as they moved against her leg. She took them out when she got into the lift, and found the one that fitted into the panel. She pressed the number fifteen, the sweat prickling in her armpits and on her palms, and a sudden sickness curdling her stomach as she moved faster and faster away from the ground.

She stepped out into the huge room. The shiny floor slid away towards the tall windows with the view that stretched over the domed trees in the park and the jumbled rooftops, to the mountains in the distance. And a telescope, she noticed, outside on the balcony. She moved carefully along the curving back wall towards the bedroom, keeping as much distance as she could between herself and the long drop to the car park below. She slid back the paneled door, her hand gliding across its smooth surface. The room was as she had left it, the bed carefully made, the pillows arranged in a casual heap. She walked to the wardrobe and pulled it open. His clothes hung in neat rows. She recognized some of them. The soft suede coat he had worn the day he had taken her to see the house on the canal. The rough linen jacket she had felt briefly against her arms the night they went to dinner. She touched them all, gently, as if they were living creatures, whispering a greeting to them, then leaning in closer, breathing in their smell that had been released by the movement of air from the open door, wanting to get inside the wardrobe with them, wrap them around her, stay there until he came back.

She walked from room to room. Each was furnished in the same unadorned style: polished wood, white walls, brightly colored rugs. At the end of the corridor was a solid metal door, bolted at top and bottom. An emergency exit, she thought, stepping quickly away from it as she remembered the external staircase she had noticed spiralling down the outside of the building. Above her in the ceiling was a trapdoor, leading to the roof space. She backed away from it too, her heart leaping in her chest as she thought of how high up she was. She walked quickly back towards the bedroom, looking through the door into a smaller room, obviously a study or workroom. A desk, a computer, a filing cabinet. And on the wall a series of black-and-white photographs. Children in uniform outside a large red-brick building. She scanned the faces and found Matthew. The same sleek hair cut in a long fringe that fell over his dark eyebrows. And there was one picture, washed-out color, taken with a man and woman. He looked as if he was about twelve. He was wearing long trousers and a V-necked navy blue sweater. He looked angry, sulky. Would they have been foster parents? she wondered. And on the other wall a painting of an old house. Somewhere in the country. Three stories, mansard roof. A flight of stone steps leading to a large stone porch. Beautiful.

She walked back to the bedroom and sat down on the bed. She looked at the silver box. She picked it up and saw her face as she had seen it before. Moving, changing, growing and shrinking. She tried the lid. It was still locked. She had asked him that first night they had spent together what he kept in it. He had smiled at her and pulled her close, kissing the top of her head and whispering in her ear, so his breath tickled her skin.

"Everything that's made me what I am."

She put her hand in the pocket of her skirt and took out his keys again. She spread them out beside her, separating each from the others with the tip of her finger. She picked up the small silver key. She fitted it into the little fleur-de-lis-shaped hole on the silver box. She turned it. She pushed open the lid. And then the phone on the wooden chest rang. Once, twice, three times. The click of the answering machine. And his voice. Saying the usual things. And the tone sounding. And his voice again. Speaking to her this time. Guiltily she snapped shut the lid, and heard him say, "Are you there, Anna? If you are, pick up the phone. Please. I want to speak to you."

She lay back on the bed, cradling the receiver between her cheek and her shoulder, while he told her he missed her, he wanted her, he needed her.

"How did you know I'd be here?" she asked.

"I just did. I wanted you to be in my room, with my things, and you were. And I've a surprise for you. Put your hand under the pillows. On the bed, just beneath your head. What do you feel?"

A small box, leather-covered. Square.

"Open it."

"Oh."

Almond-shaped, silver filigree. An inch long on a chain. She held it towards the light. It wasn't solid. She shook it gently. There was something inside it.

"Open it."

She pressed the tiny clasp and the two halves sprang apart. Inside was a fly, its wings made of silver and mother-of-pearl, its body of agate and jet.

"It's absolutely beautiful," she said.

"Put it on."

She closed the delicate case, and lifted the chain so it slipped over her head. It hung down and rested between her breasts.

"Can you feel it against you?"

She said nothing.

"Anna, please tell me."

"Yes. I can feel it."

"I'll be home next week. Will you be there for me?"

She slipped her hand into her blouse and took the silver locket between her fingers.

"Of course," she said.

28

It was the name Michael Mullen wanted, then. Five years ago. The Makepiece name. He had had his eye on it ever since he first met Adam Matthew Makepiece and his wife, Charlotte. There was something about the way it sounded, classy, but not flash. Respectable, but not dull. Descriptive, but not too explicit. Not like butcher or weaver or carter or smith.

He had asked Adam about it. And Adam had told him about the first Matthew Makepiece, his namesake. He had made his fortune from slaves at the end of the eighteenth century. A dirty business, but someone had to do it. After him came his sons, the descendants who aggrandized his fortune, diversifying into cotton, linen and hemp. Setting up spinning mills in Russia, in Nizhni Novgorod and St. Petersburg, one of the brothers moving to northern France. Then getting into light industry, the manufacture of small arms, and now land mines.

Of course, Adam had told him, the latter had caused huge problems within the family, because half of them were Quakers and didn't approve. So which half did you belong to? Michael wanted to know. The rich half, Adam said, smiling his charming, perfect, aristocratic smile before bending over the mirror, a rolled-up tenner in his hand, and carefully sniffing the snowy ridge of cocaine into his left nostril.

Drugs, the great leveller, Michael thought as he watched Adam and Charlotte, the son and daughter of blue-blooded privilege, lolling in front of his fire, their bodies strong and beautiful from years of the best of everything, and just at this moment, completely at his disposal.

"So tell me more about the Makepiece family. Are there lords and ladies in it?"

"A few sirs, that's all. The slaver Makepiece was knighted. And of course the philanthropist, he was another Matthew. Queen Victoria shook a sword over his head."

"And what did he do?"

"Good works. Asylums for fallen women, charitable institutions for orphans, workingmen's clubs, libraries. There's hardly a town or city in England that doesn't have its Makepiece building somewhere. And he was into missionaries, darkest Africa, Papua New Guinea, the South Sea Islands, convincing the natives to cover their nakedness, the usual sort of thing."

"What was wrong with him? Did he have a guilty conscience or something?"

"Probably, undoubtedly, you know what those Victorians were like. Underneath their beards and stiff upper lips lust quivered, unadulterated."

They had turned up unannounced on Michael's doorstep one fine summer's evening. It was when he was going through his country-gentleman phase, living in the wreck of a once-magnificent Georgian manor house, given to him in lieu of a debt for heroin that its owner couldn't discharge. All the best features, marble fireplaces, plaster moldings, oak floors and paneling, had been stripped and sold, disappearing into the transparent liquid that the house's former incumbent was in the habit of injecting into his collapsing veins. Adam had mentioned a few names, contacts Michael had in London. He said he thought they might be able to do some business. They ended up staying most of that summer, camping out in the huge devastated drawing room and conservatory, sunbathing high up on the roof, the blue and purple of the bogs and hills of Wicklow folding around them, like a beautiful protective blanket.

Their business arrangements had proven fruitful. Adam, for all his languid air and sleepy demeanor, knew his stuff. He seemed to be able to tap into any amount of pharmaceuticals. Acid, speed, all kinds of pills, and the finest, purest cocaine. For a while Michael succumbed to its charm, joining them as they indulged. But soon he began to see just how expendable the handsome Adam really was. Why pay the middleman? Why not go straight to the source? It was the principle upon which he had always operated. Why change the habit of a lifetime? Besides which, Adam Makepiece was beginning to irritate him. He wanted him gone and Matthew Makepiece to remain in his place. But he would need to take his time, not rush into anything.

The summer reached its height and Michael began to plan. He decided he wanted a formal garden and a pool.

There was a stream that ran through the field next to the house.

"Why not divert it," he said to Adam, "make a little waterfall and have it flow into a meandering pond? The kind of place where we could bathe when the weather was warm enough."

"Wonderful," Adam agreed, "like something Capability Brown would have designed in the eighteenth century, don't you think, Lotte my love?"

Did she reply? Michael couldn't remember, but he thought not. She probably just nodded, and rolled over, kicking off her shoes, so he could see her arched instep, and the way she stroked one foot with the other.

"You organize it, Adam, will you?" Michael had said. "There'll be a fee, of course."

"Of course." Adam smiled, his perfect, charming, aristocratic smile. "Of course there will."

And so the excavations began. Michael was surprised at how efficient Adam could be when he set his mind to it. A gang of workmen appeared and a JCB. Adam was energized. Up early every morning, starting work after a cup of coffee and a joint. Dragging Charlotte out of bed to advise him on schemes for planting. Drawing elaborate maps and diagrams with a fine-nibbed pen. Lovely things they were in their own right. Michael still had some of them somewhere. The days passed, and it was time to begin to excavate the hole where the stream would flow and the pool would form.

"Let's have a special lunch to celebrate getting this far," Michael suggested. "After all, all work and no play."

They lay on the terrace, drinking cold white wine. Pouilly-Fumé, Adam had asked for. And that was what Michael had brought. And a couple of small plastic bags.

"I'll only have the tiniest taste," Adam said. "Got work to do this afternoon."

Michael watched him as he sniffed the powder into his nostril, and stood, staggering slightly, then walked slowly back down to the hole in the ground. Michael followed him, judging how best to use the situation to his advantage. He watched the JCB driver in his cab. He was listening to music on his headphones. Scooping out a load of earth, then swinging around and dumping it. Scooping and dumping, scooping and dumping. The earth was damp and sticky. Michael watched Adam. He was standing looking at the growing pile. He was smiling. Michael walked up behind him and called out his name. Adam didn't answer. But, of course, he couldn't hear him above the noise of the digger. Michael watched the way the earth fell. He waited. Then he reached out and pushed Adam so he flopped forward on his face. And turned and walked away quickly. And before Adam could get up again the scoop had tilted, and a pile of clay had fallen on top of him. Michael couldn't see what happened next, he was too far away. But he saw the digger turn and tilt, turn and tilt, turn and tilt, before he got into his car and drove down the driveway, and out onto the road.

He went with Charlotte to identify the body, two days later, after she had raised the alarm. The house and garden were searched and finally the huge tumbled mound of earth. They took his body to the crematorium, and

Michael went back with her to the house. He lay beside the fire and watched her weep, and tried to comfort her, but she pushed him away. He prepared her drugs the way Adam did, heating the heroin, mixing it with water, carefully pushing the needle into the pale blue vein that ran through the inside of the crook of her elbow. He watched her sink back onto the cushions. He'd wait for a couple of days before he'd tell her. About the little girls that Adam liked. The places he visited when he went on buying trips to London and Amsterdam. The videotapes that he'd given Michael to mind for him. Michael had watched them all one night. They'd made him feel sick. Adam had said the kids were drugged, that they didn't feel a thing, that their parents were in on it. It was a business arrangement, that was all. But Michael wasn't convinced. He should tell Charlotte. She had a right to know what kind of man she had loved. It would be Michael's gift to her. His courtship gift. The death and the betrayal. Wrapped together with silk. And it would work, he knew it would. And it would give him the most wonderful experience in the world. Better than heroin, better than cocaine, better than them all. He'd wait, just a couple of days, and then he'd do it.

29

It's a busy life being a junkie, Alan Murray thought, as he walked from Garda headquarters down Harcourt Street, towards Stephen's Green. Already, at half past nine in the morning, he could see all the activity around the city center. Clusters of addicts, shifting, forming and re-forming like flocks of sparrows who catch sight of a handful of bread thrown down on the ground.

He imagined the map of the city spread out before him. He could list off all the areas where the dealers lived and worked, and see the interconnecting lines that the junkies drew between them. Crisscrossing, backwards and forwards, as the day passed and they stumbled from turn-on to turn-on.

He crossed the stream of traffic at the lights and walked through the gates of the Green, past the little cottage where the park keeper lived. Red-tiled roof, small sash windows and hollyhocks in the bed beside the front door. Bizarre, he thought. A little bit of country heaven slap-bang in the middle of the traffic, the dirt, the chaotic cruelty of city life. If he had been a bird, a pigeon, a starling, or one of the seagulls that flew up from the river to feed in the safety of the Green's round pond, and he had hovered over the trees and shrubs all around him, he would have seen the needles, the heroin bubbling in the base of an old soft-drink can or the bowl of a teaspoon, and the exposed veins in the arms, legs, feet, groins of the junkies crouched all around him in hiding. He knew who they were. He could name most of them and their brothers and sisters, their neighbors, their husbands, wives, girlfriends, boyfriends, sometimes even their children, if they had started young enough. And they knew him too. Probably just as intimately. And they all understood the game that was being played. The Guards couldn't stop it. It was fruitless to arrest the users, or most of the small-time dealers. They'd be in and out of prison in a matter of weeks. The only solution was to control the supply, get to the guys at the top. But that was another game altogether.

He stopped to buy Danish pastries at a little bakery on Merrion Row. They were his favorites, filled with apples and walnuts and decorated with a zigzag of icing across the crust. He gave his change to the girl who was sitting outside the door on the footpath. Her skin was gray and there were sores around her mouth and nose.

"Thanks, Mr. Murray," she said.

She'd been a pretty little thing a couple of years ago, when she'd first appeared on the scene. Decent family. Respectable, was the word that the newspapers had used when she had been found beaten half to death on the path by the canal. They'd never charged anyone with the assault. She'd been unable to make an identification. She'd gone home until her injuries healed, but she couldn't stick it. The drug was just too powerful.

. . .

"WHICH DO you like best?" He spread the pastries out on the plate Anna offered.

"You pick first, they all look delicious."

She poured coffee for him.

"Mm, the real thing. What's happened to the tea bags?"

"My boss came back from his holidays. Usually he goes to Mayo, fly-fishing near Bellacorick, but this year his wife dragged him to Provence, and he came back converted to the finer things of life. Like real coffee. He's subverted the department's budget and given us all plunge pots and a supply of beans. Now all you can hear is the dreadful screech of his electric grinder."

There was silence for a moment, then she said, "It's nice to see you, but you didn't come here to discuss the merits of beans versus pre-ground, did you?"

He put down his cup.

"Simon Woods is dead. He had an accident a couple of weeks ago. Apparently he was standing on a stepladder trying to do something with a swarm of bees when he fell and broke his neck."

"Two weeks ago?"

Murray nodded. "I've only just found out. I thought you'd like to know."

"Another accident?"

"That's the way it looks. The postmortem didn't show anything other than the damage to the neck. The inquest will officially determine whether it was accidental or not, but there doesn't seem to be anything to suggest any other explanation. Unfortunately he wasn't found until the next day. Apparently he didn't see many people out there. He was a bit of a loner."

"And nobody living in the area saw anything out of the ordinary?"

Murray shook his head, and poured more coffee. "Not a single, solitary thing."

"Poor guy." Anna put down the remains of her cake. Her fingers were sticky. She held them out in front of her, looking for something to wipe them with.

"Here." Murray dropped his handkerchief in front of her. "It's clean. Just a touch of—what's it called? That black currant drink my daughter's addicted to at the moment."

"Thanks." There was silence for a moment while Anna scrubbed at her hand. Then she looked up. "I meant to ask you, when we went out to see him, Woods, I mean, that day, you asked him if he knew someone. O'Malley or something, wasn't it? I remember he seemed to get quite upset when you said the man's name. What was that all about?"

Murray sat down again. "It wasn't very kind of me, I'm afraid, I felt pretty bad about it afterwards. I knew Woods, of course. Everyone who's had anything to do with drugs knew Simon Woods. He was quite famous once. He was a dealer, mostly cannabis, but he moved into acid in a big way. Then into heroin. Using it as well as selling it. It doesn't always happen like that, despite what the propagandists will tell you. There are probably hundreds of thousands of nice middle-class kids who smoked dope when they were students, and who moved on to California zinfandel when their lifestyles changed. But Woods was different. For a while he was very successful. Then the addiction got to him badly, and everything fell apart. He got sloppy and we got him. He was sent to Mountjoy, eight years, I think. Anyway, he signed on for treatment. Peter O'Malley was the psychologist who ran the group. He encouraged them all, no matter how bad they were. Art therapy was part of it. He got very involved with Simon Woods. Too involved. And Woods was still locked into the drug network inside the prison. Somehow or other he convinced O'Malley to move some stuff in and out. But O'Malley wasn't able for it. He was caught, fired, disgraced, and he killed himself. It was a huge scandal at the time."

"And what happened to Woods?"

"He stuck out the sentence, and when he was released he disappeared. No one had seen sight or sound of him until your husband died last April."

"So why did you really take me to see him?"

Murray shrugged. "I dunno. I thought maybe you might appeal to his better nature. And if there was more to the sending of the bees than he had told us, well, who knows? But it's too late now, anyway."

"And my husband, tell me, how did he fit into all this?"

"How do you mean?"

"Oh, come on, Sergeant Murray, I know I seem stupid, but I'm not that bad. There must be some connection. And you're not coming to see me just for a cup of my super coffee, are you?"

He smiled, and she was struck again by how different his face was when he looked happy.

"We don't know anything, really, but the Criminal Assets Bureau has been trying to find out what your husband had got himself involved in. It doesn't look too good. We know that he did the legal work for a company that owns a lot of property in this area, and a number of launderettes, newsagents, off-licenses. All small businesses with a cash trade. Very hard to keep track of the money in and out. That's all we know for sure. But one thing we do know is that there's a lot of drug money out there, and quite a number of people trying to find ways to legitimize it. Money-laundering, in other words."

"And this is what David was up to?"

"We don't know for sure, but it looks a bit like that. I'm sorry to have to add to your burden."

She was tempted to ask him if he, too, knew about David's son. Even thinking about it made her feel sick with bitterness. Perhaps this new, unknown David had shared his secrets, blurted them out to near-strangers in some pub or other. The David she had known would never have revealed such a private story to someone like Alan Murray. But then, who was the David she knew? Just one version, so it seemed, of the man, and hers had no more nor less validity than anyone else's.

She had read Isobel's version in the letters she wrote to him. There was another version in the large cardboard box that was waiting in the hall when she got back to the house by the canal. It was late. She had been persuaded to go for a drink with her boss and a couple of entomologists visiting from England. Their conversation drifted around her head. Arguments about the usefulness or otherwise of the Internet as a research tool. Her boss had the convert's zeal.

"Just think," he kept on repeating, "what's out there to be found. All you need to know is what questions to ask." She knew the questions, it was the answers that eluded her.

An envelope was stuck to the top of the box. She sat down in the chair by the window and opened it. She recognized James's handwriting.

Anna,
You might as well have these now. Please remember
   that he did love you.
James

IT WAS a busy night by the canal. A constant stream of cars moved up and down. Stopping, starting again. The women's voices floated up to her. They sounded unnaturally loud. Was it alcohol or heroin that gave them that slurred self-confidence? She sat cross-legged in front of the fire, huddling as close as she could to its warmth. She dropped her eyes to the pages of the books that James had piled into the box. Hardbacked, squared paper. David's handwriting, faded blue-black ink, crawling forward from square to square. Each one dated on the front page, with its first entry and its last. His life spelled out in short sharp sentences.

Drinks with Tony, Peter, Andy. Played cricket, got pissed. Went out with Jenny, Susan. Hot weather, exams then holidays. Going to Donegal to stay with cousins. James coming too. Such a bore, he's too young to drag around.

She searched for names she knew. And found Isobel.

Stunning woman, but too old. Fantastic fuck. Do anything. Wants too much. Possessive.

And then later on.

At last, met the niece. Everything Isobel said she was. And more.

And the nature of the seduction spelled out so casually she felt the vomit rise in her throat. And Isobel's part in it. For all those years. His constant infidelity, betrayal. But not just of Anna, of Isobel too. She lost track of the other women he had sex with. Each one was named, described, assessed. And then the reference to the child.

She wanted to call the kid after her husband, but I refused to countenance that. If I am to be screwed for maintenance at least let me have some say in this.

The detailed entries trailed off. Now there were scraps of information. The name Mullen kept on cropping up. No description of who he or she might be. And David's writing changed too. It sprawled haphazardly across the page.

Can't take it much more. Can't cope with this any longer. It's too dangerous. I have to stop. I need help. I can't tell Anna. God knows what she'd think of me if she knew. She'd leave me, and then where would I be? How could I tell her?

She remembered she had so often seen David's diaries on his desk, lying open. Or stacked in a pile in the filing cabinet. And she had never looked at them, never read them. It was a matter of honor. They were private. She wouldn't do such a thing.

She picked the books up at random, now, ripping out any pages that made reference to Isobel or to herself. And saw something that made her heart feel as if it would stop beating with grief.

Isobel told me about her brother and his wife. She is still so angry after all these years. She told me what happened. They went out sailing, her brother was very weak from his illness. He could barely speak, but he had insisted that he wanted to see the islands one more time. The weather was good, light airs, high pressure. When they didn't come back the lifeboat went out to look for them. They found no sign, but ten days later their bodies were found by a fishing boat, half a mile from the Fastnet Rock. The boat was never found. There was a postmortem and an inquest. Apparently both of them had taken a large quantity of sleeping pills and alcohol. No one could understand how it could have been an accident, the weather was too good. But, of course, Isobel says it had to be fine, otherwise the wife wouldn't have been able to handle the boat. And it didn't matter once they were far enough out. Isobel reckons she must have scuppered the boat, and floated free of it. I said to her surely Anna must know there was something odd about it all, but she says no, she was too young to be aware of what happened, and no one would ever have talked about it to her. It was better that way, that she didn't know. Isobel still carries the grudge though. She's like that. She doesn't forget or forgive.

And I cannot remember, Anna thought. Why can't I? There must be something, anything, about that time. The house had been very silent. She had gone to school every day. The teacher had told the other children that they must be kind to her. Then Isobel said that they had found her mother and father. They would be buried in the churchyard by the house. She would have to be very good and do as she was told. Could she remember saying goodbye to them, that day they went sailing? She searched her memory. But there was nothing.

It was cold now, here in this room with the high ceiling and the long windows that rattled in the wind. She was chilled to the bone. She got up and lit the fire, taking logs from a pile on the landing, arranging them in the grate like an Indian's tepee and poured herself a glass of wine. There had been wine and fire that one day that she could remember, all those years ago.

SMOKE RISING in a gray column on a windless afternoon. Rain falling in a soft drizzle. Steam hissing as drops of water danced delicately on the smoldering pyre. A man seated in a wheelchair lifted a bottle of wine to his lips. His hand shook. Golden liquid poured down his chin and onto his shirt. The small girl with the curly fair hair wiped his face with a handkerchief printed with the picture of Snow White and the Seven Dwarfs.

"Can I have some, Daddy?"

He held the bottle towards her. It was heavy in her hands. She lifted it uncertainly. Carefully, precisely, she tilted it at an angle so just enough dripped into her mouth. She swallowed, and put the bottle back down on the ground, resting once again where he could reach it, just beside his chair. She picked up a piece of charred stick and poked the pile of wood. Once it had been the arrow-shaped nose of a boat, sleek and narrow, a racing dinghy, designed to plane across the tops of the waves, responding to the slightest change in the wind, shift in the shape of the water. Once he had sailed her, his long legs braced against her deck as his sleek body hung out, suspended from the wires of the trapeze, parallel to the dark blue sea beneath him. Once he had dragged her single-handed up and down the slipway, righting her when she capsized, bouncing on the centerboard with the wind tearing at his hair, until she sprang upright. Once he had hauled sails and sheets, tested his bones and muscles as severely as he tested her wood and brass.

Now his body was without strength, as damaged as the dinghy. He had found her rotten and holed, half covered by a torn tarpaulin in the boathouse. He had made Isobel bring her out into the open. Then he had poured petrol over her timbers and thrown a lighted torch on top, yelling for Anna to stay back out of the way, flinging one arm up in front of his face to keep the heat of the flames at bay. He reached now for the bottle. His fingers grazed the top. He called to his daughter and she squatted and picked it up, gripping it with both hands, then stood and stumbled, and fell, the bottle spinning away from her, its contents draining into the ground, while she tried to stem the flow with her fingers, and heard a sound she had never heard before. She got up slowly and turned to face him, and saw the backs of his hands as he covered his eyes, and the tears oozing through his fingers as his shoulders shook until she felt that his thin body would crack and splinter into charred pieces like the burning wood. And she would never be able to put him back together again.

. . .

THE FIRE settled and subsided, the embers glowing in the bed of the grate. Anna stood up and walked out onto the landing. She switched on the light, and leaned down to fill her arms with more logs. It was bright out here now, newly painted an acid yellow.

"Who picked the color?" she had asked.

"The boss," was the reply.

"Oh." She had paused, and put down her shopping. "Have you seen him recently?"

"Yeah, of course, he was here this morning. Checking up on us, giving out because he thinks we're being too slow."

"Oh, I see. I thought he was away."

The man standing in front of her, his overalls encrusted with dried paint, shrugged, taking a cigarette from behind his ear and lighting it.

"He comes and goes, you can never tell when. He brought all the paint for the rooms downstairs. Authentic colors, he says they are. Just like the old distempers they used last century. He got them specially mixed."

But there had been no sign of him when she went to the apartment a couple of days ago to lie on his bed and rest her head on his pillow. To turn the key in the lock on the silver box, and begin to open it, then to remember. It was none of her business, whatever it contained. She had no right to pry. But he had given her all his keys, hadn't he? That was because he trusted that she would respect his privacy. The way she had respected David's. And look where that had gotten her. What was it Matthew had said when she had asked him what he kept in the box? My most precious belongings, everything that's made me what I am.

She remembered the words as she twisted between her fingers the silver cocoon he had given her, and tried to summon up his face. And to think that he had been here this morning. And left her no sign. Her legs were leaden as she walked slowly up the stairs, and into her room.

She had tried to eat that night, but her stomach felt as if it had closed over and the thought of food made her sick. She drank some wine, and lay down in front of the fire. She slept.

And woke. The sound of banging on the front door, the thump of the knocker, lifting, dropping again and again.

Matthew, it must be Matthew. She was halfway down the stairs before she remembered that he had a key. Perhaps he doesn't want to frighten me by walking in, she thought, opening the heavy door, the wind catching her hair and pulling it from its clasp. But it was a woman on the doorstep. Small and very thin. Dark curls frizzed. Heavy makeup on her cheeks, black lines around her eyes, thick crimson lipstick. The hands that clutched the coat around her neck were wrinkled, the veins standing out like thick rubber bands. But a soft sweet voice, and a smile that wiped away all fear.

"Can I come in?" she said. "I knew your husband."

30

Anna was a nectar-feeder, Michael thought. That's what she was. A butterfly, lowering her beautiful body deep into the sweet heart of a flower. And like a butterfly she had her usual habitat, her familiar feeding grounds. The banks of the Dodder, swathed in cow parsley and elder, the well-tended lawns and shaded pergola of Herbert Park, the herbaceous borders of Merrion Square, the crowded city-center streets through which she wandered.

Michael had known this from the time that he first began to watch her, before he killed her husband. He was even more conscious of it now. The simplicity of her life amazed him. It was so ordered, so predictable. He had always thought that he would be driven crazy by the limits of that kind of life. But she imbued it all with such grace, made its miniature nature so attractive.

He loved that he could think of her at any time of the day and know where she was and what she was doing. He could see her in his mind's eye, bent over her desk, her long slender fingers carefully coaxing the pinned specimens from one position to another. He could see the way she sat with her legs wrapped around each other, her shoes pushed from her feet, her long straight toes pressing down on the polished floor beneath her. He could hear her breathing as she concentrated on her task. And the little sigh that escaped from her mouth as she finished and put down her tweezers and picked up her fine-nibbed pen. He knew that as she leaned forward over her desk, his silver locket moved with her, hanging away from her skin as she bent over, then settling back into the small gap between her breasts as she straightened up. He wanted to be there too, to stand behind her as she worked and rest his body against hers, his mouth on the exposed vertebrae at the nape of her neck, his stomach in the hollow of her spine, his hands reaching round to cup her bosom, his thighs pushing hers down onto her stool. The thought made him gasp, jerked him away from the task in hand.

He knew from minute to minute what stage of her day she had reached. It wasn't just that her life was predictable. His mother's life had been that. Out on the street at six every evening during the winter. At eight from April till the end of August. The key in the door every half hour until he stopped listening and fell asleep. Their dinner together at four every afternoon, when he came home from school. And on Sundays at twelve thirty after Mass. And on Sunday night she would go out with her mates, the other "girls" who worked the same squalid territory, coming home roaring drunk after the pub shut at eleven thirty. Now that was predictable. And predictable that she would die from neglect when he was twelve. It was cancer of the cervix that killed her eventually. But she didn't have a chance, really. She never looked after herself or took care in any way.

Anna's life, however, was a harmonious discipline. She was a creature of nature. She knew a world that he could never imagine. She could name the stars in the sky, the fish in the sea, the hundreds of plants that grew in every garden and beside every road. He tried to understand what her train of thought might be as she walked from home to the museum every morning. But as much as her daily wanderings were known to him, her conversations remained mysterious and surprising.

And he liked that. And that she had no idea what he was doing or how he conducted his life. She thought she did. He had told her three weeks ago that he was going away on business. She didn't ask him for any details, an itinerary, a schedule. If she had, he would have said that he was doing deals in London, and in Amsterdam, that he might have to go to Hamburg, possibly even to the countries of the old Eastern bloc, Poland, Hungary, Czechoslovakia. If she had pressed him further, he would have said that he was expanding his business interests, making the most of the tiger economy. There was money to be made all over the world if you had capital. And he had capital.

But she didn't ask. She just said that she would miss him, and would he keep in touch, let her know when he was coming home. And she had been so excited when he had phoned her at the apartment, and so surprised that he had been lucky enough to find her there. He could have told her. Luck didn't come into it. He was in his car, which was parked across the road, and he had seen her go in, waited for ten minutes until he was sure she was upstairs and then made the call. It was that simple.

It would never have occurred to her that there was another world, a mere twenty minutes or so away from the leafy streets where she lived. It was his other world. The back room in the narrow redbrick house at the far end of the South Circular, where he had nursed his granny through her last illness, and where she had died. That was his real home. The room with the sagging sofa and the old radio still with the knobbly brown material stretched across the speakers. And his mother's tin box in the bottom of the wardrobe. He'd brought it with him after she died, when he'd left London and come to live with his granny permanently. It still contained the last few pounds she had earned. Rolled together with an elastic band around them. And a few odd coins. Reminding him of what was important in life.

Like looking after all the people who lived on the corporation estates that spread out, identical row on row, transforming the greens, browns, yellows of what had once been farmland into a dirty jumbled mass of brick and concrete, the air a sludge of polluted gray. This was where the people of his other world lived. Like Gabriel, for instance, his right-hand man, who made his pickups from all around the city. Thousands of pounds, bundled haphazardly together, carried in plastic shopping bags. Gabriel would do anything for him, for a cut or a consideration. Including getting rid of potential problems, like the bee-man Simon Woods. Michael should have realized that you can never trust an old hippie, no matter how far they seem to have moved. There's always room for a fit of guilty conscience. A crazy desire to do the right thing. But

Gabriel, for instance, didn't suffer from the same weakness. He knew just how to handle Woods. After all, he was asking for it, dressed up in that ridiculous suit. He was bound to trip and fall. A hangman's fracture, it was. If only someone had come sooner, Woods might have been saved. But he had chosen to live on his own, away from other people. It was a risk, and he had paid the ultimate price for it.

Michael thought about Anna and her insects as Gabriel drove him away from the city down the motorway towards the western suburbs. She had told him one day when they were in the museum how, as the insects grow, they have to shed their hard outer skeleton. They rest as the old skin melts away, then they drag themselves out of it, while the new skin underneath gradually hardens in its place. She told him that the period between molts is called an instar, and some insects do it as many as fifty times during their lives. How many times had he done it, he wondered, as he caught sight of his face in the wing mirror on Gabriel's car? Making the transformation from Matthew Makepiece to Michael Mullen. Or was he like the butterfly or moth who disappears into the pupa and emerges completely transformed, no physical similarity between it and the caterpillar it once had been?

He reached over and touched Gabriel on the arm, pointing to the traffic circle in front of them. They took the first exit to the left and turned off into a road, which quickly became narrow and rutted, as it wound up towards the hills. Michael nudged Gabriel again, and they turned once more into a narrow laneway, cluttered with abandoned cars, rusted heaps of metal. At the far end a man was leaning against a dark blue van. Gabriel slowed and stopped, and Michael got out and walked towards him. Andy Horgan had aged in the five years since they'd first met on the ferry, the night that Michael had got caught up in the fight with the Travellers. His belly hung out now over his belt, and folds of flesh pushed against his collar. But Michael could still remember the way he looked in those photographs, his body curving over the back of the woman, the wild, excited gleam of his eyes, and his open-mouthed grin.

Michael put his hand in his pocket and took out the envelope. Same amount, every fortnight. Handed over in different places around the city. And for that he got the gift of knowledge. How and what, where and why. Everything you've ever wanted to know about the movements of the Drug Squad but were too scared or too stupid to ask. He smiled. Horgan looked at him suspiciously.

"You're looking pretty pleased with yourself." His voice was petulant.

"And why wouldn't I be? Sure isn't it a lovely autumn day, with the sun shinin', and sure aren't we all grand and healthy?" And he laughed out loud as he heard his gran's Galway tones echoing back to him.

"Jesus fuckin' Christ." Horgan jammed the envelope into the pocket of his anorak and drew hard on his cigarette. "Let's get on with it. I don't have much time. Everything's getting a lot more difficult these days. There are new guys working in there now and I can tell you, I don't know how much longer I'm going to be able to carry on with this."

"That's fine, Andy. Any time you want to stop, that's fine with me." Michael looked closely at him. "But tell me, first of all, how's the missus?"

Maybe Horgan was right, he thought later. The cops were gearing up, taking the whole drug business a lot more seriously now. It was becoming a political issue, he could see that. The middle classes were scared it would move from the confines of the estates into their nice, safe areas, bringing with it the contamination of AIDS. The anti-drug groups were getting braver, stronger, more desperate. But not in his domain, not yet. He watched, as Gabriel drove him into the winding maze of streets and houses, the way heads turned towards them as they passed. No one yet had the energy to stand up to him. They wanted what he was selling too much. Now he was mopping up business from the other parts of the city, where the cops had moved in and the dealers had all moved out. Addicts followed the supply, like seagulls the fishing boats.

The car slowed down as they approached the end of their journey. A small crowd had gathered around the gate of Gabriel's house. He looked to see who was waiting to see him. He knew them all. Their strengths and weaknesses. The ones who were reliable, whose habit made them straight, and those who were crooked, whose habit made them devious. He had noted all their little foibles. Like Anna with her collection. There were parts of it that she knew by heart. She knew their characteristics, their habits, the way they mated, reproduced, grew and died. He could say the same thing about these people who lived out here, only a matter of miles from where she lived, but a world of difference between them.

But they all shared one thing. A weakness, he would call it. She wanted to be loved and appreciated as much as they all did. He saw it in her face, the way she smiled at him. Two nights ago, he had opened the door from the street just after eleven. Walked quickly up the stairs. Paused on the landing, saw the pile of logs heaped neatly in the corner. Listened and heard the sound of a woman's voice singing. Used his key to open the door. A fire burned dully in the grate. He turned towards the bedroom. A soft light shone from the lamp by the bed and a glow from the half-open door to the bathroom fell across the floor. He tiptoed towards it. The room was filled with steam. Candles flickered at each end of the bath. She was lying with her back towards him. She lifted up one long narrow foot and turned the tap with her toes. Water gushed out. She sat up and reached forward to turn it off. Her back was very white and the bones of her spine stood out clearly. She lay back again, lifted both her hands and freed her hair from the knot on the top of her head. It tumbled into the water. She slid down so her whole body and her face were submerged. He tiptoed forward and crouched beside her. He picked up the bottle of shampoo that stood on the shelf above the bath, and tipped some into the palm of his hand, and as she raised herself, opening her eyes, and turned her face towards him, he reached over and began to lather her hair. She opened her mouth and smiled, and he kissed her, lifting his other hand to gather up all the stray locks, and draw them too into the soapy bubbles. As her mouth drew him into her, and her hands caught the back of his head and pulled him closer and closer.

When he had rinsed her hair, wrapped her tightly in a bath towel, piled more wood on the fire, he told her stories of his travels. The places he had visited, the people he had met, the money he was going to make. And she told him about the woman called Charlotte who had come to see her. Who said she was the mother of David's son. She was angry. He had never seen her like that before.

"Why weren't you here?" she said. "I needed you, I wanted you. You shouldn't have left me for so long."

"And I promise I never will again," he said. "I want you to come and live with me now. I want you to be there all the time. So I can look after you, like this," he said, as he picked up a brush and began to pull it gently through her hair. Then laid her down on the rug and kissed her, lifting the towel away so he could see her pale skin. And the glint of his special silver locket in the hollow at the base of her neck.

"Why do I feel like this about you?" she asked him, later, and she sat up and looked down at him, running her fingers over his chest. He smiled up at her and thought of the others. Tessa, Máire and Charlotte. They had never known what he had done. Perhaps now was the time to move on to the next test. What would she do if he told her? Would she still love him as she said she did now?

He pulled her down beside him and kissed her eyes shut.

"You are my nectar-feeder," he whispered. "You draw the sweetness out of me. Sleep now. And sleep well."

31

Nothing would ever be the same for Billy after he'd been in the hospital. He wished they'd never told him, that he'd never found out. He didn't want to know. He supposed they must have asked his permission to do all the tests. He didn't remember. He had been in so much pain, and everything had been so confusing, that he couldn't be sure what anyone had said. Until the day when he heard the doctor's squeaky shoes coming closer and closer on the linoleum floor and the rattle of the curtains on the rail, as they were pulled around the bed, and the muffling of all the banging and clattering in the ward, the radio on the locker next to him, the nurses' shouted instructions and laughter.

He would have to be very careful from now on, they told him. Come to the clinic regularly, make sure he took all the drugs. And, above all, protect others from contact with his blood. He thought of it now, the stickiness on his fingers and his neck the day that Anna had cut him while she was shaving him. He hadn't seen her since. She had come to visit, he knew. Old Winnie next door had spoken to her, and said he wasn't at home. Winnie knew what had happened. She was good to him, these days. She did his shopping when he couldn't face going out, and she helped him count all the pills, noting the times he had to take them, which ones needed to be swallowed before food, which ones after. And she put him to bed when he was tired, and lay beside him, holding his hand and crooning an old lullaby she knew from the old days.

She helped him in other ways too. Went out to the amusements in Dun Laoghaire and picked up his parcels, brought them back to the flat, then took them to the little cemetery in Donnybrook, placing them underneath the old dried-up wreaths and pushed in between broken slabs of headstones. It had been a bit of a brainwave to use Winnie for this. It was the guy who had come to see him who had suggested it. The guy who the boss had sent. Winnie didn't mind. She liked the few extra quid and she liked having something to do. She wasn't worried that the Garda station was next door to the graveyard. "Sure they'd never be bothered with an old woman like me," she said to him. And she was right. And it was so easy for the stuff to be collected from there. The boss's friend told him about the old convent right behind the low gray wall, formal gardens with clipped yew walks and a row of cypress trees along the boundary. There were no nuns left there now, he said. No more nosy old bags, fiddling with their rosary beads as they watched everything and anything that moved. It was the simplest thing to hop over the wall, he said to him, and find the plastic bags. Nothing to it.

But now Billy wanted to see Anna again. He was feeling a bit better, a bit more like his old self. He knew she would understand, and she'd get used to it. She wouldn't hold it against him. He still loved her and he was sure that she cared about him. She'd want to help him, she was that sort of person. He was going to tell her, when it was the right moment.

It was windy today. A blowy southwesterly. He hadn't realized when he was inside. But he knew when he felt it against his cheeks and the way it lifted the hair from his forehead. Winds from that direction were generally warmer and wetter than the northerlies and easterlies. He had the compass directions all worked out. He would stand in the open space outside the flats and spin around on his heels, finding the wind. South and west were in the direction of the city center and the park. North and east were towards the river and the harbor where the big boats tied up, the ones that had the loudest hooters. The easterlies stirred the little bell outside his door. The westerlies caused the smoke in the chimney to billow back down into his room, making his eyes water and catching in his throat, so he would have to stand on a chair and open one of the windows, just a crack at the top, to create the right kind of draft. Old Winnie had told him what to do. She knew all about drafts and fires. She had been a maid in a big house in County Kildare when she was a girl, lugging coal scuttles up four flights of stairs while young ladies the same age as she lay in their beds till all hours. She was outside watering the last of her petunias as he came out and locked the door behind him. He could smell the lavender perfume escaping from the neckband and sleeves of her crocheted cardigan, mixed with the tang of the peat moss in which she grew her plants.

"Bye-bye, Billy," she said. "Will you be home later?"

He didn't answer. He turned away, reaching down to

take hold of Grace's harness, feeling the comforting sensation of the metal and leather in his hand. He hitched his bag over his shoulder and pulled the door again by the handle just to make sure that it was completely closed. "Forward," he said to the dog, and together they walked slowly away.

He waited for Anna at the museum gate. It was lunchtime and he knew she'd be out soon.

"Grace, my sweetheart," he heard Anna's voice, her pleasure at seeing them making it lift and rise. "And Billy, what a surprise. I've called to see you so often recently but you were never there."

He didn't reply. She put her hand on his arm and he felt her close by him.

"Where are you going now? Are you going into town busking? Are you looking for company?"

"Would you like to come for a trip with me? Would you like to come out to Dun Laoghaire?" His voice sounded stiff and creaky, as if he hadn't used it for days. As if he were speaking a foreign language, and had to think before he pronounced each word.

"Well," she paused, "why not? I'm taking the rest of the day off, I've been working weekends for the past few weeks, so I reckon they owe me a bit of time to myself." She paused again. He waited. He knew her pauses. "And, anyway, I'm glad I met you. I've got something I want to talk to you about."

HE SHOULDN'T have brought her out there with him. Not really. But he wanted her to know that there were people other than her who liked him. The girls in the café, the man on the carousel, the bouncers by the slot machines. He could tell she was surprised. And a bit impressed, he thought. By the tone in her voice.

"They know you. Everyone seems to know you here."

They sat in the café. The girls brought him his usual. A large Coke in a waxed paper container, and a plate of chips. Put them in front of him, with a straw already sticking out through the slot in the lid, and a wad of paper napkins so he could wipe the grease from his hands and face when he had finished. He sat close to her, and from time to time put his arm around her shoulders. He remembered what old Winnie had said, how pretty she was, and the note of envy in her voice. He was proud that she'd come out with him. They'd all be looking at him, wondering who she was. She was chatting away, feeding chips to Grace, and then he felt a hand on his shoulder, fingers that brushed against his ear, his cheek, that smelled of cigarettes and paper money. And heard the scrape of a chair being pulled out on the other side of the table. And Steve's voice saying, "Who's your friend, Billy? Are you going to introduce us, or what?"

Before he could say anything he heard her speak, say her name, then the rustle of her sleeve as she held out her hand. He listened. To the dull thud of the music, the screech of the machinery that carried the rides, the shouts of children and the roars of their adult companions. To her voice. Chatting away to Steve, about the tourist trade, the weather, telling him about other amusement arcades she had been to, how she could never go on the big roller coasters because she was so scared of heights. He listened to Steve's voice as he replied. His tone was friendly, interested, lighthearted. Steve liked her, Billy could tell.

"But do you know," she was saying, "do you know what I really love? The bumper cars. What do you say, Billy? Will your friends mind Grace for a few minutes while we go and have a ride?"

He hadn't realized it would be so much fun. She took the wheel for the first few turns, spinning them around and around, their bodies moving together in the same direction. Then the bang and the bump as they crashed into another car. At first it made him breathless. Then he began to laugh too, while all around them loud music blared out, punctuated by the crackle from the electricity powering the cars, and the screams and shouts from the other people.

"Come on, it's your turn now." She made him change places, putting both his hands on the wheel, and her hands over them, so at first they turned the wheel together, until she said, "It's all yours," and let him do it by himself, while she laughed and he laughed, and all those wonderful sensations ran through his body. The bangs and crashes from the other cars, the electrical crackles and splutters and the screams coming from every direction around them.

It was afterwards when they were on the train back to town, and his heart had slowed to its usual pace and the smile had begun to die back from his face, that she told him. That she was thinking she might move again.

"That's good," he said. "It's not nice there by the canal. It's not a good place to live." Maybe, he thought, maybe now was the time to tell her. He put out his hand and touched her arm.

"Yes." She laid her hand on top of his. "You always did say that, didn't you? And you were right, really. I can see that now."

He had rehearsed so often what he would say. He had repeated the words and phrases over and over in his head. But now he was struck dumb. His mouth was dry, his throat tight. He forced open his mouth to speak.

"You see, Billy, it's this man I've gotten to know recently. I really like him, and he likes me. And he wants me to go and live with him, and I'm thinking that I might. It'd be a new start for me, Billy. What do you think?" She squeezed his hand. "I feel different these days, Billy, like a different person. And it's good for me."

What was she saying? Who was she talking about?

"I'm happy now, Billy. Can you hear it in my voice?"

He listened to the sound of the train. The track whistled beneath the wheels. He knew where they were. Between Blackrock and Booterstown where there were no longer any high stone walls hemming them in. It was always much quieter here, out in the open. Except for the wind that rushed in from the sea and shook the carriage.

"Did you hear what I said, Billy?" She squeezed his hand again. "It won't make any difference to us, you know. We'll still always be friends, won't we? And I'll still always come and see you, and go to the park with you and Grace. Some things will never change, no matter what."

He could hear the train slowing as it approached the next station.

"You can't do it, Anna, you mustn't. You don't know what's going on. This man you're talking about, what do you really know about him? What do you really know?" He was shouting now, grabbing hold of her face and pulling it close to his, so he could smell her skin and feel her breath on his mouth.

She jerked away from him. "Don't touch me like that, don't."

"Anna, listen to me, I know who he is, and he's no good for you. Stay away from him. I mean it." He stood up, jerking Grace to her feet.

"What is it?" She half rose to her feet. "Where are you going? This isn't your stop."

He didn't answer. He pushed past her, and stood by the door, holding on to Grace with one hand, until they slowed to a stop. He reached for the button, feeling the smooth plastic beneath his fingers. He pushed it. The door slid back. He stepped out and walked away. He heard her calling his name, but he kept on going. It was too late now. Far too late for anything that she could do.

32

It was a wonderful invention, the video camera, Murray thought. Even if the downside was sitting for hours in a stuffy little room that stank of other people's aftershave, trawling through the tapes it spewed out. The upside was that sooner or later, if he was lucky and the god of CCTV was feeling benign, he'd find something. The name, the face, the car, the situation that would bring the whole fuzzy picture into sharp focus.

But when? He'd been at this off and on for days now, first thing in the morning before he began work, at lunchtimes and sometimes staying late for an hour or so in the evening. And so far he'd been proved wrong. He'd found nothing.

He pressed the *eject* button on the machine, took out the cassette and flung it carelessly on the pile on the floor. He picked up another one and slotted it in. He pressed *play*. He sat back and watched.

Cars, cars, and more cars. Streaming beneath the bridges over the wide new road that bypassed Bray on its way south. The cameras weren't immediately noticeable. They were placed at each side so they picked up the cars as they travelled in both directions. No attempt was made to conceal them. But there didn't need to be. At the speeds at which most people drove they wouldn't have the time to look away from the road and up at the brackets attached to overhead beams, and the small rectangular objects whose lenses flashed from time to time in the sun.

Murray spooled through the tape. The date and time flicked past in the top right-hand corner. It was the day that Woods had died. There were a number of possible routes to his house. Whoever had killed him could have gone the mountain way, taking the back roads. But that might be more risky, Murray reasoned. Fewer cars travelling more slowly. He was more likely to be spotted and remembered. Whereas this way, just one of a steady stream of traffic heading out of the city, paradoxically made him more anonymous.

It had taken Murray a while to convince his boss that Woods hadn't died accidentally.

"Look at it my way," he said to Jim Farrell, his inspector. "There's just too much coincidence involved. And I don't trust coincidence. I want to go back and have another look at his place at the very least. We all know Woods had been a dealer for years and years. He dropped out of sight after he came out of prison, and he obviously wasn't into heroin or cocaine any longer. If he was we'd have heard something, I'm sure. But drugs and everything and everyone that goes with them were his way of life. Just because he started beekeeping doesn't mean he gave up the rest of it."

Farrell wasn't impressed with his argument. Murray persisted.

"Look, just let me go back with a warrant and search the house and shed. If there's nothing there I'll forget it."

There was nothing there, because someone had beaten them to it. The front door was shut but unlocked. Floorboards had been lifted and carelessly nailed down again. Wood panels had been pulled from the wall of the bedroom upstairs. A small safe in the back of a cupboard stood open. And the hives had been upturned, the wooden combs smashed, wax and honey a sticky mess on the meadow grass.

Farrell still wasn't convinced.

"It doesn't prove anything, Alan. I accept it looks suspicious, but it could be purely opportunistic. Some old mate of Woods, who heard about his death and reckoned there'd be some goodies lying around. That's all. Really. Give it a rest now."

But Murray wouldn't. He had faith in the all-seeing eye of the camera, even though his head ached and his vision blurred as his eyes followed the constant movement of the cars.

He sighed and peeled the foil lid off a pot of yogurt. He dipped his plastic spoon into it and took a mouthful. It was peach. Emily's favorite. And what do we have here? Murray leaned forward, his spoon hovering in midair. He pressed *stop*, then *rewind*, then *pause*. The cars were approaching the bridge. There was one in the central lane that caught his attention. It was some kind of a Ford, a Mondeo perhaps. Nothing unusual there. But it was the driver he noticed. Murray knew his face and his name. Gabriel Reilly, he was sure of it. Dark hair going gray, stocky build.

About five foot ten, eleven. He'd been a regular in the District Court for years. Petty theft, larceny, assault. Then he'd begun to show up on drug offenses. Possession mostly. They'd never been able to get him for dealing. And they hadn't seen much of him for a while now. Murray spooled the tape on and paused it so he could write down the license number on the car: 91 D 362,782. He took the tape from the machine and put it in his pocket, then scraped the last morsels from the sides of the plastic pot. The sweetness clung to his tongue and the roof of his mouth. He could see why Emily cooed every time she saw the peach-colored containers in the fridge. He felt like cooing too. Although, he had to admit, it wasn't just because of the yogurt.

ANNA WOULDN'T have much to take with her to Matthew's. If she decided to go there. Just her clothes, a few pieces of old jewelry that had belonged to her mother, her books and a couple of boxes of odds and ends of letters, papers, photographs. She had dumped the presents, payments, that David had given her while they were married in the rubbish bin, wrapped in newspaper. They were bad luck, those brooches, earrings, gold chains. No one should ever wear them again.

But she kept on hearing Billy's words. Why had he said those things? What could he know? She tried to remember if she had ever met Billy when she was with Matthew. There was that time when Matthew had come with her and waited outside. They had talked, she remembered, standing on the walkway. Had Billy overheard their conversation?

She had gone yesterday to his flat to see him, but there were no lights on, no sounds from inside when she lifted the letterbox and peered inside. He's not well, she thought. Since he was attacked he hasn't been the same. He's too nervous for his own good. But she couldn't stop seeing the look on his face, and feeling the way his fingers had gripped her chin. He needed help, a doctor or social worker.

Matthew had come to meet her after work again.

"It's getting to be a habit, a routine, isn't it?" she said to him, as he stepped forward into the light from the glass doors. He just kissed her and pulled her close to him, sliding his hand under her shawl to rest against her breast.

"Should I carry you over the threshold?" he said to her, as the lift slowed and stopped and the doors to the apartment slid open. She didn't answer. The ground fell away beneath her feet. She was suspended in midair. She reached out and grasped the doorjamb, feeling the slots into which the metal panels fitted.

"You'll have to get over it, your fear of heights, my precious one, if you're going to live here. Won't you?" He took her by the hand and pulled her out. "You shouldn't let it dominate your actions in this way. You have to face it, confront it, and then you'll defeat it."

She smiled. "You sound like something from one of those Victorian allegorical children's stories. Cowardice, the thief of manhood, is vanquished by Bravery, the prince of hope."

"Or how about a bit of common sense and faith in technology? The lift is not going to plunge fifteen floors to the ground, the bottom is not going to fall out of it, the lift shaft is not going to crumble. And nothing bad is going to happen to you here. You are perfectly safe with me, my love."

David had said that too. She had believed him. Foolishly. She thought of her conversation with the woman called Charlotte who had come to see her two nights ago.

"Why did you come?" Anna asked her.

"Because the girls out there," the woman gestured to the dark outside the windows, "told me about this woman they had met who was kind to them and friendly. And I saw you one night when I was out there too. You were sitting in the window reading, and I remembered that once David had brought me to the house. He thought you weren't there. We had gone in through the garden, but you were in the kitchen. We could see you clearly through the glass. And I recognized you again. And I thought you had a right to know."

How her husband had known David years ago in England, had gone to school with him. How he had helped them with their business when they first came to Ireland. How her husband had died. It was an accident. He had been making a garden for a friend with a beautiful old house in Wicklow. He had fallen, banged his head, and a load of earth had been dumped on him. It was a terrible time but David had been kind to her. He had helped her to get through it all. And then she had gotten pregnant, and he wanted her to have an abortion.

"I wouldn't," she said. "I wouldn't do it. I couldn't. It didn't seem right."

"And where is the child now?" Anna asked.

"He's in England with my mother. I can't look after him."

"But why are you like this? Surely you don't need to be. You're . . ."

"I'm not like the others, is that what you mean? I came from a good, loving family, I went to university. I could do something else with my life."

Anna shrugged. "I suppose what I mean is you have choices."

"Do I? I don't think you understand. I fell in love, that was my undoing."

"With David?"

"No." Charlotte smiled. She took off her jacket, and held out her arms. Anna looked at the dark bruised patches.

"That's it," Charlotte said. "My one true love for which I will do anything and which eventually will kill me."

"YOU'LL BE all right here on your own for a bit, will you?" Matthew got up from the table. "I've a bit of business to see to."

"Oh?"

"Yeah, new tenants for one of my houses. I just want to check that everything's all right for them."

"Will you be long?"

"A couple of hours, that should do it. But before I go, come with me, Anna. I want to show you something."

He took her hand and they walked along the corridor. He opened the door at the end. "Here," he said. "If you decide to come and live with me this will be your room, for your work." The walls were lined with bookshelves and there was a large desk in the middle of the floor. "Sit down," he said, and pulled out the chair for her. "I want to see how it will be when you are here, in this room, so I can think of you and picture you." He put his hands on her shoulders, then knelt down beside her.

"See, I'm like the baby in the picture." He unbuttoned her blouse and put his mouth to her nipple, sucking it hard. He slipped the other hand under her skirt. "And here, I'm holding on to my goldfinch."

She looked down at him, at the way his fingers curled around her bosom, then cried out as his other fingers, hidden from her gaze, grasped hold of her.

He pulled her down beside him. She reached up and slipped her hand inside his collar. She felt the cold chain beneath her fingers. She pulled it out. The key dangled in front of her eyes. She felt it graze her forehead, then delicately touch her nose and come to rest on her lips. She reached up and began to undo his shirt, slowly maneuvering the small white buttons until she could touch his bare skin. She lay down and watched the key again. It began to move, dancing up and down, jerkily now, on the end of its fine, silver chain.

SHE WOKE much later. It was very dark. She was lying where he had left her on his bed. He had covered her with the quilt and kissed her on her forehead, saying he was sorry, but he was late already. He had to go but he wouldn't be long.

She hadn't meant to sleep. She was going to read and wait until he came back. But somehow she had drifted off. She pulled herself up slowly, disturbed by the unfamiliarity of her surroundings. She wasn't even sure if she was alone or not. She reached over, and felt for him. But he wasn't there.

She switched on the lamp beside the bed. The clock said 3:40. She sat up and looked around. The room was as it always was. The walnut wardrobe where he kept his clothes, the walnut chest by the bed and the silver box shining like the moon in the reflected light from the lamp. She picked it up and rested it on her knees. Her face looked up at her. Swollen, distorted in the box's gently convex lid. She pushed at it with her thumbs. It was locked, as always. She got out of bed and walked into the sitting room next door. The city lights flickered and sparkled at her out of the darkness. They could be a million miles away, she thought. They could be the dying gasps of a solar explosion, light-years separating us from them. She found her bag lying where she had dropped it on the sofa. She put her hand inside and felt the bunch of keys. She walked back into the bedroom, sat down on the bed and spread them out beside her. She picked up the smallest, the little silver one, the size of a paper clip. A copy of the one that Matthew wore around his neck. She fitted it into the keyhole in the box. She turned it once and heard the tiniest little click. She took it out. She pushed the lid with her thumbs. She opened the box.

. . .

WHAT WAS it Matthew had said to her that the box contained?

"My most precious belongings, everything that's made me what I am."

What had she expected? Now she wasn't sure. Love letters, maybe. A reminder of a past relationship. The kinds of mementoes that she knew would have twisted her stomach into a sick knot of jealousy. Confirmed why she should not have breached his privacy.

Or perhaps there was something to do with his childhood. A photograph of a baby, or a young woman that would have given him some clue about his family, some scrap of comfort.

She pushed back the lid. An aromatic scent filled her nostrils. The inside of the box must be made of cedarwood, she thought. Like the ones that contained David's best cigars. She remembered how they had looked. Like fat indulgent fingers. Rich men's treats.

But there were no cigars in this box, no letters, no faded photographs. Just four cassette tapes in their plastic boxes, and four clear plastic wallets. And a notebook, small and black, with a thick elastic band snapped around it.

She picked up each of the tapes in turn. They were numbered: 1, 2, 3, 4. She turned them over, examining them for any other kind of identification. She took each one out of its box. The cassettes were numbered neatly too. She put them down and picked up the plastic wallets. They contained two strips of negatives, also numbered, 1 to 4. She opened the one with the 3 on it. She held the flimsy piece of exposed film to the light from the lamp.

Faces looked back at her. Dark patches for teeth and mouths, blobs of light where eye sockets stared out. She put it back, and tried each of the others in turn. They all showed the same kinds of detail. They were all people. Some were women, she could tell from the shape of hair and body. She turned finally to the notebook. She slipped her finger underneath the band. And then she heard it. The sound of the lift. That soft mechanical whine. And a slight thump as it stopped. Silence for a moment. Then the low whistle as the doors began to slide open.

Carefully, quickly, she put everything back into the box. She closed the lid and heard the faint click of the lock catching. She put it back on the walnut chest. She lay back on the bed and reached up to turn off the light.

And heard footsteps. And twisted around and saw Matthew standing in the doorway, a smile brightening his face, as he held out his arms and walked towards her.

33

Trust. How did that kid in Zoë's class define it? It's when you pay the hit man before he's done the job. They had laughed about it at the time, sitting in Zoë's sunny kitchen, watching Tom play with his new kitten while she talked about her pupils. The ones who came to her from the outer suburbs, victims, she kept on stressing, of their families' inadequacies.

"Makes me feel I was lucky to have been brought up the way I was. At least, although the nuns were strict, cruel in some cases, at least they were consistent. And they genuinely had our best interests at heart." She paused and poured more coffee. "The problem was, I suppose, that their view of what was in our best interests was quite often completely different from ours."

"And what did you think about trust?" Anna had asked her. "Did the fact that you knew so little about your parents make you suspicious of people? Did it mean that it was hard for you to trust them?"

Zoë had cut more slices of her favorite chocolate cake, licking the icing carefully from her fingertips before answering.

"It's hard to say. Life in the children's home was so

ordered, so routine. There was no question of choice. And that was a freedom in its own way. You never had to think about what you were going to do, or even how you would respond to anyone. There was no choice in relationships. We feared and respected the nuns. We liked the kitchen staff who gave us extra pieces of bread and jam. We knew all the girls in our dormitory, who were friends and who were not. We trusted the friends, of course we did. We all fitted neatly into a kind of hierarchy. It was just like that. From the first moment I can remember."

"But afterwards, when you left, what was that like?"

Again more chocolate cake, and another cup of coffee. Zoë liked it strong and freshly brewed.

"It's hard to explain, looking back now. I was, I suppose, very innocent. But I was also very knowing. I knew how to survive. I knew how to make myself liked, how to protect myself. So it wasn't that I didn't trust. It was more that the whole question of trust was incomprehensible to me. I had never come across it."

ANNA THOUGHT about their conversation now as she walked across the playground towards Zoë's classroom. She had arranged to meet her at four. Already it was four thirty. She had been late for everything all day because she had lain awake for most of last night, listening to Matthew's even breath beside her. He had turned to her again and again, holding on to her in his sleep. Occasionally he had half woken and kissed her cheek, her shoulder, her arm, before turning away again. And when he had woken properly in the morning, the words she had wanted to say had melted away, as he held her tightly, and kissed her. She shouldn't have looked. It was none of her business. He was entitled to his secrets, just as she was to hers.

She stopped outside the school building and peered in through the windows. Zoë was standing at the blackboard, the duster in her hand, carefully wiping with long, smooth strokes the last of the chalk from its shiny surface. The classroom was very bright. Fluorescent lights fixed to the ceiling spread their glaring light across the battered chairs and tables, arranged in groups on the stained linoleum floor.

She often came to see Zoë when school was over. Watched her go through the ritual of restoring order, readying everything again for the new day to come. Zoë was good at it. She had the knack, the touch. She could always see exactly what was needed and with a few simple movements and gestures make good whatever depredations had taken place. She was good with the children she taught too. Anna had watched her: the easy way she sat beside them at their small tables, her large soft body inclined towards them, so they could smell the warm sweetness that rose up from her bright clothes, hear the care and kindness in her voice as she took them through their work, praising, encouraging even the ones with the most problems sent to this special school when no one else could cope with them.

Anna stepped away from the window and walked around to the swinging doors at the front of the building. The smell of the school enveloped her in its fusty warmth as she walked down the corridor. What was it Isobel always called it? The smell of small boys, that was it, accompanied with a fastidious wrinkling of her nose. She felt sick as she thought about Isobel. There had been no contact between them since that night, after the dog had died, that night of anger and fear. It wasn't right, Anna thought. No matter what happened, Isobel was still her aunt. And this must mean something. It must matter in some way, she was sure of it. It was important that she had her father's eyes, her mother's hair, her aunt's bony grace. That she could see the family resemblance. And did David? She wondered, anger suddenly replacing regret. When he fucked the one, did he think he was fucking the other?

"Anna, is that you out there?"

The door opened and Zoë beckoned her in.

"Sorry, sorry, I know I'm late." Anna held up her hands in mock submission.

"It's okay, I'm only just finished myself. It's been one of those days. Just hang on a couple more minutes, will you?"

Anna walked to the back of the classroom, and leaned over a large rectangular aquarium case on the table underneath a hand-painted sign. "Our Favorite Insects," it said, in straggling red letters. She stirred the carefully constructed woodland habitat with the tip of her finger.

"The kids all love them, you know."

Anna looked up. "The stick insects?"

"Yes, they're so proud of the fact that you bred them especially for us."

Anna prodded what looked like a long thin piece of

bark and watched it move slowly away from her prying finger.

"And," Zoë continued, moving around the room, piling colored blocks into neat skyscrapers, "that's why I want you to come out to look for Eugene. He's better at taking care of them than any of the others. He never usually misses his turn. And he's been gone for three days, no explanation."

"So why don't you just ring up his mother and ask where he is? Or get onto the social workers. Isn't it their job to go out after your kids? Whenever there's a problem?"

Zoë sat down at her desk and opened the top drawer. She pulled out a file and leafed through it, then jotted something down on the back of an envelope.

"Come on," she said, "it's time to go. I don't want to be back too late for Tom."

THEY HAD driven away from the city center towards the west, where the sheltering line of hills gave way to the flat, unbroken plain that stretched from Dublin to the River Shannon. Here were the endless rows of two-story houses, each with a picture-book pitched roof, large front windows and chimney stack, each with its regulation front garden, low breeze-block wall and iron front gate. On the desolate open spaces between the streets, they could dimly see wrecked cars, abandoned, and the ghostly shapes of tethered horses.

It had begun to rain. Heavy, bloated drops of water flung themselves against the windscreen. Anna shivered.

"There must be something very special about this kid to be bringing us out here on a day like today."

Zoë fished in the glove compartment for a packet of mints. She maneuvered one out of its foil tube and waved them in Anna's direction.

"Eugene likes mints. He told me it's because they make him feel so nice and clean when he's eaten them. He says he never feels clean any other time."

"And why is that?"

"He won't say. He doesn't say much at all, but he writes me little notes. He tells me that he loves the color of the sky when there's a full moon."

Anna smiled. "What a sweet thing to say."

"Yes, isn't it? And you'd like him, Anna. When the comet was here in April I lent him Kevin's binoculars so he could watch it every night. He was in love with the comet. He was so upset when it left us. He couldn't believe that he couldn't see it anymore."

"So has he run off in search of intergalactic adventures, would you say, or what?"

Zoë shrugged. "I don't know for sure, but his parents split up a few months ago. His mother has a new boyfriend living in the house. Eugene doesn't like him. I think maybe he's gone to his father's, and his father is a pretty rough character. In and out of prison."

"Have you ever met him?"

"He came to the school when all the trouble with the mother started. There was a terrible scene. He forced his way into the classroom, said he wanted to take Eugene away there and then. I had to call the police."

They drove on. The streetlights had come on, casting pools of orange light, bright circles that did nothing to dissipate the deepening gloom of the evening. Anna peered out, trying to find some landmark among the jumbled shapes of houses.

"I've never been out here before," she said. "Incredible when you think of all the years I've lived in Dublin."

"Not really." Zoë peeled off another mint. "You've never had a reason. And we're all creatures of habit, aren't we? We don't make voyages of discovery until it's absolutely necessary. Look at me and Tom, and all the people we've met since he started going to the HIV clinic in James's Hospital. One minute you're sitting next to someone who could be a schoolteacher or a doctor or a civil servant and the next you're having cups of tea and a gossip with an addict, all tattoos and pasty face, the kind of person you'd once have scurried across the road to avoid. It's been a real eye-opener for me."

"And how is Tom?"

"A lot better these days. The drug therapy they have now seems to work. No one knows for how long, but because he's so young, perhaps they'll have found a real cure by the time he's grown up."

"And what about all the others who got it from the plasma? How are they?"

Zoë didn't answer immediately. When she spoke her voice trembled. "Most of them are dead. A whole generation of hemophiliacs wiped out just like that."

Anna reached out and touched her arm. "I'm so sorry," she said.

"Don't be. As I told you, there's really no rhyme or reason to who gets it."

"But surely there are those whose behavior puts them at risk, and then there are true innocents like Tom."

"Yeah, and people like your blind friend Billy—isn't that his name? How do you think he got it?"

"What?" Anna's voice was incredulous. "What on earth are you talking about?"

"Shit!" Zoë banged her fists on the steering wheel. "I shouldn't have said that. It's an unspoken rule in the clinic that you never tell. I shouldn't have said anything."

"But you have, you have, Zoë. Tell me, are you sure it's him?"

"Yes, of course I am. He's been coming to the clinic for about a month now. I've seen him three or four times. But please don't say anything. I shouldn't have told you. Don't ask him. If he wants you to know he'll tell you himself."

Anna felt sick again. She remembered the blood on her fingers and how he had pushed her away. She remembered the expression on his face in the train when she told him about Matthew. Every time she had tried to see him since then he was never at home. The old lady next door had popped her head out when she heard Anna ringing the little bell. "Will you tell him I was looking for him?" Anna had asked her. "Please tell him."

Winnie, that was her name, had nodded, the crystal earrings hanging from her pendulous lobes bobbing up and down.

"I don't know, Anna, but I think I'm lost." Zoë had

pulled into a narrow cul-de-sac. She slowed the car and stopped. In front was a large open space, grass kicked into mud. Beyond it in the distance more houses and streets. People straggled towards a large metal container rigged up as a temporary shop. They could hear voices. Laughing, shouting.

"Have you any idea where we are?" Anna asked.

"I thought I did. I was pretty certain that Eugene lives over there in those houses. I was here before a few months ago. Mind you, it was daytime then. And it was summer. Even here summer makes a difference. I'll go and have a look, see if I can find anyone to ask." She pulled her coat up over her shoulders and buttoned it, wrapping her shawl around her head. She picked up her bag from the floor.

"Wait for me," she said, as she banged shut the door.

Anna leaned back and closed her eyes. She wished she was anywhere other than here. She felt ill at ease and out of place. She needed the comfort of the familiar around her. Like the garden ant who spends its days scurrying along the same path, in and out of its nest, never looking to right or left, only ahead, and is completely put out by the appearance of anything different or unusual in its way. That is what I am, she thought. As Zoë said, a creature of habit, pure and simple.

Time passed. Billy, poor Billy, she thought. She could see him sitting in the hospital waiting room, his eyes swivelling from side to side the way they did when he was anxious. He would be holding his whistle, his fingers moving up and down, pressing hard on the different-sized openings, making little circles, indentations in his skin. Grace would be leaning against his legs, her head lying on his feet. Anna could have been there with him if he'd told her. She could have helped him get through it, if he'd trusted her enough. But there it was again. That deficiency of trust.

She stretched her legs out as far as they could go in the cramped interior, flexing her feet up and down. Then she pulled them up underneath her, twisting around to rest her forearms and head on the back of the seat. She closed her eyes and listened. Sounds from far off. The low moan of traffic on the motorway, half a mile away. The whistle of a gust of wind as it swooped around a chimney and slithered over the roof tiles. She felt so tired. And now she knew the reason why. She had done the pregnancy test this morning when she got to the office. And watched as the bright-pink positive ring appeared in the little container. She had known already what the result would be. Her body had told her. Her breasts were tender, hurting even now underneath the strap of the seat belt. And was it her imagination or had they already begun to grow? She thought of the painting that Matthew had told her he loved. The *Litta Madonna*. Soon her breasts would push through her dress, heavy with milk, the way they did in Leonardo's imagination.

She closed her eyes and rested her head against the cold glass of the window. She dozed. Then jerked awake. The sudden blast of an electric guitar from a car radio as a door opened nearby, then slammed shut again. Footsteps passing on the concrete footpath and the exhausted choking cry of a baby. And then something else. She lifted her head and listened. Men's voices. Shouts. Coming together in a rhythm. A chant. The sound of drums. Car horns as a counterpoint. The call of a siren, waxing and waning, rising and falling on the wind. And in the distance, across the verge, she could see through the gaps between the houses the flare of torches and the shape of people moving together like birds massing at sunset.

She had watched Zoë pick her way delicately across the mud, her arms held out on either side of her bulky body for balance. Now she followed in her path, looking down at her feet to avoid stepping in the coiled mounds of dog dirt that littered the waste ground. Two streets away she could see the lights and hear now the words of the crowd.

"Pushers, pushers, pushers. Out, out, out."

And a single voice crying, *"What do we want?"*

And the response: *"Pushers out."*

Again the voice by itself: *"When do we want them?"*

And the roar of the hundreds of people who filled the road, pouring up and over the footpaths, trotting along behind the figure up front with the megaphone. And screaming, *"Now."*

She stood in the middle of the street looking at the faces as they shoved past her. Features blurred by anger, smeared with rage. Bodies barely able to contain their hatred. Melding together, waiting for the signal to explode as one. Hands held cigarettes to mouths, the red dots of light revealing skin gray with neglect. Children shrieked at each other as they rushed by, dancing in front of a television news crew that had appeared from nowhere, lit up for an instant by the harsh light on the top of the camera, then back into the dark again, cannoning into adults who called out threats in harsh monosyllables.

Anna twisted around trying to single out the one familiar face and shape among the hundreds of others. She wanted to call Zoë's name but she was silenced, her voice dying in her throat as the crowd pushed forward, carrying her along, contained within its invisible boundaries.

And then she saw her. She was standing on the front step of the house before which the crowd had now stopped. A powerful light played over the reinforced door, glinting on the exposed silvery metal. Two women and a man leaned out of an upstairs window, screaming abuse at the crowd below. And Zoë stood still and silent, her arm around the shoulders of a boy whose white face was without expression.

The man with the megaphone held up one hand. Silence fell slowly. He waited until no voice competed with his. Then he began to speak. Articulate, passionate, controlled. They had come, he said, because they had proof that heroin was being dealt from this house. That the people who lived in this house had brought others into the community who were pushers, parasites preying on their children, corrupting them, destroying their future, filling their lives with pain and death. And he turned to the crowd and said, quietly, "What are pushers?"

And the crowd roared back, *"The scum of the earth."*

Again he said, quietly, "What do we want?" And raised his hand, and as he brought it down the crowd screamed out in unison, *"Out, out, out."*

The people in the upstairs window fell back out of

sight, as the crowd surged forward, carrying Anna with them, through the gate and down the gentle incline towards the front door. Zoë and the boy disappeared from view behind the crush of bodies. Anna reached out, feeling her feet lose contact with the ground as the people around her dragged her with them. She began to slip and slide as the rain, which had slackened to a gentle drizzle, began to fall again in dense, heavy drops. Now she called out, her voice hesitant at first, then louder, more insistent. And heard her name in response and the cry, "Help me, please, help me." And when she pushed again, using her elbows and her fists she found herself at last in front of Zoë, the child no longer by her side, and her face a shocked milky white.

"Where is he? Where's Eugene?" Anna screamed at her, as loudly as she could above the shouts and roars of the crowd, the insistent baying of a police siren and the drums beating out a rhythm that matched the chant.

"I don't know, someone grabbed him. I don't know." Zoë's face disappeared again behind the crowd. Anna pushed and shoved again, reached past a tall man with a shining gold earring in one ear and a woman whose face was seamed with fault lines of anger and despair. And felt at last beneath her fingers the soft folds of flesh around Zoë's wrists, grabbed hold of them as tightly as she could, then turned and thrust her way through the crowd, dragging Zoë with her, until they were back on the street again, running, zigzagging through the onlookers, standing in groups, away from the main body of the march. They heard, before they saw its headlights, the car that was driving towards them. Faster and faster down the middle of the road, people scattering, pushing backwards out of the way, panic spreading in ripples through the crowd, as its engine screeched, and she saw the faces of the two men in the front. The gaping holes in their masks where their eyes and mouths looked out, with fists raised, threatening as they swerved from side to side, the horn blaring, the smell of the tires dragging over the tar macadam. And she saw how it was heading right towards her. Her legs were useless, no connection between her desire to move and her ability. And then just as she thought the metal of the front hood was sure to smash into her, she saw the man next to the driver jerk the wheel, and spin the car away, and on down the road, the sound of its engine fading into the cacophony of the night. The crowd surged once more around her, and she turned quickly, grabbing Zoë's hands, and saw suddenly a familiar figure. Standing in the window of the house, looking out at the crowd below. She knew the shape of his head, the angular planes of his face, the dark gleam of his hair as he leaned forward into the light, then drew back, pulling the window shut and stepping into the darkness again. It was Matthew, her Matthew, whom she had last seen that morning, drinking tea and eating toast, standing beside the tall windows with the sun shining on his face, saying, as she pulled on her coat and picked up her bag, "I'll see you this evening, won't I? You will be here for me when I get back, won't you? You do promise me?"

He came to the door of the lift and reached in and kissed her quickly on the cheek. She watched him as the lift doors slid shut. His feet were bare, his hair was wet from the shower. He smelled of clean skin, like a baby.

She stood in the middle of the road. Rain sluiced down her face. She looked at the house again. All the windows, top and bottom, were dark. Beside her Zoë sobbed quietly, pulling at her sleeve. Around her, on all sides, the crowd was slipping away, like drops of water rolling off a piece of polished wood.

"Come on, Anna, let's go home." Zoë tugged her hand again. Anna turned back once more, towards the house, then away again, and followed Zoë down the road towards the car.

34

The boat was big and very beautiful. It rested at its mooring like a giant swan. Its white sails flapped as it turned slowly into the wind. Then it let slip its line and began to sail, its canvas ballooning, stretched tightly. It moved slowly away from the shore. And as the wind blew harder and harder and the sails got bigger and bigger, the boat lifted up into the sky, gravity releasing it, letting it go.

She laughed out loud and turned to the man standing beside her. "Look," she said, "how can that be?"

He shrugged his shoulders and smiled. She looked closely at him. He was familiar but she couldn't think of his name.

And then she looked up again and saw that as the boat reached the clouds, the sails were beginning to flap freely, and suddenly it was dropping, faster and faster, heading for the water. And she reached out to the man, clutching his arm, waiting for the sound of the boat exploding from the impact. Shattering into planks, beams, shards of wood. She began to cry, tears as salty as the blue sea spread out in front of her.

ANNA WOKE. She lay still, the bedclothes tucked tightly around her body. She moved her head gently on the pillow and watched the sycamore branches outside the window slowly waving to her in the wind. It was still dark even though her clock told her that it was after eight in the morning.

She sat up. Saliva filled her mouth. She swallowed hard and quickly got out of bed. She rushed into the bathroom. She shuddered and gasped, and a thin stream of vomit poured from her, trickling down her nose. She leaned over the toilet bowl, holding on to it with both hands, her body shaking with each racking spasm. Then she collapsed, exhausted, on the floor.

It had been very late when she got back to the house on the canal. She had driven Zoë home. Kevin had been waiting anxiously, Tom curled up half asleep on his knee. Anna had tried to explain, but her eyes were drawn to the television set in the corner. A reporter stood, microphone in hand, in the middle of a dark, crowded street. His voice was shrill. There had been a riot on the Swan's Nest estate. Anti-drug campaigners had attacked a house. A number of people were injured when a car was driven at high speed into the protesters. Extra police were drafted in to cope with what he described as "running battles," which had been going on all through the evening. Anna watched the pictures. Torches flared, faces appearing in the flickering lights. Some were masked. She walked towards the screen and squatted down in front of it. She wanted to be able to hold her magnifying glass to the crowd. To single out the face she had seen at the window.

The picture changed again. She saw a mass of people walking, in orderly lines, then chaos, the sound of an engine, a horn, shouts, cries, shrieks, as the crowd disintegrated, separated, then formed again, and there, in the middle of it all, her own white face looking back at herself. Her hair caught the light from the streetlamp, refracting it in a rainbow that spun out around her head. Like the corona of the full moon, she thought, half smiling at the incongruity of the image.

"See?" she said, turning back to Kevin, who was cradling Zoë's head on his chest, stroking her face and murmuring comforting words in her ear. "See what it was like?"

The bathroom tiles were cold and unforgiving, pressing into her legs. She stood up and looked at herself in the mirror. The man from her dream looked back. She reached out to touch him, but saw instead her own hand, her fingers pressed against the glass. Who was he? She should have asked him. If only she hadn't woken when she had, maybe he would have explained himself to her.

She pulled her nightdress over her head. Was it her imagination or had her body begun to change already? She could only be a few weeks pregnant, six weeks or so at the most. Was it possible that already the tiny embryo embedded in the wall of her womb was making such a mark? She remembered an article she had read once. It explained how the natural defenses of the body are lulled into a false sense of security by the hormones the pregnancy triggers. In spite of itself the host welcomes the invader. It reminded her now, as she stood under a scalding shower, of the way the parasitic wasp behaves, paralyzing its victim, preventing it from developing, weakening its resistance as the wasp's eggs hatch into larvae and gradually begin to consume the body, which has given them a place of refuge.

She looked down at her stomach, placing both her hands over it, fingers spread out, thumbs touching. What was inside her? Was it beautiful and good? Would it make her life whole again? Or was it alien and dangerous, something to be destroyed? She crouched down beneath the stream of water, put her hands over the top of her head and began to rock backwards and forwards, sobs of grief pouring from her mouth.

MICHAEL STOOD on the staircase that led to the museum's upper gallery. The old wood creaked loudly as he moved. The mammals were displayed up here. Squirrels and stoats, otters and badgers. And all the native birds of prey. He began to walk slowly along one side of the museum's inner rectangle. It was dark today. He looked up at the apex of the glass ceiling. It was as if the gray clouds that covered the sky were hanging right above it, keeping all the brightness away.

Brightness came from below today. He leaned on the mahogany balustrade and looked down. Anna was directly beneath him. She was standing beside a scale model of a rock pool. Around her clustered a group of small children. He could hear her voice clearly. She was identifying all the creatures that lived within its limpid water. He listened.

"Periwinkles, coral worms, common starfish, daisy brittle stars, dead man's fingers." There was a chorus of oohs and aahs from the children.

"No, no, it's all right. It's just the name for another kind of starfish. Listen, listen, hermit crabs who steal other shells to live in, and whelks and mutton shells. And all the different kinds of seaweed. Bladder wrack, that's like a little water pistol, great for squirting people, and club-leafed sea wrack, aren't they all pretty?"

Michael watched her. She was wearing a narrow gray skirt with a cherry-colored sweater. The sleeves were pushed up from her wrists, and he could see the pale skin of her forearms and hands. The children clamored for her attention, leaping up and down beside her. She was telling them stories, making life in the rock pool seem as interesting and exciting as if it were science fiction. She moved away, and he walked above her, watching her, wondering when she would feel his gaze on her back and turn to look up at him. It would be soon, he knew that. Very soon.

"I SAW you there," she said. The children had gone. They were alone, apart from the security guard half-seated on a high stool by the front door. "I saw you in that house. The one the crowd was attacking. I couldn't believe it was you, but I saw you clearly. You were in the upstairs window, just after the car ran into the crowd."

His hands were in the pockets of his leather jacket. He took out his gold watch. He looked up at the large round clock on the wall above her head. He snapped open the case and moved the hands with one fingertip. He closed it again and began to wind it, using the little knob on the top. She could hear the rasp as metal meshed with metal.

"I want to know. What were you doing there, in that house?"

"I could ask the same thing of you." He swung the watch gently backwards and forwards on its golden chain.

"Don't be ridiculous." Her voice was unusually grating. She didn't look well, he thought. Dark smudges under her eyes aged her. He could see what her face would be like when she was an old woman.

"Why is it ridiculous? I saw you on the TV news. You and your friend, the teacher, you were in the crowd."

"We were looking for someone, a child, one of her pupils. We didn't know what was going to happen. It was dreadful, so frightening."

"And for me too." He stepped closer. "I was giving a lift to one of the guys who works for me. A painter. He got a call from his sister to say that she was in trouble. His car had broken down. He was really worried, so I said I'd take him. He swore to me afterwards that he didn't realize what was going on. It was the sister's boyfriend they were after. Apparently he's been dealing for ages. It's a way of life for a lot of people who live out in those estates. They don't think about it the way 'respectable' people do, the way the cops and the politicians do. It's all they have."

He stepped closer. He reached out and touched her cheek with the back of his hand. "I'm sorry you were frightened. But, really, please believe me, I was just as frightened as you. Those people in that house were under siege. And the police will do nothing to protect them. The anti-drug groups are nothing short of vigilantes, for all their rhetoric. It's mob rule they're advocating, and the

cops are letting them do their dirty work." His hand
moved from her cheek to her shoulder, then traced the line
of her collarbone underneath the fine wool of her sweater.

"I thought you'd be waiting for me when I got home
last night. I was so disappointed that you weren't there.
Please, come after you've finished here. You look tired.
I'll cook you a meal, and make you feel better again." His
hand dropped to her breast. Rested for a moment, then fell
away. Lifted her hand, turned it over and kissed her palm,
tracing the fine lines with the tip of his tongue. He closed
her hand and pressed her fingers down. "That's to keep
you going until later."

She watched his tall thin figure walk quickly down the
long room. He paused at the double glass doors. He
looked back and waved, then turned again and pushed his
way through them and out. She wiped her hand on her
skirt.

IT WAS four o'clock when she left the museum, nearly
dark on this dull autumn day. She turned right to walk
towards Baggot Street. The lights of the cars that passed
her by glowed with an unnatural brilliance. She walked
quickly, her shawl wrapped tightly around her hair, her
face lowered. She picked up a taxi and gave him the
address. Usually she would have enjoyed the walk from
the museum to the apartments where Matthew lived. It
was a route which took her through her favorite parts of
Dublin. Over the hump-backed canal bridge where
Baggot Street and Mespil Road met, down Pembroke
Road, along Wellington Road, the ground beneath her

feet thick with sodden leaves from the cherry trees which in spring gave her such pink-and-white pleasures, then through a network of laneways until she came to the wide gates and car park that surrounded the apartments. But today was different. Today she would not dawdle.

The building loomed above her and when she leaned back to look up at it she could swear that it moved. Just a little bit. Swayed gently as a chilling gust blew in from the sea. She leaned forward to rest her neck and looked up at it again. Blocks of light were piled one on top of the other, but the highest windows were dark.

A car pulled in through the gate. She turned to face it, the headlights dazzling her eyes, star shapes, followed by large spots of black. The car pulled into a space. The engine stopped. Silence again, just for a moment, then the click of doors opening, the scrape of shoes on the hard surface, and the slamming, in quick succession, of the doors. A man and a woman passed her by without a glance. Elegantly, warmly dressed, the woman's perfume hanging in the cold night air. She followed in their wake past the security guard, across the polished floor and into the lift, its doors open. The man reached out a stubby index finger and pushed the button for the fifth floor. Anna took out her little key and turned it in the slot beside the fifteenth. The lift doors slid together. Smoothly, with a hiss like an intake of breath. She saw herself reflected in the polished steel. A shadowy insubstantial figure, that wavered from side to side as the lift rose silently. Up and up and up. And came to a stop as the number five above the door lit up. There was a moment's pause before the doors slid apart. The man and woman stepped out. Again the pause. Her heart shuddered in her chest. She could feel the drop beneath her feet, as if there was nothing underneath her. No metal, no wood, no tiles. Just the long empty shaft and at the bottom of it the hardness of concrete. The doors closed. The lift began to move. She pressed herself into the corner and held out both her palms, pushing her hands against the smooth marbled walls. They were cold to the touch. She counted out loud, trying to control her breathing so the dizziness that threatened to overwhelm her was kept at bay. She tensed her thighs, pressing herself hard against the tiles. It is my will, she thought, that keeps this metal box moving upwards. That is all. If I was to stop for a moment, to relax my vigilance, that would be the end of me. We would fall, the lift and I, down to the bottom, to smash into tiny pieces. My bones, its steel. My flesh, its wood. My blood, its glass and wiring. Just as she felt that she would begin to disintegrate, the lift stopped. It shuddered once and the doors slid smoothly apart. She reached forward carefully, first one foot, then the other, stepping out into the apartment that was waiting for her.

It was dark in the room into which she stepped. The view of the city and the mountains hung in front of her, like a huge painting of grays and blacks, stippled with sparkling yellows and reds. She took a step forward, then stopped. She could feel the floor begin to lurch and tilt. It was as if she were on the rim of a waterfall, and at any minute she would begin to slip uncontrollably over its edge. She moved backwards against the wall and began to slide herself along towards Matthew's bedroom. At least here, no matter what else she had to face, she would be away from those terrifying windows.

And this was what she had to face. The silver box, and its contents, the tapes, the negatives, the small black notebook. It was much darker in the bedroom, but she did not switch on the light. She sat down on the bed, took the key from her bag and fitted it in the lock. She opened it and put her hand inside. And felt not what she had been expecting but a small, hard, rectangular object. She pulled it out, holding it up in front of her face. It was a tape recorder, the kind O'Dwyer used for dictating memos to the staff. She pressed the *eject* button. A tape was in place. She pressed *play* and listened.

It was Matthew's voice, and he was speaking to her.

"So," he said, "your curiosity has finally got the better of you. I was wondering when it would. You resisted for longer than I had thought was possible. You have impressed me with your honorable refusal to pry. But now you, like everyone else, have given in. And you want to know what I keep in the box. What it is that has made me what I am. Well, Anna, you will have to go up into the attic. You know how to do that. Go to the trapdoor in the ceiling. Reach up and catch hold of the handle and a ladder will be released, and it's easy after that. But before you do anything, remember that you have a choice. You could decide not to go any further with your quest. You could decide that whatever is in the box is nothing to do with you, and if I wanted you to know I would have told you myself. You could make that decision. Couldn't you? And remember, Anna, that the consequences will be on your own head. That is all I have to say. Except this. In the words of the Chinese poet your husband told me often that he loved so much,

> *Since you, sir, went away,*
> *My gauze curtains sigh in the autumn's wind.*
> *My thoughts of you are like the creeping grass*
> *That grows and spreads without end.*

"Remember this. And remember me."

She stood up, the tape recorder dropping from her hands. It clattered noisily on the wooden floor. She bent down and picked it up. She rewound the tape, and placed it back in the box. She locked it again.

She went into the bathroom. She closed the door and switched on the light. Saliva poured once more into her mouth and she bent over the basin, spitting first, then vomiting. Her throat burned. She turned on the cold tap and held her hands under the gush of water. She gulped noisily and splashed her face. She picked up a towel from the rail and held it to her cheeks. It smelled of Matthew. She flung it down, turning on the tap again, and again sluicing water over her skin, then walked towards the door, drops falling from her nose and chin. She switched off the light, paused, listened, but all was quiet.

Quiet, too, at the top of the steep metal staircase to the attic. And cold. Dark as well, so she stepped forward reluctantly, away from the comforting square of light that came from the open trapdoor. Something brushed against her hair and she flinched, a small cry bursting from her throat. But it was only a swinging light switch, hanging within reach. She twisted it around her hand, then stopped. A shadowy figure waited against the far wall. Tall, slim, wearing some kind of light-colored dress.

"Who are you?" Anna's voice was suddenly loud in her ears. "Who are you? Did Matthew send you? What do you want from me?" She was trembling, her legs shaking uncontrollably. She was conscious of how far above ground she was, here, up in the roof of this building that terrified her. She wanted to fling herself on the ground, and hold on tightly with her fingernails. Anything to stop the vertigo that flooded her body. Again she called out, but still there was no response. She tugged the cord. Light flared in her eyes, blinding her for a moment. She covered her face with her hands, then peeped like a child through her fingers. A tailor's dummy stood in front of her. It was wearing a dress that was instantly recognizable despite the jagged tears through the fine white satin. It was her wedding dress, clumsily tacked together with large uneven stitches. Last seen abandoned on the bedroom floor in her old house in Anglesea Road. She could still hear the whine of the razor blade through the material. She remembered her anger and her pain. She stepped forward and touched it gently, as fear washed over her.

She looked around at the huge open space beneath the roof. Pipes wrapped in silver insulation ran along one wall, and bundles of wires, some caught inside lengths of plastic, others in gentle swags, draped the other. Farther away were the jumbled shapes of boxes and what looked like stored building materials, piles of wood, tins of paint, bags of cement. And at her feet another tape recorder was waiting for her. She picked it up and again pressed the *play* button.

"So," Matthew's voice again, "you've made your decision. Well, I hope you'll be able to live with it. And tell me, Anna, are you pleased that I rescued your dress for you? It seemed like such a waste to throw it away. It was once so beautiful, and I can imagine how you looked in it. I thought I should take care of it for you, and maybe one day you'll wear it for me. What do you think about that idea?" There was a pause. He cleared his throat. "Are you ready now? Are you sure you've made up your mind? Because it's not too late to back out." Another pause. "All right, well, this is what you do. Move the tailor's dummy and you will find everything you need. But just one final point, Anna. Don't think that you can do this and then abandon me. It doesn't work like that. You'll find out what I mean. Very soon."

There was silence. She put down the tape recorder and walked towards her ruined dress. She bent down and felt beneath it. Her hand found a large parcel wrapped in brown paper. She stood up slowly and tore it open, grabbing at its contents as they tumbled to the dusty floor. There were the tapes, one with her name printed on it. Packets of negatives. And a photograph torn in two. She recognized one half of it immediately. She had seen it before, that night, just after David had died. In the garage when she thought she had been dreaming. The other half she had never seen before showed Isobel, gazing lovingly at David. Here too was the notebook from the silver box, and a scrapbook. Bigger, stiff cardboard covers. She turned over the pages. They were filled with newspaper cuttings. Death notices, she saw, and longer articles. She turned the stiff cardboard pages slowly. Then heard a sudden whirring and grinding, coming from somewhere above her head. The lift, she thought, remembering the shape of the building from the ground, and the ugly hut-like structure that interrupted the smooth line of the roof. The noise got louder and louder. She imagined lengths of steel wire coiling tightly as they pulled the metal box and its occupants up and up and up. She could feel the tension in the twisted skeins, the weight testing, stretching, and the labored response of the electric motor. Rising higher and higher, the cogs of one wheel grinding against the other. She waited for it to stop, at one of the floors beneath. And realized that it wasn't going to, that it was coming all the way to the top, to her.

She turned, holding the tapes, the negatives, the scrapbook, the notebook pressed against her stomach. She stepped out onto the ladder, pulling the trapdoor closed behind her, jumping from the last few rungs onto the floor. She turned and ran towards the door that she had never seen open. The one that led out onto the emergency staircase that spiralled down outside the building. She had seen it from below and it had made her feel faint and dizzy just looking at it from the ground. But now, as she heard the lift slowing, she shot back the bolts and stepped out.

Onto a metal platform barely big enough for two people. Wind pulled at her hair, wrapping fine strands around her eyes and mouth, and spatterings of rain stung her cheeks. She stepped forward towards the top of the spiral, barely able to keep her eyes open, the sight frightened her so much. Below, a dark emptiness broken here and there by patches of light and the humped shapes of houses and cars. She pressed herself against the door, feeling the heavy metal handle biting into her. She wanted to turn away, and open it, fall backwards into safety. But she knew that safety was not behind the door. Safety lay out here and below, at the bottom of the spiral beneath her, and once she had begun there was no going back. One hand sliding down the metal rail, the other holding tightly her treasures from the attic. She kept her gaze fixed downwards, counting out loud, fixing her thoughts on the numbers as if they were holy talismans, protection against evil, until the ground was there before her eyes, solid, unmoving, bearing the weight of her body. And she had done it.

35

"Once upon a time there were twelve beautiful princesses, and they lived in a huge castle with their father, the King."

It was story time in Murray's house. Emily had been in and out of the bath and now she sat on his knee, her red hair slicked back from her smooth round face.

"Read-y book, Da Da." She banged her hand down on the shiny illustrated pages. "Read-y book."

Murray pulled her closer and continued. "Every night before the princesses went to sleep they put their little shoes neatly at the ends of their beds. And they were perfect. But every morning when their nurse came in to wake them up, their shoes were filled with holes and had to be thrown away. And their father, the King, was very angry."

Sarah was on night duty. He wished she wasn't. She was four and a half months pregnant now, much bigger than she had been with Emily. And tired. "Could you not give up work, love?" he'd said to her. "After all, you've been having a hard time. Surely they'd all understand if you decided to take a break for a couple of months."

But she had refused. They were short-staffed at the hospital. They needed her. She'd had to drop out of the operating theater because she couldn't really stand for long stretches of time any longer, but she didn't mind being transferred to the wards for a couple of months. "It's easy, really. Nights are quiet. Anyway, we need the money."

That put an end to the discussion. Murray tried not to hear the reproof in Sarah's voice. Maybe it was his imagination, but he seemed to notice it more and more these days. The why-did-I-marry-a-Guard tone. The terrible-shifts-lousy-money-dangerous-and-antisocial edge to her voice. He kissed Emily's soft cheek and lifted her Mickey Mouse drinking cup to her mouth.

"No, Da Da, Em'ly do that." She pushed his hands away and took the two handles of the cup in her own. She tilted it back and orange juice ran down her chin, dribbling into the folds of her chubby neck, then dropping onto the pages of the book. She laughed loudly, and he laughed too, as he took out his handkerchief and wiped the tear-shaped drips away. If Sarah had been here he wouldn't have been reading to her like this. Sarah always said that his choice of stories was too grown-up. As far as he was concerned that was rubbish. Emily loved them, and so did he.

He read on. The story unfolded with precision and certainty. The mystery of the worn-out shoes. The challenge laid down by the King to find out what was happening. The reward offered: the hand of one of the princesses in marriage. The arrival of the wily old soldier, aided by the witch. His discovery of the magical world, where the trees were laden with branches and leaves made of gold, silver and diamonds, and the castle where the princesses danced all night with the young princes. And the happy-ever-after ending when the soldier gets to marry the oldest of the sisters.

Emily was asleep long before he reached the end. But he kept on reading out loud anyway. If he had been challenged he would have said it was because the child was lulled by the sound of his voice. But the truth was that he was lulled, soothed and calmed by the familiar story. And the notion that charmed him. That there could be worlds that existed side by side, in parallel, the inhabitants of one oblivious to the existence of the other.

He felt like that about the suburb in which he and Sarah and Emily lived. He liked the way he could turn off the dual carriageway at Loughlinstown, leaving behind the hectic streams of traffic, and within three minutes he'd be pulling into his own road, slowing almost to a walking pace in case a football might roll out in front of him, followed by one of the children who played in each other's front gardens, winter and summer, and spilled onto the grass verge at the slightest opportunity. He could imagine Emily in years to come, out here with all the others. He could see her sitting on the low pebbledashed wall with her friends, rushing to the ice-cream van on warm summer evenings, flirting he was sure with the little boys in whose sandpits she now played. It made him feel happy and secure to think of it, so far removed from the world in which he spent most of his waking hours.

He could name all his neighbors, the twenty-odd families that lived on his street. He knew the cars they drove, the way they spent their weekends, the friends and relations who came to visit. It was a habit, really, the gathering of information. One that all Guards develop soon after they put on the uniform, and one they never give up. Sarah hated it. So he didn't let on how much he knew about them all. He'd try and look surprised when she said that the Morans in number twenty-eight had bought a new car. And not tell her that he'd already memorized the license number, 97 D 282,576. Make: Renault Mégane. Color: navy blue. When she told him that Derek Owens from number sixteen had left home and was living with another woman in a flat in Dun Laoghaire, he kept his mouth shut about how he'd spotted him on more than one occasion, parked by the seafront, the windows steamed up, and seen him sleeping in the car a few nights in a row.

It was a habit, that was all. Part of the way that Guards live. Making connections, putting two and two together, joining the dots to make up the picture.

And the picture that the dots were making was beginning to look very, very interesting. Emily sighed, her head lolling against his arm. He stood up slowly and carefully, cradling her limp body. He walked up the stairs, watching her face, the way she frowned as his footsteps disturbed her sleep. She reminded him suddenly of his mother, whose pretty round face could be transformed by the slightest displeasure, her eyebrows coming together across the bridge of her nose, her lips pursing with irritation.

He sat beside her crib and watched her, as she twisted and turned, making a little nest of the bedclothes, then lying completely still, facedown, her thumb in her mouth. It was warm here in her little bedroom. Clean and pretty, with its nursery-rhyme frieze around the wall, and matching curtains. He stood up and opened them slightly, looking out at the houses across the road, their curtains pulled tight against the cold night air.

It was quiet here now, the children all in bed. Unlike the road where Gabriel Reilly lived. There, the noise never really stopped. There was always someone shouting, someone angry. Cars arriving and leaving, and a gang hanging around the front gate. Murray had been watching Reilly now for the best part of a week. Following him in and out of town, watching where he was going and whom he was seeing. He'd drawn a little map for himself. The names of the people involved and a series of arrows that showed how they were related to each other. There was Billy Newman. Reilly had visited him a couple of times in his little flat in Cherrytree Court. He didn't stay for long, a few minutes at the most. And then there was the tall dark man, the good-looking one, whom Murray had seen in Reilly's car, and going into and coming out of Reilly's house. Murray had recognized his face, but it had been a while before he could put a name to it. He'd taken some photographs and shown them around the office. It was Mick Finnegan, one of the old lads, who'd come up with the goods.

"Mullen," he said. "Remember his grandmother had that shop on the South Circular years ago? She was a dodgy old bird. A moneylender, she'd half Dolphin's Barn flats on her books. And a couple of heavies with iron bars to do her collecting. Michael was her daughter's kid. Lived in London most of the time, came over here for holidays."

"And does he have a record?"

Finnegan shrugged. "Probably. Most of that crowd from around there do."

But Records didn't come up with anything, even though he'd got onto them a couple of times, asking them to look for his file. He'd thought it was their usual snail slowness, but the clerk he spoke to got quite pissed off about it, said they had nothing on the name he'd given her. That he must have been mistaken, and who did he think he was speaking to her in that tone of voice?

He was pretty certain when he thought about it that it was the same guy he'd seen waiting for Anna Neale outside the museum a few months ago. And she was Billy's friend. And he was sure that Gabriel Reilly had something to do with the death of Simon Woods.

But perhaps it was all just a coincidence and he was making mountains where there were only pimples. He turned back to Emily and bent down over her crib, covering her again with the quilt, then walked downstairs and into the kitchen. He pulled a can of Heineken from the six-pack in the fridge. He jerked off the ring-pull. White foam poured out all over his fingers.

"Shit," he said, and shook off the drops, watching how they spattered the tiled floor. He lifted the can to his mouth and licked away the bubbled froth. He poured the rest into a glass, and began to tidy up, gathering together Emily's toys and books, all the paraphernalia of her young life.

He went back into the sitting room and switched on the television, flicking from channel to channel. It had been odd when he went to see Billy yesterday. It was the middle of the afternoon, but his curtains were pulled shut. Murray had banged on the door. He could hear the sound of voices, loud, arguing, but there was no reply. He banged again, and again, and the old lady who lived next door stuck her head out and shouted, "What are you doing? What do you want? What are you making such a racket for?" She leaned on her stick and glared at him, while a small tortoiseshell cat curled itself, vinelike, around her legs.

"I'm sorry." He found himself apologizing, intimidated by her fierce expression. "I'm very sorry. I hope I didn't frighten you."

"Frighten me? Who do you think I am? No, you just woke me up. It's hard enough to get a decent sleep around here without fellas banging on my door."

"Uh, it wasn't your door, I'm afraid, it was your next-door neighbor's. I can hear voices in there, but I can't get an answer."

"That's just Billy's telly. He's probably lying down. Here." She dragged herself to the door and bent over, pushing open the tarnished brass flap on the letterbox. The cat mewed softly as she called out Billy's name. Murray squatted down and scratched behind a pair of upright ginger ears, moving around its face to the clean white chin underneath. The cat purred appreciatively and arched its back with pleasure. Murray ran his finger along its bony spine and down onto its tail. The cat's purr increased in volume.

When the door opened the cat jumped ahead of him over the threshold. Murray watched the black Labrador get up from her cushion by the stove. She stretched out her nose and sniffed the air. Then her tail began to wag. Billy stood in front of him. He was pale, his hair lank and uncombed. His eyes swivelled from side to side.

"It's me, Billy, Sergeant Murray, remember?"

Billy turned and shuffled back to the unmade bed. He lay down, resting on a jumble of pillows. The cat sprang up beside him. Loud applause came from the TV set behind him. He turned around to look at it. Oprah Winfrey was standing among her audience, microphone in hand.

"I was wondering if I could have a word with you."

A man stood up. He was small and very fat. He began to cry. "I just want to thank you, Oprah," he said, his voice breaking with emotion. "You have saved my marriage today." The studio audience began to applaud.

Billy lifted his hand. He was holding the remote control. "Crap," he said, "fucking crap." He pushed the button. The picture disappeared. There was silence. "Put the kettle on, Mr. Murray, if you wouldn't mind, and make us a cuppa."

Murray had asked him, when they were drinking tea and eating some chocolate biscuits that he had found in the cupboard, why he watched television.

"Why wouldn't I? Sure there's just as much talking on the telly as there is pictures. Sometimes I go to the movies too. They even let me bring Grace in with me. I like that." Billy drank carefully from his mug, holding it with both hands. He reminded Murray of Emily's proud mastery of her cup. "Do you like the movies, Mr. Murray?"

There was plenty of chat from Billy today. About everything except the subjects that interested Murray. Like Gabriel Reilly and his visits.

"I don't know who you're talking about." Billy's eyes moved uncontrollably in their sockets. "I don't know anyone called that."

"But I've seen him coming in here. Twice—yesterday and a couple of days before that."

Again Billy's eyes rolled from side to side, but his voice was steady. "Sorry, Mr. Murray, but I can't help you. I don't know anyone who's got that name. I have a few friends who come to see me, and there's my new social worker from James's Hospital. A nice guy. Tony Doran is his name. He comes to see me regular."

"And then there's Anna Neale, isn't there? Has she been here recently?"

Billy sat up straight. "What's it to you? It's none of your fucking business." He drank noisily and held out his mug, his arm rigid and straight. "Gimme some more tea."

Murray poured. Billy leaned back against his crumpled pillows and pulled his knees up to his chest. He was wearing a pair of thick woollen socks, brightly colored in reds and blues.

"Nice and warm, are they, your feet in those things? Did someone knit them for you? Your little old lady next door?"

"No, they were a present from Anna. She was away somewhere with her husband, somewhere with snow and stuff. She bought them for me."

"She likes you, doesn't she? She told me herself, that time when you got the beating, she told me how much she likes you. She said you were a wonderful person, and she said you were one of her favorite people in all the world."

Billy's face brightened. His eyes fixed themselves on Murray's, holding still just for a moment, and for that moment they were the clear blue of the sea in summer.

Then they began to move again, and his expression darkened. He reached down to the cat lying beside him on the bed, and pulled it up and onto his chest. "I don't believe you, you just want something. I don't believe you and I don't believe her. She's just a fucking old slag like the rest of them. She can't keep her legs closed. I hate her." He bent his face down to the cat's sleek back and rubbed his cheek against it. "Get out of here and leave me alone." His voice was muffled but the tone was unmistakable.

Murray stood up. "Okay, Billy, whatever you want. But listen. I know what you're involved in, we've all known for a long time what you're up to. But it's not you we want, do you hear me? We've nothing to gain by arresting you and charging you and putting you away. There's nothing in it for us except grief and hassle and bad publicity. It's the guy you're working for, that's who we want. We'll get him sooner or later, Billy, I can guarantee you that. But it would be much better for you if you gave us a hand now. We'd remember it and we'd be grateful." He went into the kitchenette and rinsed out his mug. He walked back into the room. "So I'll tell you what I'll do. I'm going to give my card to old Winnie next door. It has my phone number on it, and when you're ready give us a call. Okay?"

MURRAY GOT up from the sofa and went into the kitchen to get more beer. He paused at the foot of the stairs and listened, but there was no sound from Emily's room. He walked back into the sitting room. And saw suddenly a familiar face. Christ Almighty. It was Anna Neale. They were showing footage from that anti-drug march out in

Swan's Nest a couple of nights ago. And there she was, slap-bang in the middle of it.

Murray had missed the whole thing, thank God. He needed to get caught up in a messy situation like that like he needed a hole in the head. The Commissioner was going mad about it. The problem was the protesters were more effective than the Guards. Forcing the pushers out of the suburban estates, getting the local communities to fight back, setting up their own nightly patrols. It was well organized and managed. But why wouldn't it be? Local intelligence had it that the Provos were heavily involved. Still—Murray sat down and opened another can, carefully this time—you had to hand it to them. They'd turned drugs into a national issue. It was no longer simply a question of a crowd of gurriers, whom no one cared about as long as they stayed in their own miserable estates and didn't impinge on the rest of the population.

He watched the Minister for Justice answering questions. He looked uneasy, self-conscious. Out of his depth. Murray couldn't figure out what Anna Neale would be doing there. Just another stupid coincidence. He'd make a note in his diary. He'd call in on her tomorrow. Now he was tired. He lay back and closed his eyes.

AND OPENED them, suddenly. He sat up. His neck was stiff and aching. It was cold now, the dying embers of the fire showing a dull ruby through the gray ash. The phone was ringing. He reached for it and looked at his watch. It was four A.M.

What was it the voice had said? "It's your wife.

Something's happened to her. We're not sure exactly what, but she's been assaulted. It happened here in the hospital. You'd better come immediately. We've been onto the Guards. They're on their way."

Too late to call a neighbor to mind Emily. He'd have to bring her with him. Bundling her into a blanket, strapping her into her car seat, panic flooding his body with sickening adrenaline as he reversed out of the driveway and onto the street, accelerating towards the main road.

Then the second phone call, as he was halfway there, on his mobile phone. A man's voice. What exactly did he say? He wished he'd been able to write it down.

"We got her, that pregnant bitch you're married to. It's lucky she's already carrying your bastard, because if she wasn't, she'd be giving you a nasty little surprise. This is a warning. Next time it'll be Emily. You know Emily, don't you? Your cute little red-haired daughter. Remember this now. Remember what I'm saying."

Through the red lights, his hand on the horn, the sound of the tires screeching on the wet surface. Stopping outside the main door to the hospital. Dragging Emily from the back of the car, her screams loud and urgent in the quiet, cold night air. Running along the corridors, his heart pounding, the breath catching in his throat, pushing past the nurses, looking at Sarah's torn mouth, the tears seeping from the corners of her eyes. And crying then, sobbing into Emily's warm back, until the nurses slowly led him away.

36

Footsteps running across the wet road, leaves slippery under her feet. The distorted blare of a horn as a driver swerved to avoid her, his fist shaking at her face through his smeared windscreen. A stream of traffic, swishing carelessly through pools that spread from gutters blocked with more fallen leaves. Waves of murky water lapping up and over the footpath, catching her unawares. Rain dripping down her forehead, her hair sticking flatly to her skull and revealing its bony contours. A woman coming towards her, wearing a long gray coat like hers, the same kind of lace-up boots, carrying a bag that looked so familiar. But this woman was old, worn, her features twisted and distorted, her body hunched over as if in pain. Yet she moved as Anna moved, stopped when Anna stopped, lifted her hands to her mouth to hold back the cries of fear that burst involuntarily from her. And closed her eyes with the same kind of exhaustion as Anna, when she felt the cold glass of the long mirror in the ladies' toilet against her cheek.

IT WAS so bright inside the Stephen's Green shopping center. Light and sound bounced back from all the hard and shiny reflective surfaces. Anna sat at a small round table on the second-floor balcony. She looked up at the domed glass ceiling high above her. Outside all was blackness. Inside all was brightness. Outside it was as cold and empty as outer space. Inside it was warm and comforting, flooded with music and conversation, the sound of tills opening and closing, the rattle of cups on saucers, glasses on marble countertops. She picked up her drink and took a deep swallow. It was Black Bush, the label on the bottle behind the bar beckoning, comforting her with its familiarity, reminding her of David. He always used to drink it on Christmas Eve. They'd go to Midnight Mass at St. Bartholomew's, and come home and eat mince pies and have a couple of glasses before bed. Or they used to. Last Christmas had been different. She'd waited for him, but he hadn't come. So she went by herself, the tears streaming down her face as she sang. She stayed up till late, then fell asleep on the sofa. And he had woken her. She smiled now when she remembered it. He had been wearing a red Santa hat, and he had pulled her to her feet, and pushed her up the stairs, saying, "Time for bed, or Santa won't know where to find you."

He had smelled, she remembered, of alcohol and something else. A strange, bitter, chemical scent, but before she could ask him what it was he was already asleep, passed out fully dressed beside her. And the next morning he had been all contrition, the apologies flowing from him like a soothing balm. Why had she always believed him? She couldn't understand it now. Zoë had been right, after all. She had said to her more than once, sometimes with anger, sometimes just with an exasperated acceptance, "You don't live in the real world, do you? You haven't a clue how people conduct their lives. If they were insects you'd know everything about them. What they ate, how they mated, where they laid their eggs, how they raised their young, how and when they would die. And yet you have no curiosity about human nature. It means nothing to you. You haven't a notion."

Anna drank again. But now there was no warmth or comfort as the whiskey spread through her body. She felt sick. And remembered the bundle of cells, dividing, dividing, dividing within her. Growing, taking her over. Forcing her to protect them, even if she didn't want to.

She looked at her watch. It was seven forty-five. She had left the negatives she had found at the One Hour Photo shop on the floor below. They would be ready in half an hour. She put down her glass and reached into her bag. She took out the scrapbook. She opened it.

Death notices. Four of them.

1 January 1983. Christopher Walsh, beloved youngest son of Brian and Joan.

25 May 1988. Liam Ward, dear son of Peadar and Éilis, and fiancé of Máire.

16 August 1992. Adam Matthew Makepiece, adored husband of Charlotte.

9 April 1997. David Sebastian Neale, sorely missed by his beloved wife, Anna.

She stood up, involuntarily. Her hand swept across the table, knocking her glass to the floor. Faces turned towards her. Curious, alarmed. A babble of voices.

"Are you all right?"

"Can I help?"

"Let me give you a hand."

But she brushed away all concern and knelt down to pick up the shards of broken glass, piling them into a sticky heap, then taking the dustpan and brush offered by the barman and sweeping them together.

"I'm so sorry," she said, "so silly of me, so clumsy."

THE CAROUSEL of photographs shuffled mechanically forward. Each print hung limply like a butterfly's new wings. She peered in through the plate-glass window and watched them. She walked up and down, waiting. Her bag felt heavy, as if there was a large stone weighing it down. She rummaged inside, checking that the scrapbook was still there. She looked up at the huge Perspex clock suspended from the glass roof. Twenty minutes more.

She put the headphones of her Walkman into her ears. She inserted the tape marked "1." She listened. The crowd flowed around her, like river water avoiding a fallen branch. Backwards and forwards she walked, her feet stepping precisely on the shiny tiled floor.

Don't step on the cracks, you'll break your back. Was that what the kids in school used to say? She changed the tape. She listened again. Her reflection swam up in front of her in a shop window. Her hair had begun to dry. Fine fair tendrils stood up around her pale face. There were deep shadows under her eyes. She was so tired. It's the thing within me, she thought. Secreting progesterone, tranquilizing me, making me sleepy and passive, so I'll conserve my energy. Save it all for the incubus that he has laid there.

She looked at her watch again. Soon it would be time. She changed the tape again. And heard this time a woman's voice she recognized. She listened, saliva filling her mouth so she had to pull a tissue from her pocket and spit into it.

Ten minutes more. She felt in her bag again, and took out the tape labeled "4." She listened. Suddenly her body sagged. She lurched from side to side, her careful path disrupted. She stared at her plate-glass self. She wanted to walk into it, and smash it, destroy what she saw in front of her, as completely as the sounds she heard in her ears were destroying everything else.

She pulled the headphones from her ears. She looked up again at the clock. It was time.

THE MUSEUM was dark. No lights anywhere. She let herself in through the side door. The guard raised an eyebrow as he wrote her name in the book, noting the time.

"Working late?"

"Never stops. Got a paper to finish for O'Dwyer. You know what he's like."

She switched on the lamp in her office. She would be safe here, in this room that was more familiar to her than any other, her books and papers around her, the copper tap's rhythmic dripping in the square enamel sink in the corner. She dropped her coat and shawl in a pile on the floor and lined up her treasures on the desk. The cassette tapes, the photographs, the scrapbook, the notebook. Where would she begin?

With David, of course. The last set of pictures. She laid them out in front of her. And put her hands over her eyes, unable to bear what it was she was seeing. David, backed against the wall, his hands up, palms facing out, his face contorted. David on his knees, begging, his hands clasped as if in prayer. David, bent over so his head touched the floor, his arms spread out on either side. David with his mouth open, his eyes shut tight, like a child waking suddenly from a nightmare, one hand clutching the opposite shoulder, the other hand held out as if to protect himself. David, ripping his shirt from his body. And what was that she could see? She picked up her magnifying glass, and held it over the photograph. It was the gold watch, still in his pocket, the one her father had left her, that she had given to David on their wedding day. She began to sob, moans of fear welling up from her throat, as she looked at the last of the pictures. David, the way she had found him. Lying with his eyes wide open, and an expression that she did not have the words to describe carved on his face.

She picked up the phone, leafing through her diary, looking for the numbers she knew she had written somewhere. Her voice shook as she asked for Sergeant Murray.

"He's not on duty now. Can anyone else help you?" She hung up without replying. There was another number he had given her. His mobile phone. She punched in the digits, and heard a neutral recorded voice: "The number you have dialled is unavailable. Please leave a message after the tone." She opened her mouth to speak. Her lips were so dry that barely a sound would come out.

"Please, Sergeant Murray, I need you. Please help me. I'll phone again later."

Footsteps outside in the corridor. A knock on the door. The handle rattled. Her heart leaped in her breast like a trapped frog.

"Would you like a cup of tea, Anna? We've just brewed up."

"No, really, I'm fine, thanks."

There was a pause. Then, "Well, if you change your mind, the kettle's just boiled downstairs."

She waited until there was silence again, then she went back to the scrapbook. Newspaper reports of the four deaths. Photographs of the deceased and their families. Reports of the inquests. The coroner's verdicts. And a face she recognized. Younger, his hair long, but still the same glossy brown. The same thin face and dark eyes, and a lift to his head that reminded her of the seals her father used to take her to see, out past the islands in the bay. The man she knew as Matthew Makepiece, the same name as the man who had suffocated beneath a mound of clay. The man the newspaper called Michael Mullen, who stood beside the woman called Charlotte, the same woman who had come to see her that night, who had told her about David and the child. The man who was the friend of Christopher Walsh who had drowned in the canal, the employer of Liam Ward who had died in a fire. Who was, she realized, the man with whom David had begged and pleaded for his life. That she had heard on the tape marked "4." Who was the reason that David had said, "I'll give you whatever you want. You can have the house, anything, I promise, I'll pay you back. I'll make it up to you. You can have her. Do you want her? Anything, just don't do this. Please, Michael, I beg you."

She opened the notebook. Inside the cover the word "Sightings" was printed in small neat handwriting. She turned the pages. The entries were precise, clear and simple. He had been watching her and the other women too. For years altogether. She thought of the telescope on the balcony. What had he said to her, all those months ago when they first met in David's house?

"There's a wonderful view. I can see for miles in every direction."

And what he couldn't see he imagined.

She stood up and went over to the window. She leaned her head against the cold glass. And felt, as she moved, the locket that still hung between her breasts. She took it off and opened it, looking closely for the first time at the insect cocooned. She leaned over to her desk and picked up her magnifying glass. She held it over the silver shape. And saw the male dance fly, *Hilara maura*. Who wraps his dead prey in silk and presents it to the female, mating with her while her attention is distracted. While she is still fascinated with his courtship gift. And will not resist him.

37

Billy was good at waiting. He had learned the skill early on in life. How to wait, how to be patient. But now it seemed that the only thing he was waiting for was to die.

They had put him on a whole pile of new drugs at the clinic.

"It's really important, Billy," the nice nurse who smelled of chewing gum and cigarettes said, "that you remember to take all your pills at the correct times. You can't afford to miss them. If you remember, and do as we're telling you, chances are that you'll stay healthy, and who knows, in years to come maybe someone will find a cure and then you'll be completely better."

But he didn't believe her. Besides which the drugs made him feel sick. Rotten in his stomach. Like when he was a little boy and he had a passion for Jaffa cakes, the ones with the stuff that tasted like oranges in the middle, and he ate too many. Ma Mullen in the shop gave them to him, taught him how to play the whistle, rewarded him with biscuits when he remembered her favorite tunes.

"Play them for me, Billy, 'The Drunken Landlady' and 'The Blackberry Blossom' and the slow air I love the best, 'Mo Mhuirnín Bán'—My Fair-Haired Love." Until he was dizzy from the music, and sick from the sweetness of the biscuits.

Nothing they could do for him in the hospital could make him feel better. He wanted Anna, but it seemed like weeks since he had last seen her. Walked with her, felt her long legs and arms beside his, as his hand gently cupped the bones of her elbow and his nostrils were filled with the sweet scent of her hair and her breath. She had promised him that she would bring back some water from the holy well near her aunt's house in the country. She had said that everyone believed that it worked, that it restored sight. She wasn't sure herself, she said. As a scientist she couldn't really believe in miracles, but there was always the power of the mind over the body. And, anyway, it was lovely water, clean and pure. There would be no harm in it. But she hadn't done what she had said, and now she was gone from him. She hadn't told him who it was she had left him for. But he knew. He'd recognized the voice of the man who had been waiting for her one day when she had come to see him. He had tried to tell her that day on the train, tried to warn her. But he was frightened of Michael, once his pimp, now his boss. The person he feared above all others. Now he had Anna too. And she didn't want Billy any longer.

Billy couldn't understand why. It must be, he thought, that she had found out about the virus and she was scared of catching it. Maybe her friend, the teacher with the little boy who was also HIV-positive, had told her that they had met in the clinic. That she had recognized him, and come over to say hello, that the little boy had played with Grace.

Anna's friend, Zoë she said was her name, had told him that the boy had got it from contaminated blood, given to him for his hemophilia. She didn't ask him how he got it. But of course, she wouldn't. No one ever asked that question. But if Anna found out, she would want to know. And what would he tell her? That it was all the fault of Michael Mullen. Who had come to live with his granny when his mother in England died. Who first began to slip things into his bag when he was going on the bus to the school for the blind. Little parcels that someone, he didn't know who, would take from it as it hung on its peg in the cloakroom. Michael Mullen who gave him a place to stay when Billy's mother who couldn't cope anymore had disappeared. Put him up in his granny's back kitchen, telling the social worker who came to visit that he was doing fine, that he didn't need any help, that he didn't want to go into a special residential unit. Sure, wasn't it best for him to be with people he knew, and who knew him? Billy had smiled as he listened to Michael's voice.

"My understanding, and of course, correct me if I'm wrong, is that in the majority of cases, institutions, no matter how well-meaning, cannot replace the love and affection that the family unit or even, as in this case, the surrogate family unit can supply. Billy has lived in these streets all his life. He is an intrinsic part of the fabric of the community. A close-knit community as I'm sure you're aware. What on earth is to be gained by removing him?"

He listened while Michael started talking about books he had read, quoting names and case studies, until eventually the social worker conceded defeat.

"Fine, okay, as long as you're prepared to continue caring for Billy as you are now, he can stay. There will, however, be regular fortnightly visits. And if we feel that his situation is deteriorating in any way, physical, emotional, psychological, we will of course take steps to remedy it. Is that understood?"

How Michael had laughed. Particularly when he heard that they themselves had become part of the fieldwork in some thesis the social worker was writing.

"Do you hear that, Billy? We're going to be responsible for making that arsehole a doctor. A doctor of fucking social science, whatever that is. You and me. A winning combination."

It was good when Michael was happy. The world was a warm, loving place, full of nice food to eat, and music to play, and a feeling of belonging, of being part of a family. He liked it best on winter evenings when they were alone together. Michael would get a big fire going, roaring up the chimney, with so much heat coming out of it that Billy would have to sit back and away, turning first one side, then the other to the flames. But Michael would sit right beside it, at a small round table. He'd be quiet, sometimes humming one of his granny's tunes under his breath. And there'd be the sound of the blade on the chopping board. Cutting up the smooth slabs of hash that smelled like dried grass on a summer's day. Making the ten-pound deals. Getting more for his money. Always beside the fire, so, Billy knew, if there was any commotion at the door he could just fuck the lot of it into the flames and that would be that.

Not that it ever happened. Michael was too clever for any of them. The cops, or the other operators. Michael had it up top. That's what he'd say to Billy, and he'd bang his knuckles down hard on Billy's skull. "Do you hear that, Billy? Hollow. Not like mine. Mine's full to the brim."

And then there were other nights when Michael would have all his mates around. Steve and Gabriel and Joey and the ones whose names Billy never knew. There'd be cans of lager and bottles of vodka and whiskey. And there'd be joints passing around and as the night wore on someone would sit beside him and an arm would go around his shoulders, and a hand on his leg. And then they'd go into the front room, and Billy would stay there and wait for the next and the next and the next. Not Michael, though. Michael didn't do that. Not that Billy would have minded. He loved Michael, then, in those days. And then Michael started taking him out, to other parties that he went to, and from there somehow all the other stuff started to happen. The trips to Phoenix Park, cold nights along the Quays, the noise and smoke and smell of the bars they visited.

Billy thought Michael would never leave him, but Michael was moving on. "You'll be all right, Billy, don't worry. I've been onto that guy again, you know Mr. Ph. fucking D. He owes me. He'll fix you up in a flat right in the middle of town. You've got your dog now, and I'll still have work for you, as much or as little as you want or need. It's better this way, really."

But it wasn't. Not really. And the time had come to do something about it. He stepped outside onto the balcony. There was a smell of baking coming from the direction of

Winnie's front door. He knocked three times and waited. Tomorrow or the next day they would go on a little trip, Winnie, Grace and himself. Out on the train to Howth. He would be able to smell the sea and hear the sound of the wind pushing the waves up against the wall. Then he would hear a car door slamming, and the sound of footsteps. And a voice would call out to him, "Hallo Billy, and how are you today?"

"I'm fine, grand," he would say.

They would sit down, the three of them, on one of the wooden benches there beside the harbor. And the voice would say, "So, tell me why you've dragged me all the way out here, Billy. What is it I can do for you?"

"It's not what you can do for me, Mr. Murray, it's what I can do for you."

He smiled as he thought of it, and he knocked louder this time on the old lady's door.

38

Michael sat in the dark and waited too. He leaned back into his chair and lifted a glass of wine to his lips. He watched the lights of the cars on the road that led from the city. Even now at this late hour they flowed ceaselessly beneath his windows, a constant stream of gold and crimson. He lifted his gaze and looked for the outline of the hills against the sky. It was barely visible, but soon the winter sun would begin to struggle towards the horizon and he would see clearly the familiar undulations. Soon he knew the phone would ring, and one of his people would tell him what must be done. Meanwhile, he sat and drank and thought of what had come to pass.

What was it that Gabriel's son had said to his teacher? Something about how trust was when you paid the hit man before he did the job. That was it. Michael had laughed when Gabriel told him, that night the marchers arrived at the house. Gabriel didn't think it was funny. "You shouldn't be saying things like that to outsiders," he said to the kid, and gave him a belt across the back of his head, and kept him out of school even though the kid had cried and said he wanted to go, until Gabriel hit him again, and the kid shut up.

Who to trust, that was always Michael's biggest dilemma. He had wanted to trust Anna. About everything. But he had to be sure. So he had tested her. For a while she resisted. She wanted to believe, he knew, that he was the person she thought he was. So unlike her husband. Warm and loving and different. No past hanging over him. No secrets. And maybe if she hadn't seen him out there in the house in Swan's Nest everything would have been as she had wished. That was the biggest test, and the one she failed. She didn't know that he had been here in the apartment block the whole time, waiting for her to come. Sitting in the little office behind the front desk, watching all the pictures from the security cameras. He had seen her face as she waited for the lift. He had watched her as it rose higher and higher. He had seen the panic, the terror. There was a button somewhere among all the others that Dessie had on the console in the office. If Michael had pushed it he could have stopped the lift dead, between floors. That would have been fun. But he didn't. He let her go right to the top. And picked her up again in the bedroom, saw her open the box, play the tape, watched her reaction. Switched over to the camera in the corridor, watched her go up the stairs into the attic. Waited for her to find the light switch, then watched how she responded. She could barely stand she was so frightened, especially when she saw her dress, and the way he had carefully stitched it back together again. That was a good touch. He was glad he'd bothered to pick it up from the bedroom in the house in Anglesea Road where she had left it.

And it was then that he left Dessie's little room and got

into the lift and rode up and up to the fifteenth floor. And that was the only moment in the time he had known her that she really surprised him. He had thought to confront her there and then, as she came down the steps. He would be waiting and it would all be over very quickly. But she didn't come. He couldn't quite believe it. She had gone through the fire door and down the outside staircase. He opened the door after her and stepped out onto the metal platform. A wind was blowing from the northeast, and it flattened his hair against his forehead and caught at his trouser legs. Down below, the bare branches of the trees crashed together like reindeer's antlers at the rutting season, and the lights from the street jigged between them, casting shadows that jumped from place to place. His first instinct had been to follow her down those twisting metal steps, but he slowed himself down, calmed his breathing. No, better to wait. There weren't many places she could go. He knew them all. He could cover them all. He had the people and the contacts. Far better to stay here, make a few phone calls and wait.

He got up, went into the kitchen and took another bottle from the cupboard. He broke the surface of the cork with the sharp, pointed end of the corkscrew. Then he pushed hard and twisted. He had never killed anyone like this. But of course he had never actually killed. He had put in place the necessary circumstances. He had stood by and watched. The closest he'd come was that night in David Neale's house. He'd watched him as he opened the padded envelope, leaned with his back against the door so he couldn't get out of the room that had become his place of execution.

But he was curious. He'd seen a television program once: Ukrainian peasants who had been used by the Nazis to exterminate the Jews in their own village. One of the men, elderly now, was asked why he did it and what he felt. And he said, "It's a kind of curiosity. You're not sure what will happen, but you pull the trigger and the man just falls."

So simple. You pull the trigger and the man just falls.

You stand by the canal and you watch as your friend's lungs fill with water and drag him down.

You see your enemy lying asleep on the bed, and you light the cigarette and drop it. You smell the smoke as you walk away, but you just keep walking. He doesn't scream or cry out because he is already unconscious.

You watch the load of earth bury your rival. You know that it is filling his nose and mouth with sticky clay, so his airways are blocked, and he can make no sound. His arms and legs are immobilized and he cannot free himself.

You watch the bee circle and you see it land. There's a cry, then the man who was once your mentor and confidant falls. His blood pressure collapses, and his heart stops pushing oxygen through his blood vessels to his brain. Five minutes later he's dead.

Michael jerked the cork from the mouth of the bottle. He walked back into the sitting room. He sat down and filled his glass. And waited for the phone to ring.

MURRAY WAS awake too. He stood in the corner of the room where Sarah lay and listened to the sound of her breathing. She was sedated. She wouldn't wake for hours. Beside her in a low cot Emily was also asleep.

Sarah had been questioned. She told them everything she could. She had been making up a bed in an unoccupied private room at the far end of the ward. She saw a masked face reflected in the window. Before she could turn around she was forced to the ground and raped from behind. A gloved hand kept her mouth shut. No words had been spoken. No weapon had been used. She had been bound and gagged and left in the bathroom. It was four hours before she was found.

No one in the hospital had seen anything unusual. It was a busy night. A pileup on the Stillorgan road, a fire in Dun Laoghaire. As many people as possible had been questioned. Tomorrow the net would be cast wider. Meanwhile Sarah lay flat on her back, her stomach a gentle rise beneath the hospital quilt.

The doctor had said that no damage had been done to the baby, as far as they could see. "We'll get the bastard who did this to you, I promise, Sarah." Murray knelt beside her, holding her hand. She did not speak, just looked at him with an expression of such hurt that he could not return her gaze.

"We'll keep you in overnight," the doctor said, "just to make sure that your pregnancy isn't compromised. All right, Sarah?"

She nodded and still did not speak, but when they came towards her with a hospital gown and began to take off her own soiled uniform, she said, clearly and distinctly, "You do it, Alan, please, I don't want anyone else to touch me."

He waited beside her until she was asleep, standing uneasily looking out of the window, then lay down on the bed, cradling her head in the crook of his arm, listening to the sound of her breath. Until he too slept.

THE PHONE rang. It was as Michael had predicted. Now he drove slowly through the rain-soaked streets. Solid, Victorian Dublin. Redbrick, semidetached, bay windows upstairs and downstairs. Occasionally a moment of Gothic folly. Like the house he now stopped in front of. It was taller than the others in the road, with a mansard roof and dormer windows, and a small clock tower over what had once been the stables. He pushed past the overflowing rubbish bins, walked through the front gate and around the side of the house to the back. He pulled a bunch of keys from his pocket and let himself in. The corridor was dark, lit only by a lamp on a low table. Four doors led from it. Three were closed. He listened. Music was playing faintly in the distance. He could smell perfume, air freshener, scented oils. He peered around the open door. A fire was burning in the grate. The room was warm and comforting. A woman sat beside the fire, and another lay sleeping on the sofa. He walked forward slowly.

"Hello, Charlotte," he said. "Is everything all right?"

Charlotte looked up at him. She smiled. "Absolutely fine."

"It happened as I thought?"

"Just as you thought."

"How is she?"

"Exhausted, frightened, angry."

"Pity to wake her."

"A pity, but we need her out of here, she's interfering with business."

"And is it good tonight?"

"Never better."

He leaned over and kissed her on her cheek. "Thank you, I'll remember this."

"Will you?"

"Of course, I never forget a favor."

He knelt down beside the sofa and touched the sleeping woman's hair.

"She's so pretty, isn't she? Such a sweet thing." His finger traced the line of her nose and rested on her upper lip.

Anna stirred and moved, then slowly opened her eyes. She looked at him, then towards Charlotte. "But you know what I told you." She pushed herself back and away from Michael's hand. "What he did to your husband, and how he used you. How he has continued to use you. You know this now."

Charlotte bent over and put a twisted piece of paper into the fire. She waited for a moment until it caught, then held it to the tip of her cigarette. The planes and angles of her face were crudely highlighted in the sudden flare of yellow.

"I've always known," she said, "always. And I told you before. There's only one love in my life. And it's over-powering. I would do anything for it."

HOME WAS what the man Anna had known as Matthew called the place to which he took her. The rectangles of light that looked down over the park and across to the house where she had once lived with David. He held her arm as they walked across the foyer and she twisted in his grasp and tried to attract the attention of the doorman who was sitting behind his desk, a magazine spread out in front of him.

"Is it Dessie you want to talk to, is that it?" The man she had known as Matthew led her across to him, leaning over to pat his shoulder as he said, "How's it going, mate? Everything all right tonight?"

Dessie smiled, nodding and giving him a thumbs-up sign.

The man she had known as Matthew turned back to her and said, "Dessie and me, we go way back," as he pulled her towards the open doors of the lift. And home.

She had never realized before how secure the apartment was. Up high on the top of the building. A lift that could be locked into place. Windows through which she dare not look, let alone venture. And the twisting spiral staircase with its impenetrable metal door, bolted shut and padlocked now at the top and bottom. The trapdoor to the attic was nailed tightly shut. He twisted her head, catching her just under her ears with his thumbs, to look up at it.

"Who are you?" she said. "Who are you really?"

He smiled and took her arm to lead her back to the sitting room. "It depends on the circumstances. My old friends, like Dessie there down below," and he pointed to the ceiling rose above, "who's watching us now—wave to him, go on—and who can watch us in every room if I want him to, Dessie knows me as Michael Mullen. But the people from whom I buy property and to whom I sell property, they know me as Matthew Makepiece. Your husband knew me as both. He approved. He thought it was fun."

"So you did know him."

"Ah, yes, I knew him well. I knew all his little secrets."

"And why did you kill him?"

"I didn't kill him. The bees did that."

"Stop." She jerked her arm from his hand. "How dare you carry on like this now? I know what you did, not just to David but to all the others. And what you did to those women. The same thing you did to me. You're disgusting. Revolting. Obscene."

She flung herself at him, hitting out with her fists, kicking, reaching up to scratch his face and tear at his hair. He was laughing at first, putting his hands up to ward off her blows, falling backwards, his legs weak. Until she began to hurt him, her fingernails gouging skin from his cheeks, the toe of her boot connecting with his kneecap. He lunged at her, then hit her hard across the face so that her mouth filled with blood, and grabbed her by the scruff of her neck, forcing her towards the windows, wrenching them back and dragging her out onto the balcony, pushing her from behind so her body was half lifted up and over the iron balustrade while she screamed and screamed, her legs and arms flailing uselessly. He could smell her fear. She stank of it. It reminded him of the way her husband had smelled that night all those months ago. He had wet himself, a dark patch suddenly appearing on the front of his trousers. So funny to see him like that. The great David Neale. Exposed for what he really was. A cheat and a coward. Begging for mercy, promising him everything, anything. Even his wife.

She was crying, too, and screaming. He pushed her just a bit more so her body bent farther over the rail. He twisted his hands around her arms. She was cold, icy to the touch. David had been cold too, but pouring with sweat, drops rolling down his forehead. Michael had offered him his handkerchief, a nice folded linen one, and David had wiped it over his face and around his neck inside his collar. He had even wiped his forearms with it. It was perfect. So when Michael opened the box and the bees flew out, the first thing the queen did was to head for the scent that only she could smell. The perfume of queen substance. I couldn't smell it, he thought, David Neale couldn't smell it, but the queen bee could. It had been all over the handkerchief, and now it was all over David Neale's skin. The queen did what all queens do. She killed her rival. Her long hypodermic syringe pumping venom into him.

It was the chemist, Beaker they all called him, after the character in the Muppets, who had come up with it. He had been a friend of Adam's. He could make speed, ecstasy, acid. So Michael had shown him the formula for the queen substance. Trans-9-keto-2-decenoic acid.

"Can you make this?" he had asked him. "There'll be a bonus in it for you."

And Beaker had pushed his glasses to the top of his head and said, "Sure, no problem, piece of cake, man."

"Stop, stop. Don't do this. Matthew, Michael, don't do this." Her voice caught in her throat.

"Why not? Why shouldn't I?"

"Because."

"Because why?" He shook her, feeling how she was beginning to slide from his grasp.

"Because," she screamed at him, "because I'm pregnant. I'm having your baby."

"You're what?" His grip slackened for a moment. She began to move, away from him, gravity dragging her headfirst towards the ground.

"Your baby, I'm having your baby. Please, believe me." Her voice came from her mouth in sobbing gasps.

"Why should I believe you? Give me a reason."

"Why should I lie? If it wasn't true I would have no reason to want to live. Not after what you've done to me."

He leaned forward and wrapped first one arm then the other around her waist. He pulled and pulled, until she was there in front of him, her legs collapsing underneath her as she sank onto the balcony's tiled floor.

He walked away and inside. He sat down on the sofa and watched as she crawled in after him. Her face was white and streaked with tears. She looked old and frail as she curled herself up in a ball and lay with her arms wrapped around her legs, shaking and sobbing.

A baby, of his very own. And she was carrying it inside her. The last thing she would want. But it was there in spite of her wishes. And he would keep her alive. Until the day came when it would burst from her. Then she would be of no further use and he would discard her. Fling her to one side like the skin of an orange or the empty shell of a nut.

He stood up and went into the kitchen. He made tea, carefully, the way she liked it. He poured her a cup and added sugar. For shock. He walked back into the sitting room, and smiled at his reflection in the long dark windows. Yes, he liked the idea. That was the way it would be. And all he would have to do was wait.

39

"Tell me again, Billy, let's get this all straight, right from the beginning. Tell me everything you know."

It was bitterly cold by the sea at Howth. Billy and old Winnie and Grace had been early for Sergeant Murray. Winnie had said they should go into the café by the DART station to wait, but Billy wouldn't. He wanted to stay out in the open, away from anyone he didn't know. So they walked towards what Winnie said was the harbor. It was very noisy, the wind making everything rattle and bang and clang.

"What is it? What's that clinking, tinkling sound?" Billy grabbed hold of Winnie's furry sleeve.

"It's the rigging in the yachts, that's what it is."

"And what's rigging and what's yachts?" She tried to explain and he tried to understand. If he stood with his arms outstretched and his coat unbuttoned he knew how the wind would fill it and make him rock backwards and forwards, unbalanced. Imagine moving like that across vast stretches of water, with nothing in the way to stop him. The thought made him feel sick and a little bit dizzy.

They walked closer to the edge of the pier. The sound was different here. There was less of an echo from the hard stone, and he could hear the slap, suck, slap, suck of the sea against the walls. And there was a smell that caught in the back of his throat.

"Is that fish?" he asked, standing still for a moment, his feet planted squarely, his nostrils widening in the breeze.

"That's right. The timbers of these old boats are saturated with the blood and guts and oil of cod and haddock and mackerel and whiting."

It was Murray's voice he heard now above the frantic clanging and the eerie whistle as the wind rushed in from the sea. Billy turned around. He was confused. He hadn't heard any of the usual sounds, the car door banging, footsteps getting louder as they came closer. He didn't like it here now. His hand tightened on Winnie's sleeve. Why was he doing this? It was wrong. He'd be in trouble when Michael found out. And he would find out, he'd know who it was who'd done the damage.

But it was too late for all that. He'd made his mind up. And he was worried about Anna. He'd gone looking for her. First to the house on the canal, but when he rang the doorbell it was a workman who answered. "The blonde girl from upstairs, is that who you're looking for? No, she's left. We're doing up her place now. Sorry."

And no one at the museum had seen her for a couple of days either. The security guard leaned down to rub Grace's ears, then straightened up and said, "No, we got a call to say she was sick. Flu or something. She won't be in for a while."

Murray took him by the elbow. "Why don't we sit in the car, out of the cold? Here," Billy heard the clink of coins passing from hand to hand, "you go off and have a cup of tea, love. He'll be all right with us."

"Us?" Billy's voice rose. "Who's with you?" He reached out and cast his arm around in a wide semicircle.

"Just a friend from work, Billy, I was going to introduce you. This is Danny Riordan. Here." Murray took Billy's hand and pressed another one into it. Billy felt a cold, hard grip, and a voice equally cold greeting him.

It was warm in the car. Billy and Grace sat in the back. Murray began the questions. Over and over, the same things, time after time.

"Tell me again, tell me again, it's important we get this right, tell me again."

It seemed like hours later that they finished. Billy heard the Angelus ring, but still they continued. The other man had got out of the car and come back with fish and chips and cans of Coke. And still they continued. Finally Murray said to him, "You'll come into Headquarters and sign a statement, won't you? You don't have to worry, we'll look after you, we won't let anyone hurt you."

Billy didn't answer.

It was the other man who spoke. "You have to do this, Billy. Everything you've told us, it's useless unless you swear to it. Do you understand what we mean?"

"Of course I do, I'm not fucking stupid." He put one hand on the door handle. The other grasped hold of Grace's harness. "I have to go now, my friend is waiting."

"Hold on a minute." It was the same man, Riordan, who spoke. Billy felt his breath in his face as he leaned forward.

"It's all right." The seat's upholstery squeaked as Murray pushed him away. "Whatever you like, Billy, that's fine by me. Go home and think about it, and I'll phone you later and see how you are. Okay?"

But it wasn't really OK. It wasn't what he wanted. He wanted to hurt Michael, up close, to hear him cry out with pain, to beg for forgiveness. This wasn't enough, this question-and-answer session that seemed to be going nowhere. He slammed the car door shut behind him, and tightened his hand around Grace's harness. They walked together in the direction of the station, and he heard Winnie's hesitant shuffle fall in beside them.

He rested his head on her shoulder as the train gathered speed towards the city again. He was so tired. He slept, just for a few minutes, woke and said to her, "I want you to get off at Pearse station and go home without me. There's something I have to do. On my own." She began to protest, but he put his hand against her mouth, gently, firmly. He listened to the sounds of the track beneath the wheels. He didn't know these stations on the north side of the city that well, but he could tell when they got to Pearse: the sudden change in sound as the train went in underneath the station's high glass roof, voices echoing around him as the doors slid open and passengers poured noisily into the carriage.

"Goodbye, Billy, I'll see you later." Old Winnie's wrinkled lips touched his cheek, and she was gone. He put his hand in his coat pocket and took out his tin whistle. He began to play, jigs, reels, dance music, his left foot tap, tap, tapping, in time to the tune. And then one of Ma Mullen's slow airs. She loved it when he played them for her. He could feel her big hand on his head, smoothing down his hair. "You're my Mo Mhuirnín Bán, aren't you, my little lad?"

He was excited by the time he got to Dun Laoghaire. He hurried Grace along the familiar seafront walk, the wind tearing at his hair and making his eyes water and sting. Steve would be surprised to see him, he thought. He hadn't been out here for a while now. He'd be wondering what he wanted. And when Billy told him what he'd done he'd be angry. But he'd do what Billy wanted, take him where he had to go. And he wasn't frightened of any of them now.

He could hear Steve's voice already, shouting at him. "What the fuck did you do that for? You stupid cunt. You're not going to make any kind of a fucking statement to the cops. Are you? And you want to see the boss, do you? Well, I tell you, he's going to want to see you, that's for sure."

One arm around his waist, Steve marched him outside, his feet half lifting from the ground, then pushing him into the back of the van. Steve drove fast. Everything shook and rattled. Billy sat on the floor, holding on to Grace. He listened to the traffic all around them, but after a while the road began to get much more quiet. Just the rumble of the tires on the rough surface beneath them, and the splatter of rain on the windows. He could just about hear Steve's voice on the phone, the anger in his tone, but not the words he was saying. He was sure it was Michael he was talking to. He leaned his head on Grace's rough back. He could feel her heart beating slowly and steadily beneath his cheek. "I love you, Grace," he murmured. "You're my true sweetheart, aren't you?"

The dog turned her head and rested her nose, cold and wet, on his forehead.

Billy was calm and controlled by the time the van stopped. He breathed slowly, deeply. He wiped his palms on his trousers and put one hand in his coat pocket. He was ready. He hummed the tune of Anna's hymn under his breath.

> *He who would valiant be,*
> *'Gainst all disaster,*
> *Let him in constancy*
> *Follow the master.*
> *There's no discouragement*
> *Shall make him once relent.*
> *His first avowed intent*
> *To be a pilgrim.*

"Get the dog and come on."

"No, Grace stays here."

"Okay, whatever." Steve took him by the arm and began to pull him forward. Billy shook himself free.

"Take your fucking hands off me." He pulled himself up to full height and took his comb from the inside pocket of his jacket. He ran it through his hair. He straightened the knot of his tie. It was important that he look right, today of all days. He could hear Steve's feet ahead of him, first on gravel, which slipped and slid beneath their shoes, then clipped and staccato as he walked up a flight of steps. The stone was hard and unyielding. Billy paused at the top and turned back, the wind cold on his face. He breathed in through his nose, smelling the countryside. Wet earth, wet grass, and above his head the melancholy sob of a crow.

"Come on, for Christ's sake, let's get this over." Steve tugged him forward, their footsteps loud on bare boards. It was as cold inside as it was outside. Billy stood still and waited. There was silence. Then the sound of leather soles and metal clips at heel and toe. A hand on his face. Fingers gripping his chin, digging into his cheeks. He raised his mouth and felt Michael's soft lips on his.

It happened so quickly that he wished he could have slowed it down so he could enjoy it more. But, of course, at the time, it had to be quick. Otherwise it wouldn't have worked so well.

His right hand was in his pocket, gripping the smooth haft of a penknife. Anna's knife, that she had left behind one day in his flat. She had used it to open a bottle of wine, and he had come across it when he tidied up his table afterwards. He had put it in his pocket and kept it. He knew it would come in handy one day. And this was the day.

Michael was pulling him closer and closer. And Billy was carefully opening the knife with one hand, as he had practiced and practiced. And then quickly, before Michael or Steve could see what he was doing, he lifted his hand and struck. He knew exactly where to aim. The neck. The only exposed piece of flesh on such a cold day. Three, maybe four inches between ear and shoulder. Arteries, veins, tendons. All contained so neatly. All vulnerable to

Billy and his penknife. He felt the point rest delicately against the skin, and pushed and twisted, then jerked it backwards and forwards and felt Michael's fingers loosen and fall away, and his blood pour out, warm, sticky, all over Billy's hand and arm. And as Michael dropped, so Billy went too, kneeling over him. Until with a roar like a wild thing Steve was on top of him, pulling him away and hitting him, hard, again and again, so that soon there were no more sounds, no more cold, no more anything.

NOTHING BUT the howling of the dog, the one long note, over and over, accompanied by frantic, urgent scrabbling of claws, muscular foot pads pushing against the van's metal door. And a bark, once, twice, three times, then back to the howling again.

"Will someone do something with that animal? Let it out. Anything. Just get it to shut the fuck up."

It was the doctor who said it, as she knelt beside the two blood-soaked bodies on the floor. It was hard, Murray thought, to believe that either of them could be alive. He hadn't been sure, when he got there, whose blood it was, and where it was coming from, they were both so drenched in it. He cursed himself, as he watched the doctor's dark head, bent over Mullen's milk-white face. It had never occurred to him that Billy Newman might do something like this. React with violence, anger, jealousy, all the emotions that sighted people possess. It was my prejudice, pure and simple, he thought. Deciding that the blind were helpless, passive, pathetic creatures incapable of taking the initiative. Why, he wondered, should Billy Newman's feelings be any different from his own? He looked down at Michael Mullen's inert body. He wanted to stand on his face and grind it to a pulp with his heel.

Billy lay beside him. The knife was still in his hand. Murray knelt down and pushed the hair back from his forehead. Billy's eyes were open. His skin was cold and damp. He was whispering something. Murray leaned down and put his ear against his mouth. He heard the words of the hymn: *"Valiant be . . . 'gainst all disaster . . . constancy . . . follow the master."*

Murray's father had sung it too. *The Pilgrim's Progress* was his bible. He knew most of it by heart. Bunyan was a real saint, he used to say. Forget about all your Catholic plaster gods. Bunyan knew where truth and honor really lay.

Billy cried out. His chest shuddered convulsively. Then he was still.

Murray stood up and walked away. He turned his face to the wall and covered his eyes, his palms flat against the hard bone beneath his eyebrows. How had he let this happen? He had known where Billy was headed. He knew Billy wanted to tell Michael what he had done. To show off, to rub his nose in it. And Murray had let him. Riordan had followed Billy and the old lady onto the train, and Murray had radioed ahead, calling for backup. He had driven out along the sea road to Dun Laoghaire, perfectly sure that everything was in order. Billy would take them to Michael Mullen. It was as simple as that.

"Hang back," he had said to Riordan, "hang back. Don't rush it."

But he hadn't reckoned on Billy. What he would do. Where he would lead them. To this wreck of a house near the Sugar Loaf, with its beautiful formal garden. Another of Michael Mullen's secrets.

And now Billy was dead. And still the dog howled. Murray walked down the steps and across the gravel to the van. He slid back the door, and Grace leaped up at him, her tongue lolling out of her mouth, then jumped down, running in wide semicircles, her nose sweeping just above the ground. He stood and watched her, as the ambulance men carried the two stretchers, awkwardly angled, out of the house. Billy's body was wrapped tightly in a plastic sheet. It looked like something that might have come from an Egyptian sarcophagus. Too small for an adult, the size of a prepubescent boy, and vulnerable, defenseless, despite its impermeable covering.

Murray looked for the dog. She was over at the side of the house, her nose still to the ground. She was whining softly, scratching at something with her left paw. Murray walked towards her and squatted down, his hand on her harness. The dog was standing on a large metal door, laid horizontally in the gravel. Murray took hold of the loop of rope that lay on top of it. He pulled and the door opened, falling back onto the ground with a loud bang. Beneath it were shallow steps and a sloping passage, which, he could see, ran towards the house. Grace whimpered, then pulled him with her, their feet scattering the fallen leaves that had piled up against the walls. It was cold and damp down here. Bare lightbulbs hung from the vaulted ceiling. Doors opened on either side, into small dark rooms like cubbyholes, filled with heaps of rubbish, stacks of empty milk and wine bottles, mounds of tin cans. The last door was closed, a heavy padlock snapped shut around the bolt. Murray lifted it up and it banged loudly. And a voice shouted, "Help me, please, let me out."

It was a voice he knew, screaming louder.

"Please, please, let me out. Don't keep me here in the dark. Please. I'll do anything you want. Anything."

A sledgehammer thudded against the lock, again and again. And as the door splintered, then burst open, he saw Anna, sitting on a camp bed, her hands and feet shackled, a bucket on the flagged floor beside her, and a beautiful silver box on a small table in front of her.

40

Days passed, weeks passed, months passed. And still it grew. The thing inside her. She had seen it, the murky swirls of light gray and dark gray that twitched and jerked in the scan's triangular beam.

"Look," the nurses said. "Isn't it wonderful?"

But she had turned her head away and saw only Michael's face, screaming with rage, as he answered the phone. That last day, out in the house in Wicklow.

"WHAT WILL you do now?" they all asked her, Zoë, Sergeant Murray, James, even Isobel, who had come to see her in the hospital where she had been taken.

She didn't know what to say to any of them.

They let her out to go to Billy's funeral. A beautiful day, bright and clear, mild even though it was the beginning of December.

"It's like one of St. Martin's days," the nurse said, as she helped her on with her coat and wrapped her berry-red shawl around her shoulders. And Anna remembered the story. How St. Martin had torn his cloak in two and given half to a beggar. And God had protected him, by giving him seven clement days until he could find himself another cloak to wear.

Sergeant Murray picked her up and drove her to the church on Westland Row. They were both silent, the radio on, music blocking out the noise of the traffic. The winter sunlight angled through the windows, warming her bare hands, which were clasped loosely in her lap. And then they heard the ten o'clock news.

"A Dublin man, Michael Mullen, with an address in Donnybrook, has been charged today at a special sitting of the Dublin District Court with the kidnapping and unlawful imprisonment of Ms. Anna Neale earlier this month. He has been remanded in custody pending further court appearances. Our crime correspondent says that further charges in relation to drug-trafficking offenses may be forthcoming. A second man, Steve Brennan from Dun Laoghaire, has been charged in connection with the death of Billy Newman, who died four days ago from injuries received in a brutal assault. Gabriel Reilly, from the Swan's Nest area of the city, has been charged with possession of a quantity of heroin with intent to supply others."

Murray glanced sideways at her. Her face was without expression. She had looked like that, he thought, ever since he had taken her from the basement of the old house out in Wicklow.

They sat up at the front of the church beside Winnie. Someone had brought Grace, and she pressed herself against Anna's legs, resting her heavy head on her knees. Anna stared at the coffin. She couldn't believe that Billy was inside it. She thought of him the way he always was, lying on his cushion in front of the fire, or standing on Grafton Street, his tin whistle in his hand. She wanted to hold him close and kiss his forehead. Tell him she was sorry that she had hurt him, that she had never meant to be cruel. Tell him how she missed him, how she would always remember him. She looked around her at the congregation, scattered thinly among the dark wooden pews. There were the old people from the flats, some of the regulars from the street, a slim woman with fair hair who looked familiar. Anna stared at her, trying to think where she had seen her before. Murray followed her gaze. "That's Billy's sister, Tessa."

"Oh."

"She saw his picture in the paper and contacted us. Apparently they'd lost touch. She hadn't seen him for years."

Lost touch, what an appropriate way to describe it, Anna thought, watching the woman as she stood and knelt and stood again, her hair flopping forward over her face, the way Billy's flopped over his. And remembered where she had seen her before. Among Michael's photographs, her small pallid body curled up on an unmade bed, her breasts little more than a gentle swelling beneath the dark knobs of her nipples.

She didn't go to the cemetery, the woman with the fair hair and the thin closed face. She slipped away after the Mass was over, her heels tapping neatly on the church's tiled floor. Anna watched her leave, and was glad. She didn't want to get too close to her, knowing what she knew. It would make her think again of Michael, feel again his hands on her body, and remember what he had done to her. And to the others.

THAT WAS months ago, that fine mild day, a brief respite before the Atlantic depressions flung their storms across the countryside. Christmas came and went. Anna spent it alone. Just her and the growing baby inside her. Isobel had asked her to come and stay, but she had said no. Zoë, too, had offered. But Anna wanted time, to settle into her new home, a flat at the top of one of the Georgian houses in Merrion Square. It belonged to the museum, the cold, quiet basement where once cook and kitchenmaids had labored, and the high-ceilinged rooms on the first and second floors used for storage. Crates of specimens, hundreds of thousands of insects, imperfectly cataloged, waiting to be assigned their place in the order of things. And high above them, looking out over the browns, grays and glaucous greens of the square's winter tapestry, the dusty, empty space where now she lived.

She could not have gone back to the house in Anglesea Road or the flat by the canal. Michael's property would be seized by the state. Part of the new anti-drug laws, Murray had told her. Besides which she could not have lived somewhere that Michael had been and left his mark. Invisible to her eye, it might have been like ultraviolet light, but still she would have known it was there and felt tainted, dirtied by the proximity. O'Dwyer had offered her the flat. Came to her when she was still in the hospital. Told her not to worry, that her job was always there, "No matter what," he said, reaching out to take her hand. Then said that if she needed somewhere to live, the old curator's residence was empty. He didn't want it, his wife wouldn't leave her garden, but she might like to move in. "Just until you've got yourself straight, m'dear. Of course," he continued, "it might not suit you, it's very far from the ground, up at the top of the house. It might upset you, in your, um, condition."

No, she had replied, and told him that she didn't mind any longer, that it didn't bother her the way it used to. So she spent Christmas making it her own, these rooms that offered her the possibility of a home. Moving the furniture until she was happy with her sitting room, her kitchen, her study, her bedroom. And the smaller one next door with a barred window that looked back over the gray and purple slate roofs of the city towards the gray and purple mountains to the west. Already painted white, with a small cast-iron fireplace, decorated with birds and flowers.

"You'll have to make up your mind soon," Zoë kept on warning her. "Don't leave it too late, you won't be able to do anything about it then."

But she couldn't decide. And still, inside her, it grew. Changing the shape and feel of her body, making curves where before there had been only flat planes. Filling her, in spite of herself, with a feeling of well-being and satisfaction.

She walked to Grafton Street on Christmas Eve in the late afternoon. All day long she had watched the traffic from her windows as it washed out of the city, like the neap tide of the winter solstice. She saw how the offices across the square closed down, their lights disappearing as, room by room, they were abandoned for the holidays. And when twilight and the mist of evening began to make the streetlights glow and glimmer like those on the huge Christmas tree she could see outside the National Gallery, she called Grace and put on her lead, walked down the three flights of stairs and out into the cold, calm air.

The pavement was wet underfoot, and slippery. A heavy dew and the beginnings of the frost, she thought, and watched where she placed her feet. She raised her eyes to the sky above the playing fields of Trinity College. It was gold streaked with bright pink and a tinge of pale green, the colors picked up and reflected back from the shop windows she passed, and the same colors on the Christmas decorations inside. And fewer and fewer people the closer she got to the city center.

Grafton Street was virtually empty, just the last stragglers lurching by, laden with carrier-bags and bunches of flowers. And more flowers, a small mound placed carefully in the spot where Billy used to stand. She bent down to look at them. White lilies, yellow chrysanthemums, a wreath of holly, bright with berries, red roses and bunches of freesias whose scent rose up to fill her nostrils. A candle flickered, grease making a waterfall shape down its side. Grace shuffled and sniffed too. She whined softly and pulled away. Anna stood still, her head bowed, the tears slipping down her cheeks.

Then she turned and faced the gentle slope that ran northwards past the front entrance of Trinity College and the Bank of Ireland, down to the river. On the other side of the Liffey the ground rose gradually again. At the top of the small incline stood Mountjoy Prison, and inside it the man responsible for all this suffering and hurt.

She began to walk with the dog by her side, their steps even and matched. The city was quiet and empty now, all the shops closed, hardly a car passing. The streets revealed themselves to her as if the buildings were natural structures, growing out of the ground, permanent and fixed forever. When she reached the river she stopped suddenly, as if a rope had been tied around her ankles and tugged hard. The water flowed slowly, sluggishly. It gleamed like a piece of black taffeta, with greens, reds, golds rippling through its warp and weft. O'Connell Bridge was empty. All was silent. She looked around. She and Grace were completely alone. She took a step forward and stopped again. Her heart fluttered and she felt sick and weak. It was no more than half a mile from here to the prison. Bricks, stones, metal separated them. But it was as if he were standing beside her. She could see the lift of his dark head, the shape of his eyes, his smile widening in greeting. She could feel the touch of his hand and smell his skin. The bridge yawned in front of her, a wide space, the traffic lights at either end changing automatically like Christmas decorations. She folded her arms across her stomach, then felt in her pocket for the card that had been waiting for her on the flagged hall floor that morning. She had slipped her finger under the flap of the envelope and felt fragments of glitter, rough against her fingertips. The card was handmade. A round and jolly Santa, crudely drawn with a red face and a huge sack, smiled up at her, strewing in front of him a path of silver and gold. She opened it and recognized the writing. It was small and neat, the letters carefully formed. Ten words, that was all: *Don't forget me, Anna. I'll be back. For my baby.*

Still it grew, the thing inside her. But now she could feel it, fluttering first of all, like a butterfly trapped inside a fist, then beating and banging with a tiny foot or elbow against her ribs. She lay awake at night, watching her belly shift in sudden rolling spasms from one side to the other. Waiting.

Until the night, or was it the early morning, when she woke and felt the first contractions, and knew that soon the waiting would be over. Ten more hours, the pain growing in intensity. They asked her in the hospital if she wanted someone to be with her. But she shook her head, catching her bottom lip with her top teeth, bending over with each contraction, squatting in the corner of her room, then walking backwards and forwards until the next pain came. Until she could move no longer and the nurses helped her onto the bed, as she pushed whatever was inside her out.

"Show me," she screamed at them, and they held him up to her, his body red and slippery, his dark hair matted with blood and mucus. They laid him on her stomach and she felt his skin next to her own, and began to cry, tears of sorrow that dripped down onto his crumpled face.

"I'm so sorry," she whispered into his small, creased ear. "I didn't want you, I didn't love you. But I'll make it up to you, I promise." And she held him to her breast, squeezing her huge brown nipple between her first and second fingers until he turned his mouth towards it and began to suck.

41

The birth notice was in the newspaper.

> NEALE—Anna, is delighted to announce the birth
> of a beautiful son, Julian Bartholomew, born 12th
> June, in the Rotunda Hospital, Dublin.

She cut it out and propped it up on the mantelpiece. She
sat in the rocking chair, the baby held close, and watched
the jades, emeralds, mottled verdigris of the square's summer coat. And at night half awake, half asleep, until the
sky turned to pearl-gray over the rooftops, the streetlights
faded and the song of the thrush and the blackbird ceded
to the urgent rumble of the city's morning traffic.

They all came to see her. Zoë and little Tom, James,
Isobel, wanting to stay, O'Dwyer and the others from the
museum across the road. And Alan Murray. He brought
plastic bags stuffed with baby clothes. "You might as well
have them. Our little lad is well grown out of them
already. And I think it's unlikely we'll be having any
more."

"Thank you, they're great." She tumbled the little tow-
eling suits, woollen cardigans, bonnets, mittens and multi-

colored socks out on the floor. "That's really kind of you. Your wife doesn't mind?"

"She suggested it. She's always asking me how you are. She's very anxious for your safety."

They were both silent. Anna kissed the top of the baby's head and curled her index finger into the palm of his hand.

"How is she these days?"

"Not great. Emily and the baby keep her busy during the day, but it's at night that it gets bad." Screams of fear and pain echoing through the house, until the doctor had prescribed sedatives that knocked her out so in the morning her face was white, her movements sluggish and uncoordinated. "If we'd been able to charge someone with it, she'd have felt better, I'm sure of it. She couldn't make an identification, and there was no available forensic evidence. I suppose I should be pleased that the guy used a condom, but if he hadn't at least we would have had that."

"And Emily, how's she?"

He smiled, then winced slightly, easing his shoulders inside his summer shirt. "She's wonderful, a bit too wonderful. She made me take her to the beach at Killiney yesterday. And I very stupidly lay down, took off my shirt because it was one of the few days this summer that the sun actually shone, and I promptly fell asleep. And when I woke I was burned, my poor white skin all pink. And it's so sore now."

"And Emily was all right?"

"Yeah, she was, perfectly. The funny thing about her is that although she has inherited my red hair, the rest of her coloring is her mother's, so her skin just gets lovely and golden when she gets out in the sun." He paused. "It's funny that, the way they get bits here and bits there, from both parents, and from each family too."

He stopped, a flush rising up his face. She was staring down at the baby. At the dark fuzz of hair on his head, and the opaque blue of his eyes.

He stood up. "I'd better go," he said, suddenly awkward.

She put out her hand and caught hold of his jacket. "You're not going away anywhere, are you? Not for the next few weeks?"

"No, I took all my leave when Sarah was pregnant."

"It's just, sometimes," she paused again and looked back down at the baby, "I like to know that I can get in touch with you."

HE THOUGHT about what she had said, later that night when he was in bed, Sarah fast asleep beside him. She had taken her pills. She would not stir now until the morning. He could picture Anna in those beautiful rooms high above the square, the baby on her knee. He wondered if he should make her move. Somewhere where there were more people around at night. A housing estate like this, with neighbors, other children, lots of sociable comings and goings. He would ring her in the morning and suggest it.

HE THOUGHT about it again, when he got the phone call, just after twelve o'clock the next day. The last thing he had expected or had wanted to hear. Mullen had been taken to the District Court, a hearing for a further remand. Routine, nothing special. But this time his barrister had made an application to the High Court for bail. They hadn't been prepared for it. They didn't have their objections in order, and the judge adhered to the letter of the law. Bail had been granted. The prosecution had stated that a man with Michael Mullen's history of violence could not be allowed out pending his trial, but the judge disagreed. Mullen had no convictions for crimes of violence, and the defense had given assurances that he would not attempt to make contact with any of the witnesses in the case. Given these circumstances, to deny him his freedom could be construed as a violation of his constitutional rights.

"You'd better get round to the girl." Inspector Farrell's voice was unusually high-pitched. "Get round there, and warn her. And you'd want to be keeping an eye on her. We don't want anything nasty happening."

SHE WAS like the tethered heifer, beautiful and white, that had once been the river nymph Io until Jupiter changed her shape to hide her from his jealous wife. She was the bait that Michael Mullen would not be able to resist. She lifted her head and gazed around. Watching the trees and shrubs shake and shiver. Was it a breeze? Was it something else? She was calm now. Waiting. Soon it would all be over. And she would have peace again.

had expected, or had moved on. Tom Alaline had been taken to the District Court. She had sat in the courtroom...

42

A heavy thundery shower darkened the sky. Hailstones crashed against the top windows and the roof, waking her from a drowsing nap in the rocking chair, the baby curled against her belly. She was hungry. She walked out onto the landing. Evening light flooded through the stained-glass skylight, casting squares of burnished gold and imperial purple across the white walls of the stairwell, and over the face of the man who had just climbed down through it and stood now in front of her, breathing heavily. Who reached out both his hands and took the baby from her arms, holding him to look at him, then bringing him close, resting his cheek against his soft skin, sighing deeply and saying, "He smells so good, he looks so lovely. And so do you."

The baby hiccuped a couple of times, small gasping sounds from his open mouth.

"Where have you been?" she asked. "It's more than two weeks since you got out. I thought you'd have come before this."

He didn't look well, she thought. He didn't look the way she remembered him. He seemed smaller, thinner. His hair was lank, without any shine, and his face was pale, smudged shadows under his eyes. His clothes were dirty, and there were dark ridges beneath his fingernails. When he turned away she saw the long, puckered scar that stretched from his neck underneath the collar of his shirt. But still when he smiled he was the same Matthew, and he smiled now, as he looked down at the baby in his arms. "Isn't he beautiful?" he said. "And do you know, he's the image of me when I was his age."

She sat where he told her to. In the rocking chair by the window.

"You just stay there and behave yourself and everything will be fine. I know they're watching. I've been watching them, too, for the past couple of days."

"You like that, don't you, watching people. How long did you watch me? And how much did you know about me?"

"Enough to know you'd be a pushover. And you were, too."

She twisted and turned in the chair, watching his hands around the baby's small body.

"You came through the attic. That was smart. They told me if you tried to get to see me it would probably be through the basement."

He smiled at her. "You know me, Anna. Always unpredictable. But I was surprised that they didn't know that the roof space in these old houses is open from one side of the square to the other. I was expecting to meet some kind of reception committee, but there wasn't a soul."

"So you've come for the baby?"

"That's right."

"And do you really think that I'm going to give him to you? Just like that. After all I've been through. After all the pain and suffering, the agony of the past year."

"What choice do you have, Anna? Remember where he came from. I put him there inside you, just like one of those insects you told me about. I put him there so he would be fed and nourished by you, so he would grow and get stronger and bigger. And now I want him back."

"You're mad," she said. "You're completely mad. You disgust me. But this is as far as it goes between us. You know that, surely. You killed my husband, and even worse, you made me betray his memory with you. You took everything from me, you took his future and you took our past together."

She made as if to get up from the chair.

"Watch it," he said. "Watch where I'm putting my hands."

He put his thumb and first finger over the baby's nostrils, and began to pinch them gently together.

"No, don't do that. Please, don't." She sank back down again.

"That's better, that's much better." He lifted the baby up and kissed him gently on his forehead, rubbing his chin against the fuzz of dark hair on the baby's head.

"You were saying, Anna, you were blaming me. But I didn't betray you. It was David who did that. He lied to you and cheated on you, and laughed at you. He did the same things to me too. You don't know how much I cared about him. He was my guide, my mentor, the man I wanted to be. And what did I discover? That he was stealing from me, abusing my trust. In the way that all the others abused trust too. I did you a favor, if you could only see it. And then you betrayed me too. So go on, tell me some more about how I disgust you. That's not what you said to me before, is it? Do you remember all the things we did together? Do you remember what it felt like? I've thought about it a lot over the past few months. And do you know what I did when I got out? I got my collection of videotapes, my special ones, and I watched them all. Do you want me to tell you what you said to me, then?"

The baby stirred and began to whimper. Michael kissed him again on the forehead. Anna could feel his lips on hers, his hands on her body. Saliva flooded into her mouth, and the hairs rose on her arms. The baby puckered up his tiny lips and twisted towards Michael's chest. "See?" he said. "He wants me."

"He needs to be fed. Give him to me." She straightened in the chair.

Michael held out the baby towards her.

"Get up slowly and come here." He watched her stand, swaying slightly from side to side. She slid one long bare foot in front of the other across the floor. When she was close enough to touch he reached out and took her by the hand, pulling her into him, his fingers gliding up the smooth skin of her arm, touching her breast, feeling the wetness of the milk as it spurted from her nipple. He moved his hand up to her throat.

"You know, Anna, it really doesn't take very much to kill someone. All I would have to do would be to squeeze you here." His fingers twisted into her skin, making her gag. "Or maybe I'd just give a little jerk and a twist."

"Aah." Her head was bent back by the force of his grip, and slowly he pushed her down onto her knees, as with his other hand he undid his belt and opened his trousers.

"Now," he said, "it's been such a long time since I felt your sweet mouth on me. There was no one in prison remotely as lovely as you, my Anna. No one who knew so well how to make me feel good. So here, how about a welcome-home present?"

MICHAEL LAY on the sofa and watched her feeding the baby, how she cradled him close, supporting his head with the palm of her hand until he had managed to take the whole of her nipple into his mouth. He saw how the milk gushed from her heavy breast, too much for the baby to swallow all at once. He wanted to taste it. He crawled over to her, below the level of the windowsill, and put out his tongue to catch the drops before they rolled down onto the white linen of her blouse.

"Get away from me." She jerked back, but the baby lost his grip and began immediately to cry, high-pitched shrieks of disappointment. Michael sat back on his haunches. He ran his tongue around the inside of his mouth. He didn't like it. He had thought it would be sweeter. He watched the way the baby's body tensed, his legs and arms pushing out, his head thrashing from side to side, until she coaxed his mouth back into position and he could suck again.

And for the moment all was silence, just the creaking of

the chair beneath her as she rocked backwards and forwards, and the click of Grace's claws on the floorboards as she padded into the room and collapsed with a small sigh in her usual place beside the window.

"Ah, Billy's faithful mutt. You've inherited her, I see. She's not much use, is she, as a guard dog. She's never going to spring at my throat and tear me to pieces. Still, I suppose she'll be company for you after we've gone."

She didn't reply. She looked down at the baby's pale face. He had fallen asleep, the effort of feeding too much for him. A small bubble of saliva rested on his bottom lip. His eyelids fluttered, his eyeballs flickering from side to side beneath them. He flung out his left arm, his tiny fingers, wrinkled like a starfish's legs, she thought, spread wide. Then he opened his eyes and looked up at her. She leaned over him, pulling him back towards her breast and a lock of her hair fell down across his chest. His fingers grasped it and tugged, as his mouth fastened onto her again, and he began to suck.

And then the phone rang.

"Answer it," he said.

She stood up, the baby still held to her breast, and walked towards the table by the window. She lifted the receiver and looked out. She could see Sergeant Murray standing below, leaning against his car. He waved up at her, as she heard his voice in her ear.

"Everything all right?"

"Fine, just fine."

"Baby okay?"

"Yes, really. I'm just feeding him again."

"Greedy little devil, isn't he?"

"Yes, I suppose he is."

"Now, remember the routine, Anna. What we agreed, if he shows up. You do know what to do, don't you?"

"Of course, everything's fine."

"And listen, Anna, if you decide you don't want to do this, you can leave. At any time. It's not worth risking you or the baby, do you understand?"

"Yes, I understand completely. It's fine, everything's perfectly all right up here."

"Okay. Well, I'm off now, but Reardon and Donnelly will be here and I'll be back in the morning. And you have my mobile number, haven't you?"

"Of course I have, but really everything's okay up here with me. I'm just a bit tired now. I'll be going to bed soon."

Murray put his phone back in his pocket. He looked up at the window high above the street. He could see her standing there, her white skirt and blouse shining in the evening sun. She waved down at him and he waved back. Lucky baby, he thought, to be loved so much after all that she had been through. He had wondered, he and Sarah had talked about it. Would she have an abortion?

"You could hardly blame her if she did," Sarah said. "Poor girl, what kind of feelings could she possibly have for a baby conceived like that?"

But somehow through the months that passed he had seen her come to terms with it. And now, well, it was written all over her face, her body. The magic had worked. She'd do anything for her son now.

Including this. He still wasn't sure about it. It was very risky. They'd go through the night, but first thing tomorrow he would go and see her and tell her it was all over.

"How's she doing?" Reardon stood beside him lighting a cigarette.

"She's fine. Look, I'm off. Give me a ring if there's any problems."

"There won't be, I think you've got it all wrong, Alan. He's not going to show up here, he's too cute."

"Well," Murray shrugged, "who knows? Anyway, you know where all the lads are placed, and there's panic buttons in all the rooms, if by some miracle he manages to get in. I'll phone you later."

"Don't, there's no need. Go home, relax, have a break."

Murray looked up at the windows one more time as he opened his car door. The shutters were closed. She'll be heading for bed, he thought. Good girl, she needs all the sleep she can get.

IT WAS dark inside now, only a small lamp brightening the sitting room. She laid the baby on a folded blanket on the floor and took off his nappy. She watched the way he moved his legs and arms. Straightening them, flexing them, testing their strength. Michael sat and watched too. She looked up at him, then back to the baby boy. She began to sing, softly. Snatches of lullabies, nonsense rhymes. The baby stared at her, suspending his thrashing movements, then started up again, kicking out, twisting and turning his plump arched feet, making little ooh sounds, his mouth rounded. She sang on and on,

> *Lullay, lullay,*
> *My dear son, my sweeting,*
> *Lullay, lullay,*
> *My dear son, my own dear dearing.*

Repeating the same few phrases over and over. And watched Michael. The way his eyes were beginning to flicker, to close for a couple of seconds, then jerk open. To close for a few seconds longer, opening slowly again, his gaze unfocused. She watched how his head lolled against the back of the chair, then over to his shoulder and back again. Watching him while she kept on singing and slowly, gently, dressed the baby. Wrapping him tightly in his blanket. Picking him up, holding him close, carefully, slowly getting to her feet, backing away, still singing, tiptoeing, quietly, quietly, carefully towards the door. Out onto the landing, the stairs dark and steep beneath her. And heard his feet behind her, and felt his hand on her shoulder, his fingers digging into her neck.

"And where do you think you're going?"

"It's okay, it's okay, really it is, I was just going to put the baby down for a while, and I was going to make you something to eat. I thought you might be hungry."

"That's surprisingly considerate of you."

"Then maybe we could talk, Michael, sort this whole thing out."

"Of course, of course we can, sort the whole thing out perfectly."

"Look, you go into the kitchen, there's wine or beer if you prefer in the fridge. I'm just going to put him in his carrycot in the bedroom."

"Come on, Anna, what do you take me for? I'm not letting you go anywhere in this house by yourself."

"Okay." Her voice was angry, impatient. "Whatever, but I'm going to put him down. Come with me if you want."

He walked behind her up the stairs to the rooms above, and watched as she carefully laid the baby in his little bed, covering him with a crocheted blanket, switching on the bedside lamp.

"You're not really going to take him, are you? You're just doing it to frighten me. That's it, isn't it?"

He took her by the hand and led her out of the room and into the dark stairwell again. "Is it? Think about it, Anna. Why should I give a fuck about you? You were going to betray me and my secrets. Weren't you? You were going to tell the police about everything that was in my silver box, everything that made me what I am. So why should I care about what you think or feel now?" He pushed her, so she tripped and stumbled, then jerked her upright again, twisting his fingers through her hair. "Now where's that food you were talking about?"

He waited until she had closed the shutters over the window in the kitchen, then sat down at the table and watched her as she moved around the room, opening cupboards, bringing out eggs, bacon, bread, butter. Her movements were graceful and precise. She was slim again, except for the full curve of her breasts, and the roundness of her hips.

"I'll do that," he said, taking the knife from her hand to cut the bread, then butter it. He stood back and watched her place the frying pan on the electric ring, adding butter until it sizzled, then the rashers of bacon, and a few minutes later an egg. He sat down and inhaled the delicious smells, listening to the splutter of food frying, turning the knife this way and that so the light gleamed from its blade.

"Tell me," he said, "what happened to my box? Who has it now?"

She shrugged her shoulders, then bent down to open the fridge, her face suddenly illuminated in the bright light that came from inside its door. He heard the clink of bottles. She straightened up, holding beer in her hands.

"I don't know, I suppose the police kept it." She turned to the drawer in the kitchen table, rummaging among the cutlery.

"Careful." His hand was on her wrist. He pushed her aside and found the opener. He pried the top off the bottle, hastily putting his mouth to the foam as it poured out.

"Do you have a glass?"

"Of course." She turned to the cupboard on the wall and reached up to it. He watched her rise on tiptoe, the muscles of her back and shoulders tense. She leaned forward. And then there was darkness. Sudden and complete.

DARKNESS TO protect and save. To wrap her tight. To cover her movements. She had practiced, the way Billy had practiced. Her hand in her pocket, opening the knife, fitting her fingernail into the slot, pulling out the sharp blade. Over and over again. The way he had done it. The same knife that had belonged to her father. She had forgotten where she had left it. Murray had shown it to her and she had recognized it, and asked if she could have it back.

"I don't see why not," he had said. "We don't need it for evidence now Billy's dead." She had kept it close, knowing that sooner or later the time would come when she would use it.

And this was the time. Her hand in the cupboard. Reaching for the switch that controlled the main fuse. Pushing it up, so the darkness swallowed them both. Turning quickly, throwing herself on him. The sharp point of the blade ripping into the skin of his neck. The same place that Billy had chosen. Tearing at the muscles, the sinews, the veins, digging into his windpipe, so he could no longer breathe.

"No," he tried to say, but there was blood everywhere. He stood up, and dragged her with him, the knife gashing now across his throat, slicing into his larynx so he was speechless. He fell backwards, and she fell with him. He tried to push her away, but now he had no strength. It was darkness outside, and darkness within him too. And he heard her voice up close in his ear. What was she saying? He heard the words and remembered them.

"You said it to me then, when you had me in that cellar. And you laughed when you said it. The difference between us is this, you said, it's all in the imagination. Where yours ends, mine begins. That's what you said. Well, Michael, Matthew, whatever you are, you misjudged me that day. And you misjudged me today. Because my imagination is boundless."

"No." He tried to get the word out, and pushed her again, and this time she fell back and he was half on his feet, but he didn't have the strength to stand. There was wet stickiness everywhere, and his feet and hands slipped as he crawled, slowly away from her. Just a few inches, and then it was too late, and he could move no more. And there was nothing else that he could do but let his head fall to the floor, and close his eyes. Bright lights for an instant, then darkness again.

MORNING SUNLIGHT creeps down the stairs. Shines on the rich red pool that has formed, coagulated, begun to harden. On the man's body lying twisted, curled up, the open savage wound in his neck laying bare the muscles, the flesh, the bone of his spine.

A narrow beam glances through the open door and inches across the floor to the rocking chair by the shuttered window. It picks up the white dress that the woman seated there is wearing, decorated as if with huge ornamental petals of Oriental poppies or peonies or full-blown roses. The light slips up across her body, over the sleeping baby in her arms, to her face. Her mouth is open. She is singing,

> *Lullay, lullay,*
> *My dear son, my sweeting,*
> *Lullay, lullay,*
> *My dear son, my own dear dearing.*

Over and over again, repeating the same words, the same phrase. Until she closes her eyes. And she, too, sleeps.

EAGER TO PLEASE

JULIE PARSONS

Available in hardcover in October 2001
from
Simon & Schuster

Turn the page for a preview of
Eager to Please. . . .

JULIE PARSONS

EAGER TO PLEASE

JULIE PARSONS

SHE REMEMBERED the way it was the first time she ever saw the prison. It was through the mesh that covered the windows of the van in which they brought her from the Four Courts that day all those years ago. It was winter. It was late afternoon, early evening. Rush hour in Dublin. It was dark. Or it should have been dark. Instead it was very bright everywhere. Shining white lights flooding the tarmacadam when the van stopped at the gate, so she could see out, and see the high cross and the gravestones set into the scraggy grass.

What's that? she asked the prison officer.

The tall, well-built woman shrugged and said, *Kevin Barry. Monument to him.*

Who? She tried to think. *Who?*

You know, Kevin Barry, the hero of the War of Independence. He was hanged here and a load of others too. Against that wall.

She tried to stand up to get a better look, but the officer tugged at the chain that joined them at the wrist.

Where do you think you're going, eh? Sit down and mind yourself.

A snigger ran around the van. She looked at them all, the other women who'd made the short trip from the court to the prison. She had tried to sit away from them, to keep a distance between their tracksuits and trainers and her best black skirt and jacket, to keep the smoke from the cigarettes that drooped from their mouths and tattooed fingers away from her nostrils and eyes. But there was no distance in the van, no means to separate her and her shame from them.

And then the van began to move again, through the high metal gates, past the tall stone building that looked like a church, the cluster of makeshift sheds at its side, and towards the metal cage that surrounded the entrance. It was interesting, she thought, remembering back, how quickly she had become used to the metal. It was everywhere. Steel, she supposed. *A malleable alloy of iron and carbon* was the way her architectural textbooks had described it, *capable of being tempered to many different degrees of hardness.* Incapable of rust. Beautiful too when used with glass the way her heroes, Le Corbusier and Frank Lloyd Wright, had employed it. To create palaces of light and space. Ugly now in this place of containment, where it couldn't be pulled apart and used as a weapon of defense or attack. Interesting too how she had adapted to all the hard surfaces. The tiled floors, the bars on the windows, the upright chairs, the wooden doors, three inches thick, decorated with locks and spyholes. Even the pad, as the padded cell was known, wasn't soft. Walls, floors covered with hard rubber. Nothing she could use to damage herself, or anyone else, that first night. After they had taken away her clothes and handed out her prison issue—a clean bra and pants, as if she needed them. A tracksuit, as if she ever wore one. A nightgown and a dressing gown, as if she didn't have her own, at home, lying across the bed, her own bed, that she had hoped she'd sleep in that night.

That she had hoped she'd sleep in that night. That she had been sure she'd come home to. That at the end of the trial the jury would believe her. That she hadn't done what the prosecution said. That she didn't take the 12-gauge shotgun and shoot him, first of all in the right thigh, severing the femoral artery so his blood pumped out on the floor. Then as he screamed and weakened and fell back, that she didn't shoot him again, this time in the groin, tearing his genitals apart, so there was a lot more blood, spattering her clothes with small tear-shaped drops. And some of the jury, two, to be precise, believed her and not them. One of the women, older, pale-faced, wept as the foreman stood and delivered his verdict.

How do you find the defendant, Rachel Kathleen Beckett? Guilty or not guilty of the murder of Martin Anthony Beckett?

Guilty, Your Honor, by a majority of ten to two.

And the sentence?

The judge with the ruddy face and flabby jowls leaned forward across the bench.

I have no choice in this case, when the verdict is guilty of murder, there is a mandatory sentence of life. And this I shall impose on you, Rachel Kathleen Beckett.

Life or death? Which began and which ended on that cold November afternoon twelve years ago? She still could not decide.

Form P30. That was what it was called, the stiff piece of cardboard which was slotted into the outside of her cell door. Everyone had one. It stated registered number, name, and religion. It stated when committed and for what sentence. And it gave the particulars of discharge, sentence expiration, and earliest possible date of release, with a box beside for the day, the month, and the year. The other women, those who weren't lifers, had numbers written in the boxes. But she didn't. Hers were blank. She stood and looked at the piece of cardboard, put up her hand to touch it, then pulled it from its slot and tore it into tiny pieces, shoving them into the pocket of her jeans. Behind her she heard the laughs, the taunts, the insults, and heard the shout of the officer she remembered from the van.

What do you think you're doing? Who do you think you are? As she grabbed her by the arm, pulled her into the office, dragged the pieces of cardboard from her pocket, and said, *Here, you, Miss High and Mighty. Think you're better than everyone else, do you? Think you can do what you like with prison property. Well, now, have another think while you put it all back together again.*

Handed her the roll of Sellotape, made her stay there in the stuffy little office, until the jigsaw was complete, then forced her back out onto the landing. The women lined up on either side, jeering and shouting as she walked up the first flight of stairs to her cell. She took the piece of cardboard and put it back where it had been. And looked down and away as the officer, Macken, that was her name, said loudly so that everyone else could hear, *You'd better start using your brains and using your education, Beckett, and finding out how best to please us. You'd better be bloody eager to please me, or else, Beckett, your life sentence is going to last a lot longer than anyone else's. Do you hear me now? Do I make myself plain?*

Pushed her into the cell, followed her, and said, *It's a funny thing about time, isn't it? Right now it's standing still for you. The hands of the clock aren't moving at all. And they won't until you get your attitude straight. Do you hear me now? Do you read me loud and clear?*

She was right about that, Macken the bitch, as she was right about most things. It was such a long time, her first night and first day. Her first week, month, year. So long till Christmas, Easter, New Year. So long that she hardly noticed her daughter Amy's birthday. And the anniversary of Martin's death. When all she wanted to do was stay in her cell, turn her face to the wall, and weep. Because she missed him, because she had loved him. Because she had lost him and everything else.

She didn't remember much of any of that year, or the one after that or the one after that. Time passing had no meaning for her now. No meaning at all. The only thing that meant anything was the mood, the atmosphere, the feelings around her. Sometimes they were good. Most times they were bad. What was it all about, she wondered, these waves of tension that washed up and down the landings, dragging the women with them? She watched how they would congregate outside one cell or another, how huddles would take shape in the far corner of the exercise yard, in the laundry in the basement, or in the showers. They would turn to her when she approached, sometimes laughing, joking, their faces animated with an inner glee which frightened her with its excess. At other times they would turn on her, far too ready with their fists and feet. And their needles. Although they were much too careful of their precious spikes to waste them on an outsider like her.

An outsider? Hardly. Not when she slept every night behind a locked door. When she woke every morning to the sound of a key. When her prison sentence drifted out in front of her like a piece of seaweed in mid-ocean as she lay in her bed in the dark and conjured up the sea beneath her. Felt the lift and surge of an Atlantic swell. Heard the rush of water beneath the keel, the breath of the wind on her face, the sudden lurch in her stomach as the boat heeled over and she felt as if she would fall, tumble headfirst down through white water, green water, and into the blackness of the deep from which there was no way up. No way out. Not now. Not for her.

The Outside. What could it possibly be like, now, after all these years inside? She remembered how in the beginning she would try to stand as close as she could to the prison officers, so she could smell the freshness they brought with them every day. She tried to ask them what it was like outside, beyond the enclosing stone walls which leached out even the brightest color. Was it raining, was it sunny, from which direction came the wind? She wanted to know in early summer if the dew was thick on the grass in the mornings, and in midwinter if they had to scrape the ice from their windscreens. In the beginning they shrugged off her questions, suspicious of her motives. But most of them softened, gradually, came to see that all she wanted was the raw material with which to imagine.

Most of them softened, and some even came to like her. She was different. She wasn't the same as the other women. They were in and out of there every few months, prison a respite from the demands of the street, a chance to rest and sleep and eat, maybe even go to school for a few months, catch up on a bit of the childhood that so many of them had missed.

They talked about her, some of the prison officers, and speculated why she had done what she did. But that kind of interest wasn't encouraged. The tall, well-built woman who had brought her to the prison, Macken, Macken from the van as she called her, put it into words for the others.

You're kidding yourself if you think any of them are like us. They're not. They're different. They think differently, they act differently. None of us will ever end up here. Don't start getting into a "there but for the grace of God" kind of mentality. And as far as Rachel Beckett goes, forget it. She killed her husband. She murdered her husband. She stood over him when he was drunk. She loaded his gun. She took off the safety catch. She aimed at him and she pulled the trigger. Twice. Stay away from her, I'm telling you all. And what's more, Macken said, *will she admit it? Will she take responsibility for it? For what she did? She'll no more do that than saw her way out of here with a nail file through the bars.*

And they turned from their cups of tea and watched her as she slouched with the others against the wall of the landing, her expression as blank and withdrawn as any one of the rest.

The exercise yard on a dull, blowy afternoon. The women, twenty, thirty of them, standing around, smoking, bored, idle. Gossiping, moaning, complaining. And Rachel, by herself, in the corner, reading. Then a voice began to sing a favorite song, a song of defiance. And soon another had joined her, and another and another, until there was a circle of women, arms linked, all singing. Throwing their voices

out and up towards the windows of the men's prison next
door.

Oh no, not I,
I will survive,
As long as I know how to love
I know I'll stay alive.

Waiting for the voices of the men. Roaring the chorus back
at them.

I've got all my life to live,
I've got all my love to give . . .

Shadows seen against the windowpanes. Their words muffled by the iron mesh.

And I'll survive
I will survive.

The expressions on the women's faces. Joy, pleasure,
exhilaration. The faces she was beginning to sort out and
differentiate, assigning them names and histories. Patty,
Tina, Lisa, Molly, Denise, Bridget, Theresa. Who now
looked over to where she leaned against the wall, laughing
out loud, clapping in time. Stamping her feet on the
asphalt. Singing along with them.

And they held out their hands to her and sealed her into
their circle. The vibrations shook her throat and diaphragm
as she shouted as loudly as the rest. And they stamped and
roared as one voice and swung their arms backwards and

forwards, until the screws came through the meshed gates. Five, maybe six of them in a group, shouting at them.

Break it up.

Quiet it down.

Come on.

Inside now.

It's teatime.

And Rachel watched the way the women opened their circle, then closed it again around the screws, singing more and more loudly, while the men's faces pressed against the bars of the windows that looked down on them, singing too, chanting out the words, their voices low, resonant, ferocious, beautiful.

And the circle got tighter and tighter, pushing in closer, trapping the screws, so they began to twist and turn, this way and that, suddenly small and defenseless, just women like their prisoners, their uniforms meaning nothing, their fear plain to see. As the volume of the singing rose even louder and the chanting from the men above became less and less musical, more and more staccato.

She felt it there, for the first time on that dull, blowy afternoon in the exercise yard. The charge of energy when the group forms, becomes a mass, and realizes its power. She watched the women's bodies. They were growing, changing shape, there in front of her. And the officers could see it too. They knew what was happening. They stepped this way and that, their faces pale, their attitude defensive. She could see the way they were trying to catch the attention of individuals, break them from the group, calling out their names.

Hey, Jackie, Tina, Molly. Hey, Theresa. Hey, I'm talking to you. Hey, calm it down. Break it up, or else.

Or else? Or else what, she wondered as she watched. These women were beyond or else. And everyone out there knew it. So she waited, tense and expectant, not sure what came next. Asking herself, What will I do? Where do I stand? Her hands clenching into fists, the muscles in her legs tightening.

And then, suddenly, it had ended, as quickly as it had begun. The women made the decision. They had had their fun. They knew there was nothing further to be gained, so they unlinked their arms and moved apart. They stopped singing and they walked quietly back inside. She smiled as she followed them indoors on that dull, blowy afternoon, hearing the jeers and catcalls of the men who watched. They wouldn't have walked away from it. They would have taken it to the limit. But they would have been beaten. This way, she thought, the women had it all. They'd flexed their muscles. They'd shown their power. And they'd do it again. Singly, collectively, one way or the other. It was always there. A choice. A possibility. Never to be forgotten. Ever.

She had asked to see the psychologist. She had faith then. Back at the beginning. Faith in her own kind. Reasonable people with education and understanding.

Why? The response was polite but disinterested.

I need help.

Really?

She had waited. They were short-staffed. There was a list. Her name was added to the bottom. The day came. She had prepared what she would say. She had practiced the words, remembered the vocabulary.

Look, I shouldn't be here. I'm not violent or dangerous.

This is a mistake. I didn't kill my husband. It wasn't me. Yes, we had a row. Yes, I was angry. But I didn't kill him. Please, don't you see? I'm not a psychopath, a sociopath, someone like that. Don't you see that I shouldn't be here?

The psychologist's report had stressed her state of denial, her inability to accept responsibility for her actions, her lack of remorse.

She waited to see what would happen. Time passed. She asked to see the Governor.

Surely, she said, *surely the psychologist has told you that I am innocent. That I didn't do this. That I shouldn't be here.*

Rachel. The Governor's voice was kind, concerned. *Rachel, I don't think you quite understand what this is all about. You have been tried by a court of law. You have been found guilty by a jury of your peers. You have been sentenced to life imprisonment. That is the only reality. Anything else is the stuff of dreams.*

It was a long time before she willingly went to see another expert. There were duty calls that had to be made. And sometimes they made her laugh, the students, sent on work experience or placement, so serious, so concerned. The do-gooders who thought they could relieve her burden of guilt. The priests and nuns who came to offer succor. She'd smile at them all and imagine the conversations they'd have when they went home.

You'll never guess who I met today.

Do you remember her?

Yes, that's right, the one who shot her husband.

Life sentence, that's what she got.

Nice? Oh, she's lovely. Very polite, well spoken. You'd never guess, ever.

It was boredom really that made her go the last time, and the recommendation from the others.

You should see this one, Rachel, they all said. *He's different. He's nice.*

He was older than the rest. Just doing a locum, he told her, filling in for a while, needed a few bob. He looked through her file. She watched him. He looked tired, ill. His clothes were shabby. He was a smoker, nicotine stains on his fingers, yellow marks on his teeth. He slowly turned over the pages, then he looked up and held her gaze.

The time has come, he said, *for you to admit your crime. You've been here for too long for your own good. Your sentence was reviewed after seven years by the Sentence Review Group. It was reviewed the following year and the year after that. They decided against probation. And do you know why?*

She nodded.

Of course you do. You're not stupid. But you're too clever to be here still. Next time you're looking in the mirror think about what you see. Think about the lines on your face, the gray in your hair, and the wrinkles on your hands. Think for once about your future. Then ask to see the Governor. Tell him you're ready to accept responsibility for killing your husband. You're ready to admit your guilt and that you now feel genuine remorse. And as you say the words they will transform you. They will make you worthy of pity and redemption. And maybe not tomorrow or the next day or the next, but someday in the still-to-come, those words will release you. Now go away and think about what I have said.

The Governor had sent for her. Told her he had good news. That the Sentence Review Group had made a recommendation. She was to be made ready for temporary release. Or perhaps she should think of it as release on license.

You understand, don't you, Rachel? Your life sentence will always remain. But if you behave yourself, follow the rules, you will be able to live once again as others. Well, almost as others.

She was to learn how to shop and cook, handle money, use public transport, pay bills, look after herself once again. That twelve years after surrendering her life to the institutions of the State, they had now decided to return it to her.

Did she want it? She lay on her bed at night, securely locked in, and let her eyes wander over the familiar marks on the walls and stains on the ceiling. She had been in this same cell for nine years, eleven months, and two days. It was on the top landing, in the corner nearest the road. Not that she could see beyond the walls during the day. But at night it was different. At night she could see the lights of the airport, and the planes as they landed and took off. By day they were insignificant smudges, an occasional flash as sunlight glanced off a metal wing or superstructure. But at night she could follow with her eyes their lights as they rose through the air, up and up and up. And she could go with them. To London or New York. To Paris or Rome. To all those cities she had once visited, all those years ago. And she would summon up from her memory the names of the streets, the buildings she had studied, analyzed, wondered about, admired, and she could smell the air, feel the warmth of the sun on her arms, the light dazzling her eyes. Now she stood and went to the window, pushing it open through the bars as far as it would go. It was cold, but she didn't care. She raised her eyes to the blue-black sky. The moon was in its dying phase. She could clearly see the Copernicus crater and the crater named after Kepler. Martin had loved the moon. He had shown her through his binoculars the seas and craters and named them for her.

One of the things that fascinates me about it, he had said, is the way it's always there, even during the day. You can't see it because of the light from the sun, but it's always out there, waiting till night comes, and then it can reveal its face again. It's the way a good surveillance officer should be. So carefully concealed and camouflaged that none of the people you're watching can see you, until you want them to. He had said it to her in the days when he still talked to her, shared his work with her. Told her everything.

Jackie the probation officer, the one she had known the longest, said to her today, *You must have some friends, some family, someone you can reestablish contact with. You're going to need them now, when you're out. It's very hard to get by on your own. I know you've been lonely in here but loneliness on the outside is a completely different kettle of fish.*

Had she been lonely in here? She tried to remember, to compare the way she felt now with what had gone before. All around her she heard voices. Women's voices. She knew them all, their names, their ages, their crimes. She had sat with them in the dust of the yard and listened as they told the stories of their lives. She had told them stories too, the stories her mother had read to her when she was a child, which she in turn had passed on to her own daughter. "The Frog King," "The Twelve Dancing Princesses," "Beauty and the Beast," "Bluebeard," "The Princess and the Pea." She had watched how their faces softened and their eyes closed as they lolled against each other and dreamed. Now she heard them calling out through their windows to the men behind the gray walls of the prison across the yard. Brothers, boyfriends, husbands. Men she had come to know through the letters she had helped their women write. Puzzling over the words, fingers clumsy with ballpoint or pencil.

Dear Johnny, I love you. I can't wait to get out of this kip and be with you again.

Dear Mikey, how's it going? Are you any better? Are you going to the hospital and taking your tablets like I told you?

Dear Pat, I'm sending you all my kisses and hugs. I miss you. Do you miss me?

Are you listening? the women shouted now. *Are you listening?*

Sometimes she felt like joining in, even though she had no one of her own behind the barred windows opposite. But sometimes she just wanted to hear the sound of her own voice, calling out, waiting for an answer.

Who would she call to now?

Are you listening, outside world? I'm coming back. Are you listening?

**Visit the Simon & Schuster
romance Web site:**

www.SimonSaysLove.com

**and sign up for our
romance e-mail updates!**

Keep up on the latest
new romance releases,
author appearances, news, chats,
special offers, and more!
We'll deliver the information
right to your inbox—if it's new,
you'll know about it.

POCKET BOOKS

2800.02